ISBN: 978-1-951213-18-3
eISBN: 978-1-951213-21-3

Maharidge, Dale, author.
Burn Coast : a novel / Dale Maharidge.
Description: Los Angeles : Unnamed Press, 2022.
Identifiers: LCCN 2021041170 | ISBN 9781951213183 (hardcover) |
    ISBN 9781951213213 (epub)
Subjects: LCSH: Country life--California, Northern--Fiction. |
    Counterculture--California, Northern--Fiction. | Missing
    persons--Fiction. | Marijuana--Growth--Fiction. | LCGFT: Noir fiction. | Novels.
Classification: LCC PS3613.A34928 B87 2022 | DDC 813/.6--dc23
LC record available at https://lccn.loc.gov/202104117

Cover Photograph by Danielle Starkey.
Designed and Typeset by Jaya Nicely.

Manufactured in the United States of America

Distributed by Publishers Group West

First Edition

BURN
COAST

a novel

DALE
MAHARIDGE

The Unnamed Press
Los Angeles, CA

AUTHOR'S NOTE

This is a work of fiction about a special place that may never have existed. Any resemblance to living or dead persons, including the author, or their actions, legal or illegal, is coincidental. Thanks to the Corporation of Yaddo, where much of this novel was conceived, and to editor Chris Heiser.

To the Cottage

CONTENTS

BURN
COAST

Burn Coast (n.): *A region of California where three tectonic plates meet to form a triple junction fault zone. The Athapaskan people arrived here during the Ice Age, when one-third of the planet was frozen and it was a treeless land except for tan oaks in the canyons. They netted salmon and harvested mussels. Carbohydrates came from acorns, ground in stone mortars and then boiled to remove tannins, for flatbread.*

With the retreat of the ice starting ten thousand years ago, two aggressive species of fir migrated south, century by century, from the boreal regions. When the fir reached the triple junction, they began overtaking the valued tan oak. In late summer the low dead branches of the invading fir curled down as the trees struggled to conserve water, marking the time for the Athapaskans to set fires. For generations, infernos swept the coastal hills, incinerating young Douglas and white fir. The dominant feature of the landscape, thanks to the diligent burning, was grassland. In the spring the hills were as bright green as rock kelp; at late summer sunset, the color of ripe persimmons.

And so it was until 1857. In that year, Elwin Edwards and the Jones clan rode horses over a ridge and set sight on the triple junction's grasslands. They invoked God and praised Him for creating so much natural bounty for their cattle. By 1861, the men had exterminated most of the twelve hundred indigenous people. A band fled south. In one account, they were driven by white pursuers into the sea and drowned. In another, they were buried or tied down in the sand amid the rocks and then the tide came in. In both versions a woman about to die issued a curse: "The white man is doomed to never prosper here."

Flash-forward 110 years: On June 27, 1971, pilot Les Hall revved the engines of a DC-3 for takeoff from a new landing strip, created for a subdivision under construction by R. J. Beaumont and Associates and World Leisure Time interests on the coast south of McGee Ridge. Three crew members and twenty-one executives and salesmen were aboard. They'd come for a weekend tour. It was a scam. Most lots were too steep to build on. Insiders called the operation "the Show," and they flew in the salesmen to avoid having them experience the horrible roads leading to this wild coast. The aircraft wouldn't lift. It careened off the runway, crashing into a rock offshore. The DC-3 split open, spilling its passengers, some of whom were beaten to death against the reef by the savage surf—the same rocks where the last band of Athapaskans perished at the hands of Edwards and the Jones clan. Only seven people survived.

1
METHOD LIVING

She spent the afternoon playing the tuba, seated on the rusted springs of what remained of a couch perched at the edge of the bluff nine hundred feet above the surf, as an emerging cold front blackened the Pacific sky. When daylight began its retreat, the wind picked up; gusts shot her long white hair straight back as she stood and faced the coming storm. A ritual of purity was needed. At the forest edge she harvested dark green stringers of yerba buena poking through the winter-browned rattlesnake and velvet grasses. She chopped the tiny spade-like leaves of the herb on the Ark's worn Douglas fir plank countertop, boiled water, made tea from it. After burning sage, she sat in the dark sipping the hot drink, usually calming. Yet tonight she remained deeply troubled. Rushes of Arctic wind slammed the Ark. The eleven buckets that captured drips from the leaking roof each had a unique pitch, a tempo that accelerated or diminished with the intensity of storm surges as night came on. She struck a Diamond match, put flame to the charred wick of a kerosene lamp, replaced the globe. In the maturing orange glow, she stared at the long white rectangular box set atop the Steinway. The previous day the box had arrived at the post office, down in the hamlet. Before she even opened it, the name on the shipping label was upsetting: "Arden Vanderlip." A handwritten note on a large yellow Post-it was inside the box:

> *Dearest Arden:*
> *I was cleaning out the hall closet and found these*
> *things. I thought you should have them.*
> *Warmly,*
> *Richard*

When they'd talked by phone ten days earlier, Zoë insisted that Richard have the co-op, but she reluctantly agreed to take what remained of the investments from that poisoned money. She had not, however, agreed to take these things. Why Richard insisted on calling her Arden, a name she had disavowed fifty years ago, was beyond her. And yet its contents were already pulling her back.

Zoë went to the piano and again peered inside the box; among the items were a white parasol, white gloves, and a white ball gown. She stripped and put on the gown, carried the oil lamp to the bathroom, and stood before the mirror. Decades of being a billy goat on the ridge had kept her trim, her body the same shape and weight as at seventeen. Not that the gown inspired any sense of longing for another time in her life, even if it fitted perfectly. She returned to the piano and slipped on the gloves, which reached her elbows. Clutching the parasol, she plunged out the Ark's front door and into the squall, neglecting to bring the Petzl headlamp with her. Opening and twirling the parasol, Zoë stumbled down the steep, harrowing untrailed route to the ocean. The dress flapped in the gale, and the parasol was shredded to its wire frame. When she reached the beach she waded into fifty-two-degree surf. She curtsied to the fierce sea, tossed the parasol against the wind onto a cresting breaker, where it was lost in the crashing foam that surged around her waist. The power of the withdrawing water and the force of the moon pulled her out to sea. She fought the current, fought to regain the shore, fought for life. Then she let go. For once, she gave up. The moon replied, *No...* and the Pacific thrust her back into the shallows. She gasped and spat, crawled crablike with numbed clubs for limbs to the cold reaches of the highest wet sand. She cursed the heavens. It had been so peaceful, letting go.

Zoë climbed her way back up the near-vertical headland, difficult to scale even in daylight, doubly so with the onset of hypothermia. Rain prickled her flesh. Her tongue drank the ancient waters from coyote bushes, salal, and fir saplings. It was just before eleven o'clock when she made it back to the Ark. The gown was caked with mud, torn by thorns of blackberry and wild rose; the white gloves, blackened from clawing at the earth where she needed to pull herself up. She shivered violently while making a fire in the cast-iron stove. She stripped and hovered next to the flue pipe, taking in the emerging warmth. When a substantial bed of coals formed, she stuffed in the gown and gloves, leaving the door open as the damp cloth smoldered and smoked before igniting. At the piano, she played Wagner's *Lohengrin*, eyes going between the keys and the wet cotton crackling in the firebox. She had failed.

Lara called to say she couldn't get a hold of Zoë. It had been four days since anyone in town had seen or heard from her. She asked if I would go check on her. Things like this you never wanted to handle alone, and my first instinct was to telephone Likowski, but the last time I tried that, he slammed the phone down when he recognized my voice. Instead I called Eddie. His truck wasn't running, but he said he could ride Buck the back way through the woods. I hurried up my road on foot, out of breath by the time I reached Zoë's gate. The shiny stainless steel shackle on the brass combination padlock was open. Zoë never left the gate unlocked, especially now with Klaus in jail, J.D.'s lawyer hassling her, and the spate of violence between the Bulgarian mobsters and Mexican cartels. I hiked up the rutted track until her house, called "the Ark" because it was built to resemble a ship, came into view over the crest of a hill. Her black 1994 Volvo hatchback was parked in front of the barn. "Zoë!" I called out.

I peered through the porch window and saw nothing, went to the ocean side of the Ark and looked in those windows. I didn't immediately enter for fear of what I'd find, but everything appeared in order. I opened the lockless door and stuck in my head: "Zoë?"

The place was empty. I went out to the barn. The heavy door's bearings squealed as it rolled back. A flock of startled bats blew past my face as my eyes adjusted to the dark chamber: tack hung on wall hooks, piles of moldy boxes, rusting equipment in the corners, plus an ancient Brush Hog, a posthole auger, a fire dripper, a discer from Helmut's failed attempt to start a quinoa farm. But no Zoë. I opened the unlocked driver's door of the Volvo. Escaping heat rushed into the fifty-degree air—the sun had been out all morning. The keys were in the ignition, which was where most of us normally left our car keys.

I went back to the Ark. It struck me that the interior appeared exactly as it had early Wednesday morning—the last time I'd been here. I pulled on the stove's heavy iron door. The stubs of burned branch wood ends were those that I'd placed on the embers. It was clear another fire had not been built. I'd used the last of the wood that night and more had not been brought in. In the bathroom, Zoë's robe hung on a hook. I inspected the rest of the Ark, climbing a ladder to a hatch leading to the roof deck. The faux mast had snapped off in a storm a few years earlier. Behind the splintered trunk was a cabin patterned after a ship's bridge. Access to it was disconnected from the rest of the house save for the route I'd taken. It had been Klaus's bedroom. I'd never been inside. The walls were covered with fading yellowing posters for metal groups. The recognizable ones: Motörhead and Slayer. The room appeared unchanged, either in homage or due to neglect, since the mid-1980s.

Hooves on the road. I went to the rail and spotted Likowski atop AOC, his new mare, a quarter mile distant. Likowski's fiancée, Lara, must have called him. He was in full cowboy mode, wearing a white ten-gallon hat and boots; still, he wore dark sunglasses with small square lenses. AOC was at a gallop. Likowski was inside by the time I made it down the ladder. His still-blond hair fell straight almost to his shoulders and his face was narrow—at this point in life he resembled Tom Petty. We didn't utter a word. I stood next to the stove while he made his own search: on the roof, out to the barn. When he reentered the Ark, he removed the sunglasses and stared at me for an uncomfortably long time, as if on a dare to see who'd speak. He broke: "Is her purse here?"

"Haven't seen it."

We searched under the bed, in cupboards, everywhere. No purse. But then it was hard to remember the last time we'd seen Zoë with a purse. We ended up back in the main room.

"Her cell phone?" Likowski asked.

I shrugged. "Tried that too. No luck."

It was then I noticed a glaring absence: Zoë's tuba, which usually hung on the wall, was missing. I asked Likowski if he'd seen it in his searching. He hadn't. He glanced out the window at the Volvo. "Have you tried starting it?"

Likowski went out, got behind the wheel, and turned the key. Nothing happened. He pulled the hood release. The positive terminal from the battery had been disconnected. We stared at the dangling cable.

"We should report this," I said.

"They won't do shit." His tone was withering, just as it had been weeks earlier when he'd told me to fuck off and kicked me out of his sweat lodge. The anger in his voice made me wince.

"I'll check out the Hildegard cabin," Likowski said, turning abruptly. The cabin was a tiny (and, frankly, creepy) house deep in the canyon south of the Ark. I went to the bluff where Zoë always played the tuba, walked through brush on the steep downslope. After half an hour of searching the acreage, I had one more tense exchange with Likowski before he wandered away again. I ended up back inside the Ark at the piano and the box, some three feet long, two feet deep and wide. I pulled it down, sat on the floor, and started going through it. Objects were scattered beneath tissue paper, fancy department store gift wrap: a U.S. Army dress blues jacket with one star on each shoulder and a billboard of service ribbons from campaigns in Italy and Germany. The jacket smelled of age, motor oil, and wet dog. Beneath were Italian lira and German reichsmark notes. A menu and bill for dinner in 1943 at a restaurant in Palermo, Sicily. Other menus, train schedules, camp rules for German POWs. A swastika flag with a handwritten note in a cellophane wrap paper-clipped on to it: "From ruins of Gestapo HQ, Prinz-Albrecht-Straße, Berlin." A distinguished service award signed by General George S. Patton; clipped to it, a picture of Patton with another military man in the bombed ruins of Berlin.

Zoë's father.

He was handsome and tall. The men, arms around each other, are smiling.

A packet of letters bound in string, all in German, in thick blue or black fountain pen, addressed to "Herr Gen. H. S. Vanderlip" from various addresses in the United States, postmarked between 1950 and 1961. A program from the Debutante Cotillion and Christmas Ball at the Waldorf on the night of December 22, 1959. Near the bottom was a note on a contemporary Post-it, in ballpoint, apparently from the sender: "Arden, we had someone cut open the safe in the office. It took the man hours to do it. That safe was built like Fort Knox! There was just this inside. You had better be sitting down when you read it." I peeled off the wrapping paper. An inch-thick hardbound volume was inside. Written on the front: "Diary—General H. Spellman Vanderlip, 1942–1958." By the way it was still wrapped, Zoë had not even tried to look at it. She seemed to have gone no deeper than the top of the box.

I knew Zoë's father had died years earlier. Why was this stuff just being sent now? A stack of unopened mail was piled next to the box. I riffled through it. Mostly it was junk and bills, but there was a registered letter from Allianz Global Investors in New York City. I stared at the letter. Had I been the last person to see her?

She had called me Tuesday night, weeping, asking me to come over. I was surprised—she never showed emotion like that. Zoë was total WASP, a stoic East Coast blue blood regardless of her outlaw hippie trappings. I stayed with her until dawn. Two days ago. I wondered if she'd killed herself, but I shook off that thought partly because I didn't want to believe that, partly because she'd had a habit of ghosting herself before, and partly because I didn't want to think the worst. I pocketed the letter just as I heard someone ride up and yell, "Hello?"

Eddie was dismounting his very large frame from Buck, an appropriately massive black stallion. I always admired the beast for bearing Eddie's weight. I hoped Eddie was all right. He had been on haloperidol, then graduated to new antipsychotic medications, and he was clearly keeping to his regimen because one of the side effects was weight gain. Easily pushing 240 pounds, Eddie was now a wire-haired Russian razorback boar of a human. He nodded at me standing on the porch.

"Saw Likowski," I said. "He walked home for his truck, went to talk to the cops in person. They wouldn't do a damn thing if we just called it in."

"They won't do a damn thing either way," Eddie mumbled.

"He said we should go to the beach, look there," I said.

I hadn't been on a horse since Likowski taught me how to ride in the early aughts. I knew enough about the animals to be scared of them, and I vowed never again to get on one, but AOC was gentle. I mounted her and followed Eddie up the road. We went north to where an old brushed-in jeep route jagged off the headland to the beach. The plan was to double back south on the sand; it was too steep for horses in front of the Ark. Regardless, I was in for a sore ass. In moments like this I was critically aware that I wasn't actually one of them. People like Eddie and Likowski had always been here, it seemed, along with their saddle-hardened buttocks. I had an ominous feeling as AOC followed Buck through the brush of that old jeep trail that was still navigable only because a rancher's cows used the route as a path.

"If she did get caught up down there, she'll wash up, just like that girl we found last year," Eddie said over his shoulder. The woman, who'd been killed by a gunshot to the head, remained unidentified. Authorities believe her body was dumped in the ocean at the beach trailhead, but nothing had been published about the case in months. "Vultures were on her," Eddie continued, his stutter springing up momentarily. "There's a m-minus tide this afternoon. We should look for vultures."

I stared at the shiny rear end of Eddie's black horse and the large form of the rider atop the animal, and we continued on our way to the beach.

It was the week before my water tank was delivered. I'd fetched the mail from my post office box in the hamlet. On the way back up to the ridge I stopped at the road edge directly in front of Eddie's place. I faced a colossal rock henge and two massive eucalyptus trunks, amputated fifteen feet off the ground. He'd carved the three-foot-diameter stumps with a chain saw and ax into faces that resembled mo'ai, those big-eared Easter Island monoliths, and painted them bright green. Their elongated blank eyes unsettled tourists who braved the miles of winding roads through the dark redwood and Douglas fir forests of the coastal mountains. Behind the rock wall were two other stump artworks. Both had flat-topped heads and were painted turquoise. One had ghostly eyes, the paint having dripped as if crying. The second was reminiscent of a native person, with a red face and blue-black eyes.

I drove on. At the bridge, I spotted Eddie wading across a shallow pool out to the river bar, an expanse of cobblestones silver white in the high noon sun. I parked on the far side of the bridge where the truck wouldn't be seen and, binoculars in hand, scrambled down the bank where I sat in the Pacific willows. I rested my elbows on my knees and trained the glasses on Eddie a good quarter of a mile downriver. A red-winged blackbird alighted on a branch and began singing. There was the pleasant sound of flowing water. The bird flew off. Eddie was bent over, studying the rocks. He picked one up and then summarily dropped it. Eddie waded into the channel and found a wet boulder, hoisted it atop his shoulder. The stone was the size and shape of a compact automobile's transmission. Sixty pounds was my guess. I knew the weight because of hauling rock when I developed the springs on my land. Eddie struggled beneath the boulder. He staggered a few steps, stopped to rest, then resumed a slow march. He was stout. Yet it wasn't an obesity of the type one sees in city people. It was the beastly manner of a rural creature that eats excessively to sustain toil. His gray-brown beard hid a round and what would have otherwise been a plain face if not for his dominating eyes—they burned with an intensity like that of a person who'd just discovered a lover had cheated on them. Eddie reached a pool of knee-deep slack water at the edge of the north bank. The oxbow channel was about two hundred yards from the main stem of the river and carried current only during the winter rainy season. The water was muddied from the trips he'd made that morning across the pool; he picked up speed to propel the rock atop the shoulder-high bank. The rock rolled backward. He pushed hard against it, forcing it to come to a rest. He dropped into the water, panting, legs against the bank and beads of sweat running down his face. A breeze came upcanyon from the ocean. His gaze fell upon Edwards Mountain, rising to the south. When his lungs ceased heaving, Eddie grabbed the exposed root of a Pacific willow that jagged from the earth like a twisted human elbow and pulled himself up the bank to the boulder next to a deep-bellied wheelbarrow, rusted and dented, patched with plates of welded steel. There was a booming metallic thud when it dropped into the wheelbarrow, loud even from a distance. He grabbed the gray and splintered handles and propelled the cart down a trail through a spindly riparian forest of red alder and vanished. I imagined him emerging in the meadow south of his house. The weather-beaten dwelling belonged in a Walker Evans photograph from 1930s Alabama. The house had been visible from the main road just out front. But now it was hidden behind that arcing wall comprising thousands of river rocks. A dozen feet tall, ten wide at the base and tapering to a foot or so at the apex, it more than half encircled the house.

The notion to build the wall came one night in 1989, six years earlier. It was just after two o'clock in the morning. Eddie was seated next to a wood-burning stove, an Uzi in his left hand, his eyes on the ceiling. This time they'd gotten inside the house. He loudly chambered a round, and the scuffling ceased. "B-bastards," he stammered, and held his breath in the ensuing silence. Then he grabbed the phone and spun the rotary dial frantically to call Doc Anderson, who sleepily answered.

"They're up there, D-Doc! They're up there! Come help!"

"Who? Eddie, who?"

"Indians! They're—"

Now they were dancing.

Eddie screamed. Gunshots filled the doctor's ear as Eddie blasted rounds into the ceiling. The Uzi wasn't on full auto. He didn't want to waste ammo in case they came down the stairs. The doctor tried to keep Eddie on the line, but Eddie hung up. By the time the doctor arrived, perhaps trusting a bit too much that Eddie would recognize the sound of his voice as he cautiously entered the house, he discovered that Eddie had pushed furniture against the door of the stairwell leading to the second floor. The Uzi remained pointed at the ceiling. Doc got Eddie to put down the weapon, tried to calm him by inviting him to come sleep at his place. Eddie declined. He had to deal with the Indians. There was no running from them—they wanted revenge for his great-grandfather's part in the massacre of the Native Americans who were driven into the sea and drowned. If he left, they'd simply follow him to Doc's house, putting him and his family in danger. Worry filled Eddie's face in response to Doc's continued skepticism.

"I'm not on meth, I promise! Not on nothin'!" he pleaded. "I've been doing good. Don't tell Kow!"

"V-vultures," Eddie stammered, pointing to the southern sky beyond a jutting headland.

We dismounted on the soft sand at the bottom of the old jeep road. I squinted. A distant raptor and then another came in and out of view, riding thermals, hidden now and then by the thousand-foot-tall gray belly of the Franciscan rock formation from the Jurassic period.

"Looks like they're right below Zoë's place," I said.

We hurried, not that getting there rapidly would change anything. I flashed on the last words I had with Zoë days earlier, seated on the edge of her couch that dawn. She locked eyes with me and said, *Thank you for coming.* I still didn't want to admit this had happened—that she had called me and I'd gone to the Ark that night. As far as I knew, I was the last one who had seen her alive.

Eddie's stallion was much faster than AOC, kicking up clumps of wet sand as we galloped down the beach, though she made a good effort. The blue plain of the Pacific was on our right; to the south, headlands stretched into an unpeopled, roadless mist. A series of canyons, each like a knife cut, were forested and dark in sharp contrast to the golden ridges, which resembled yeasty challah bread in the midafternoon sun. The tide, at minus 1.2 feet, was nearing slack. The reef before us was an expanse of mussel-crusted rock stretching out nearly a quarter of a mile.

"There!" I yelled, pointing to movement: a vulture perched on a sea stack. We tied the horses off on coyote brush and ran across the sand to the tide pools. I hit the reef ahead of Eddie. The rocks were slick with kelp and other seaweeds, thick with blue and horse mussels, patches of drooping sea palm. *Thank you for coming.* My heart raced as I went around a large tide pool filled with hundreds of turquoise sea anemones. The vulture flapped its wings; two others ascended from the other side of the sea stack that was an island at high tide. I slipped and caught myself, nearly face-planting in a bed of razor-sharp mussels. Finally, I went on all fours across the top of the rock, white with the shit of buzzards and cormorants.

The body was mostly eaten. Bones glistened in the sun. I sat, panting; my chest heaved.

"Sea lion," Eddie said nonjudgmentally from behind. I hadn't realized he had caught up with me. We picked our way slowly back across the reef. "So you two still aren't talkin'?" Eddie asked as he went around a tide pool.

"I'm talking. It's him who's not talking. He's still mad at me for listing my place."

"Kow says it's more than that. Says you weren't being honest."

Irritated by his echoing what Likowski had turned into a mantra, I took it out on Eddie because I could: "You don't think I'm honest, Eddie?"

"I didn't say that."

"I've always been straight with you guys." I itemized my defenses, in particular that I was really no different from Likowski and most of the other hippies who came here two, three decades before I showed up. "Except for you, Eddie, we're all on the run from someplace else," I said with an edge in my voice.

"I wish I was from someplace else," Eddie said plaintively. His burning eyes softened for a moment. His wistful gaze melted any anger that I had, as Eddie shook his head. "Likowski just thinks that you didn't say what you were actually doing."

"Come on! I told you all exactly why."

"That's not exactly the same as *what*. He says you were keepin' things secret."

I laughed tiredly. "You could say the same thing about him."

Eddie chuckled. He knew as much as I that Likowski was the one with the actual secrets. Difference between me and Eddie? I was nosing around, while Eddie didn't care about Likowski's past. Eddie was like a puppy in the best way possible—he lived in the moment, something I envied. I've always seemed to be living for the future, a week, month, or year beyond where I am in life, a distant point in time when I'd be content, satisfied with my career, and not having to worry about money. But for one very important portion of my existence—moving to this wilderness coast—the problem was that I wasn't thinking far enough ahead. After almost twenty-five years of being here, in a sudden rush of existential crisis, I realized I had to leave. Likowski had been the first person I'd told. I counted the days—it had been nearly three weeks before Zoë vanished.

The vultures circled a thousand feet above the sea lion corpse. We were directly below the Ark now, though it wasn't visible from the reef. I studied the headland and tried to imagine how Zoë negotiated the thick chaparral in the dark. Something now told me she didn't come back to the beach Wednesday to drown herself. Yet we did due diligence and spent the next two hours searching the high tide line. "That girl's body drifted south," Eddie said. "That's where the current goes."

We dismounted to inspect each driftwood pile and tangle of kelp, rode along the brush line where the sand dunes met the palisades. We didn't talk, absorbed in the search, and ended up nearly three miles down the coast. The rolling marine layer thickened a mile or so offshore, and the sun, an hour from setting, was a dull orange globe. Suddenly, the fog raced in and enveloped us as if it were nearly night. Eddie called it "Black Fog." Somewhere out on the reef, a colony of sea lions barked desperately. The incoming surf sounded like Midwest thunder.

We galloped north. Eddie drove his horse hard as if specters were chasing him and was soon lost from sight. Fog billowed past my ears. My hands were numb, spine sore. AOC slowed to a steady canter. I had no idea where we were until Eddie and his horse materialized before us.

"That's the trail up," he said, pointing. Then he rode off, and I was alone.

AOC picked her way up the cow path. It wasn't unusual on such paths, at certain times, to feel less than alone, watched, even followed. You got used to it. But now, I kept looking back, a tingle prickling my neck until we reached Zoë's gate. There was a fenced five acres where AOC could graze, and I topped off the water trough. After that, bowlegged, exhausted, I went home, lit a few oil lamps to conserve power in my L-16s, and pulled the letter from Allianz Global Investors that I'd pocketed from the Ark. Why had I taken it? Because, as Likowski would tell you, I'm a snoop. I arrived here a snoop, and I'll leave as one. It's all I know to do, no matter who my friends are.

I slid a finger along the seal of the letter. Inside was a statement outlining Zoë's share of her father's estate along with a notice imploring her to contact the company for it to complete its fiduciary duties. It was so strange. Her father had died in 1999, so the estate should have been settled twenty years earlier. I thumbed through the pages, adding up the accounts, nearly $3 million. I knew Zoë had money in other banks—she'd told me about the accounts that summer we were lovers. She had whispered it like a confession, a source of both shame and willful pride. Zoë, it turned out, was rich—or, at least, rich in comparison to most of her neighbors, and at the time I must admit I had felt a little privileged to be taken into her confidence.

If something bad happened, only one person stood to gain financially. He was in jail. But that didn't mean that others couldn't do the work on his behalf. It was a shitty thing to think of someone's own son, but then I'd come a long way in my opinion of Klaus.

Soon after, I fell asleep, the letter from Allianz Global Investors still in hand.

Long before we met, I heard Zoë.

It was weeks after I bought my fifty acres on that brittle edge of the continent, a late summer afternoon in 1995, when the anemometer registered zero during one of those atmospheric inversions that locks over the California coast, when the temperature climbs into the high nineties on the normally cold Pacific headlands and time seems suspended and the rush of air from a faraway raven's wingbeats can be heard. Surf strikes the ear as if it's yards away, not one thousand vertical feet below; all sound carries for great distance in the stillness.

I took a break from shoveling dirt to sit in the shade side of the new water tank, the day after it was delivered from town by flatbed truck. My flesh dripped sweat that mixed with dust; the sunscreen was wearing off and my arms were turning red. I was exhausted from digging a massive hole in the meadow to partially bury the five-thousand-gallon poly tank so that during an earthquake it wouldn't roll down the mountain in a direct line to the cabin site. I calculated the weight and the math was terrifying: over twenty tons of water would reside in the cylinder on which I rested my back. As I imagined the crushing force of that mass—plenty of justification for all the shoveling—the distinct sound of a tuba emerged from the south. (I later learned that it was Rimsky-Korsakov's "Flight of the Bumblebee.") A tuba? I began tapping along with the beat, and then a grower a mile higher on the ridge joined in with bongos.

To better hear it I walked out to the western edge of the meadow, where the land fell steeply toward the ocean. Clambering up on a split rail fence corner at the outer line to my property, at the rusted gate where my easement went across Lauren McGowan's place, I got a 160-degree view of the Pacific: some four and a half thousand miles due south was Easter Island; west, mainland Japan. The headland plunged steeply to the beach. It was a favored spot. I couldn't see the sunset from my house site—it had a north-facing sea view— so the fence rail was an excellent perch for watching the sun dip into the ocean or, more commonly, becoming lost in the mist of the marine layer that hung miles offshore. This day the horizon was a sharp deep blue line. I closed my eyes and listened to the tuba and bongos, now going at a crazy pace—nothing less than free-form jazz and a marvelous hippie moment in the wilderness.

When I opened my eyes, I spotted a man on a white horse far below. A brown pack horse trailed behind, tethered with rope to the first; that animal was laden with supplies. The lead animal picked a course amid the coyote brush and juvenile fir dotting the grassland, coming up the mountain against the deep blue of the Pacific, right in my direction. The man never looked up. The horse chose the route. The rider wore a black cowboy hat, black shirt, and leather chaps abraded by years of assault against chaparral. Nothing about him said it wasn't 1888, until his face lifted and I saw the mirrored sunglasses. He was ruggedly handsome, could have been a Marlboro Man in one of those old 1960s television commercials. His beard stubble was tinged with gray, though most of the hair sticking out from the hat was dark blond. The man raised his head when the horses came to a halt about twenty feet from where I sat. The rider and I were at eye level because of my elevation on the fence rail.

"You're the newbie. The writer," the man announced in a tone that was curt, possibly hostile. He took no joy in pronouncing the word "writer."

"Will Specter," I said, giving as friendly a little wave as I could.

"Likowski," the thin man, who was easily over six feet, replied. In the long silence that followed, I stared at my reflection in his shades.

"Nice-looking horses," I said in a grasp for small talk.

"Abbie." He nodded to the horse on which he sat.

"Great name."

"After Abbie Hoffman. And that's Malcolm," he added of the young brown horse.

"After X?"

"Yep."

With that, Likowski flipped the reins to continue on his way.

"Hey," I said. "Who's playing the tuba?"

"What tuba?"

Which is when I noted that it had gone silent, along with the bongos. And a moment later, Likowski was gone as well.

I had assumed I would get a chilly reception when I moved here, though the previous owner of my land, a man named Baker, seemed to think otherwise. I was concerned about being the outsider amid a self-exiled group of sixties refugees who had built their off-grid homesteads in the early 1970s and survived in the underground weed economy. Before signing the final papers, I asked Baker, "What about my neighbors? I'm not going to grow. You think they'll accept me?" And Baker replied, "Won't matter if you grow or not. That ridge is full of outlaws. You're gonna be one of 'em just by being there."

My transformation into an outlaw occurred quite rapidly, at least in the eyes of the government. Black helicopters sprouting machine guns, operated by the Campaign Against Marijuana Planting, often hovered over my property while I built the cabin those first two summers. In mid-August of the second year, a chopper dropped off six CAMP commandos on the meadow, thick with golden velvet grass laid flat by the machine's blades. I walked up to meet them as the chopper rose and flew away. The captain talked with me as his men used machetes to bushwhack into the poison oak thickets of Elk Creek Canyon, to eradicate one of my neighbors' patches somewhere down in that fog of brush. I informed the captain that I was a half-time professor at Stanford University a few months of the year (even though I didn't feel at all like a professor, the truth being I was very much a masquerading academic, with no higher degree than the one bequeathed by the school of life) and that I was not a marijuana farmer, so they could move on without concern, thank you—the last two words said with a fuck off inflection.

The captain smiled. "Have you seen Chelsea?"

I had not. I'd spotted Secret Service guys in suits, plugged into their electronic earbuds, standing outside classrooms, but in her four years at Stanford I would never set sight on the daughter of the president of the United States of America, a country out there beyond the Redwood Curtain sinking deeper into its abyss.

I could tell by the amused glimmer in his cop eye that he was sure I was a Clinton man, even though I wasn't—I had always tried to be no man's man. He decided to play good cop, clearly trying to dig up information on my neighbors. I begged off and went back to building my cabin with solar-powered tools (the nearest power lines were miles away). I'd already wasted too much time on those cops. I lived by the sun. I had only four hundred watts of photovoltaic panels and two L-16 batteries. That meant I could run the table saw from about ten in the morning to three in the afternoon. Two more batteries and three more panels would have changed everything, but that was $2,500 I didn't have. The chopper returned late that afternoon to take away the commandos and armloads of skunk weed, the entire annual income of Brett, a kid down on his luck, who was staying with Likowski that summer and who would plunge further into depression and financial ruin because of the loss. With lessons like that, it didn't take long to realize that I was exactly like my grower neighbors in my motive for fleeing to this shore of broken pieces, this damagedland of hurt souls. We hated them, the forces of power out there. If I hadn't come primed to feel this way, those helicopters would have been reason enough for conversion. I'd spent my life figuring out if it was push or pull that motivated me to be an outsider, so it made sense in a lot of ways that I ended up on this ridge very much in solitude most of the year, over a half mile (as the flicker woodpecker flies) from Dan Likowski, my secretive neighbor who never went by his first name and who lived deep in Elk Creek Canyon below my place. Likowski was the nearest human to me, but it would take years for us to get close.

"I'm so terribly sorry to hear that Arden is missing."

Richard was shocked when I called. I had no idea who he was other than the man who had sent the box of old things to Zoë. Richard told me he was the widowed husband of her estranged half brother. "So you've had no further contact with her?"

"None."

"Are there any other living relatives?"

"The lineage ended with Jonathan and Arden. I am sure there are no other immediate relatives."

"Thank you for calling me back so late East Coast time."

"I may long since be retired, but I continue keeping theater hours."

Richard launched into what he knew of Vanderlip family history. He related a lot, much of which I had never known, especially as it had to do with Zoë's inheritance and her father. "The general, as a final insult, didn't leave anything to Jonathan or Arden in his will. The general disowned both of them and took up with a much younger woman after Zoë's mother died—a woman in her thirties. But he never formally married her, and the will only specified the benefactor as his legally married spouse. *That* will hadn't been updated since the death of Barre, his first wife. So Jonathan challenged it and won. It was just the beginning. The attorneys embezzled money. There was another lawsuit. Everything dragged on. It consumed Jonathan's life in his last years. But he wasn't suing for the money. Financially, he and I were well-off. He did so on moral grounds. He got to live long enough for the final victory, but he suffered a stroke the day after Christmas, two weeks before our anniversary. It left him in a coma from which he never recovered. He died on January 2. When I telephoned Arden, she was bitter. Simply bitter. 'I don't want that money,' she told me. 'Do you have any idea where that money came from? It's ill-gotten. There is blood on it.' She told me to keep it. I had no legal right, no moral right, to it. I couldn't do that. I told her that I was carrying out Jonathan's final wishes. 'His intention was to donate his half to the American Civil Liberties Union, a wish that I am going to honor. He was eager for you to have your half. I don't want to impose myself on your business, but perhaps you should think about doing something similar. Donate it to a cause.' She hung up on me."

I parked next to Eddie's truck, spray-painted fluorescent orange— every square inch with the exception of the window glass and headlamps, the brake and turn lights. It was an unusual color, to be sure, for somebody who wanted to stay as hidden as possible. I once asked Eddie why he did that. *'Cuz I need it that way at night,* he responded. Beyond the truck was an expanse of gravel filled with rusting farm equipment, stacks of rotting boards, a cast-off plastic septic tank. Next to this mad assemblage was an old-style California redwood barn circa the 1920s with a steep metal roof, tinged orange with rust, that swept out at the bottom.

I hobbled to where the rock ended next to the eucalyptus tree trunks carved into the Easter Island heads. I could barely walk—muscles I'd forgotten existed were stiff from the ride down the beach with Eddie. I had to pull aside a barrier, made of two-by-ten planks, in a three-foot gap in the rock wall. The front door of the house was off its hinges and wired shut. Plywood nailed to interior walls blotted the windows. The glass was still intact. On the north side was another door. I knocked. Eddie, in a white T-shirt and boxer shorts, appeared. He rubbed his eyes. Even tired they were fierce.

"Hey, Will," Eddie mumbled, waving me in. He disappeared into a bedroom to get dressed. It was only seven in the morning. I was the first one to arrive. The ceiling was stained yellow from the leaking roof, but at least Eddie had spackled the bullet holes from when he'd shot at the Indians. He hadn't, on the other hand, sanded or painted the plaster that was hand-slathered in place. The Jøtul in the living room was open full throttle, nearly glowing red, and the house was overheated. The place was a time capsule of the 1950s and early 1960s. There was a black-and-white Philips television just like when I was a kid. I had no idea if it even still worked. The dark brown mahogany end tables, with sharp angles popular in that era, were worn and stained from innumerable spilled beverages. Burn lines showed traces of generations of forgotten cigarettes. Stuffing erupted from an abraded couch next to the Jøtul; fir branch rounds were stacked next to it. All off-gridder houses smelled moldy, but the odor of Eddie's house was of rank decay.

I wandered a ways down the hall, dark because of the plywood-covered windows. Enough ambient light existed for me to once again study the paintings that hung there: watercolors on cotton fiber paper of spirit faces akin to the two trees on the north side of the house, evocative of Munch's *The Scream* but lacking emotion, simply staring with huge, drooping blank eyes. One was a Ghost Dancing Native American figure with raging spiral-like black eyes. I hadn't been inside Eddie's much, but every time I visited, the paintings startled me. I asked once about what inspired them, and Eddie had only muttered that he'd done them after his mother died. It was clear he didn't want to talk further about them.

Eddie materialized silently, wearing blue jean coveralls of the type favored by Midwest farmers. "Making coffee," he said with an intensity that was almost humorous.

The kitchen was decayed Betty Crocker. An art deco–style Frigidaire. A sloping once-white metal counter and porcelain sink, both yellowed, paint chipped. Eddie put water on to boil, scooped coffee from a can into a metal stovetop Drip-O-Lator, just like the one my grandmother used. He poured boiled water over the grounds, put the lid on, kept the pot on a burner while it finished dripping. We drank the strong coffee at the kitchen table, talking about weed—the falling price and the black market, in which Eddie remained firmly based. Much to Likowski's displeasure, he was growing indoors.

Eddie took me out the side door, each of us carrying our mugs. We went around the spirit heads, past the Easter Island faces, with their large carved ears listening for sounds only Eddie could hear. At the barn, he rolled open the ten-foot-tall door, and I studied what at one time had been the center of the Edwards family's ranch. A rusting tractor that hadn't been fired up in decades had a seat crusted with the shit stalagmites of swallows. There was a hay bailing machine, a discer, a loft filled with rotting hay. Eddie had had three horses at one point but had to give them all away when he went to jail for his meth conviction. Now he just had Buck, in a different barn. A plywood partition, unpainted and bright yellow, blocked the rear half of the barn. We entered the moist, warm air of the chamber, where there were rows of foot-tall plants in buckets beneath bright white grow lights. This was his weed, Mellow Yellow, which he'd bred with the help of Likowski, and he was proud to show me once again. Any time I visited, Eddie showed off his plants as if for the first time.

Eddie's cell phone rang before I could comment. It was Likowski. "Dude's like my conscience, man," Eddie said with a sigh, and put it on speaker.

"Of course the cops aren't gonna do jack!" Likowski spat out without saying hello. He sounded like he was driving, I assumed back from town. "I asked them, 'Can you come out and study the house and car as a crime scene?' And they said, 'We don't know if a crime has been committed.' So I said, 'How will you know whether or not a crime has been committed unless you investigate?' Detective Harris said a bunch of horseshit about how they have too many cases and too few detectives, blah, blah, blah. I told him Zoë isn't a grower, and they lied and said that didn't matter. Harris said they were going to classify her as a 'voluntary missing adult,' to check back in two weeks! Two weeks! I said, 'People just keep disappearing in this county and you don't give a fuck.' And the detective, he got all bent, started laying into me, saying for me to watch my language. So I said, 'Fuck you!' and walked out."

Both Eddie and I shook our heads ruefully. None of it was a surprise, neither the detective's lack of interest nor Likowski's ill-advised rebuke that would likely guarantee him getting raided that coming summer.

We returned to the kitchen as the others began arriving: Bill and Alma, and then Andy. It was going to be up to us—the neighbors—as was usually the case on this coast south of the Cougar, the road that crossed the Coast Range and connected us to the distant town—to America. Eddie poured a new pot from the Drip-O-Lator in mugs, and all of us sat around the gray Formica kitchen table, except for Bill, who was pacing back and forth in front of the stove. He had a round, wilderness-weathered face and a robust white beard, having come to resemble a mountain man from a nineteenth-century painting. "Thoughts, people?"

"I think she's had enough of Klaus," Andy said immediately. He had the same white beard as his brother, Bill, but his face was thinner and less sun ravaged. "A few months ago I ran into her on the beach. She was saying she was thinking of going back to Berlin to live out the rest of her life. She said she was done with this country. She didn't mention Klaus, but if Klaus is going to spend twenty or thirty years in prison, she has no reason left to be here."

"No mother would do that, certainly not Zoë," Alma said. Alma had long brown hair that flung wildly when she danced at the hippie gatherings, usually wearing a skirt made from 122 ties that had belonged to her father who had worked on Wall Street.

Though the same age as Bill, she looked fifteen or twenty years younger. "Zoë might not bail on Klaus, but he could have done something to her."

Nobody said anything. Alma went on: "After what he did to Tammie, I think he's capable of anything. He hates women. Maybe he finally unloaded on his mother. Or—"

"That could be a whole crowd of people," Bill interrupted.

"Let me finish," Alma said in the half-exhausted tone of a long-partnered woman, a woman who was tired of being interrupted by a man. "Or it's J.D.," she finished. "He's pissed that Zoë sued him."

I shook my head. I'd been following the situation on J.D.'s large-scale operation. J.D. was the reclusive billionaire with a mansion up higher on the ridge and aspirations for the legal cannabis market beyond our ken, or even Klaus's. But things in that respect had settled. I said, "J.D.'s not taking any water out of McCabe Creek for his operation. It's all coming from Elk Creek. That lawsuit is in the process of getting thrown out. The steelhead are vanishing for some other reason."

"But it's costing him," Bill said. "He has those two very expensive lawyers. You saw how monster they were at the hearing."

"I'm sure that doesn't matter much to him," I said. "That's not motive to kill." I added, "She's taken off without telling anyone before. Remember when she walked the Camino de Santiago? No one heard from her for two months."

"Then why is her car still there?" Alma asked.

"She didn't take her car that time either," I said. "She walked and hitched to town."

"We should check with the police to see if she's used her passport," Alma said.

"Ha," Andy said. "The cops aren't going to lift a finger."

"Lara speaks some German. She's going to make some calls," Bill said.

Alma gave her husband a steel-gray side-eye. "It's not a spontaneous vacation. This feels different and you know it."

Bill poured the last of the Drip-O-Lator into his cup. He now stopped pacing, stood in the center of the kitchen.

"Okay, let's go there. Let's talk about the fuckin' elephant in the room," Bill said. "I really think she's offed herself. She can't stand the idea of her son being a rapist. And what's she got left? She lost it a long time ago."

Now I realized why I didn't want to talk about my late-night visit with Zoë. I feared it would lend credence to suicide. Something told me that she didn't go back to the beach after I left. I stayed quiet as a debate ensued over Zoë's capacity to kill herself. Eddie never spoke. He walked down the hall and stared at one of his watercolors for a long time. I had a feeling he saw an answer in those eyes on the wall.

It took another fifteen minutes before things settled and everyone agreed that there was nothing left to do but look for our old friend and longtime neighbor. Alma took charge of marshaling volunteers. More of our neighbors arrived, and she set Johnny Gray and his partner up with heading the search in the forest around the Ark; Craig and Maggie Johnson, who had a big spread on the river, were already driving north to town to post flyers with Lara, Likowski's fiancée.

"Tammie's going to meet them in town," Alma said.

"Is that a good idea?" Andy asked.

"Tammie has issues with Klaus, not his mother."

Eddie and Bill would go on horseback to the beach and do another search. That was a task I didn't want—I wasn't able to imagine another minute on a horse.

"Will, you go with Likowski," Alma said with a little smirk. "He's almost back from town."

I shrugged and went out front to wait for him on the gravel shoulder. I didn't have to wait long. His battered 1968 Toyota 4x4 pickup pulled up, and even through the windshield I saw his face drop at the sight of me. I hopped in his truck without asking and let him know the plan: I'd help him flyer the 101. He looked none too pleased about it, but he was stuck with me. As he drove, I studied one of the flyers, pulled from a stack on the seat between us, with Zoë's picture in color.

HAVE YOU SEEN?
MISSING PERSON

ZOË VANDERLIP, AGE 76
HAIR: WHITE / HEIGHT: 5'10" / WEIGHT: 122
LAST SEEN FEBRUARY 11
$10,000 CASH REWARD FOR INFORMATION
SECURE EMAIL: DEATHWISHDAN@protonmail.com

In silence, Likowski navigated the potholed road destroyed by overweight Mack delivery trucks servicing the industrial grows with liquid fertilizer and soil. In places he had to slow so much we would have made better time walking, but with good reason; the previous month I'd blown a tire on my way in. The looping road led us ever higher into the coastal mountains. Near the summit we stopped for a pee break. There was no sign of humanity other than a huge industrial greenhouse far below in a forest clearing, gleaming white in the sun. Likowski's eyes were on it.

On the long grade down to the redwood forest, I peered out the side window, catching glimpses of other greenhouse complexes in the canyon. Once we entered the old-growth redwoods, a species of tree that infests this coast, we stopped at a trailhead signboard and put up the first flyer. Likowski's staple gun evoked pistol shots: *thwack! thwack!... thwack! thwack!* We went south on the 101, stopping at every interchange with a gas station or tourist attraction. Our destination was a town at the bottom of the county, the gateway to the Redwood Curtain; all travelers in this corridor had to pass through it. A casual glance and you feel like you're back in 1969: a hemp shop; a tie-dye boutique with a rainbow of color and a keep-on-truckin' hippie couple wearing bell bottoms on the sign; a crystal store; a health food market with a giant peace sign; the Emerald Inn, a quaint mom-and-pop hotel; the requisite free love–looking hippie hitchhikers with dogs and packs on either set of off-ramps; flower children smoking weed in a park. But on closer inspection things weren't at all what they seem. The flower children were actually gnarly homeless dudes and haggard women, severely mentally ill at best. The hitchhikers: meth freaks. The cute hippie shops were empty of customers: many of them pandering, cynical fronts for washing black-market weed money. No sane tourist would stay at the trashy Emerald Inn—most of its visitors booked rooms to engage in black-market buys, which blew up with the in-the-cellar price of $1,000-a-pound toxic industrial gangster bud that came with heavily taxed legal weed.

We struggled to find blank spots on poles and walls; Zoë's missing flyer was nudged in along the many others, eight of them young trimmers, all women. The most plaintive: PLEASE HELP ME FIND MY DAUGHTER, over a picture of a freckle-faced woman-child, missing since 2012 (though the poster was new). Pine utility poles were more rusting staples than exposed wood, thousands peppering each one from years of flyers being tacked to them. Some sheets for the disappeared had been up so long they were yellowed and faded, ready to blow away in the next strong wind. At one pole, a picture of a dark-bearded man: WANTED: POT THIEF. CHECK HIS BAG IF HE TRIMS 4 U!!!! Something about all of it enraged me. *Thwack! Thwack! Thwack! Thwack!* The hipster weed stealer was gone, covered by Zoë's fresh face, photographed in the magic glow of sunset. I recalled that first time with her, over two decades earlier, on the red couch in the exact same light and spot where Lara took the picture I was now staring at. My eyes teared and Likowski, looking in my direction, turned away quickly.

"We were together one summer," I said to his back. "1996."

Zoë desired couches. Lots of them. Before I came into her life, Zoë already had a collection of sofas scattered all over her 160 acres, each in a different stage of decay. Couches were in the forest, down by the creek; two were out at the bluffs at the western edge of her property, on a point above the breakers. That's where she favored sitting at sunset, playing the tuba. Each year she set out fresh couches wherever she fancied, and the more moldy and rotten they became with each passing season, the better. She'd been buying them secondhand in town, so she was keenly interested when I told her about an excellent and free source at Stanford University, a rather well-kept secret. It was spring and I had mentioned this casually one afternoon, having been invited to the Ark for a supper with some of the neighbors.

How I came to be appointed distinguished visiting professor at that august institution was, I suspected, less interesting to Zoë than details about couch procurement, but she asked anyway, which was a story that began in the 1980s, a Venn diagram of bad shit that led to severe burnout from years of war correspondence and a near-complete breakdown that led to my quitting my job at L.A.'s paper of record. Zoë wondered, in a consoling tone, how it could have gone any other way... if you had a gram of empathy. As for Stanford, the only reason I had the job was a substantial endowment by the McClatchy and Chandler families; those funds bequeathed by two California newspaper dynasties had to legally be spent annually, and there was no diverting that money to what the new chair saw as serious academic matters; the funds were mandated solely for a real journalist. In this small way I was still sort of being paid by the Los Angeles Times. "And the couches?" Zoë could not help but finally ask. I leaned in closer and told her the secret, and she laughed a long and throaty laugh.

And so there I was a month later, at another spring quarter's end, about to start my second summer on the ridge. At cessation of the school year, when students vacated, they hauled perfectly useful household goods and furnishings to the dumpsters behind the residential houses. Numerous couches ended up next to the bins. I cruised the campus and picked out a red vinyl midcentury modern, strapped it into the bed of the pickup, and the next morning drove it across the Golden Gate Bridge.

It was an hour from sunset when I opened Zoë's gate and piloted the bouncing truck down the precarious road to the Ark. Zoë emerged, standing at the aft of the home that was square like a normal dwelling, opposite the long pointing bow. The house had begun decomposing before it was even completed twenty years earlier and had been watertight for exactly just one year, when the roof began leaking. Buckets occupied permanent places in the bedrooms and kitchen and bathroom. The Ark had settled unevenly, and its rooms tilted noticeably toward the sea. A carelessly placed egg would roll off the counter and smash on the floor, and there was the sensation of being on an actual boat when walking across it, a deck swaying starboard from an ocean swell. Now it gleamed like driftwood in the sun, resembling a marooned mariner's vessel from ancient legend. Her once-blond hair was as white as the splintered siding. She was frightfully thin. The couch was heavy even for me, but she showed no sign of strain when she lifted her end; we carried it to the bare ground in front of the Ark and placed it next to a fire pit.

"Let's face it to the sea and sit to watch the sunset," Zoë said.

She procured a bottle of Jameson and made heavy pours in two jelly jars. We sat on the red couch. The sun was warm. The whiskey warmer. My eyes were on the horizon. I was exhausted from finishing up with teaching and the long drive, the last two hours on steep, winding roads that were made by men with shovels and horses and carts to create a wagon route over the Coast Range and barely improved on with the passage of eight decades. Zoë was to my left, and her head suddenly snapped in my direction. She was kissing me before I realized it. I was taken aback; this was not something I expected or, up to that moment, entertained. Sensing protest, she pressed her right index finger over my lips.

"Shut up. You like powerful women."

She pushed me backward onto the flaming-red Naugahyde and ripped off my clothes, quite literally—shirt buttons popped, scattering in all directions, and the fabric tore at the shoulder. I liked her—she was beautiful and smart—but it seemed too complicated to start something with Zoë. Don't shit in your own nest, the old cliché goes—but on the ridge, it was doubly true. In my experience, intimacy made people unreliable in practical ways. And on the ridge, we needed to rely on our neighbors. Could I have halted things from going further? Of course. I considered that option all the way up to the instant that we were naked and she straddled me...

I turned my head to the ocean and watched the last edge of the orange ball, faint in the marine layer, sink into the sea. Our naked bodies embraced tightly against the growing chill in the enveloping dusk. The next thing I remember was awakening hours later at two in the morning in her bedroom. I studied eight water stains in the ceiling by the glow of two oil lamps on a dresser. The stains varied in size, from a dinner plate to the width of the mouth of a fifty-five-gallon metal drum. The largest had a black center where the Sheetrock had been drilled through from the leaking roof, with concentric outer rings ranging from yellow to orange. Chopin's Nocturne in E minor filled the Ark, blending with the sound of crashing surf. A bat swooped low. I felt wind from its wings on my cheeks. The sheets smelled of must. I rubbed my stubbled face, stood to lean against the bedroom doorframe, and watched a nude Zoë at the Steinway, placed near the bow of the home—the only nook where the roof didn't leak. She was hot; she had a youthful body from all the wood hauling and splitting, from mucking out spring boxes and hydropower ponds and tanks. She didn't acknowledge my appearance. Her eyes were intense on the keys. She burst into Beethoven's Piano Concerto no. 5, her hands moving in a wave across the keyboard, a tsunami of sound. Later we wrapped ourselves in a blanket and went outside to stand on the ocean-facing side of the Ark, bracing against the fifty-two-degree wind that loudly snapped the Earth First! flag on the mast. We faced Sagittarius. The Pacific was nearly black. Photovoltaic panels on the south-facing roof, reflecting starlight, were deep phosphorescent blue.

I said, "This could end up messy."

"We will be summer lovers," she replied a little distantly. "We will have a lovely three months. We will have sex one last time before you return to your students. Farewell sex. Then we will pretend that none of this ever happened."

Likowski listened without interruption as I told him about the summer I ended up in Zoë's bed. He expressed no reaction whatsoever to my confession. When I finally stopped, he only said, "I was with her when Klaus was in high school. One year."

We stared at each other. This could have been taken as one-upmanship on Likowski's part, but I knew better. It was a peace offering, or at least the makings of one. We went back out on the 101 and hit some off-ramps north of the road we'd taken to the highway. At some point, I admitted what I had not yet spoken out loud to anybody.

"I think I was the last one to see her."

"Yeah?"

"She called me over that night. The last thing I wanted was to go out in that storm, but she was crying."

Likowski nodded with understanding—imagining Zoë crying was next to impossible. "Why'd she call you over? What did she talk about?"

I shrugged. "Almost nothing. The main thing she said was that she should never have left Berlin."

"That's it?"

"And she was soaking wet. She'd been down there. In the middle of that storm."

"She was in the water?"

"Yep. And came back up."

"Which is why you're going to say she didn't kill herself," he said wryly. Something in his tone told me the peace offering was being revoked.

"You're full of news," he muttered finally. "As usual."

Likowski had been behind the wheel all day as we'd flyered the 101, so I offered to drive that last hard part on the way home. Without a word, he tossed me the keys, got in the passenger seat, and shut his eyes. They remained this way, even as I raced the Cougar's gauntlet, but he couldn't have been sleeping, not on the Cougar. Jesus, or could he? Visibility was three car lengths. It's good there were no other drivers stupid enough to be on the road in that fog—Likowski's grille would have ended up in their asses. There was always fog on the Cougar, but the fog this night was ridiculously thick, even for a Black Fog. You go into the clouds on the Cougar, ascend to the realm of the moon and sun; and after you get to know it, after years of driving that snake, you embrace risk. Otherwise it takes two hours to get home. You can make it in an hour and a half (an hour fifteen if you're really crazy), if you've got it down, have the entire course imprinted in memory, keep a foot on the gas, and have fast reflexes. *Left, sharp right, sharp left, a straightaway for five hundred feet, you're okay in here; hairpin left, right, right; up, up, up; more up*—Christ, it never ends, like a video game. Get it wrong, however, and false familiarity will kill you in one second; one left instead of right, you're zapped, over the edge, *adios, motherfucker*, for real. Forty miles of for real. Forty miles of unrelenting being on game.

When doing the build back in the 1990s, I returned from town with eight hundred feet of two- and four-inch PVC pipe in ten-foot pieces, to run from the big water tank to the house. I bought the big pipe, no pressure line loss, because I needed every ounce of head from the tank just 44.2 vertical feet above the cabin. The pipes were lashed with come-alongs, hanging out of the truck's bed, strapped tight—until they weren't. On one of the hairpins the bundle let loose, flying across the Cougar like a game of snow-white pick-up sticks. After scrambling to pull them all to the side, I went to the edge and peered over. It was an absolutely straight one thousand feet down, with just two feet of shoulder, no guardrail. It made me dizzy. Drop-offs like this lined the entire Cougar, and if you thought about them on the outside curves, about the two feet between you and the edge, you'd never drive that road.

If I happened to launch Likowski's truck over the brink, we might not be discovered for years, if ever, no matter how hard anyone looked, unless the truck exploded and started a forest fire. Old wrecks with skeletons inside were occasionally found deep in the canyon, solving long-ago missing person reports. The Cougar was built with Chinese hand labor, men who came to redwood country seeking employment after they finished chopping and blasting Leland Stanford's railroad across the Sierra; these were men who understood how to chisel paths with hand tools on cliffs where no paths had a right to exist. The road was not much improved from their excellent work with shovels and pickaxes, save for pavement, crumbling and marked by thousands of potholes. The road had no base; asphalt had been laid over the clay wagon road. Not long after the Chinese men finished making the Cougar, in 1885, an edict was issued that all "coolies" had twenty-four hours to leave the county. The order was no idle threat—it was decreed by those who slaughtered the native population over two decades earlier.

We crested the final hill that led down into the hamlet. I was eager for home and sleep. But Likowski awakened about a quarter mile from the Purple Thistle, and instead of driving on I slowed. "Want a drink?" I asked.

I took his silence for a yes and pulled in front of the bar with its bright purple neon sign of a flowering thistle, genus *Carduus*, the common prickly invasive species found all over North America, glowing over the entrance. It was the only public gathering place in the hamlet since the hippie Dugout closed in the aughts, becoming the "in" spot for new money, and yet it remained a redneck joint. The words "redneck" and "hippie" had long since become meaningless in terms of telling by sight who belonged to which tribe. Hippie men from the seventies now had short hair and drove battered pickup trucks; some called themselves "bluenecks." Many pioneer family men cultivated marijuana and their hair was long.

The Thistle also harbored some bad memories—enough for me not to have been back in four years. The last time we were here Klaus assaulted a woman in the bathroom—a young trimmer none of us knew. Though she hadn't filed charges at the time, apparently too scared of retribution, it appeared she was part of the district attorney's case against him, though nobody knew for sure.

Tonight the place looked dead. We could see inside through the front plate glass: just one guy seated on a barstool. We found a booth near the rear with a good view of the sterile interior, more like a Denny's than a bar. Likowski took the war correspondent's seat—back against the wall. Even with neither of us having been around in years, Jake still recognized us. "Gentlemen," he shouted from behind the bar. "Wellers?"

"Feeling poor tonight," I hollered back. "Whatcha got on tap?"

We gave a flyer to Jake, who immediately posted it at the Thistle's entrance. Likowski stared into a Redwood Curtain pale ale; a Six Rivers was in front of me. We drank in silence. Three weeks had passed since our argument, started in Likowski's sweat lodge when I'd blurted out the news that I was putting my land up for sale. Likowski had first called me every dirty name he could think of related to my being a journalist. I shrugged, prepared for that abuse. But then he suggested I was selling to J.D.—an offensive idea I had not anticipated. A bitter shouting match ensued; I had left and hiked back home.

Likowski finally turned his face to me and locked eyes: "I'm going to tell you something you don't want to hear. We're wasting our time. I think she offed herself. She may not have gone back down to the ocean that night. There's places on the ridge where nobody's been since the Indians. She shot herself, she's back up in there, we'll never find her body."

I shook my head.

"Don't give yourself so much credit," Likowski said, giving me a rare sneer, especially cruel on his Marlboro Man face. "You weren't going to save her. I'd like to believe she's alive. But I know her. You know her. Her only son's going to prison for *rapes*, plural, not to mention he's a scumbag. And she's right. She should have stayed in Berlin. She's getting old. Everyone she knew when they built their homesteads is dead or about to die. She picked her way to go out."

"So where's the tuba, then?"

The sneer remained on Likowski's face before giving way to sadness. "It's with her. That's all. It's with her bones in the woods."

The bar began to fill up with about two dozen young people, a third of them women who looked like trimmers. Three men seated at the bar talked in what sounded like Russian, but we knew they weren't. They looked vaguely Euro, and each wore a silk running suit: bright blue, yellow, and tan. Their footwear resembled slippers, no laces, made of velvet, burgundy, and black, which was how we confirmed they were Bulgarians. They got the slipper shoes from France, and most of the Euro mobsters were partial to them. Kid Rock's "All Summer Long" dropped on the jukebox—*We thought those days would never end...*—while people kept pouring through the door. All of them were total strangers to me. When I arrived over two decades earlier, I soon recognized the faces of everyone in their cars or trucks. Now the valley was filled with aliens coming at my windshield.

Jake, possibly out of pity for the gnarled older-timers we were, brought over Wellers, on the house. "To Zoë's safe return," he said, lifting a glass before drifting away.

Likowski and I had stopped speaking for so long that it surprised me when I heard his voice again: "There's a shitstorm coming to this country. You don't want to be out there. There's no better place than here. We can hunt, fish, grow our own food. We don't need the outside world."

For all his anger, I could see Likowski's sincerity. He truly didn't want me to go, to put myself back out there. Just as he didn't want to believe that Zoë had left. He'd prefer to believe that she had called it quits altogether and done herself in, not because he didn't care about her but precisely because he did. After all, I knew it was his final retirement plan.

"We aren't an island," I said quietly. "We have to go to town for everything. Or order it from Amazon."

"Where are you gonna go that's better than here? Safer?"

"Safer? We're in a bar with Bulgarian mobsters for regulars."

The stark truth was that the hippie refuge had morphed into a macabre reality show, weed meets *The Wire* in the woods. Zoë vanishing, whatever was going on with her, was the latest weird thing to happen. Violence increased in the wake of legal weed that tanked the price. Alongside the Bulgarians, there were Mexican cartels, a rash of disappearances, near weekly homicides, among them an SUV recently found burning at the side of the road, two bullet-riddled bodies inside. I repeated all these things. Likowski replied, "We're okay out where we are. We're out there at the edge, you, me, Bill and Alma. Those assholes can do what they want."

We had our backs to the sea. I couldn't pretend being at the edge protected us from what was happening to the east. But that wasn't the only reason I was selling.

"Have you thought about getting old?" I asked.

"What's old?" he replied fast, before I could continue.

"I mean with Lara."

His fiancée was nearly half his age. He was pretending to keep up and failing at it. His homestead was decaying around him: the roof truss and beam ends were dry-rotted, the metal roof nearly rusted through in spots, the barn so infested with termites that it now leaned, his road in serious need of some bulldozer work. He simply chose not to see these things. "She knows what she's getting into," he said into his Weller, and I could tell that Lara was the hope, the spark keeping things on the ridge alive for him. But would she stay?

"Look, I'll speak for myself. The last twenty-five years have been hard."

Likowski evinced a nasty, mocking pout that made the previous sneer seem almost friendly.

"I'm not crying about it. It's just true. But I'm thinking about the next twenty-five. Alone."

Likowski stared at me, and his face again filled with sadness for a brief moment. "You're alone because of what you do." And then anger replaced it: "You just came here to do research. And now you are going to do another book, tell the world about the 'secret lives of weed farmers.' *And* sell your place, cash in on the Green Rush, and leave."

"I don't recall cutting my wrist and signing a blood oath that I'd never sell," I shouted.

The ensuing argument was a replay of the sweat lodge weeks earlier, shouted over Ted Nugent's "Wang Dang Sweet Poontang" and featuring a diatribe about the limited possibilities of a financial windfall from any publishing venture, much less this one. It didn't matter.

"You're just a spy," Likowski concluded again. The accusation was both true and untrue: it was my nature.

"It's all material, as Nora Ephron said." I gave him a far weaker sneer of my own. It was true. Every moment of revelation, confusion, questioning, pain, pleasure—from birth until you can no longer tap at a keyboard to put it all down—goes in. But it was untrue that I'd planned to write a book when I came in 1995. The book revealed itself. When? I have no idea, but the point came where there was no *not* writing it. I knew this: my intention of writing a book had nothing to do with setting off Likowski. It was other things—one of them being I had betrayed him simply by putting my place up for sale. And there was more. Despite the long-ago summer of sex with Zoë, by my end days on the ridge I'd grown much more intimate with Likowski, if betrayal is indeed the measure. Downing the last of my Weller, I owned it angrily: "I know this much: Dan Likowski isn't who he says he is. No database reveals anything in California beyond the property record. There are two Daniel Likowskis in Ohio and Pennsylvania who are twenty to thirty years younger. The only age-appropriate match is on Ancestry.com, for a Daniel T. Likowski who died as an infant in Cleveland. You don't really care that I'm selling. You just know I'm closing in on your past."

"Fuck you," Likowski said.

For a moment I thought he might strike me. Instead, he stormed out of the booth and toward the exit, only to reel back as the Thistle's front door blew open. Klaus Vanderlip, wearing aviator sunglasses, strode in and hung a black leather jacket on a peg in the wall. If he saw the flyer for his mother, he made no indication. Instead, his angular chin slowly rose as he scanned the room. Flanking his rear were two of his foremen who doubled as heavies when he was in public.

"Mayor!" someone shouted. He'd bestowed this unelected title on himself about a year before his arrest, his expansive greenhouses having made him the largest employer in the valley. He could call himself anything he wanted. Soon there was a unified chant of *Mayor! Mayor!* A thin, satisfied smile came to his face. Someone rushed up to him with a drink and slapped him on the back. Likowski looked on with horror as the reality must have dawned on him: the high-priced lawyers had finally paid off and gotten Klaus bail after being in jail for five months.

This wasn't the shy, grunge outcast kid whom I hired to help me raise the center roof beam and to put on the roof when I built my place back in 1995. Nor was it the kid who'd been Likowski's protégé and mentee, in desperate need of a father figure. In those days he resembled Kurt Cobain, with straight-as-vermicelli blond hair hanging like sad puppy tails on either side of his ears and falling forward to conceal his face, perpetual blond stubble on his chin. He was awkward but nice, the kind of kid who'd shake your hand twice, even three times, when you said goodbye. This Klaus was confident and commanding. The old Klaus was as dead as Kurt Cobain.

Over his shock, Likowski went straight at him, and for a moment, it put fear in the younger man. "Stay the fuck away from me, Kow!" Klaus snarled, as the two men stood, chests nearly touching. "Everything would be fine if you just stayed the fuck out of my business!"

I half expected bitch-slapping tweaker rage from Klaus, based on when I'd seen Klaus lose it before. But it was still Likowski, the only adult male who treated him seriously when he was a kid. As they glared at each other and everyone in the bar stopped, waiting for the fight, I rushed in and pulled Likowski out the front door. Under the purple neon of the bar's sign, the fight in him drained almost instantly, and he went to his truck without bothering to ask if I was coming. He knew I wasn't. There was work for the spy to do, and as I turned to go inside I heard Likowski's truck door slam in goodbye.

Klaus pushed aside his acolytes and approached the moment he saw me returning to the booth I'd just left. "Will!" he shouted, breaking into a broad grin.

I forced a journalist's smile. We fist-bumped and I asked when he got out.

"Friday night. That lawyer Mom hired worked his magic. What the hell you and Kow doing out so late?"

I studied him for a long moment before answering: "We're looking for your mom."

Klaus looked puzzled as he sat opposite. I slid him a flyer.

"No one told you yet? No one's seen her in days. We spent the day posting flyers up and down the 101. You walked by one in fact, coming in here."

Klaus shook his head, and a wry smile came across his face. "You all really have too much damn time on your hands up there on the ridge."

"What do you mean?"

Klaus looked at me evenly: "I talked to her on Wednesday about the lawyers. She told me she was going away for a few days, maybe a few weeks."

"Where?"

"She didn't say. You know how Mom is."

"But her car's still there."

"She's probably on a vision quest or..." He trailed off, and I suddenly saw the little boy inside Klaus. "She'll show up. She always does."

A woman grabbed Klaus by the arm and started dragging him out of the booth to dance. He shook her off.

"What time on Wednesday did you talk to your mom?"

"Ten or eleven," Klaus said. "I could check my phone and tell you exactly."

He was a total poker face. It was impossible to tell what he was thinking, so I tried to rattle him. "Some people think you had something to do with it."

"Are you fucking telling me you think I did something to Mom?" Klaus's tone was on the edge of frightening—the first time he'd ever raised his voice with me.

"That's just what some people are saying."

"People like Alma? She believes every fucking conspiracy theory she hears. People like Kow? Doc? Were you part of their getting Tammie to go to the DA?!"

"I'm just a writer," I said as flatly as possible. I relaxed a little when he didn't press the question. The woman was again tugging on his shoulder.

"Mom is fine," he said tersely as he stood to go dance with the woman. "Jake!" Klaus barked toward the bar.

Jake's head jerked up, startled, like a private being yelled at by his platoon sergeant. Klaus pointed at me. "Weller! On me."

I nursed the new Weller, replaying the conversation and grimacing at the shitty jukebox music as it grew increasingly louder with more Ted Nugent. There was nothing in his voice that gave any hint that he was faking his ignorance. But then Klaus was a practiced liar. A song or two later, he went out front to smoke. I watched him through the plate glass, between dancing bodies. His face, purple from the neon, was grave as he talked on his cell phone. He waved his arms. When he reentered the bar, he broke into a broad grin and hugged a woman who'd just arrived, a frightfully thin girl in a pink silk dress, her hair dyed purple. Seeing her with Klaus made me shudder. Didn't she know what he was charged with? Or perhaps she did and didn't care. Or, like Jake, didn't have much choice—being anti-Klaus wasn't much of an option here.

I stared into my drink, my head spinning—the long day had taken a toll. Only the sound of the Harley Fat Boy firing up and Klaus roaring away spurred me to look up, and when I did, a woman was standing there. She was tall, maybe five-nine, and very thin, her black hair tinged henna around the bangs and front edges. She wore a black top and a short black skirt with black nylon tights. She was Chinese or Chinese American, at least fifty, which made her out of place among the twenty-something women in the crowd. Still, she was easily the most beautiful person in the room. "May I?" she asked, pointing to the empty side of the booth.

As she sat, I introduced myself.

"I know who you are, Will."

She sipped the drink in her hand—a gimlet—pulled the lime off, sucked on it, then dropped it into the glass.

"Your name?" I asked.

"You need to know something," she replied, ignoring the question.

"What do I need to know?"

"Sotirova might have kidnapped Zoë. And you should know that Klaus has enemies. He's in a bidding war for the Thistle. Do you know who Sotirova is?"

Everyone knew who he was. I answered like a schoolboy reciting before the blackboard: "Sotirova is a lieutenant for Bulgarian mobsters with a big grow to the south, in the inland mountains."

She nodded approvingly. "And Sotirova may have kidnapped her for leverage on Klaus to back off bidding for the bar."

"Klaus doesn't seem too worried about his mother. He says she's on vacation. Or a vision quest."

In lieu of a dismissive shrug, she sipped the gimlet.

"Besides... this joint? It's not worth it," I added.

"You certainly don't understand the three cardinal rules of real estate: location, location, location."

I was puzzled—and it probably showed. "Pretend I'm stupid, or drunk—or both."

"I'll just say this: it's a whole lot more valuable than what the P&L says. It's losing money, hemorrhaging money. Jake's been skimming. Even if he wasn't, it's not profitable. But it's worth a lot."

"Why?"

She laughed. "I'm not doing your job for you. If you think about it, you can figure it out."

I sighed. My entire goddamn career as a journalist, no one ever made it easy. I was so tired I couldn't think about it. "If they want to own a bar, one of them could just buy the old Dugout and reopen it. Cheap. It's still filled with everything, just like the day it shut down."

"When it closed, the property reverted to residential. It was out of compliance," she said. "The zoning board won't allow it."

"Here? They don't give a shit," I said.

She laughed. "Have you been reading the news? They're using Google Earth to do what CAMP never dreamed of doing— enforcing everything now. They want the taxes. *Dude*, it's not 1970 anymore."

I began laughing. The woman asked why. I just laughed some more. It was a ridiculous scene. She was hot. Mysterious. Full of inside knowledge. "I've lived here for years. How could I not know who you are?" I finally asked.

"Let's just say I'm before your time."

"How is that possible?"

"And a concerned citizen. And someone who cares about Zoë."

"What am I supposed to do?"

She smiled coyly and rolled her eyes. If she didn't scare the shit out of me, I would have said she was flirting. She stood. "I just want to say: check out Sotirova. But hurry. He might be dead before the end of the week."

With that she winked and walked out of the bar. I thought for a moment, then left the half-consumed Weller and followed her. She was getting into a fancy convertible, the top up because of the cold night. I don't know cars. I pulled out my smartphone and took a picture as she opened up and blew past the Thistle, heading south. Soon, I'd figured out it was a Ferrari Portofino, a quarter of a million dollars' worth of machine.

For my part, I began walking home, remembering when things had really started to change. Back at the Thistle, I had told Klaus that I was just a writer, but I couldn't pretend to myself anymore. I was caught up in a vortex of lives, like it or not, something that I was now realizing happened almost the instant I moved here. A long time before, a lot longer than last summer, I had ceased being a mere observer. My life would be easier if I was just a writer.

That night our world started spinning, Likowski and Lara huddled with Tammie in her yurt, not far from Klaus's grow where she worked. Tammie was still sobbing. It had been roughly three hours since the violent assault. Tammie was grasping for what to do, and though it seemed obvious that calling the sheriff's office and pressing charges were what had to happen next, she wasn't sure. "I am afraid they will put me in prison," Tammie said with sadness.

"Because of your immigration status?" Lara offered gently.

"I have no status!"

"I'll bail you out," Likowski said quickly.

Lara hushed him with a glance.

"Please, let's go to Doctor Anderson for him to examine you," Lara said. "And you can choose not to go to the cops, but we should photograph those marks on your neck so there is evidence."

"Now?"

Lara nodded, and Tammie pulled her shirt low around her shoulders. Lara adjusted a small table lamp with an LED bulb, better illuminating the bright red welts where Klaus's thumbs dug into her throat. Lara raised the camera shakily; the shutter clicked.

Likowski telephoned Doc and they got to his office just after midnight. The clinic was in a cottage that resembled something from early last century: old oak cabinets, glassware, an examining table of faded chrome and cracked red Naugahyde with a gleaming white paper covering it. Tammie sat on the edge in a patient's smock.

"I'm going to ask some difficult questions, Tammie," Doc said, still rubbing sleep out of his eyes. "Are you okay with that? With us trying to help?" Regardless of whether she was okay with it, it was her best choice.

The next evening, a meeting was held at the community center. Most of my neighbors came down from McGee Ridge, and a dozen others from the valley also showed up. We argued about how best to handle Klaus attacking women. There were others besides Tammie, and there was no doubt that a report should be filed with the sheriff's office, but would it do anything? Unlikely as that was, Tammie had decided that she wanted to press charges and we wanted to support her.

An indifferent detective took a report. Three weeks passed with no word. Tammie was now living in the pottery studio down in Likowski's big-leaf maple forest, where there was no landline or cell service. She slept a lot and visited only with Lara, ascending the steep track to make a call on her phone at Likowski's. The detective didn't answer. She left a message. Days passed. She left another message. Finally we wrote a letter to the highest authority in the county—or rather, I wrote one on behalf of the neighbors—imploring District Attorney Robert Bogel to act. I doubted anything would come of it. In fact, we were all convinced it would languish as nearly all these cases did.

And yet, two weeks later, my phone rang. It was Doc. He told me, "Klaus has been arrested."

The beginnings of ends are often difficult to mark. The old adage posits that the two best times in a boater's life is the day he buys a boat and the day he sells it. Something happens in between when it all goes to shit and it's never clear exactly when. The best day of my journalism life is easy to identify: November 17, 1978, my start date at the *Los Angeles Times*. The end date? I forget exactly, sometime in early April 1994. For what happened in between, I think of an interview I did when I was twenty for a freelance piece in the weekend arts section of the *Cleveland Plain Dealer*, with a septuagenarian radio personality named Armstrong who'd worked for every station in town over a half century, quitting and moving on when he was no longer treated well. He told me many things that I wouldn't understand until after that old man was long dead, among them: *one day you are soaring with an eagle, the next, beneath the belly of a snake; you are the same person with the same talent, but they suddenly no longer see you that way; it is they who have changed, not you; you have to be willing to walk; it's like gangrene, get it on your leg, you cut off the leg, move on.* I'd allowed the gangrene to fester but can't exactly remember when the rot started. If you were involved with some dark news event, be it economic, criminal, or ecologically destructive in nature—fires, earthquakes, floods, hurricanes, wars— there was a very good chance that Will Specter showed up at your door in the 1980s. There wasn't a disaster in the Bible that I didn't cover, save for a plague of locusts.

Yet it was much more than simply the demons I'd collected in those years of reporting for the *Times*, a blur of PTSD-inducing assignments; it was the change in newsroom culture. There was a new top editor, a bald man who wore suspenders—a corporate clone in over his head whose insecurity made our lives miserable. I couldn't take it any longer. I went into the newsroom at three A.M. and slipped my resignation letter, along with my LAPD and CHP press passes, beneath the door of Mike's glass office; he was the editor who'd hired me and the sole editor I still respected. I went back to my desk and sent a system-wide message to the entire building: "It's been nice working with some of you." And then I left the newsroom for the last time, wheeling all my files out with a hand cart.

Walking home from the Purple Thistle that night, I struggled to remember the exact date I left the *Times*, then I thought that maybe it didn't really matter. Mike also couldn't take it any longer, but there was a different way out for him. About a year after I left, he swallowed a bottle of pills and ended zipped up in a coroner's body bag. I couldn't bring back Mike. I couldn't change that past. What mattered now was this: this end was different. It started at the very beginning, the day in 1995 when I drove off the mountain to the general store to put up a HELP WANTED sign on the bulletin board. I was ready to give up on off-grid living. I had no fucking idea what I was getting myself into and I knew it, which filled me with a sense of dread and a mean case of buyer's remorse. In that moment I was doubtful if I'd even get the roof on before the rainy season. I was a pilgrim, desperate for assistance. (Owning a bungalow two blocks from Sunset Boulevard is diametrically opposite to that of a wilderness cabin deep behind the Redwood Curtain.)

Only one person answered my posting, and so there I was at four o'clock one afternoon, after having started work at seven that morning, resting with a young Klaus Vanderlip in the shade of my south wall, right after we'd winched the thirty-foot-long ten-by-twelve-inch roof beam into place. It was his first day on the job. Klaus, skinny and shirtless, asked if it was quitting time, and when I responded that I thought so, he pulled two cold Sierra Nevada pale ales from a cooler in his truck. As we emptied the cooler of the beers Klaus had brought, I learned about the outlaws in the surrounding hills and the vagaries of guerrilla weed farming. I also learned a little about Likowski, whom Klaus still looked up to: *The best weed man north, south, and east. West if there was a west from here.*

I grew fond of him, in large part because he helped make it possible for me to have a roof and get through that first winter. And I believe Klaus favored me for a simple reason as well. Unlike everyone else, from his mother to his teachers to his so-called friends, I never judged him. Still, I had a feeling about him. There was a coming storm, recognizable in the attitude, the dangerous chip on his thin shoulder, when he talked about someday being respected, having money, power. He had something to prove and, together with a festering inferiority complex, I knew the kid had potential to veer wildly out of control.

I'd conducted hundreds of reportorial autopsies on people who'd blown through the guardrails, reverse outlining what led to decline: why that angry white drifter returned to the Stockton schoolyard of his childhood to shoot all those Asian children; why that NBA basketball star put the gun in his mouth and pulled the trigger; the perverted, megalomaniacal course that led the cult leader to amass a fortune while raping thirty-four straight male followers whom he lured to his rural compound. In thousands of interviews I dissected rage, despair, greed, vengeance, and Caligulan desire that resulted in bleak outcomes, and I did it all on newspaper deadline. In 1995 with Klaus, I was looking at Chekhov's gun on the wall long before it was fired. I knew enough to start taking notes in my journal that first night after Klaus and I raised the roof beam; for the next quarter century I filled journals—dozens of them.

I didn't come with a goal of writing about my new community, no matter how much Likowski believed that to be the case. I simply kept a running diary of my life. At first, I remained in the spirit of the daily journalist, who examines events and composes snapshots. Frozen in a moment, the published story always remains incomplete. A news hole must be filled. You feed that maw and then you do it again the next day. And the next. In my case, I did it for decades for different publications: one-long-constant-motherfucking-deadline. The daily journalist deals with the grist of the moment untethered from any meaning that pleases the historian or novelist. At some point, I realized I was no longer that daily guy. In my time living on the ridge, it became for me a retooling of research, observation, documentation, immersion. I was transfixed with Klaus, Likowski, Zoë, and Eddie and how their beginnings, so far removed from one another, intertwined with their conclusions. I found myself absorbed by their histories, dissecting their existences not as snapshots but as a movie reel with tens of thousands of frames. Just as there is method acting for the screen, there is method journalism (or perhaps it was simply method living).

The first five miles after the Thistle was the easy part of the walk, following the relatively level road along the river. My phone battery had died after googling what kind of car the mysterious woman was driving, but I guessed it was about four in the morning when I neared the sea and the long grade up to the ridge. The fog was so thick I couldn't see the road and kept walking into brush at the edge. The ocean was loud somewhere below.

I recalled the early days and weeks in 1995, when, despite my being overwhelmed by the construction, there was magic; when every sensation was new: sleeping beneath the stars in the meadow after escrow closed, waking up to a still and dewy dawn; climbing to the topmost reaches of an old-growth Douglas fir as fog boiled off the ocean, the mist broken into fragments by the ancient forest, the pieces becoming flying white-sheeted cartoon ghosts weaving through the trunks below. And there was sound: hundred-mile-an-hour wind rushing through the fir during a Pineapple Express, those hellacious storms that blow in from Hawaii—*woo-woo-WOO!*—as a gust neared, passed, and rolled over the ridge (wind is the language of this wild place); the cry of the red-tailed hawks that nested near the cabin; the screech of a saw-whet owl; coyotes howling in the canyon on full moon nights. Feel: the roughness of lichen and Franciscan sedimentary rock when I lay naked on an exposed outcrop in the meadow, the prickle of nettles, the Pacific air on my skin. And smell: the oily peppermint of yerba buena, the balmy pitch of fir, the salty sweet of thimbleberry as I crawled on hands and knees searching for the springs that would become my water supply.

That was the first job I tackled. I hauled hundreds of pounds of rock by wheelbarrow down the mountain and bags of Portland cement and beach sand, from which I made two massive stone spring boxes with lids, which poured through black poly pipe to a four-hundred-gallon holding tank, which in turn was piped into a small pump house containing a football-sized Dankoff pump that ran off twelve-volt direct current from solar panels, the device somehow miraculously promising to propel a steady stream of water uphill via poly pipe. After hauling all that rock and laying all that pipe and cable down from the solar panels, there came the excitement of seeing the tiny spark when I touched the positive wire to the pump's motor. I black-taped the connection and ran uphill through the forest. In the meadow, as I neared the five-thousand-gallon tank, the sound of falling water. I pulled the poly pipe from the intake and stared at the gushing liquid, pushed 174 vertical feet up from the pump house. I held the pipe overhead and allowed water to pour onto my tongue. When I'd drunk my fill, I spat a mouthful at the sun. I whooped. I made that water happen. It was so fundamental, a primal joy unknown to city people. Yet remembering the elation of those initial days was like trying to recapture the exhilaration of first love: recalled, but not felt in the soul. The conclusion of my time on McGee Ridge, however long it took to sell, was a task to be endured, like the cessation of a long-term relationship. Then Zoë vanished and changed everything.

Dawn's light was breaking when I opened the door of the cabin. I collapsed on the bed and slept until four in the afternoon. I ate a meal and waited for night. I walked to the Ark. There was a half-moon and I didn't need a headlamp. When I crested the hill, the structure was dark. And creepy. But I went in and I started with the box, extracting General Vanderlip's diary, other documents. And then I spent the next two hours going through cabinets and drawers and tripping over buckets. The hydro was still working, and I collected the three electric lamps, carrying them to Zoë's bedroom, where I used a PDF creator app on my phone to copy all the pages through the rest of the night. I might have been a spy, but a thief I was not.

I placed all the items back exactly where I found them. I wasn't yet ready to start the autopsy—that would require trips to Berlin and New York City long after I sold my place on the ridge. But I had my clues.

2

1943–1980

It was a moment her father had been waiting for all seventeen years of her life and she desired to take a taxi! *General H. Spellman Vanderlip's daughter will not show up at the cotillion in a taxi!* thundered the general, who was fond of talking of himself in the third person, especially after having consumed too much Canadian Club, which meant any day of the week past two in the afternoon. General Vanderlip had booked the limousine back in July. Even then he feared being too late. Everyone would be trying to rent a limo for the Debutante Cotillion and Christmas Ball at the Waldorf in Manhattan on the night of December 22, 1959. Arden Rutherford Vanderlip would step out of that hired car with her escort, William, the general and his wife, Barre, behind them as cameras flashed. It was simply how it would be. He needed to have her name in the papers. A publicist had been hired to be certain she made the *Times*. The publicist would leak that President Eisenhower was one of those who had nominated her, even though the president despised General Patton.

Arden was forged in war, conceived on the eve of Patton's campaign leading the U.S. Seventh Army in northern Africa against the troops of Field Marshal Erwin Rommel. Vanderlip had not yet been promoted. He was a full colonel when he had a conjugal visit with Barre Rutherford Vanderlip, his wife. As Patton's confidant, he enjoyed certain perquisites. Barre wasn't ready for a child, not in war, maybe not after. It was the dangerous time of month, but there was no avoiding sex with her husband. Just before the Sicily campaign in 1943, Patton promoted Vanderlip to brigadier general. In the press, Brigadier General Hobart Gay was publicly Patton's chief of staff, but it was Vanderlip who was really his most vital aide, tasked with carrying out many top secret assignments. As such Vanderlip could take many liberties. Another conjugal visit was arranged for the newly minted general in Palermo. Patton personally ordered a Lockheed Electra to transport Barre, along with their baby, from London. If Vanderlip needed to get laid, he would get laid. A nurse was charged with taking care of the infant girl. The Vanderlips dined that night at the best restaurant, while armed U.S. soldiers stood guard in front. The couple started with maccu soup, moved on to pasta con le sarde, then pesce spada alla ghiotta, and finished with pignolata Messinese. Two bottles of Magma Nerello Mascalese, the grapes having been grown on the slopes of Mount Etna, were consumed. They returned to the best hotel in town, which Patton had commandeered. It would have been romantic, but it wasn't. It was more than the soldiers with M-1 rifles outside their door that ruined the mood. She was simply exhausted.

Before they left the penthouse off Central Park East, the general joked about Arden and William kissing after the ball. Arden restrained herself from bursting out in laughter. Only she knew that William was a homosexual.

To say the grand ballroom of the Waldorf was pink was to understate, like describing an eastern deciduous forest as merely "green" during spring leaf out. The room was a riot of ebullient pink. Tablecloths. Napkins. The candelabras over the dinner tables. Streamers of pink satin ribbon exploded from the ceiling; above them tulle netting had been crisscrossed to form a rose cloud, beyond which were thousands of twinkling lights. The streamers danced in a gentle wind created by unseen fans. The stage was edged by hedge-like shrubs; despite the season, there were rows of pink azaleas in bloom, quince trees with pink blossoms. Tall Grecian columns, wrapped in silver smilax, stood on either side of the red-carpeted stairs. One hundred and three debutantes in matching flowing white ball gowns and elbow-length white gloves were presented by their mothers in a receiving line. Arden ascended the stage and played the piano as a quartet of men in tuxedos sang about flowers. The general nodded approvingly, not so much out of fatherly pride, but with satisfaction at making a good investment; all those years of piano lessons were worth it. Six of the debutantes and their escorts performed the Coming Out Waltz. The young women twirled white parasols and waved ostrich feather fans. When the presenting to society began, each woman, carrying a garland of flowers, climbed the stage. When her turn came, Arden curtsied as she had been taught in practice. After the last girl took a curtsy, the debutantes and their escorts retired to the Jade Room to dance a Viennese waltz played by an orchestra.

Arden despised the general that appeared when the drinking started in the afternoon and went into the deep of night. The morning general was at least tolerable. The morning general was who she wished her father was all the time. The night general was scary, especially when the Nazis showed up. They came every few months for evening cordials during her early years. Arden sat near the door outside the parlor, perched on a brown-upholstered Victorian daybed that had belonged to the general's grandmother, pretending to be reading Emerson or Thoreau. From what English that was spoken at the start of evenings, she gathered they had all met in Bavaria at the end of the war, when the Germans in the room had been detained in displaced persons camps. After cordials, the men graduated to Johnnie Walker Black Label, *General Patton's favorite,* a German-accented voice once said. *Patton often said we destroyed the wrong enemy,* her father said another night. He was rabidly anti-Soviet. He often made the papers when McCarthy was in the news, quoted about the threat posed by communism. As the drinks flowed, the use of German increased until it was exclusively spoken. She understood a few words. One was *Juden.* She heard *Juden* this and *Juden* that—and by the sharp tone of the voices and the laughter that sometimes followed, she knew they were talking bad things.

She was forbidden from going into the general's office, with its near-black mahogany shelves filled with books, first-edition classics ranging from Dickens to the initial American translation of Balzac. The books were reason enough for trespass, but the room's main window offered a view of the park. She was often left at home alone, and though the office door was always closed, it was left unlocked. She stole into the office to read, seated in the high-backed black leather chair at the desk where her father wrote the many volumes he authored about the dangers of communism. She was careful to leave no trace of disturbance, lest the general start locking the door.

There was a safe built into the wall of the bookshelf opposite the window, belly-height to the six-foot-one general. Often when she slipped into the office, she pulled on the safe's handle in the hope of seeing what was inside. She must have done that a hundred times, a hundred and fifty. Two hundred? Always it was locked. Two months after the cotillion, a blizzard struck the city. Schools were closed. She was home reading in the parlor when the telephone rang. It was her aunt—her uncle, the general's brother, had gone into cardiac arrest and was undergoing emergency surgery at Roosevelt Hospital. She called out with alarm for her father and handed the phone over. He said, *Yes, yes, yes,* and then he raced out the door. Her mother was at a social function.

Arden went to the kitchen of the penthouse and poured Canadian Club into a water glass. She'd been drinking it now since her freshman year in high school. So much whiskey was consumed by her parents that they never noticed the depletion. Whiskey sloshed as she went down the hall to the office to sit at the desk, put her long legs up on its surface—she was nearly as tall as her father—and watch the snow fall on the park. She was happy to be alone.

As always, she absentmindedly pulled on the safe's handle. She expected the hard tug to support her weight, but she nearly careered to the floor when the door flung open. Some whiskey spilled in a small puddle on the oak floor. She looked at the open safe, disbelieving. Her father must have not spun the cylinder in his hurry to reach the phone. On the left were eleven packets of one-hundred-dollar bills with $10,000 bands wrapped around each. To the right, bound volumes. She raced to the bathroom for a washrag that she wetted to wipe up the whiskey. Then she pulled the stack of papers and sat at the desk. On top was a photostat of a diary—Patton's. She sped through it. On one page he called Jews a "sub-human species." He wrote, "I have never looked at a group of people who seem to be more lacking in intelligence and spirit." He favorably described how American soldiers had beaten Jews with rifle butts in the camps run by the United States because they didn't keep their quarters clean. Next in the stack was an eight-by-ten bound volume marked "TOP SECRET: OPERATION OVERCAST." Inside were orders addressed to her father from General Patton to expedite the emigration of German POWs. There were contact names at the Office of Strategic Services. The Germans on the first pages were priority cases: members of the Schutzstaffel, Luftwaffe, and Kriegsmarine; asterisks next to names indicated those who were to receive forged passports and transportation to Argentina and Paraguay. Pages of names followed: Popple, Schulze, Jungert, Schreiber, and so on. Next to the names was their specialties: guidance systems, satellites, biological weapons, synthetic fuels, aeronautical engineering. Most were to be designated "War Department Special Employees" and transported by both the U.S. Air Force and Navy. Others were to be sent to Mexico City and then on to the border metropolis of Ciudad Juárez, where the U.S. consulate office would shepherd their paperwork to get them into El Paso by land and then on to various War Department bases and research facilities.

There was the sound of the front door opening.

She hurried to replace the volumes in the safe as she had found them, exited the office, and clicked its door closed with time to toss the washrag into the bathroom. She was two steps down the hall when Barre rounded the corner. *What's wrong? You look like you've been up to something.*

I'm just upset about Uncle John, she blurted out, explaining about his heart attack. Her mother consoled Arden, who realized to her horror that she'd left the water glass of whiskey on the desk. But half-finished glasses of whiskey were always being left across the penthouse, and the general wouldn't notice another one on his desk when he came home. But Arden's initial horror wasn't anything compared with what she felt about what she'd found inside the safe, and she counted the days before she could escape the general.

Of course she got into Radcliffe. Her admission was guaranteed: three previous generations of Vanderlips had graduated from Harvard. Arden Rutherford Vanderlip matriculated into the Class of 1965. She was a dual English and Germanic languages and literatures concentrator, She made the dean's list each term. She was a good girl who studied hard, didn't like most boys, and would rather read books than listen to a man blather about this or that, things of no interest to her.

But in her junior year she started seeing Arnold Cohen. He wasn't at Harvard—Jews still had trouble getting into the institution, and most went to Columbia, the "Jewish Harvard." Cohen attended Boston University. She certainly wasn't in love, nor did she really like him very much. The day after Kennedy was assassinated, Arden phoned her parents to say she was coming home for Thanksgiving, but that because of her studies, she would return that evening. She left out that she was bringing a companion, Arnold Cohen. Arnold was far shorter than Arden and a bit heavyset. She positioned herself behind him, her head entirely above his, then pushed the buzzer on her parents' co-op door. The door swung in. The general stood before them. Her gaze was nearly even with the old man's.

"Hi, Daddy!" Arden exclaimed cheerfully. "I brought a friend along. His name is Arnold. Arnold Co-hen."

She carefully watched the general's face, heavily lined around the eyes—far more than should have been normal for his sixty years—because of the Canadian Club. His training as a lawyer had taught him to conceal even the slightest hint of revelation. His adherence to this affectation occupied all aspects of his life, either in official capacity or at home. Arden, however, knew how to read those lines, far better than her mother. Barre was an idiot about her husband. A sixteenth of an inch up or down in the corners, Arden knew if the general was approving or disproving. The lines revealed anger—but only for a flash. No one else would have detected it.

Arnold thrust out his right hand. *Pleased to meet you, Mr. Vanderlip.*

The general shook the boy's hand with vigor. *Come in. Let me get you a drink.*

The general clasped Arden's hand with both of his briefly. They went into the parlor and an array of liquor bottles. Arnold chose the Marie Brizard Cherry Cordial. As her father poured it, Arden glumly grabbed a bottle of Gordon's and splashed some into a glass.

His father escaped from Mielec early in the war, she said, sipping the gin. Again her eyes locked on to those of her father. This time the lines didn't move one bit. He was now ready for her, knew exactly what his daughter was up to. *He's too damn smart,* she thought.

The general went on talking with the boy and was his usual charming public self. She could barely get through the turkey dinner her mother had had delivered. She feigned sleep on the train ride north so she wouldn't have to talk with Arnold. Two weeks later, she dumped him.

When Arden came home during the intersession in her senior year, the general incessantly hounded her about postgraduate plans. She'd lied and told him that she was going to apply to law schools. She took the LSAT to appease him. But she had no intention of carrying through with applications to Harvard, Columbia, or Yale, the only three law schools he would have her attend, he insisted, if she were to enter politics. He dreamed of Senator Arden Rutherford Vanderlip. If he didn't have a son from this marriage, at least he would have that. Women, after all, were increasingly assuming positions of power. It was certainly not beyond the realm of the possible. She listened sullenly. The only thing she hated worse than the thought of becoming a lawyer was the notion of entering politics. She was eager to return to school. She loaded the spring term with classes on poetry, literature, and history.

Arden was obsessed with Germany. Besides studying the language, she audited a course on the war, taught by a Jewish studies professor in the Divinity School. It was controversial because the course questioned common assumptions; in particular, it was critical of how the Allies knew of the extermination camps but did nothing.

Also, Arden began having sex, and to her mild surprise, she enjoyed it. She met Robert in Dr. Rolf von Eckartsberg's class on Rilke. Robert had a Beatles haircut. He was cute. Von Eckartsberg and his wife were experimenting with a drug called LSD at an estate in the town of Millbrook; a few undergraduates like Arden and Robert were invited with some other postdoc students one late March weekend. Arden and Robert were given a room in the mansion and then introduced to Timothy Leary. That night the group read poetry. Leary talked about the heightened state of "aesthetic receptivity" that acid gave him. Von Eckartsberg focused on its impact on sex between him and his wife, who was seated at his side. *In the proper setting it can create a fusion of mystic unity. The effects can be like those of hatha yoga.* He told of increased kinesthetic-muscular responsiveness. Arden and Robert had been lovers for three weeks, just getting over the awkwardness of being new at it. Robert wasn't much more than a virgin himself, having only one previous girlfriend and only for a short time. Sex that night after taking LSD made them feel like reincarnated souls who had been lovers in six different lifetimes. How would it ever be again as good? Her head exploded. She wasn't sure she'd ever do LSD another time, but she'd become aware of another dimension of herself.

During spring break, against her better judgment, she went home. On the second day, the general summoned her into his office. She sat in an overstuffed walnut Victorian chair. The high-backed black leather chair behind the desk elevated her father so that he loomed like a presiding judge. *What plans, pray tell, do you have for after graduation? You are becoming rather bohemian.*

Whatever words she uttered, he was prepared to smash her argument with a verbal sledgehammer, one that she would be defenseless against. She'd felt its weight numerous times growing up. She couldn't, or wouldn't, bring up what happened those nights when she first reached puberty and he was blind drunk; even as her mind raced it did not go there. It happened, sure, but because she didn't want it to have happened, it did not occur; it was blotted. But it existed. She could, however, say this: *I know what's in that safe.* She pointed accusingly to her left. Her voice came out stronger than she expected. His eyes widened. She'd never before seen them like this. The lines went insane with emotion.

You're bluffing.

So they pay you in cash. Who do you work for?

Now fear in the lines. For once, perhaps the only time in his life, she thought, he was at a loss for words. *Yes, yes, yes!* She fought the urge to smile, then the impulse to laugh with hysterical glee and stamp her feet at the same time. The general merely stared, dumbfounded.

Is it those Nazis who used to come here? Or the government?

Young lady— His face was flush. He went back as best he could to being the unflappable general. *Daughters should not know some things about their fathers. I do not owe you any explanations. The subject of this meeting was not to be about my employment. It was to discuss yours, your future —*

You brought Nazis into this country! I saw the list of names. Hundreds of them —

There were higher issues at stake. We had to beat the Russians! You don't understand. The Russians, they wanted to, and still want to, crush us. We needed their expertise. Do you realize what von Braun did for us? How all of the others helped? Some things are more important —

More important? They gassed millions of Jews!

To quote de Gaulle, "No nation has friends. Only interests."

So the ends justify the means?

Exactly.

And so you brought those awful Nazis here, rewarding them —

I will not discuss that matter any further. If you do not plan on attending law school, I will not subsidize your increasingly beatnik lifestyle. How do you propose to make a living writing poetry about drugs and sex?

You... you snuck into my room! You spied on me!

This trait appears to run in the family.

I don't care about money! I'm going to Berlin!

There is nothing in Berlin. The Communists have choked off the western sector. No sane person would go there. Berlin is lost. With the wall, it is isolated, a rathole. A dead end.

That's why I'm going! she shouted as she stood. Then she lowered her voice and glared. *I'm going there to fuck a Jew. Lots of Jews. Communist Jews!*

She packed her things, stormed out with suitcase in hand, and caught a train to South Station in Boston. Her father watched her go with the faintest of derisive grins, but she wasn't bothered by that. She was in fact terrified about money. In the short term, her schooling, lodging, and meals were paid through graduation. She had enough in her bank account to purchase an airline ticket to Paris. From there she'd somehow find a way to reach West Berlin. In the long term, her grandmother Lauranne had created a trust account of $150,000 solely in her name, which she could access on her thirtieth birthday.

She read poetry and took long walks with Robert along the Charles River in the emerging spring afternoons. They sat and watched the scullers. Was she in love? She wasn't sure. But Robert soon announced that he was going back to the girl he'd lost his virginity to. After that, during rainy May afternoons, Arden spent most of her free time inside, writing poetry.

There were no Jews in West Berlin immediately available to be had as lovers. They had all been killed or had fled Germany. She was embarrassed by her naïveté, which quite possibly explained the weird grin on the general's face.

But there was Bruno Schöen. They shared many things in common besides a love of poetry and literature—chief that they were estranged from their fathers. Bruno's dad had been an officer in the Schutzstaffel. He hated the old man. He'd fled to the western sector to escape conscription by the West German government. He'd been denied conscientious objector status by the authorities in Bonn. There were many like him in Berlin. Bruno abhorred violence because of what his father did for the SS. He couldn't even stand it when other squatters in his building trapped mice. He wanted to catch them alive and let them go elsewhere. Now he was a carpenter and there was plenty of rebuilding going on.

Arden met Bruno in a café not long after she'd hitchhiked into West Berlin. He was reading Kafka, and she struck up a conversation. He spoke in long existential soliloquies about his place in life on this planet. *I'm seeking a simpler existence. Not the life that we find in books, no. No. The one we live by doing, seeing, feeling—touching. Wanting greatness, seeking approbation, lusting for money, is what has gotten the world into the trouble we have seen. It means tonnages of bombs falling from the sky. The deaths of those who have done nothing more malicious than wanting to breathe the air, to exist. I do not wish to partake in any of that. I want to stand apart. Be outside of any system. That is my purpose in life: to find a new system.* Then he stared at her like a watching bear, not a bear that wished to consume her, but with eyes that dared her to say something equal in return.

They met up again, and he offered to cook her dinner. He led her through a neighborhood that grew increasingly unreconstructed, past roofless shells of buildings bombed twenty years earlier. They came to the Potsdamer Platz. Bruno pointed to the wall, built by the East Germans, that encircled the city. They were on a landlocked island, isolated. This thought elated her. She was surprised to learn that in fact it was a series of walls. The one closest to them was covered in graffiti.

His squat was in a four-story building. The exterior brick was pocked by hundreds of bullet rounds, and bigger chunks had been blown out by bomb and mortar shrapnel, but the structure had never sustained a direct hit from above—the roof was intact. Glass had been replaced in the windows by squatters, mostly German draft resisters; they occupied the top two floors. Turkish construction workers were in the bottom ones.

Bruno cooked sausages and potatoes on a steel barrel that had been converted into a wood-fired stove by a welder; the chimney vented out a window. As darkness fell, he lit oil lamps. There was no electricity. They ate at a table made from a door salvaged from a bombed building. It was romantic. Bruno was tall and thin, with blond hair and chiseled features. He looked like those war cartoons of the savage Aryan, except that he was sweet. He wore perfectly round glasses, like John Lennon. She thought they made him look cute. She later learned those were the standard-issue frames under socialized medicine. She ended up in his bed that night. By that fall of 1965, Arden was pregnant.

She grew used to living without electricity or a phone. For some reason the water in the building still functioned and the toilets flushed. Winter was cold in the squat, but if they sat close to the steel drum and kept it stoked, it was okay. She helped Bruno haul timbers and boards from ruins, even when she was in her seventh month of carrying the baby. Bruno used a hand saw to cut the fuel into pieces small enough to fit inside the stove. He also brought home end cuts and other wood scraps from construction sites. Arden began tutoring the German draft resisters who wanted to learn English. She excelled at speaking German. The first summer after Klaus was born, she found old car fenders that she lugged to the roof. Bruno carried up buckets of dirt. She planted gardens in the hollows of the metal, and thereafter for much of the year they had fresh lettuce, tomatoes, beans. They ate well and were even saving money in a bank account.

In 1968 they bought a motorcycle. When Bruno was at work, Arden put Klaus in her lap and rode the motorcycle to the Spree River, where people skinny-dipped. One July afternoon, Arden was lying naked on a blanket with Klaus next to her, when three German women pointed out that American soldiers on a hill were watching them with binoculars. The women wondered aloud why the soldiers didn't just come down to the riverbank and get naked with them. *Weil sie Amis sind,* Arden said in flawless German—they were simply being Americans. The German women laughed. They thought she was German. Arden stood and put her hands over her head, wiggling her breasts and hips in a show for the soldiers. *Blöde Amis! Sie wissen nicht, was sie verpassen!* she said, to more laughter as she mocked the dumb Americans. She blew the faraway men a kiss.

U.S. draft resisters began showing up in Berlin, along with American women who wore colorful skirts and beads. Several Americans moved into Arden and Bruno's building, taking over the rooms on the first floor that had been occupied by Turkish workers who went back home. Arden avoided them at first, pretended to be German. She wanted no contact with America. She in fact had been shunning news from back home and didn't know much save for the assassinations of Bobby and MLK. Berlin had become her lost desert island after all, even as Bruno was becoming more distant, brooding. He sensed something had changed in her. Maybe it happened after Arden began talking to the American women. From them she learned of riots, the protests on campuses, the election of Richard Nixon. It sounded like a foreign nation and became suddenly far more appealing. Arden started dressing like the American women. She found a white blouse and skirt in a secondhand shop and tie-dyed them.

She spent her days teaching English to Germans and reading to her boy. Klaus was three. She studied books on homeschooling, but that idea was unpalatable. She wanted her boy to have a proper education. For that she feared they'd have to return to the States. She also wanted him to be closer to the natural world, removed from the society that was collapsing. A friend from college had sent her the *Whole Earth Catalog*. She wondered about communes, living in a dome. She had to find some way back to America. She mentioned this to Bruno.

Moving to the United States was out of the question for him. Even though he hated that his father had been an SS officer, he had lost too many friends in the Dresden firebombings. *How can I go live in the nation that did that? They incinerated thousands of civilians. Your country is as morally bankrupt as the Nazis! Your President Roosevelt turned away a ship of Jewish refugees before the war! Look at what your country is doing to the people of Vietnam!*

But look at what is going on right over there, she noted, pointing out the window to the wall. *It's all going to blow up. The Russians are just waiting for the collapse of the West.*

East, West—it did not matter. All systems were going to implode. She didn't want their child to endure that horror. They had to seek a place of ultimate refuge. They needed to be utterly apart from any society. There was no place like that in Europe.

The arguments grew increasingly acrimonious. Bruno spent less and less time at home. On January 2, 1970, she awakened alone on the mattress on the floor of the squat. When she stood to wash her face, a note was pinned to the wall next to the mirror: it was from Bruno. He'd left for Tangier. She learned that he'd run off with a British woman who was squatting in a building near the Alexanderplatz.

Arden took up with new lovers. The first was a woman. One night in bed, Arden told her lover, *I no longer want to be called Arden. I do not want to be referred to by the name of his dead mother. It reminds me of him. I shall now be known as Zoë.*

Her girlfriend was compelled to ask, *But why not then entirely change your name? Shed yourself of Vanderlip as well and become any last name of your choosing. Call yourself after a constellation, an exotic bird, a sacred mountain, a fairy witch. How very exciting that would be.*

Zoë responded, *I am proud of my long family history, and I will not let him take that from me.*

Months later, Zoë met Helmut, a West German draft resister whose father was Heinz Linge, Hitler's valet who was in the Führerbunker when his boss killed himself. If Bruno had bear eyes, the eyes of Helmut were like those of a mountain lion caught in the headlights: fierce, intense, and they nearly seemed to glow blue in strong sun. Helmut also made a living doing construction work, also read poetry to Zoë in coffeehouses, and she began sleeping with him. She didn't tell her girlfriend about the affair for two months.

I am not a lesbian, Zoë declared when they finally talked.

I did not believe so, the woman responded.

Helmut moved into the squat. One attraction of Helmut was that he also sought to escape society, and he had no problem with going to the United States; he was, like many Germans, fascinated by the American West. Books about the region stacked up in the squat. An article in the popular magazine *Stern* caught special attention: "To reach this crazy place, you first drive to the rural country outside of the city," the article began, speaking of the California coast north of San Francisco. "And then you keep driving. Beyond the country. And then you keep going on winding and forbidding roads. This place is not rural. It is wilderness."

Don't grow up to be a man. Her gaze was on the concrete and cinder block wall a few blocks to the east, the razor wire–topped fence beyond, and the towers with machine gunners. She turned to her son, his blond hair orange from the glow of the low winter sun reflected from the windows of a just-restored building near Potsdamer Platz. Klaus was at the dinner table, a twelve-centimeter-thick fifteenth-century door salvaged from a shrapnel-scarred church, set on sawhorses. Her eyes, with prosecutorial intensity, were a legacy of her father; his came from Bruno, deeply set and Aryan, projecting both love and terror and, in the past year, increasing indifference.

Don't—

It was early December 1972, a few days before they left Berlin. They stared at each other in the ensuing silence, in the squat where he was birthed six years earlier with the help of the hippie Austrian *hebamme*, who was a friend of a friend and agreed to assist with the delivery for an ounce of Bruno's weed from Morocco.

Ich habe noch eins gefunden! Klaus cried one afternoon, eight months after they arrived on the lost edge of the American continent. A place called McGee Ridge. A place that, in Zoë's awestruck opinion, no magazine article, regardless of language or understanding, could appropriately describe.

Speak in English! Helmut yelled over the force of the wind and the crashing surf, in an accent so thick it almost sounded like he was uttering German.

It is the other part! the boy shouted in Germanic inflection as he ran over the dune, carrying a stone object over his head. *I found one! The Indians! The Indians!*

The boy held his prize in outstretched palms: a smooth stone pestle. The color of the rock was an exact match for the mortar Helmut discovered in the dunes the previous day, amid ancient, bleached mussel shells, middens where the Native Americans dumped shells for centuries. Mortars and pestles, tools of the Athapaskans, decorated the front porches of many of the hippies—the ones who had homes and were not living in tents.

Zoë emerged from behind a pillar of rock rising near the shore, where the reef extended a half mile out at the lowest tide. She dragged a hatch from a midsized fishing vessel. *We can use this!* she exclaimed. Any salvageable flotsam would go into the home they were building of found objects and forest timbers.

They gathered a large bucket of horse mussels to roast on a grill set over a fire. The shellfish, some as long as a woman's hand, were as tender as the smaller California blues. They found perfectly round pearls in several mussels. They believed that they'd always find pearls.

Zoë took to bedding down under the stars, as she imagined the Native Americans must have done, alone in the open meadow. One morning she awakened and gazed across the golden grasses at the skeleton of studs of their home under construction. She imagined where they would place the ship's hatch: *In the roof, over the second-floor bedroom, where we can build an observation deck.* She had a sudden inspiration. *It is an ark, sailing upon a sea of this timeless wilderness. We must make it a worthy one.* At that moment she decided that the south side of the structure had to come to a point, like the bow of a ship. The many components that had washed ashore were just part of the influence. The other was the collapse of civilization. The end had begun before she was born, her belief and proof rooted in the seeds of her father's sins, and the 1970s were simply a decade in an ongoing process of de-evolution that might take a century to reach its bleak conclusion. To accommodate the change, Helmut tore off the south framing, reconfigured the foundation piers, and rebuilt from scratch. *This Ark will be our lifeboat. We will dance upon its deck amid the slow-motion apocalypse.*

That night, to commemorate the decision, Zoë stood on the topmost rafters of the emerging dwelling, holding the collected works of Shakespeare, and spoke to the orange ball of the sun about to drop over the blue horizon of the Pacific.

> *This earth of majesty, this seat of Mars,*
> *This other Eden, demi-paradise,*
> *This fortress built by Nature for her self*
> *Against infection and the hand of war,*
> *This happy breed of men, this little world,*
> *This precious stone set in a silver sea...*

She levitated, airborne an inch, perhaps two, though her back actually never left the soil of the meadow beneath it—she had sailed heavenward, bonded for a microsecond with this block of the American continent, moving in tandem with the plate. Within seconds the shock wave from the earthquake somewhere offshore reached the crest of the coastal range ten miles inland, and a flash of sheet lightning blew off the summit as electricity shot into the atmosphere.

She worked herself with two fingers, thinking not of Helmut but of a past woman lover in Berlin. She was suddenly aware of someone coming toward her in the moonless dark, from the direction of the just-completed Ark. Helmut's naked form stood over her, his erection silhouetted against the Milky Way. His penis was small, thin. It pointed south. They had not made love in months. She did not desire to make love. *Not with him.* He tried to take her, but she pushed him so that he fell on the dried rattlesnake grass; she quickly mounted him, pinning his arms. She arched back, hips moving increasingly faster, grinding him into the prickers and stickleburrs; her eyes not on him but on Andromeda and the stars curving toward Perseus. What was beneath her she wished to grind into the earth until nothing remained.

One year had passed since Zoë kicked Helmut out. Ronald Reagan was running for president. It mattered not if Carter somehow pulled off a miracle. They were all the same.

This is not America, she told Klaus, just after his fourteenth birthday. *That country out there—it is not for us.*

She refused to acknowledge the fact that they now lived inside the legal borders of the United States. But practical matters would force the country upon her.

That country beyond did indeed seem alien to the young Klaus. Town was two hours to the north on twisting roads hugging steep canyon walls. They visited that small city only once a month. Town was to be shunned other than for picking up sacks of beans and flour, barbed wire to pen in the goats, or other things they couldn't make, grow, or harvest. She distilled salt from seawater. They survived by shooting deer, catching cabezon and surfperch, collecting mussels that crusted the reef by the acre; greenhouses and gardens perpetually grew lettuces and potatoes and kale. She abhorred when they had to move to town, synonymous with *out there*; town, this fog-bedeviled epicenter of the logging industry eradicating the last of the old growth, the main drag carpet-bombed with McDonald's, Burger King, Taco Bell, Longs Drugs, Shell, Arco. Yet they had to leave the protective wilderness of their coast and live in town for the same reason they abandoned Berlin, and that was for her boy to have a good education. They would live there for the four years of high school, after which Klaus would matriculate to Harvard just as she had, and her father before, and his father before. Klaus needed immersion in a good American school. She worried that his mind drifted, that he couldn't handle speaking both German and English and learning the classics. How could he have already forgotten German?

Don't grow up to be a man, she said that late August day, the week after they moved to town, sitting at a brown Formica kitchen table with Klaus. Her eyes were on a distant line of redwoods on a ridge ten miles east; below, stretching to the water, a collection of Victorian and Craftsman homes, square midcentury fourplexes, and the distant plaza.

I don't understand what you mean, Momma.

You know what I mean.

No, Momma, I don't!

She remained mute. The boy was angry. He believed she meant that she didn't want him to become taller, to grow up. Only later he realized she had meant all the men she had chosen in her life. For now, he simply wished to be larger.

Because he was small for his age, he often took this to be a kind of curse. He was often mistaken for being ten, though he was about to become a freshman in high school. He was tiny but had full teenage desires, which made him excited about living in town. There were lots of girls there—girls and the Cineplex and the video arcade and hamburgers and hot showers, objects of desire that didn't exist near the Ark.

Town did hold two things of value for Zoë: two bookstores and the Fault Zone, a coffeehouse in a Victorian near the college, where she drank large cups of locally roasted coffee and read German classics. She sat between the fireplace and the window looking out at college girls in heavy green U.S. Army wool coats, smoking cigarettes on the rain-drenched patio. She saw her reflection in the water-spattered pane; her long blondish hair framed her face with the high cheekbones of her father. These made her a strikingly attractive woman, but she hated that she had the general's face.

A steady stream of books came home in her pack, penned by Balzac, Maupassant, Cervantes, Goethe, Tolstoy. She read them to Klaus in the evenings, during his freshman fall and winter. She'd given up on trying to get him to read them all on his own; the boy had trouble concentrating. She mandated that he read one book solo each week, but it often took two, three weeks. He seemed otherwise quite smart, and the pace of his reading ability was frustrating and confusing to Zoë. She reasoned that by reading books out loud to him, he might learn more, faster, a foie gras approach to literary immersion. She carefully chose the books for him to read on his own. She brought home Faulkner because it would be easier. Weeks later she grilled the boy:

Do you think Joe Christmas was African American?

Yes, Momma.

Who set fire to the house? Was it Joe Christmas? Or was it Joe Brown?

I dunno, Momma. I don't think the writer wanted you to know.

Why do you think Joe Christmas was blamed for killing the woman? Do you think it is the same as with what happened with Virg?

She did her best to connect the stories to their lives. But this complicated things too.

Kinda?

Could it be because Virg is the only black man on the ridge?

Everyone blamed Virg for stealing Thomas's weed, Momma. But I think it was one of Jenny's guys. It's kinda the same as the book, the white guy getting away with it. But nobody killed Virg.

The small home in town was on the grid and had gas furnace heat, but Zoë felt compelled to have a fire each night, for ambiance, and the fact that wood heat is more satisfying; she also chose to illuminate the room not with incandescent electric lights but with oil lamps, just like they did at the Ark and in the Berlin squat before that. It was necessary that things feel exactly the same as Berlin and on the ridge. This would have to do while she prepared her boy for Harvard. It would be the final fall that Klaus was a boy. His tiny frame would blossom, and by the middle of his sophomore year he'd reach six feet. But that late October night of 1980, he was still her small boy. Zoë set *Light in August* on a table, and the mother and child stared at the flames consuming Doug fir rounds.

Momma, why did we come here?

So you could go to high school —

I mean why'd we leave Berlin?

You needed to be in America, to get a proper education.

But we aren't really in America down there with just the wind and the
goats and all the chores—
Splitting wood is good for you.
Maybe we should have stayed in Berlin.
Maybe—yes, maybe we should have.
I love you, Momma.
You are my boy.
Do you love me, Momma?
You are my boy.

3

CROSSING THE LINE

Finding Viktor Sotirova proved to be easy—maybe too easy, I thought, as my truck ascended the coastal mountains on the winding road. No one in my circle knew the identity of the woman who had tipped me off. Sure, I had sources, but I came up empty on that one. My research on Sotirova was more fruitful. I found an online press release from the sheriff's office about a bust in 2012—a grow with six greenhouses. Twelve workers were arrested, 675 pounds of bud confiscated, and 985 plants destroyed. Severe damage to the landscape was noted: illegal roads were carved into a hillside and a creek was dammed, with all the water being withdrawn for the operation.

No criminal charges were filed. The case ended up in civil court. Velikov Manov, one of Sotirova's workers, took the public fall. He was fined $300,000 for environmental damage. No criminal case resulted, no one went to jail; it was difficult getting a jury to convict for growing, but easy for environmental damage. The report said the property was owned by Eastern Resources LLC. Its chief operating officer was recorded as Viktor Sotirova. The California Secretary of State's corporate filing division listed both his phone number and an email on the site, which was surprising. I made the assumption that Sotirova was like every other grower and used Signal, so I sent him a text message on the app. I wrote that I wanted to talk about Klaus having a beef with him, that I wanted to hear his side of the dispute. The message, I hoped, would catch his attention.

The response came within an hour: *I will talk with you, but only in person.* What followed in great detail in the next few messages were directions to a remote site far to the south. It was beyond weird. I never expected a reply, much less an invitation for the following afternoon. I did more homework. Sotirova was born in Bulgaria. There was a *Miami Herald* story about his arrest in Florida in the 1990s on a weapons charge. He was a lieutenant in a Bulgarian mob organization that first went to Miami after being forced out of Europe; it then set up operations in New York City. In the 1990s it branched out to Northern California, growing weed that was transported back east to be sold for a premium.

I had two hours to spare when I arrived in the south county, so I checked on the flyers for Zoë that Likowski and I had put up. Some were covered with posters for music events or other missing people. I stapled replacements over the music posters. I then drove east on curving narrow roads. It was gnarly country. At a crossroads there was a little clapboard market scabbed with peeling white paint; a half dozen locals standing out front glared menacingly. The directions led me through mountains on steadily diminishing blacktop, until the road turned to gravel. I passed a burned-up car that had been dragged to the side. There was a fork. I was to take the dirt road to the left, where there was a big rock formation. GPS wouldn't work here, Sotirova told me, and he was correct. I had no phone service. It was all old-school route finding. I had to put the truck into low four on a steep and rutted grade. Finally, I came to a gate that was unlocked. There was a discreetly placed camera in the branches of a California buckeye. A half mile beyond two men brandished AR-15s. I slowed. *Jesus, it feels like Salvador.* Yet I wasn't scared. I'd met with guerrillas numerous times during that civil war; it wasn't in their interest to kill me, no more than it was in Sotirova's to rub out a journalist. He wanted to use me somehow, to get at Klaus, or to throw me off course. The man on the left took his hand off the gunstock and waved me forward. I came to a flat that had been cleared of trees by bulldozers; there were eight massive greenhouses. To the south, eight yurts. Another man, a boy really, maybe eighteen, with an AR-15 over his shoulder, greeted me. I got out of the truck, and he led me to a yurt on the northern edge of the forest where I was told to wait.

I sat with my back against a fifty-year-old Douglas fir spared from the bulldozing. The youthful guard went back to his position, joined by his two comrades, who continued brandishing their weapons; the kid's remained shoulder-strapped to his body. The three were clearly nervous and I wondered why. Through the edges of the white hoop greenhouses, I caught occasional glimpses of young women preparing the site for planting. There were at least a half dozen working. Snippets of conversation in Bulgarian drifted my way.

I was nearly falling asleep when a man walked toward me, trailed by the three armed men. Viktor Sotirova looked nothing like a Bulgarian mobster, at least as one would imagine cast in a film. He was a good twenty-five pounds or more overweight, short, made ugly by a big mole on his left cheek and hair that was prematurely receding at forty-five. He greeted me with a tired hello and motioned me with his left arm to come inside the yurt. There was no brooking shaking hands. The three gunmen remained about fifty feet distant. I pulled a notebook from my pocket and a tiny stick recorder.

"Do not turn that on," Sotirova said sternly. He stared at me across a plain white plastic table with six white plastic chairs encircling it in the otherwise empty yurt. His breath was terrible; his teeth were brown at the roots.

"How do you know Klaus?" he asked. "You are his friend?"

"I wouldn't go that far. Let's just say I've known him a long time. I'm friends with his mother—"

"Who has gone missing," he helped me finish.

I nodded.

"So what does that have to do with me?" Sotirova was terse. It made me nervous, but I tried not to show it. Sotirova stood.

"I hear Klaus is pissed at you."

Sotirova's face studied me for a long time. "Really?"

"Really what?"

Sotirova broke into a loud, unexpected chortle. Then he spun on his heel and walked out of the yurt. I followed, having no indication I shouldn't. He went straight to the youngest of the three guards outside, grabbed the AR-15 from his arms. He pointed the weapon at me. I felt the dryness in my mouth turning into a desert. He took a few steps forward.

"Do you know who came to see me two days ago?"

"I'll guess Klaus?" I asked as nonchalantly as I could muster.

"Don't tell me you didn't know!"

With that the rifle jerked vertical and he popped off two rounds into the sky. My eardrums rang from the blasts but I didn't flinch. It was possible he suspected I might be in league with Klaus and part of any plotting against him.

"I didn't," I said, as if the question had not been interrupted by the shots.

Sotirova now laughed, and the three men began laughing as well. Sotirova sobered and glared at them, and they regained their stony faces. It was my turn to laugh, but I restrained myself.

"He came here thinking I had kidnapped her," he said, as if acknowledging that I was really innocent of being on Klaus's side. "You came here too—because you want to know if I did something to that woman?"

"Yes."

"What I have to say is this: you do not want me as an enemy. But will I hurt the mother of my enemy? Never. I will blow away the ass of Klaus, yes, and have a big feast of celebration that night. But do anything to his mother? No."

With that he handed the gun back to the youngest guard. "I am very busy." He turned and began walking away. When I tried to ask one Hail Mary question about Klaus and the Purple Thistle, he raised his left hand and said his men would escort me to my truck. As I drove away, the three stood with the AR-15s pointed at the ground.

On the morning of July 4, I awakened and pulled two cabbages from the Sun Frost fridge. I cut each in half and sliced the flat edges, shaving off slaw that I placed in a large bowl and salted. Four and a half months had passed since Zoë vanished. I was still digging, replacing flyers—and my place hadn't sold. One man came, a creepy dude who looked around and didn't speak to my realtor save for mumbling. The majority of my assets were tied up with the land, and I'd now become prisoner to what had for so long been a refuge. Now I was dreading what for so many years had been a highlight: the big hippie bash down on the river at Craig and Maggie Johnson's place.

The beauty of this off-grid coast, long before the arrival of the mobsters and Green Rush opportunists, was that we had long been a community and it was centered around two big events: a winter solstice fire and July 4 at the Johnsons'. Each year for a quarter of a century, I had made this slaw to take to the event. After it was desiccated enough, I poured off the salty water and added oil and vinegar, then drove off the ridge.

On the dirt road that ran to the Johnson place, I came to a high spot that overlooked Klaus's grow. I spotted several women going from one of the white hoop greenhouses to another. I imagined they were taking care of the fresh clones planted after the dep harvest (using light deprivation that mimicked fall conditions encouraged plants to flower, which meant two crops per season became possible). A half mile farther on, there was another turnout that looked directly down on Craig and Maggie's river bar ranch. I was in no rush. I got out and leaned against my fender. A big crowd of people was already gathered in the meadow.

I recalled that first July 4 there with Zoë back in the 1990s. When we arrived that day, she played the tuba, a vague rendition of "The Star-Spangled Banner." Our entrance was cheered by more than one hundred hippies, who partook in the Fourth not as an act of patriotism, but as an inversion to all that the holiday meant to most citizens living out there in a nation of fast-food chains, freeways, roadside congestion, lighting at night that consumed electricity as if it existed in unlimited supply, not by the nano-watt as measured by us off-gridders. They celebrated being outside of America. July 4 was an excuse for a midsummer party; to smoke weed; for some to play in a jug band, others to dance, wiggle their buck naked asses, show their tits and swinging dicks to the creeks, the ocean, the stars; to fornicate in the bushes along the river bar—whatever they felt like doing. There was a pig roasting on a spit, grilled corn on the cob, slices of watermelon, valley-raised roasted goat that had fed on grass and coyote brush, fresh-baked breads, salads, pies of cherry and berry; a cloud of marijuana smoke hung thick as ocean fog over the crowd. That first time, Craig and Maggie clapped their hands. *Come gather 'round*, Maggie, in a flowing blue dress, shouted. The hippies formed a huge circle in the meadow. A dead branch atop a gnarled Douglas fir that resembled a hawk's inverted talon caught the last ray of sun. A weathered barn stood next to the tree. Bats began pouring out the window near the peak, forming a swirling bat cloud. *Everyone hold hands.* I took Zoë's hand on the left. Zoë held the hand of Lauren, who in turn clasped Andy's, who in turn grasped Klaus's. My eyes continued around the circle, and new as I was, I knew all one hundred, either by sight or name.

Now, all these years later, it seemed like a dream.

I got back into the truck, navigating the dusty road down to the gathering. I carried my slaw to the serving table. Hippies sat cross-legged on the expansive meadow. A man wore a blue beret and dark sunglasses and had a white goatee that jagged off his chin like winter ice. Canes were used by some, and one person was in a wheelchair. White-haired women, with dresses so long the hems swept the meadow grass, wore purple shawls, cowboy hats, tie-dye. One woman had a turquoise-and-orange Indian sarong. Younger women wore hipster dresses. Boys had hipster beards and porkpie hats. I studied each person, the gardens, the old barn, the fruit orchard, a circling red-tailed hawk.

I took in everything with a keen eye for remembrance. An era was ending—after forty-five consecutive years since the hippies showed up on this coast, it was the final gathering of the tribe. "This is the last year, Will," Maggie confided in a whisper, when I stuck my head into the kitchen to say hello. "I don't even know half of the people who come. Craig and I want to travel."

So many of the OG hippies were dead or had moved away. In 2002 Maggie ceased asking everyone to form a circle and hold hands. No longer did she give a speech after 2006. I now understood that when I arrived a quarter of a century earlier, it was the last hours of an all-night party, that time between three in the morning and the sun breaking on the horizon, when the buzz wears off. When I dropped in, it was still Keith Richards's guitar riffs in the middle of "Sympathy for the Devil," but they now sounded like the dying chords of an era.

"Will!" Bill suddenly shouted. "Can I borrow you for a second?"

I helped him lug a massive cooler filled with ice and beer and sodas to the tables set up with dozens of bowls of salads, fruit, slaws, corn, and desserts. There were also jars filled with shake from dep crops. As we set the cooler down, Klaus arrived wearing mirrored sunglasses. It was what I had been expecting but not looking forward to. He came with a contingent of young people and his foremen, strolling with his angular chin thrust forward. He had been out on bail for less than five months and it still shocked me to see him embraced by so many.

"He acts like he owns the place," Bill said.

"Someday he might," I said, "if he beats the rap."

Klaus's land adjoined Craig and Maggie's, and I imagined he would buy it as he built his empire. Klaus went to the grill and stacked fresh-cooked zucchini on a plate. He no longer ate meat.

I popped open a beer and sat alone on the lawn near the garden, beneath a mulberry tree. Eddie surprised me a moment later by dropping his mammoth self down next to me. He said nothing, concentrating on his plate of food. For Eddie, I was a nonthreatening companion to share space with, and the feeling was effectively mutual—we may as well have been a pair of friendly dogs for all the conversation he felt obliged to make.

I watched Klaus and wondered. There were no leads, no hint of what happened to Zoë in all the months since she disappeared. It wasn't looking good. Still, I wanted to believe she was in Berlin. I'd met with Klaus several times—either he'd forgotten accusing me of being in conspiracy against him at the Thistle or he was being calculating. I'd come to believe that it was unlikely he had done anything to her. He was convinced she was off somewhere with her tuba. Once when we talked about Zoë, he grew emotional—a man who appeared to have no capacity for empathy or emotion did in fact have some for his mother. We were scheduled for the big final interview after he finished with the dep harvest; it would be the seventh time over the years that I pulled out a recorder and we talked for hours.

Klaus spotted me and beelined my way, plate in one hand, beer in the other. He set them down and pulled off his shades. "Will!"

I stood, and he reached out to fist-bump me as though it were old times and he was still helping me out, as though it were possible for me to simply ignore what he had become and what he had done. But around Klaus, I feigned almost everything, given the lurch my stomach gave whenever he came near. It was better, as long as I was living on the ridge, to keep him close. For now, I had to tolerate Klaus and everything he was. I fist-bumped back.

"Mind if I join you?"

"Pull up a chair," I said. We sat cross-legged on the grass.

"Can I tell you a secret?"

"It's my job to keep 'em."

He proceeded to say that the Purple Thistle was for sale, and he was very close to sealing the deal. I feigned surprise.

"I've got a vision," he stated unselfconsciously, holding up a vape pen. "I'm thinking of the next phase. I hate growing. This is the future. I just hope the fucking Bulgarians don't get in the way."

He held the pen's oil up to the light, looking dreamily at the amber liquid. He outlined the reason for the purchase: because it was one of the rare legal commercial properties anywhere along the coast, he envisioned building a vaping oil manufacturing plant in back, a factory that would take biomass—the shake and other waste, "and make it into this," he said, taking yet another hit. "I'm going to create a brand—kinda like the Napa Valley, but instead of wine, oil." He launched into a soliloquy about his plans to remodel the Thistle, how he'd give it character with crushed red velvet wallpaper and wainscoting, cool 1930s-style wooden booths. Klaus's blue eyes gleamed, and in that moment he looked like the child he never really got to be.

"My dream is to turn it into a community hub, kind of like a British pub."

He would have chattered on for an hour, but I cut in. "I do recall someone saying something about a 'fifteen-year-plan,'" I said of a conversation we had many years earlier when he gave me a tour of his house grow in town. I remembered that chat because the night before I'd read my notes in a journal from 1998. I hadn't just prepared slaw for July 4; I'd also prepared for this very conversation. Now I recited it back to him from memory: *I'm going double diesel, dude. I'm gonna get rich. Mark your calendar. Come 2007, maybe 2008 tops, I'm outta here. Malibu. Or Hawaii. I gotta be somewhere warm, somewhere with surfing. Somewhere that's not here. I hate it here, Will. Hate it. I'm never coming north of the Willits Grade again after Mom's gone. Never.*

A slow smile came to Klaus's face. His eyes crinkled. They'd been twitching.

"Aren't you supposed to be out of the business altogether by now?"

"Hahahaha," Klaus said, mock laughing. "I'm still on my plan, it's just delayed. Now I'm looking at 2025. I'm still gonna quit. You'll see. Right now I'm overleveraged, Will. I've got a payroll of thirty-five people, and that doesn't even count the trimmers. Once I get the court case behind me, get caught up..."

I had an idea of just how much he was overleveraged. There was a $3.5 million mortgage alone on a house on three acres in Point Dume on the Malibu coast. The house was supposed to be a secret. I'd tracked his LLC and the shell companies he used to buy it and connected him to the property records, He was piling debt on top of debt. He'd told me the last money his mother paid the lawyers had run out; he didn't know how he was going to continue hiring them. I knew he was back into methamphetamines, and there were rumors of occasional opioid use. Klaus clearly hadn't slept in days.

It was satisfying to tweak Klaus with the history lesson, but now that he revealed he was bidding for the Thistle, it was time to ask about Sotirova.

"I hear you had an interesting meeting down south with the Bulgarians a few months ago."

"How'd you hear about that?" Klaus asked, surprised.

"You know me."

Another smile came to his face, only this smile was uneasy. I wasn't going to let him know about my visit.

"Yeah," he said. He spoke in a low voice, with reluctance. "Me and my guys, we showed up there."

There was a long silence.

"Those guys are scary," I said when it was clear Klaus wasn't going to reveal any more. "Don't you worry about them?" Back when I'd hired the young Klaus to help me put on my roof, he wanted to hear war stories. I told him some, about my being in "the shit" when I covered conflict zones. So now I asked, "Given what you're doing, who those guys are, what will you do if you get into the shit with them?"

He didn't hesitate to answer: "Bury those motherfuckers in shit."

It wasn't bravado—his voice was cold and steely. Chilling.

Klaus spotted the two women he'd arrived with. "I'd better go take care of my girls," he announced, rising. He put back on the shades. "Come to the fireworks later. My gift to the community. Forty-five grand in rocketry. Next year, it will be more. A lot more. You too, Eddie."

It shook me to remember that Eddie was still sitting there, just to my right. I turned to look and was met with his piercing, haunted gaze.

Without a word, I got up and went to find another beer and to fill my plate. I wandered alone through a gate into the Johnsons' vast fenced gardens. I sat in the center of a narrow strip of mowed grass between two rows of crops: On the left was an onion patch, the newly formed globes about an inch in diameter. On the right, a bed of mixed lettuce, enough to make salads for the 150 people present. This bottomland soil was so rich. Jesus, I wished my pathetic greenhouse gardens on the ridge grew this well.

I wanted to eat my dinner alone, apart from the scene that felt more like last rites than a celebration, but I spotted Lara. It was odd Likowski wasn't with her. Her, I wanted to talk with. I waved, and before I could stand, she headed my way. In one hand Lara had a plate of roasted goat, grilled zucchini, and sliced watermelon; in the other, a Corona. Her SLR camera was strapped over her shoulder. Lara never went anywhere without it.

"Will!"

"Where's Likowski?"

"We are meeting here. He is driving down from the ridge."

Lara sat cross-legged on the grass with the plate of food set in front of her. She wore a black skirt and black tights. Her huge dark olive eyes were filled with worry.

"Something—it was very scary, it happened the last week," she admitted, more to herself than to me. "Danny and I, we were up where he grows the plants, and we hear this person yelling from down by the house. A woman. We go down, and Danny, he asks where she come from and she points. She work for the rich man up the mountain."

"J.D.?"

She nodded thoughtfully. "She says she is hiking and is lost. She needs water. I tell Danny, 'I go in the house to get the water.'" Lara said she took the woman's plastic quart bottle, and as soon as she got inside, she sneaked photos of the woman through the living room window. Lara found an image of the woman on her camera. She handed the Canon over and I studied the back screen. The woman had what appeared to be prematurely gray and straggly hair. She was white, but her skin was weathered and browned enough that from a distance one could mistake her for Latina. She was frightfully thin, wore blue jeans and a tank top. Loose skin hung from her arms.

"I came out with water and give her the bottle. She says, 'Thank you very much, have a nice day.' But she didn't care about it. She didn't even drink from it."

As soon as she was gone, Lara said Likowski phoned some neighbors. Alma said the strange woman showed up at their place too, asking for water. "You know the ridge is full of springs." Lara shook her head. "Danny is upset. He thinks that man is up to something not good." She went on, ignoring the plate of food in the grass. "I worry something bad is going to happen. This place, it has some nice hippies. But there is a lot of darkness too." She paused and looked deeply at me with those dark eyes. "I just wish Danny was not so emotional about you. He needs you now."

Ants had begun to crawl on her plate. I pointed to them. She shooed them away and began eating.

"How did you two meet again?"

"Danny and me?"

I nodded. I knew only that she was married—not to Likowski. When he first told me about Lara, he mentioned that her husband was a bail bondsman. In turn, I told him the only thing I knew about bail dudes, whom I'd covered when I was a reporter: all of them were assholes, and he'd end up facing the wrong end of a gun. He swore she was worth the risk.

"I met Danny at the studio. He come for yoga."

"Likowski—yoga?" I laughed incredulously. I had always considered Lara a photographer—she wanted to become a photojournalist—but she taught yoga in town to earn a living. That Likowski would take a yoga class had never occurred to me.

"He is a natural," she said generously, with a smile.

"I'm sure."

Lara and I had an organic connection. We'd met at Likowski's place no more than two years ago. Knowing I had worked for a newspaper, Lara had shown me pictures of a homeless family she'd been documenting up in town. The portraits were intimate but respectful, and better than the work of most *Times* photographers I knew. Soon after, I had helped arrange for her to take portraits of trimmers working for Klaus: she was interested in documenting the lives of these women. Klaus would never have let anyone take pictures in his greenhouses, but there was one exception that got him to agree: me, his Boswell. I assured him that Lara wouldn't say where she took the pictures until the day long in the future when I published my book, and Klaus was retired to Malibu, surfing. What had become of her project?

I was about to ask if I could see the pictures she'd taken of the trimmers—which included pictures of Tammie—but our conversation was halted by Likowski coming around the house. When he spotted us, even in the dusk I could see the glare in his eyes across the three hundred yards that separated us. Lara sensed it was a good time to say goodbye. She went to Likowski, and they became lost in the crowd. I stayed another hour, but I remained off by myself in the gardens, watching the gathering from afar. I don't know if word had spread that it would be the final July 4 celebration, but the crowd was subdued. I left a back way, through the meadow along the river, circling around to my truck.

I arrived home at full dark. I climbed the ladder to the crow's nest, rye whiskey on the rocks in hand. I kicked my feet up on the desk and faced east and the view of the valley. Fifteen minutes later, the first rocket of Klaus's $45,000 show shot into the sky; there was a red-spangled burst, followed by a green one. In quick succession there were two white flashes, hitting like sonic booms seconds later, rattling my windows.

For over twenty years before I ceased being a professor, I taught a narrative writing course at Stanford. I instructed students to immerse as deeply as possible in the lives of those they were documenting. They rebelled when I said they had to think about their subjects of study as "characters." They weren't your friends—they belonged in another realm. You needed distance. To the students, this sounded clinical. I explained that if you are going to be true to the story, those you write about must become characters and not people. Otherwise the work won't get done.

I didn't want to scare the students about what would happen if they were to pursue their stories for more than one quarter of instruction at a university, so I didn't tell them that if you immerse for many months—or years—there's the danger that you also become a character and not a person. At this level of forensic study, you occupy the minds of your subjects, you become them; the story becomes intertwined with your existence, and you go native.

A colleague in another department spent years researching and writing a biography of Anne Sexton, and it was clear that she had *become* Anne Sexton, if not a confessional, naked-to-the-world poet, then a confessional, naked-to-the-world writer who was documenting a poet's tragic life; at parties this professor openly talked about her preoccupation with sex, trysts with what she told me were "scandalously younger men," and how she was living on some hard edge. And there was the writer who reached out to me years ago for advice about immersing in white power movements. He was a typical young liberal journalist, and he wanted to go undercover with the National Alliance. After three years, he reemerged and asked me to blurb his book, which was strangely sympathetic to the group. I couldn't do that and we lost touch. That book came out and he began another, I was told; he next dove deep with people who eventually became Oath Keepers. I'd forgotten about him, but then years later I saw his picture in the *Washington Post*: he was arrested for storming the U.S. Capitol. He wasn't there as a journalist. He was now an Oath Keeper. There are others I could cite, but you get the idea.

Spending two, three, four years immersed is one thing; some twenty-five years is an entirely different matter. You go deep, you get close enough to cross the line, and the nonfiction writer who does this becomes an inhabitant of a novel; you are inside the heads of your characters, them in yours. I lived as a character among the characters on McGee Ridge. I was writing a book, I was living a book; this is that book. Kafka wrote, "From a certain point onward there is no longer any turning back. That is the point that must be reached." It took moving to the ridge for me to understand these words.

4

THE POINT BEYOND

A forklift lowered a pallet into the bed of the refrigerated semitruck idling next to the trim shed. Written on the side of the truck's box: NORTHSHORE FISH DISTRIBUTORS. Klaus stood next to the truck's open bay in the July sun, clipboard in hand, watching two workers jostle the pallet into position behind the first one they'd loaded.

"Four hundred and twenty-five pounds," Klaus said approvingly of the final pallet's weight. He handed the clipboard to Rob, his foreman, and walked toward what had been the Jacksons' ranch house, going straight to the basement. He kneeled, pulled aside a rug, lifted a board, and spun the dial on a floor safe that once contained $1.5 million in cash, on average. Now it was empty save for ten bundles of one-hundred-dollar bills with gold $10,000 bands around them. He extracted the money and stared for a moment at the now-empty safe. Upstairs, he tied the packets together with rubber bands. He sniffed the brick, stuffed it in his leather jacket pocket next to his nine. After locking the office door, he looked at his phone. It was only six.

He strode past the Harley Fat Boy. Everyone was gone except for Rob, who remained on guard duty. Klaus seldom had quiet moments these days. He strolled down the dusty lane past the greenhouses, to the far end where there was a south-facing hill covered in Scotch broom and blackberry brambles; the fruits were still green marbles, and there were yet white flowers, thick with bees. An old ranch road switchbacked a few hundred feet up to a flat. Halfway, he squinted against the sun to watch a circling red-tailed hawk. On the flat, Klaus sat, rested his elbows on his crooked knees. He thought of his Trinity outlaw days, the house grow, all the hard work that had led him to this point, as he surveyed his operation: the long greenhouses, the trim shed, the drying barn, the ranch house office, the idling refrigerated truck. In the distance, the gleaming white steeple of the seldom-used church, rising over treetops; sweeping clockwise, the expanse of the meadow stretching to the river, Edwards Mountain to the south, McGee Ridge to the southwest. He'd forgotten the last time he'd really taken in this kind of a slow examination of the valley. If he beat the charges like his lawyers said he would, he would kind of miss it in a few years when he left this coast behind—or maybe not. He looked forward to spending one night at his Malibu home when they drove the load south.

Klaus went back down the ranch road and jumped on the Harley. Rob waved as Klaus throttled out the gate. He opened up on the straightaway, made a series of S moves across both empty lanes. He loved the thunder of the machine.

Only three cars were in front of the Purple Thistle when he pulled up. He removed the aviator sunglasses and blinked, rubbed his eyes as he studied the neon sign in the late-afternoon light. A smile of satisfaction emerged.

"They're in the back room," Jake said when Klaus strode through the door.

"James! Bob!" Klaus said as he entered the tiny office with three chairs around a bare wooden table.

"Klaus! Good to see you," Bob, who resembled a gray-haired Cary Grant, said. His diction was precise. He'd gone to Harvard, but Klaus didn't hold it against him.

The men shook hands. Klaus thought they were an odd couple. Bob was so good-looking. James resembled a jowly Teddy Roosevelt. Perhaps he had been a handsome young man. "You drive down?"

"No. We flew in last night," James said.

"How's it feel being back?"

"Frankly, we're happy we moved to Portland," Bob said. "It's better for James's health, to be near his doctors."

"There is no graceful way to grow old," James said. "How's business?"

"Never been better. We're driving the dep to Los Angeles tomorrow."

"Shall we have a drink?" James asked.

"Tell Jake my usual."

James opened the office door and called to Jake, who'd worked for the men who had been absentee owners of the bar for over a decade. Jake promptly appeared. "For Mr. Vanderlip, can you please get him his usual. For me, ginger ale on the rocks. Bob?"

"Vodka martini, dry, olive."

"Yes, sir." The door closed.

"Does he know about the sale?" Klaus whispered.

"We're going to tell him next week," Bob said. "We warned him this day would come."

"You know he has a grow over on Nackick's Mountain."

The men looked surprised. James asked, "Has he been selling from the bar?"

"I don't think so," Klaus lied. "He'll be okay."

"Things have changed so much. Marijuana has become such a big business," James said. "It was just the hippies for so long. We never really got to know them."

"Hippies never came in here," Bob said.

"Our crowd was *so* redneck," James said. "We had to pretend we had wives up in town."

"We only read about marijuana growing in the hills. We never saw it," Bob said. "We just heard about cows and fishing and hunting."

"And sports."

"Had to always keep the television on some damn sports game."

"And logging!"

"Chain saws and bulldozers!"

"We started losing money before we moved," James said. "Jake's been almost breaking even since you started your business. You're bringing in all the customers."

The men talked about the old days, the many fights that happened in the bar.

"I had a .38 I kept beneath the register, just in case," James said. "But I never had to pull it. The fights, they were really just some kind of sport."

There was a knock at the door. Jake came in with a tray of drinks and quickly exited. Klaus picked up the Weller 107. James and Bob lifted their drinks. "To doing business."

Glasses clinked.

"We drew up an agreement. This is the formal one," Bob said, pulling out a standard real estate contract that would be filed with the title company, with $500,000 due at the close of escrow. That would be the money paid on the books, what the county would base the property tax on. "And this"—he set a printed sheet on the table—"this side contract has the balance of $750,000, $100,000 due today's date, the balance due by the end of December."

Klaus had already set aside bank money to pay the half million. He pulled the brick of $100,000 and set it on the table.

"If you don't mind me asking," James said as he tried not to stare at the money, but not concealing his delight, "do you ever worry about counterfeit bills?"

"In all the years I've been at this, I've just had a few, like two or three."

"Don't you... worry about something happening? Especially these days. We follow the news. I keep reading about all the murders, the robberies—"

"Cars burning at the sides of roads with charred bodies inside," Bob said. "Gangland-style killings. That vaping oil kingpin's body dumped on the 101 last week! Oh my. His picture looked like Al Pacino in *The Godfather*. It wasn't at all like this back when."

"Most of that stuff's happening down south," Klaus said. "Not up here."

"Don't you fear being robbed?" James asked. "You're dealing with such large sums of cash. Large amounts of marijuana."

"You want to know what my biggest problem is? Trimmers. They're gonna rip you off. A pocketful a day, it adds up—a grand or two worth. Or more. But I know their tricks. I use hidden cameras. I catch most of them. Still, I know I have loss. We have security. I never trust anyone, even Alex, my main man, to drive a big load of product south. I always go along. Biomass, I'm not so worried about. Those trucks are going all the time. The money comes back in a safe in my Tundra. I never trust anyone to run money. I can survive the little losses. Trim rip-offs, those are like mosquitoes. But a million-dollar rip-off, it would wipe me out. I can't wait until I can get out of growing. Where are you guys headed?"

"We're driving to San Francisco for the weekend, then flying home."

"Gentlemen, why don't you keep the rental and drive back to Portland. I will return Tuesday afternoon, and I can give you the balance then. Why wait six months?"

Bob and James were astonished. "You mean the entire $650,000?" Bob asked.

Klaus nodded.

"How delightful," James said. "My Lord, how this is going to save us on capital gains. And we get to spend an extra day in San Francisco."

"Sotirova offered one-point-six," Bob said. "But he wanted a five-year carry with a balloon."

"Even if we could wait that long, I didn't like him," James said. "Scary man."

"Sotirova's gonna be pissed," Klaus said with glee. He chuckled.

The men drank and made small talk for twenty minutes.

Bob looked at his watch. "We should get back to our hotel," he said.

Klaus followed them out into the bar. James used a cane, and it took him a while to reach the exit. Klaus went into the men's room. He looked at himself in the mirror. "Klaus Vanderlip, owner of the Purple Thistle. Yes! Yes! Yes!" he whispered as he splashed water on his face. He emerged and took a seat on a barstool.

"Another?" Jake asked.

Klaus leaned across the bar and patted Jake on the shoulder. "My man! Indeed."

Klaus sipped and imagined the hot bartender he'd hire to replace Jake; she would increase business. He pictured wooden booths, wainscoting. Mostly he envisioned the vaping oil facility out back. It would take two years to save enough to start construction. Klaus drank a third Weller. His fantasies now were of hoping the night would bring in some attractive women, but only a steady stream of gnarly dudes came through the door.

"Heard anything?" Jake asked.

"Nothing," Klaus said curtly. That was not what he wanted to think about, and Jake knew then he'd just pissed off his best customer, reminding him of the presence of a three-foot-tall poster decorating the wall near the entrance, featuring his lost mother's face.

REWARD
$100,000 CASH

FOR ANY INFORMATION
LEADING TO THE WHEREABOUTS
OF ZOË VANDERLIP

Below was Klaus's burner phone Signal number and other contact information. He thought about how everything bad started after Tammie went to the cops. Maybe his mother wouldn't be missing if it wasn't for her. *Goddamn Tammie.* His trial date in November had been postponed. His lawyers were damn good, but only so good--they had run out of reasons for delay. The trial date was set for February. In their last meeting, Will had asked about her, and Klaus had talked a lot. Not everything, of course. He regretted every word of it now.

She knew only that she was nowhere. That she was now nothing.

When they transported her from San Francisco International Airport to this anonymous place it was night. Two other girls sat with her on the floor of the windowless panel van. They drove for hours. If the women had to urinate, they were to use a portable toilet that sloshed near the back door. There was no stopping. The last hour of the ride was very rough. The girls lurched left, right, left, right, being thrown one way as the engine gunned, then being tossed back across the chamber. She tried counting the curves but lost track after fifty. When the van ceased moving, the girls piled out. It was so dark. Tsvetana Lazarova had never experienced such a blackness of night. The stars were the same constellations as back in Gurkovo. But her location on the planet felt so different. The air was cold and was unlike any atmosphere she had ever breathed. Each girl was given her own yurt. This pleased Tsvetana. How nice of Viktor to provide private quarters and a fine bed. She would soon come to hate the yurt.

In the morning they were fed a breakfast of scrambled eggs and toast. There was orange juice. The food was good. There were eight girls, Viktor Sotirova, and two other men. Viktor took her to one of the greenhouses. Tsvetana was shown by Boriana how to transplant starts and sex them. Males were thrown into a basket. This was the first of many jobs that she would learn. Other important work was topping the plants at the correct time, cutting the single stem so that it would branch and produce multiple kolas. There were eight long greenhouses. During all but the late hours of the night, there was the constant noise of a diesel generator.

The three new girls were told if they ran away American immigration authorities would arrest them. They would go to prison and Donald Trump would ensure they would never be released. No one spoke Bulgarian for thousands of miles in any direction, and crazy American men with guns would abduct and torture them. It was a very dangerous wilderness beyond the borders of the compound.

Viktor never packed a gun, but the other two men had ugly black rifles used by men in war. A third man, also with a rifle, sometimes was present. The men carried the weapons with straps on their shoulders, propped them against the table when they ate lunch. They slept next to them. The guns were not meant for the girls, they were told, but any thieves who might be stupid enough to try to rob them. Tsvetana wondered, The plants are now small. This is not harvest time. The men wore silk tracksuits, bright blue or gray, and velvet shoes that looked like they were bought in Paris.

Two weeks after she arrived, Tsvetana climbed the mountain above the greenhouses. No one paid her any mind—it was their break time, and though the warnings were ominous, their immediate movements weren't monitored. Tsvetana reached a meadow at the crest. There was a clear view of the world around her. Peak after peak stretched into a ceaseless distance. Forbidding canyons cleaved off mountains. The only structures in sight were the hoop greenhouses, gleaming white in the sun, far below. Tsvetana reeled as she absorbed the reality of her isolation.

She recalled the recruiter who told of the good job growing marijuana in America. But the pictures he'd shown her were of plants beneath the sun, not in greenhouses, and of a nearby village with many things to do. She would get to see America. She was excited about the adventure of traveling to California and earning U.S. dollars. Unemployment was high in Bulgaria and her parents were poor. The recruiter gave her a Lufthansa ticket after she signed a three-year contract. He took her to Sofia Airport. The jet flew to London, where she connected to a San Francisco–bound flight. She'd never before left Bulgaria. It seemed so long ago.

Tsvetana noticed that the other girls were pretty. At seventeen she was the youngest. The oldest was twenty-four. She also was pretty: tall at five-ten, with a nearly round face, deep-set dark eyes, shoulder-length chestnut hair;

her waist was the circumference of the tiny, squat, round loaves of bread the baker sold at the market in her village. She had an exuberance and intelligence that frightened many boys. She liked reading. Her glasses made her appear older. She was wise enough not to allow others to know of her intelligence if she chose not to reveal it.

When the plants reached twelve inches, Viktor came to her yurt one night after dinner. He brought an eclair that he'd purchased in a distant town. She accepted it cautiously. "I am your friend. I will bring you more eclairs." He delivered desserts each of the coming nights. A week later, when he brought a cream puff with chocolate on top, Viktor sat at the edge of the bed while she consumed the pastry. He was big of belly and he smelled. He bathed often but was the kind of man who had the misfortune of perpetually emitting the odor of a man who never did.

He placed a hand on her knee...

The greenhouses, made of PVC tubing covered with white sheet plastic, had tall ceilings. They grew sativa. The marijuana was planted tightly. There was much work to be done: leafing, or clipping off shade leaves; spraying for mold; cleaning sediment out of the water delivery system that piped in from a creek; feeding the German shepherd guard dogs; hauling fertilizer and applying it; putting on black plastic tarps earlier each day and taking them off in the morning, mimicking shortened days to force the plants to flower by midsummer; hanging the buds and stems on strings in the drying sheds; trimming. The women rotated cooking from one day to the next, so that each had to make meals about once per week. Tsvetana grew adept at each task. Viktor had installed a sound system in the trimming shed. Large speakers blasted thumping Euro-techno, like Pulsedriver's "Night Moves" and Purebeat's "AraBeat." The bass was so deep that the plastic walls shook and trim tables vibrated. Most of the women ignored using the tables and had inverted plastic trash can lids on their laps, loaded with ragged buds. Between songs, when there was brief quiet, there was the sound of nearly a dozen Wiss scissors clicking, schkk-schkk-schkk. After all the bud was trimmed, she had trouble moving her fingers. They immediately began tending to the next crop.

Viktor came to Tsvetana's yurt every few nights. He provided birth control pills. She took them because she didn't want to get pregnant—not from anyone, but especially not from his sperm. She had very little experience having sex with men before coming to America, but she knew enough to understand that Viktor was clumsy. His smelly weight was repulsive. She imagined an old hog from her grandfather's farm was on top of her. The only good thing about it was that he was fast. She just wanted it over each time.

She read her books, brought from home, by the light of a tiny halogen lamp in the yurt. When finished, she reread each. Two men escorted the girls into town to shop once per week. "There are many undercover immigration agents looking for Mexicans and Bulgarians," Viktor warned. "If they catch you, they will send you to prison for years. Trust no one. Americans hate peoples from other countries." They were to stick very close to their minders. The girls were given fifty dollars a week to buy items such as tampons, toothpaste, and extra food, like chips and candies. They were made to sit on the floor of the van, but Tsvetana perched on her haunches as much as she could to peer through the windshield, to see by the sun which direction they were headed. It took an hour and a half to reach a four-lane highway. In another hour, they arrived at a midsized town.

The other women shopped for cosmetics and clothes. Tsvetana bought books. There were none in Bulgarian. It was just as well. She wanted to learn English. She had been practicing with Boriana and another girl who spoke it. And there was a Bulgarian man now at the site who had American citizenship. She talked to him in English. One book Tsvetana purchased was a Russian-English dictionary, Russian having enough in common with Bulgarian to be of some help. Five of the books were illustrated volumes meant for American children learning the alphabet and simple words. She bought Dickens and Tolstoy, but also Lee Child and John Grisham.

Tsvetana spent every free moment reading and practicing English. She rapidly improved. She wanted to become as American as possible. She was desperate to talk flawlessly just like American girls. She wanted to blend in, get lost in the crowd of a city, all that she saw from reading and watching shows on DVDs about American culture. Yet she only knew the United States from this land of creepy redwood and fir forests, with its giant yellow banana slugs, the haunting night songs of tiny bright green Pacific tree frogs, the dark fogs rolling off the Pacific.

Her life continued like this the next year and the one that followed.

That June, the women had just finished trimming the dep crop and were planting the next, when it was announced that Viktor had to return to

Bulgaria to attend to business. Tsvetana knew from overheard conversations that he was going to meet with his mobster bosses. Her three-year contract was not yet up, Viktor reminded her before he left. She had to remain through the next season. He was to return by September. He promised her more good times in bed. She smiled, but inside part of her died when he said that, as it did each time he raped her. The other men left as well. New men took their place. They were younger, freshly arrived from Bulgaria, and full of swagger. They got very drunk after dinner the first night. Two stood outside of Tsvetana's yurt and argued over who was going to have her. Their voices rose and they got into a fistfight. Tsvetana was very scared. Velikov, a boy not much older than her, prevailed. He entered the yurt and ordered her to strip naked. He was so drunk he could not get an erection and hurt her arms by holding her down as he tried, over and over. He finally left.

Tsvetana had a bad feeling about these new men even before the incident. She'd loaded a pack that afternoon with clothes and candy bars. She wanted to take some books, but they were too heavy. The girls' money was kept in a safe inside a trailer at the front of the property, but she had hidden nearly five hundred dollars that the men didn't know about, having lied about the cost of the books; they seldom went into the stores with her. They stood outside smoking cigarettes, trying to look badass in their silk running suits, speaking loudly in Bulgarian and laughing when Americans looked at them disapprovingly. When she emerged, she complained that books were very expensive in America and they consumed all her money. These were men who, even if they spoke good English, would not read a book, so they had no idea of their value, either intellectually or monetarily—she'd spent only a few dollars each for the used ones. The leftover money was tucked into her panties and stashed in a jar secreted in the forest.

The boy on guard duty was sleeping off his binge, snoring in front of the second greenhouse. The dogs were chained near the trailer at the entrance. The shepherds loved Tsvetana. She always gave them leftover treats and paid them a lot of attention. She scratched their necks one last time and headed down the road.

The stars were thick. She felt alive beneath the sweep of the Milky Way. She moved fast, ready to dive into the forest if there was the sound of a vehicle. With each step she felt freer. She walked until dawn and slept far from the road. She knew from watching when they went to town that it would take many hours on foot to make it to the highway. She tried to sleep as long as possible, *but mosquitoes and little black flies would not allow this. She couldn't walk on the road in daylight and certainly couldn't hitchhike. She picked her way slowly along through the dense forest of Douglas fir, pushing aside dead low branches spreading like a brown cloud before her. Late in the afternoon she napped; it turned into deep sleep. The candy bars were gone. Now she wished she'd put aside food from when it was her turn to cook.*

She awoke in the night, bushwhacked out to the road. She was very hungry and became sad when she passed a closed market. She walked and walked. She knew the names of only a few constellations besides the Big Dipper. One of those was the star formation Касионея; it resembled a tiny house. She could tell by its position in the heavens that it was about two in the morning. Soon she reached the highway. She turned north. Never had she been so famished. At six in the morning, she came to a town with a twenty-four-hour gas station and market. She acted casual as she picked out two premade roast beef sandwiches, salt and vinegar chips, an apple, and a soda, all the while watching to see if the van pulled in from the grow operation. The sleepy clerk had been up all night and didn't notice his customer was nervous. After paying, she slipped behind the market and downed the food. She fell asleep leaning against the wall.

She awakened at noon, forgetting where she was. She darted across the road and went to a coffeehouse, where she ordered a cappuccino and two almond croissants. She lingered for a few hours, and then she found a sleeping spot in the middle of the blackberry brambles out back. At dark she resumed walking, going north. She slept in a redwood forest. At dawn she was able to travel parallel with the road among the big trees. She had only seen the redwoods through the van's windshield but had not touched the thick bark of one. She craned her head back and marveled at their height. She was again a child.

When she arrived on a very desolate part of the coast, she went to a grow operation where she heard there were plenty of jobs. When Klaus Vanderlip interviewed her, he asked for her name. "Tsvetana, er... Tammie. Tsvetana is my name in my country. In America I am Tammie."

"Just keep doing what you are doing. Pretend I am not here."

Tammie furiously clipped kolas, dropping them in a basket, her hands moving so fast that Lara captured the motion with a slow shutter speed. When Lara showed up that morning, there were a dozen young women working in the greenhouses, but Lara focused on Tammie. She was naturally photogenic, even beautiful. But it wasn't just her tall, thin form. There was an edge that Lara saw in the Bulgarian immigrant and connected with immediately.

"Nice," Lara said as she checked the images on the back of the camera; she blew one up, centering on Tammie's blurred hands moving fast over the plants. "Have a look."

"How can you make such a fantastic picture?"

"Thank you. My teacher at the college says, 'It is the fool, not the tool.' But this tool is a very good camera. It makes wonderful pictures."

Tammie told Lara she'd been working for Klaus for a few months and that it was much better than working for her Bulgarian boss. "We have lunch breaks," Tammie said. "I have enough to share. Rice and red beans mixed with the stewed tomatoes, and apples."

Tammie went to the shade of a nearby willow to pick up a small orange plastic lug-handled cooler. Lara followed. The women ducked under a barbed wire fence marking the boundary with Doc Anderson's land. Tammie had been taking her breaks at the swimming hole, skinny-dipping. Doc despised Klaus's grow operation, but he didn't mind naked young women in his river. Lara stripped with Tammie, hanging clothes on box elder branches. They made their way down the slope.

Tammie had a small white plastic cosmetics bottle filled with liquid and squirted it on her palm. "Vegetable oil," she said, rubbing it all over her sticky arms, flecked with specks of bud. "It takes off the resin."

Tammie soaped up to rid herself of the oil, dove into the river. Lara followed.

"I've never swum here before," Lara said when her head emerged from the water and she shook her hair. She waded across the pool to a sandy beach half in the shade of the box elders.

Tammie followed and extracted Tupperware and sodas from the cooler. She asked where Lara was from.

"Italy."

"Do you have the documentation papers?"

"I have the marriage green card, but not enough time has passed for me to live—and leave him, to be a citizen. You?"

"I am illegal."

"Do you want to stay here?"

She nodded gravely, as though it was both her deepest wish and something that was terrifying.

"You must marry an American man."

"I don't like men."

"Then you must marry an American woman."

"I have a fantasy of being in a city like San Francisco or Los Angeles or New York, to go to university. I want to become a lawyer, maybe a photographer too."

Lara noticed that Tammie ate slowly and appreciatively. She did the same.

"I do not have the internet in my yurt," Tammie said. "When I go to town I buy old DVDs, to practice my English and to dream of being a lawyer. Did you do that?"

Lara nodded. "Yes! What do you like to watch?"

"Ally McBeal and The Good Wife."

The women laughed, and Tammie blushed. "I dream of being Ally McBeal. I am embarrassed to tell you. I am embarrassed to dream so big. I am nothing in America. I have no bank account."

"Do not ever apologize for dreams. Maybe the America dream doesn't exist for Americans anymore, but for us it means something. Things are still possible in America compared with Italy—or, I imagine, Bulgaria. Maybe it is true that we will only get the scraps. But scraps are more than we can hope for back home. Americans are very stupid in their understanding of some things. They do not know what we know. You must dream, and even if all of them do not materialize, a few will come true."

"It feels scary to talk about. I have never told them to anyone before, but I am saving my money."

"Does Klaus pay you okay?"

"It is by the hour now. Ten dollars for harvest. Trimming will soon begin. That will be two hundred dollars for the pound and I'm good. I will make good money. For the first time since Bulgaria, I am able to save all that I make."

They continued talking rapidly in their Italian- and Bulgarian-accented English as they walked back to the greenhouses. Clearly, Tammie was excited to have made a friend who was also an outsider and who had created a life for herself in this country separate from the marijuana industry. Lara continued photographing the clipping. Later that afternoon the women hung kolas to dry in a hundred-foot-long shed strung with a spiderweb of thousands of feet of thin cord; the women worked fast, hanging the marijuana branch pieces upside down, using the V crooks in the limbs, on the twine. Lara reeled from the odor of bud.

"I think I'm going to throw up. How can you stand the smell?"

"I will never smoke marijuana ever again," Tammie said.

Alex, Klaus's most trusted worker, a dark-bearded millennial in a white T-shirt, watched from a perch on a barstool with a tall seat back. His arms were crossed. He had also been in the greenhouse when the women were clipping. He observed but didn't boss anyone, never yelled; there was an unspoken demand of urgency that the women understood. He just reported laggards to Klaus, and those women did not show up the next day. Lara noticed a semiautomatic rifle and shotgun in the office at the end of the drying shed when she and Tammie came in. The guns weren't brandished, but they were kept close. When a truck appeared on the dusty lane, Lara watched Alex hurry to the office and lay a hand on the AR-15, until he realized it was someone delivering supplies. Lara desperately wanted a picture of his hand on that war rifle, but she did not want to make anyone nervous. Her goal was to eventually get pictures of Klaus—good ones—because she knew he'd be central to the story her images would tell.

The sun was low when the women left the shed, after all the clipped kolas were suspended. In gratitude, Lara took Tammie to dinner at the Purple Thistle. "Danny does not like this place," she explained as they climbed out of Lara's gray 1999 Saturn. "Too loud. And rough. But it is still early."

There were just a dozen patrons, mostly older men in electric utility work uniforms, eating at two tables. The women picked a table next to the window, and Lara confessed her affair with Likowski.

Tammie asked, "You do not love your husband?"

"No. He married me because I was the trophy wife," she said frankly, and not without sarcasm.

"How did you meet?"

"Bumble. I was in New York. It was not good for me. So I came to this hippie place, to my geezer husband. And now my geezer lover."

Tammie nodded in understanding.

"This is the end of my America road," Lara said. "It sometimes reminds me of this little Spanish island called Formentera, where I lived for six months. It has a street that leads you to a lighthouse, but it seems that it really just leads you to the edge of nothing. Apparently Jules Verne was inspired by it to write The Lighthouse at the End of the World. It is like that here—we are at the edge of infinity."

"Yes, the edge of nothingness," Tammie said. "I no longer feel Bulgarian. But I do not feel American either. Like the French say, *cul entre deux chaises*."

5

1996–1998

He felt most alive when free soloing, at six or seven thousand feet, where the air was crisp, when it was just him with the hard ancient granite, the hawks, the silence. His climbing friends thought he was crazy to go into the Trinity Alps alone to make ropeless ascents. *You are pussies! I don't care if I die.* They laughed and called him a drama king, which made him double down on embracing suicide by falling. *If it is meant to happen, so it will be.* In town he believed those words. Yet on the faces, hot sun on his neck and dripping sweat, he was scared during crux moves, when his fingers strained in a crevasse and he used opposing pressure with a toe on a barest of rock knobs to pull himself up another fourteen inches. *This must mean I don't really want to die.* But if he did make the plunge, he didn't want his body to be discovered. He knew that much. *Leave a good mystery.* They'd have no idea where to look because he parked the truck and hiked in six, seven, ten miles. He fantasized about abandoning the truck and trekking east, across the Central Valley, into the lava bed country in Lassen. That would be the best way—*pretending* to have died in a fall. *Leave all of the shit behind. Let them all think I'm dead. Start over fresh where nobody knows me.* If only he had enough money, if only his crop didn't keep getting weeded.

He was quite aware that he was a shitty grower, that he'd been lazy. He now vowed to follow exactly what Likowski had taught him that summer after high school, when he apprenticed with him to help grow Death Wish in the canyons south of McGee Ridge. He'd been a most unapt pupil, planting all his weed in one spot over the previous four growing seasons. He was still living off what he earned that first season, when he was lucky and all went well; the subsequent summers were disasters. Camouflage netting didn't help; it in fact seemed to act as a bull's-eye for CAMP and the national forest rangers. They knew how to look for it with binoculars, or that sensor arm sticking out of the helicopters saw through it with the infrared emitted by the plants—whatever it was, they zeroed in on his crop. He wasn't there for the bust because he was away most of the time, on rock faces, in town in bed with women, and deer and voles had already taken advantage of his absences. By the final time he was weeded in the late summer of 1996, there wasn't much for the feds to haul away anyway.

Turning thirty changed everything. He had to stop fucking around. *Get serious, asshole!* he shouted at a bathroom mirror. He focused on a three-step plan to earn a lot of money, a *huge* amount of money, *bricks* of hundred-dollar bills, so that he could leave the Emerald Triangle behind. He'd live in Malibu and spend his days surfing. Or perhaps Hawaii, where he'd never been, but he imagined coconut trees, warm breezes, a different woman in his arms every few months; most of all, he conjured luxury. Never again would bats piss on him in bed. No longer would he endure the steady *drip-drip* from the leaking ceiling into a bucket, or shit in an outhouse during a Pineapple Express, or have to split wood to keep warm, or rely on oil lamps and candles for light, or eat steamed nettles, or put up with a dozen other indignities of life in the Ark. He would jettison all the so-called friends who laughed at him in high school, where he was never good enough for the teachers, never good enough for *her*; there were losers and winners, and money would ensure he'd get respect.

Step one: That winter he scouted the canyons off of Big French Creek near the town of Vineland to identify planting spots on cliffs; he then packed in poly pipe, emitters, fencing, and netting and was ready to go by the spring. Come summer, there would be no climbing, no rolling down 299 to party in town, no girls. He'd be focused on twenty-three widely scattered patches. By fall, if all went according to plan, he'd leave behind his Trinity outlaw days. He never worked harder those five months of tending the patches, yet never again would he feel so free. He caught rainbow trout in white-foaming waters, and he finally learned all the major constellations using a star wheel bought at the nature store in town. Here at two thousand feet, the sky was so much sharper than on the coast; night after night the Milky Way blew across the heavens. It was beautiful, but those Andromeda hours were difficult. For the first time in his life, he faced himself, the crazy journey from Berlin to the windy coast and this canyon with its twenty-three thriving patches. A flood of conversations came back— really the same conversation with his mother continued. When they were looking for firewood that last Berlin winter, he found human bones in the rubble—a skull and a femur, a few other pieces. He shouted to his mother and Helmut, *Kommt her! Kommt her! I have found a dead person!* And Helmut replied, *Put them back and pretend you never saw them.* How could he pretend he didn't see the bones of that dead person? Pretend there was no war? How could that be, with all the ruins around them, and how they lived with no electricity? *What was the war? Why did it happen?* Was it the war that made Momma and Helmut the way they were? *Why did Bruno really leave, Momma?*

Helmut was never his *vati*. Even now he could not even utter that man's name, he was "Hell-man." He'd read books about the war, the ones Momma bought for him, and he now knew what to ask: *Did Hell-man ever confront his father about burning Hitler's body? And then saluting Sieg Heil at the black-smoke inferno with the corpse in the center? Momma, how could you sleep with a man like that?*

She'd caught Helmut in the act, trying to touch her son. That had finally done it. She nearly killed him as Helmut rushed through the Ark, throwing belongings into a bag. She, however, lived in denial of what had happened. *You don't want to talk about what happened. You know what happened. It wasn't beautiful. It was un-beautiful, Momma. You've been running away from what your father did to you your whole life.* Hell-man remained a constant specter in all future conflicts.

Step two: He learned it from Rick, his friend from high school. *Fuck growing out in the woods, dude. Indoor is the way to go. Rent a big house, at least three bedrooms, so you can go full throttle. Put white window shades in the front, then gaffer-tape black plastic behind them so from the outside nothing looks wrong. You gotta keep light out, or the plants, they'll get confused. You buy grow lights, buckets or bags, poly tubes, a light timer; put down plastic sheets. You'll need metal halide lights for the grow phase, high-pressure sodium lights for the red-orange spectrum once they start flowering. Ventilation is your biggest worry. You gotta ventilate for heat, for mold. The problem is you're cranking out skunk all over the neighborhood. You might as well put a sign on the door announcing what you're doing.*

The key is a good filtration system to nip the smell in the bud, so to speak. Hahahaha. Even with the right genetic stock, you're still gonna get mold, so you have to spray. They don't grow that big inside, but you can put 'em pretty close. How many? It's all about space. You can grow three hundred plants and harvest 'em when they get a foot high; you grow one hundred and they get taller, you get more poundage. How much? About a pound for each one thousand watts of light. You can't grow that much shit out in the woods, dude. The best variety is Northern Lights—it's bred specifically for indoor. You're gonna burn through juice; they say they don't, but they look for big spikes in bills. Suddenly the electric bill goes to like eighteen hundred bucks a month. I never rent more than twelve months. You keep it going longer, your chances of a bust go up. Way up. Hardest thing? Walking away from a setup. You'll see what I mean. Best thing to do is get one of the trim hos to put the rental agreement in her name, get the electric in her name, so if they bust you, it keeps you clean. Don't pay your rent cash. That makes 'em suspicious. Last year I got eighty-nine pounds of trimmed bud outta my house, five turns. You gotta use clones to get that much, and I push 'em hard. You start from seed, you get three turns. Eighty-nine pounds versus probably fifty-some. Big diff, my friend. One-fifty a pound for the trimmers; minus the rent, the electric bill, not counting the investment in equipment, I cleared two hundred eighty grand. Do the math, bro. How much did you grow out in the woods? You don't gotta worry about helicopters. Wood rats. Deer. Poison oak. House grows, you get to live in town, drink at the Candlelight, eat sushi at the 'Ran, sleep in a warm bed, get laid, no mosquitoes biting your face all night long, no shitting in the woods...

Klaus made $51,000 from his summer's work in the canyons of Big French Creek. Not a single one of the twenty-three patches was weeded. The only raid came on his decoy spot—Likowski had taught him to create a phony patch using male plants far from his real gardens. Klaus put his a half mile up a canyon, in an open area that surely would be seen from the air, with twenty male plants. Likowski told him it made the cops feel good, like they'd gotten something, and then they wouldn't come back around to an area they'd already "cleaned." That summer Klaus transformed into Likowski's very apt pupil. His mentor provided something else: the plants were from Likowski's Death Wish stock, seeds that he'd lifted at the end of that summer working with the elder grower and Eddie in their grow spots in the canyons south of the ridge. He kept the line going by propagating it each year out in the Trinity woods. His buyer was blown away by the power of the weed, and Klaus had to bite his lip when asked about the genetics. *Trade secret,* he said, wink-wink, nudge. *You know.* He clutched the five $10k bundles of C-notes and change in twenties that came out of the buyer's Pelican case. He now could rent a grow house, purchase supplies.

Klaus wasn't yet experienced enough to get a trimmer to rent the house for him, nor did he want to take that risk. He told no one other than Rick what he was doing, and he made Rick promise to keep the secret. A bust meant returning to the Trinity woods for another grubstake or giving up. In his nightmares he was on a face, in a crux move, and his toe, with all the pressure on it, slips; the three-hundred-foot fall awakened him panting and sweating. He took that as a sign. He'd lie very, very low. Until he had the profits from the house grow buried in jars in the woods at his mom's place, where no one could touch that money, there'd be no partying, no chicks, no climbing. *This is it. The crux move for the rest of my life.* Klaus kept a keen eye on ads in the papers, postings on corkboards in the entryways of grocery stores. Rick said he had to stick with the crappiest neighborhoods, where landlords had trouble finding stable tenants—they were hungry and greedy, and many were absentee. You didn't want a local who kept checking up on his or her property. What about neighbors? *People in the hood don't give a shit what you do,* Rick said. *They're too busy surviving to be busybodies.* Klaus answered a half dozen ads by phone and none was right: the houses were too small, or the owner lived in town. He worried that rental agents were suspicious, but he started finding likely prospects and grew more confident.

Conversation with agent #1:

I'm a grad student, getting a master's degree in forestry and wildland resources.

But hasn't school already started?

Oh yeah. I'm living in the dorm, but I got stuck with the roommate from hell. You know how that is. Dude snores and smokes weed in the room. My parents gave me some money to rent a house. I can't wait to have my own space.

Conversation with agent #2:

Does the owner live in town?

Why do you want to know?

In case I have trouble. I want to be sure that things can be fixed fast.

That's why he's hired our company—we take care of all of that. You can just call us if you have a problem with anything. We have a roster of plumbers and electricians on call. Handymen.

Conversation with agent #3:

You don't have a rental history, so it will be difficult to rent to you. Do you have someone who can cosign?

No, but I can pay three months' rent in advance.

I don't think that will be possible.

Conversation with agent #4:

I understand that I don't have a rental history. But if I give you a check for twelve months' rent, do you think that would work? My parents gave me enough to cover an entire year.

Let me make a call... Hi, Mr. J—, I've got a client here, a student at the university. He doesn't have a leasing history, but he wants to pay a year's rent in advance... Uh-huh... uh-huh ... okay, thanks, bye ... Okay. Mr. Vanderlip, he says that would be okay.

I see you punched in a 415 number. Mr. J—, he must live in the Bay Area...

Mr. J's house, on Dobkins Lane, was perfect. Three bedrooms. The street was in a run-down neighborhood of homes built in the 1930s and 1940s for lumber mill workers, now occupied by immigrants. It was difficult to find parking when Klaus pulled up; the street was lined with late-model cars, some covered in grime from being broken down for so long. Latino kids played in yards; a Laotian woman in a bright purple shawl walked down the street. He thought, *If they're undocumented, the last thing they'll do is call the cops.*

Klaus bought white window shades and huge rolls of black plastic, lots of gaffer tape. He feared shopping locally for the special lights and other heavy-duty supplies—Rick warned him that cops watched for grow-related sales. People bought black plastic all the time to cover boats or leaking roofs, or to kill Bermuda grass in lawns. That wasn't suspicious. But industrial sodium grow lights? Huge fans and fancy air filtration systems? He drove to Oakland and Walnut Creek. An electric supply company had the lights; another company, the fans and filtering equipment. A garden supply center had the seven dozen five-gallon black plastic tree nursery buckets, poly pipe, and emitters, and from Home Depot he got timers for the lights, a Lawn Genie control panel, and valve heads. The pickup truck bulged, the load strapped beneath canvas rising four feet above the cab; it looked like the Joads' jalopy, if the Joads had come to California to grow weed. He blasted the Offspring on the drive up the 101. That was just the first round of supplies. He went back twice for more lights, ductwork, and sundries, spending just over $16,000.

The build-out was more work than he anticipated—running ducts, hanging lights with chain, making the filtration system function. He always needed something or another and often drove to the hardware store for chain, Romex wire, junction boxes, black tape, propane torch gas canisters, solder, flux, nails, a half dozen different kinds of screws, plywood, two-by-fours, a hot glue gun—where did he put the fucking razor knife? *Fuck! JesusfuckingChristgoddamnit*—a new razor knife—right-angle tin snips, Vulkem, RectorSeal Number 5, more solder, screws, chain. Each hardware store visit meant spending in increments of hundreds of dollars; he peeled off the Ben Franklins as if they were one-dollar bills. The little things were killing him—they added up. He hated going out so much, afraid some of his "friends" from high school would spot him buying materials that were obviously for an indoor grow. Some of those guys were the kind who, when the bud was drying, would wear ski masks and kick the door in some night brandishing guns; one of them was in Pelican Bay, but two were still lurking. He had a MAC-10 for them but didn't want to have to go there.

He hated the build-out for other reasons. His hands were all kinds of cut up, with wounds in various stages of healing, from jagged metal edges, slipped screwdrivers and pliers. *When I'm rich, I'll hire people to do the shit work! When I'm rich, I'll never have cuts on my hands ever again! When I'm rich, I'll sit behind a desk and tell people what to do!*

It cost eight bucks per seed for Northern Lights stock. He couldn't risk buying clones, which would have cost even more anyway. He began the starts even as he was finishing the last of the ductwork. *I want plants growing like yesterday.* He set seeds on wetted paper towels sprinkled with sulfur, on which were stacked more wet paper towels, placed in the just-warm zone under one of the grow lights. When sprouted, he used tweezers to put them in soil.

After the build, he seldom left the Dobkins Lane home. Trips to the twenty-four-hour Safeway were made after midnight. When the plants were small and there was no risk of robbery, he ventured into the bracing foggy air at two in the morning and walked the streets down to the bay, where he sat on a pier smoking cigarettes, watched fishing boats heading out for crab and albacore.

But mostly he remained inside. There was a mix of paranoia and continued reflection on his life as the fall of 1997 blended into the winter of 1998. Time was measured by the height of the plants. At first he swore they couldn't be growing; he used a ruler to track each millimeter of progress. The lights were on the bulk of the day and night, and they made a buzzing hum that consumed his thoughts. The fans stopped whirring when the lights automatically clicked off. He missed the stars. In the artificial night of the house, which he imagined to be a spacecraft, he'd lie in the dark enjoying the silence as his galaxy ship sped through the heavens. *I can hear the plants growing, I swear.* His thoughts on these nights, unlike in the Big French Creek canyon camp, now focused on the future and not the past, what would exist once he reached his goal. *A big house. Dozens of workers. Respect. Power. Yes, Mr. Vanderlip. Whatever you want, Mr. Vanderlip. Lots of different women.* He smiled as he drifted into sleep. With each passing sodium lamp day, the artificial nights grew longer and longer in increments of minutes as the plants were starved for light, fooling them into thinking frost was coming; buds emerged and they smelled skunk. The scent of his future riches. He often buried his nose in a kola and inhaled; nearly each time he coughed. He was coughing a lot.

The house, despite the roaring fans, was always damp. Clear plastic sheets covered the floors—the plastic was torn, the tape coming off the seams, and water from the grow pots leaked through to the once-white carpet, in places soggy. Condensation covered all walls, in the kitchen, living room, bedrooms, the main hallway, the bathroom; black mold flourished. With this came a disturbing realization: he wouldn't be able to grow when the bud was drying, or he'd lose everything to mold. Even the attic was damp, so he gave up on the idea of turning it into a drying room. He had to factor that into how many crops he'd get out of the house. He did the mathematics on a piece of paper, the exact thousands of dollars he would lose for the month or more that it would take for drying and trimming. The house was now a sea of bright green, an indoor tropical rain forest, which made him dream of Hawaii, of warm trade winds, women, surf.

But first he had to see those bound packets of hundred-dollar bills come out of the buyer's Pelican case. He wanted to hold ten of them, one hundred grand. *You haven't lived until you've gripped a brick of one hundred grand cash, moolah, dough, skins, C-notes; there is no feeling like it. Fuck drugs, fuck sex. Flip a brick of one thousand hundreds against your nose and smell that green. Money, money, money!* The more he imagined this cash brick, the more his paranoia grew. It was exponential. *One fuckup and it's over. No hundred grand. Do not pass go. Go directly to jail.* He carried the MAC-10 everywhere in the house. All sounds set him off. A horn. A car slowing on the street. A laughing woman. *Why is she fucking laughing right in front of the fucking house?!* Each time he ran to the door to peer through the peephole, weapon in hand. When the buds started swelling, he stockpiled weeks' worth of food from Safeway so he wouldn't have to leave the Dobkins Lane house in this most critical and dangerous period. He had four shopping carts that he wheeled to his truck like a rail engine pushing boxcars. He ate a lot of canned corned beef hash and canned beans and peas when the crop was drying and during the trim. He clipped to music blasting from a boom box—he played a Sisters of Mercy CD so many times that it scratched up and stopped working.

Unlike sun-grown weed, whose buds were dark green, the indoor stuff was yellow orange. He thought of something J.J.'s father told him about a Chinese parable about the plant grown inside a greenhouse: *It has not been tested by the wind, and you are like that untested plant when you are young; you grow straight and tall, but you are weak. You have to finish growing in the wind to be hardened, to survive. Otherwise you will die.* That was true, Klaus thought. Mr. Chang surely had been through a lot of storms in his life, but this weed grown inside the house on Dobkins Lane got you just as high as sun-grown shit. *Yeah... it lacks the terpenes and other noble oils and all that other shit, but most stoners don't give a fuck.*

Likowski, of course, would never brook the sacrilege of "artificial marijuana." That old hippie looked so sad back in the day when Klaus made the case for indoor, and now, for some reason, he carried on imaginary conversations with Likowski. *Things change, Likowski. That was then and this is now. You have to compete.* Klaus sealed trimmed bud in turkey roasting bags. The nuggets resembled pieces of butterscotch candy. They were beautiful, but the remaining branches of dried weed hanging from nylon fishing line strung all through the house were eternal; he scissored and scissored and scissored and fucking scissored, but the hundreds of pieces that needed cleaning never seemed to diminish. Would it ever end? He vowed that February that this would be the last time he ever trimmed. Trimming was bullshit. It made him lose weeks of grow time; it was boring. His fingers hurt, and he wanted to scream, he wanted to be on the granite, in the sun, getting laid, alone.

At the cessation of the days and nights of scissoring, after the final dried kola was plucked from the fishing line and all the bud was sealed and stacked in turkey roasting bags, he stared at thirty-two pounds of packaged bud. *Thirty-two pounds! Jesus!* This first rotation took three and a half months after the second leaf set. Klaus blasted Ministry's "Just One Fix" and danced to the hard-driving metal. He telephoned the buyer in San Francisco when the last bud was trimmed.

The next day, a knock at the door startled Klaus from deep sleep; no one ever knocked. He'd smoked a lot of weed before going to bed, not sure if it was even day or night because the sodium lights had not been on for weeks. He grabbed the MAC-10. The knocking resumed— hard pounding. He didn't look through the peephole; he stood to the side, the weapon pointed at the door. "Who is it?"

"Barry, man."

Klaus flung open the door for the same man who bought Kow's weed. The same man, in fact, who first introduced Kow's Death Wish to a few lucky consumers. "Jon!"

Jon Barry was a double for Robert Redford in *All the President's Men*, which Klaus's mom made him go see when they were in town one afternoon. This Redford was in a leather jacket and stood holding a Pelican case. "What's with the gun, man? War, it's just a shot away, Jose."

"What do you mean?"

"The Stones, man. You gotta keep the love, gov. Love's just a kiss away. I like to focus on the love, not the guns."

"Yeah, man. Sorry." Klaus, rubbed at the sleep still in his eyes, placed the weapon on the mattress and threw a sheet over it. "Coffee?"

"No, man. Can't stay long."

"Check it out—pick one, any one," Klaus said.

Barry plucked one of the stacked turkey roasting bags, opened it. He put it to his nose and deeply inhaled. Barry closed his eyes for a long time—weirdly long, Klaus thought. But Barry was like that: he acted odd, said strange things, always rhyming, always a bit off, a few buds short of a full pound. A slow smile suddenly came to the broker's face. "Strawberry Fields," Barry declared as his eyes opened. Then, dreamily: *"For-ev-errrr."*

Klaus took a pipe and lighter from a shelf.

"No need, friend. Got a long drive back."

As Klaus resealed the opened bag, Barry scaled the other bags, wrote in a ledger; he pulled the same Texas Instruments calculator he'd been using since he'd started buying from the hippies.

"One favor," Klaus said. "Don't tell Likowski we're doing business."

"No prob, Rob."

Barry opened the Pelican case for eleven $10k stacks of hundreds and change. He was soon out the door, lugging two tote bags filled with product. Klaus watched through the peephole as Barry drove away in a white van. He turned to the trim table with the money on it and exhaled. Here was his first brick of $100,000. But instead of savoring the moment, he was gripped by sudden fear. He stuffed the money into a large canvas messenger bag, along with the MAC-10 and a plastic mayonnaise jar he'd washed and saved. He left the house for the first time in weeks. He blinked from the sun as he locked the door, his trembling right hand on the MAC in the bag. *Just make it to the truck, just get there and you'll be okay.* He fumbled to get the key in the ignition; his eyes were everywhere.

He drove south below the speed limit, and he relaxed a little only once he started climbing the Cougar. The grade marked the end of regular police patrols, meant he was reentering Not America. With each left and right on the upgrade, he grew calmer. By the time he passed through the hamlet, on his way to the Ark, he sang loudly to the Reggae Cowboys in the CD player: *We are the hardcore...Searchin' for de outlaw!* He toked on a J; his head swung to the beat.

He forced himself to calm down as he ascended the grade to McGee Ridge. Zoë was surprised and pleased to see her son. She made him lunch and they caught up; he told her he came down to clear his head, that he couldn't stay long, he had to get back to work, but that he needed to walk on the beach for a few hours. When he dropped over the crest of the hill for his "beach walk" with the messenger bag slung over his shoulder, he doubled around to the trail into the canyon. The now seldom-used path was grown in with sword fern and thimbleberry canes. The creek grew louder as the path leveled. Before him was a tiny cabin of eight by twelve feet, with a roof that curled up at the gutter lines like a fairy-tale cottage fit for Hansel and Gretel. Zoë and Lauren had built it as a place for their hippie female empowerment shit, the fire pit still surrounded by three rotting couches.

One night way back, maybe in '79 or '80, he remembered sneaking down the trail to spy on the women. It drizzled, but no matter, the gathering went on. Lauren wore a white fortune teller's outfit and a white wig. Alma had on a high-necked ruffled collar, which resembled a giant inverted chanterelle and was in fact modeled after the mushrooms that grew wild in Baker's old-growth forest. Around other necks: faux diamonds, strings of plastic pearls, whelk shells and sand dollars painted psychedelic colors. Rita had earrings made from dried chicken feet painted purple, from the birds she and Johnny Gray had raised. Zoë had on a rhinestone-crusted tiara and a white cape. When Klaus heard sounds on the trail, he darted into a thimbleberry thicket. Three women marched past, covered in mud; they'd walked up to the ridge from the valley by forest trail, crossing flooded creeks, puddles, gushing springs. *We are the mountain hags!* the muddy trio sang as they entered the clearing. He watched for a long while as the women drank and talked about women things, before finally growing bored and heading back to the Ark to smoke weed.

Two decades later, it was quiet except for the creek rushing with spring runoff and a faint squeaking from Hell-man's 1968 Ford half-ton truck, suspended fifty feet in the air between two Douglas firs with steel cables. It swayed gently in a wind coming upcanyon. When the truck stopped running in 1978, Hell-man and Zoë had pulled the engine and transmission to make it lighter, then winched it up there. The vehicle was as if in midflight, nose down at a forty-five-degree angle. It had been years since Klaus had come down this trail to the fairy-tale cottage, where Hell-man made him give hand jobs. Beyond the installation was the pump house, a four-by-four shed. Klaus opened the door. The rusting shovel, used to clear out the intake, was still there. He grabbed it and scrambled downstream.

No one ever went into that nearly impassable whorl: the channel was clogged with SUV-sized boulders, splintered tree trunks driven down by flash floods, and the canyon walls were steep as a V. A quarter mile toward the ocean and a half hour of careful scrambling later was his secret spot, where he used to hide from Hell-man, from having to read books: a flat with old-growth white fir—*his* place. He dropped the messenger bag, slumped to the needled ground, and pulled out the brick of bound bundles. He put it to his nose, smelling the ink of money, closing his eyes just as Jon Barry had done after inhaling the strawberry essence of his bud. *No one can touch me now.*

He fell asleep next to the stack of bills, and when he awakened, he'd lost track of time. He'd not slept that deeply in months; he felt refreshed. He picked a spot beneath the largest white fir, a wolf tree with massive drooping branches and a trunk so rotund that it would take three and a half men holding hands to gauge its circumference. He knew precisely, because for a moment he was again a child: he went around the trunk, picking up with his left hand where his right fingertips had left off; bark scratched his face. Then he dug a hole two feet deep, to mineral soil; the loamy earth was deposited on top of the messenger bag to keep it from mixing with fallen needles. The hundred grand went into the plastic jar with the plastic cap; he kissed the blue cap, twisted it tight, and placed the jar at the bottom of the hole. After backfilling, he scattered needles and forest litter to match the surrounding ground, naturalizing the site. He stood back to study his effort and was satisfied.

Step three: Go big. Klaus saw the future and Rick, with his small-time house grows, did not. Rick argued that the medical marijuana operations were going to get busted: *Just you wait. The feds are gonna go after the 215s.*

Klaus believed otherwise—that the grow situation was ripe for exploitation, and he wanted to be ready to blow up. *No way, bro. I'll set up four ninety-nines, get my 215s in different names. They won't piece it together. I'll blow it up. It's gonna go full legal. I want to corner the market before that happens.*

His first priority was to buy the very best land, with unlimited water and southern exposure. He was talking to old man Jackson about buying his ranch. He'd need a lot of those $100k bricks. Land was increasing in value each year. Smart money knew the Green Rush was coming, and anyone who saw the future had to move fast. By the last day of November 1998, Klaus had buried a third jar beneath the white fir and another rotation was being planted.

6

SYMPATHY FOR THE DEVIL

Eddie was dreaming of Liz when the earthquake struck. She was on top, her long brown hair falling in his face as the bed rocked. The pleasant memory of sex with Liz gave way to the slow realization of the temblor. His eyes fluttered open. The joints of the house groaned, then stilled. He grew up with quakes; he knew the Richter scale by intuition and didn't have to listen to the radio news to learn their intensity. *Six-one. No, more like a five-nine.*

He thought of Liz, who went away to college and never returned, as he tried to fall back asleep, but he could only conjure Marge, a married woman who was his sole intimate contact in decades. Marge was a regular at the Candlelight, one of a row of seedy taverns with broken, blinking neon signs on the plaza, whom he saw on his monthly trips to town. Marge had three missing front teeth and wasn't particularly attractive to him (nor was his hulking body to her). But after enough Jack Daniel's and Smirnoff Limes, they saw enough beauty in each other to have sex in his truck's cab. But even Marge was lost to him— she died of an opioid overdose two years earlier.

He gave up on sleep. Dawn's light was breaking. Numerous eyes looked down at his half-comatose form. A bedroom wall was covered in pictures of three generations of the Edwards family—twenty-four photographs in frames of various vintage, some oval with ornate scrollwork and gold leaf, others from the more recent past housed in cheap black plastic. The family's economic fortunes were told by those frames. In the center was Rosina and Elwin, his parents. Flanking them was his dead sister, on the left, and him at eighteen, thin and handsome, on the right. Above, his paternal grandparents. At the top, near the ceiling, his great-grandfather Elwin Edwards. Elwin's was the largest photograph of all, his face some eighteen inches tall, in an oval frame with curved glass bubbling two inches away from the image; the beveling acted like a magnifying lens, distorting Elwin's already raging eyes to a frightful fury. Eddie was staring at him when the aftershock struck. *Clap! KABOOOMmmmmm!* The bed shot three feet into the room as if kicked by a giant's shoe, and he was thrown to the floor. Eddie staggered to his feet, gripped with sudden horror. He ran naked through the living room, out the side door, to the back: the entire west section of the wall had tumbled in an avalanche of boulders that struck the house, and Eddie cried out in anguish.

He crumpled to the ground, sobbing. Ever since he finished the encircling wall, it had kept them out. The wall pissed them off. Each night after dusk they screamed and wailed in the riparian forest. But they *stayed* there. He looked into the red alders and Pacific willows and was gripped by panic. They were out there right now, waiting for night.

He shot into the house, threw on clothes, and immediately returned, setting out to rebuild the forty feet of fallen wall. He worked furiously, pushing boulders back in place. He didn't stop for lunch; he stuffed his face with cold leftover meat loaf from the fridge, a bag of potato chips. At four the Black Fog rolled in, and dark came early. He was exhausted. He stared at his day's labor: the wall had regained just an uneven three to four feet of its former twelve-foot height. He staggered into the house, lay on the floor next to the stove, passing out from exhaustion rather than falling asleep. At midnight he awoke to the thunder of feet dancing upstairs.

The next day was sunny. A couple from the Bay Area drove by the wall of rocks still standing in front of the house, on their way to the beach campground after visiting the store in the hamlet for supplies. The sun shot straight up the river canyon and blasted the windshield. The woman at the wheel of the Subaru had trouble seeing. She wasn't watching the rearview mirror. When she glanced, a fluorescent orange pickup truck was right on their bumper. She shrieked. The woman was going thirty miles an hour, fast for that road. The truck stayed right on her, in a winding section where the road was narrow. She slowed. The orange truck dropped back, sped up to the bumper, dropped back, sped up. There was nowhere to turn off. On the straightaway she floored it into the blinding sun, the truck right on them. Her boyfriend tried to get the plate number, but the truck was too close.

A bearded man was at the wheel, screaming. The truck fell back and was lost from sight because of a hill. Shaken, the woman parked at the campsite. Cell phones didn't work at the beach. Calling the sheriff would have meant driving back to the pay phone outside the store in the hamlet, which meant possibly encountering the orange truck. They tried to forget the incident and went to bed early in a tent next to an expanse of Pacific willows.

At midnight, a howl came from the willows. Then a shrill, nearly unintelligible voice bellowed. It was angry yet plaintive. It demanded they get away. "Leave!" it cried. "Leave now!"

Inside the tent, they were frozen in terror.

A rifle shot cracked. Then another.

"Go away!"

The couple bolted from the tent and ran through the campground into distant brush. It was fifty-two degrees. They dug a shallow depression in the sand to block the wind and huddled in quiet embrace, shivering, hoping the crazy guy didn't follow. At dawn, the man told his girlfriend to remain. He crawled to the edge, cautiously peered through a break in the willows. A sheriff's patrol car was parked next to a ranger's SUV. The couple, purple from the cold, ran stiff-legged to the cops. Officers told them another camper was stalked by the same orange pickup, but that person had gotten the license plate number. A suspect was now in custody.

The earthquake had thrown a few dishes off my counters, but otherwise my place remained intact. The large temblors that shook the coastline always stayed with me for days after, though, rewiring my nerves. It was September and there was a coastal inversion; the air was still, the sky clear. I was in the wood-fired hot tub that night after Eddie's arrest, eyes on the Milky Way as I imagined Zoë walking Wilhelmstrasse past the site of the Reich Chancellery; going through the Brandenburg Gate; following the ghost of the Berlin Wall, now marked by a meandering foot-wide line of cobbles in the pavement; ending up in front of her old squat, long since torn down; finding the back streets in the eastern sector that had remnants of her 1968

Berlin, with cool coffeehouses and narrow alley walls covered with drawings, graffiti, and art installations. She dreams what could have been.

The landline rang. I debated whether to leave the hot tub, but it was near midnight. It took me a good while to make it back into the cabin. The phone went silent before I got to it. It rang again. Likowski. He asked if I'd go to town with him the next day during visiting hours at the jail. He must have been desperate. He had no one else to turn to. Lara didn't know Eddie very well, and I suspected that Likowski didn't want to subject her to more trauma—there was enough of that going on with Tammie and the upcoming trial. It was odd to hear it, but Likowski sounded *almost* scared. I agreed.

The next morning, I was out early at my gate when Likowski's Toyota pickup came around the bend, and I jumped in. He began speaking immediately. Something had changed. Eddie's breakdown was too much in a year that had delivered repeated blows to Likowski's sense of order. He blamed Eddie's going off the deep end on Zoë's disappearance—and by extension Klaus, who (regardless of his direct involvement or not) was responsible for her declining mental state. I'm sure Zoë didn't see it that way, if she was still alive. I suspected that she resented Likowski and Lara for their role in her son's takedown. If they had not been part of causing the arrest of Klaus, she could still pretend things were fine. Zoë certainly resented me—she often reminded me that I was not really part of the community because I spent those months away at Stanford each year, as if I were cheating on the ridge. Maybe Zoë resented everyone.

The conceit of a long-form journalist is to be an amateur shrink, and Dr. Specter's analysis is that Zoë felt judged her entire life. Her family was on the wrong side of history. While other generals were at Nuremberg, seeing that Nazis were properly swinging from ropes, her father was helping them escape into comfortable American lives. She ran to Berlin, straight into the *gehärteter Stahl* jaws of the dark past, and when that didn't erase the stain of her father's sins, she fled to this lost shore. Bearing the weight of societal judgment appears to be the curse of her family. The landscape of the Burn Coast is expansive but the community very small, a thousand humans along those dozens of miles of silent forest stretching north and south. It wasn't a sheltering wilderness. Despite the growing consensus among my neighbors that she committed suicide, I believed otherwise, that she couldn't handle the shame of her son's sexual predation. I was growing more and more certain she had returned to spend her final years anonymously in a place where she'd be free of all moral scrutiny: Berlin, living in a flat in the old eastern sector. Perhaps, even, she *wanted* us to think she'd killed herself; her inviting me over was part of the plan. Believing this helped me sleep better at night.

I drank black coffee from a thermos as I listened to Likowski and my thoughts in parallel. The blue Pacific flashed out the driver's-side window as the truck jerked and tossed to sea level on that rough gravel road. He was haggard, unslept. For the first time he looked like a man in his seventies—a very old seventies.

We arrived early for visiting hours. The cop behind the counter took our driver's licenses and scribbled information in a logbook. I was well aware of what we appeared to be: rough-living growers. We sat in an extended silence on hard white plastic chairs in the waiting room until a door swung open, jarring us. We entered a blinding eight-by-eight white concrete block room. A light fixture buzzed overhead. In the center of the opposite wall was a one-foot-square window. The bearded face on the other side of the glass was alien in the orange light of the room. For a moment we thought they'd made a mistake, that it was the wrong inmate, not Eddie. But no one had more intense eyes than Eddie. He was in a straitjacket. Drool poured from the right side of Eddie's mouth.

"What the fuck?" Likowski uttered.

"We have to leave! We can't stay!" Eddie said immediately upon seeing us, slurring into a round metal speaker in the center of the wire-laced glass. Likowski said we couldn't get him out now, not yet, and Eddie sputtered, "I don't mean here!" He gestured with his entire head beyond the walls. "Out *there*, Kow."

"Why were you chasing those tourists?" I asked gently.

"They d-don't belong! None of us belong! We have to leave. Everyone has to go away!"

"Eddie!" Likowski shook his head tiredly.

"They want us all gone!"

"Maybe they don't," I said quietly. "Have you thought that maybe they are protecting you? Us? What have they actually done to you?"

A twisted smile lit his face, and he looked at me with pity, eyes wide at the level of my ignorance regarding the native curse. He turned from me to Likowski: "They got Zoë! You know it, and I know it . . ."

Eddie's eyes rolled back in his head and he suddenly fell off the stool. There was a thud followed by moaning. A deputy emerged, and a moment later Eddie was gone. The jail captain, carrying a report on Eddie's arrest, came out from behind a glass booth. Likowski was full of rage. "Why's he in a straitjacket?! Why is he—"

The captain, a tall but generic white man with eyes as frozen as a statue of a Civil War general, silenced Likowski with a raised hand: "Your friend was 5150. He is not only a danger to others but himself as well." The commander leafed through the report. "He stepped from his vehicle with his hands raised and asked the responding officers to shoot him. Told them that he wanted to die. He said, 'I'm afraid I'm going to hurt someone.'"

We remained in town that afternoon to talk with a lawyer about representing Eddie. The attorney felt the best place for Eddie was jail, that he'd go over the deep end again if he got out right away. We reluctantly had to agree. Eddie had lost all his immediate family, was estranged from his relatives, had no one close other than Likowski. The lawyer said Likowski could petition to become Eddie's guardian, that it would be a difficult process, but then the lawyer could ask the court for leniency. Without the guardianship, Eddie, with his priors and the assault with intent to kill charge, was guaranteed to be sentenced to Vacaville; even with the guardianship, the lawyer cautioned, he might end up there. Silently, I wondered if he'd occupy Charles Manson's old cell.

"When he gets out, I'm going to put him in the pottery studio," Likowski said. He paid the attorney a retainer with a small stack of hundred-dollar bills. We closed the day out with an evening drink at the Candlelight. Talk was all about Eddie and nothing else. It wasn't like old times—Likowski was mission focused. I mostly listened. Likowski said he'd do whatever it took to help Eddie.

On the drive home over the Cougar, we shared a flask of Hennessy. Likowski, getting pretty drunk, took the road slow. After we stopped to piss on the beach road, facing the towering white breakers smashing against sea stacks, I took the wheel. It was close to midnight when we passed Eddie's rock wall that failed to protect him from native spirits. Likowski stared at what could be seen of Eddie's dark house. His face remained planted in the passenger-side window, looking at the night as we drove across the bridge.

I made a left on a rough dirt road heading up Elk Creek Canyon, about a mile before where I usually turned to take the main gravel road that went to the ridgetop. I'd driven this back way to Likowski's only once before and it was challenging enough sober, in daylight. Any equal portion of the Baja 1000 in Mexico has nothing on that jeep track. Elk Creek was a trickle because of J.D.'s big industrial grow; the channel was filled with boulders. I powered down into low four-wheel creeper gear in the red alder forest. There was the grind of the transmission as we started the long crawl up the switchbacks, at a speed not much faster than walking. Then the forest of big-leaf maple, a West Coast species of tree whose muscular torsos were like sculptures, contorted arms and legs so heavy that they grew downward to rest on the earth; in the flash of the headlights, elbows with vertical forearms, fists raised in triumph or resistance, and bended knees sprouted from the duff and loam. The tight switchbacks ceased. Now the Doug fir forest. We rounded a bend. The lights raked Likowski's home, sited on a rare flat in that canyon. I'd seen it hundreds of times, yet I marveled as if it were the first.

Something came back from my childhood. My mother had bought what was then a very high-tech "painting": a two-by-three-foot flat box with a glass front; behind was a plastic film with a translucent image on a roller, driven by a motor that plugged into a wall socket. On the plastic sheet was an imposed 360-degree panorama that included a country home in the forest, impossibly cute and cozy, a serene retreat that surely could not exist anywhere on Earth. The dwelling scrolled past a backlight, followed by woods and deer and a pond. It was Thomas Kinkade before there was Thomas Kinkade; and now I realized that Likowski's homestead was Kinkade in cannabisland,

and if that con man of an artist would have lived longer, he would have forked over folding money for the right to paint it. At least in my opinion.

"Wanna come in?" Likowski asked.

The sound of the surf was louder than at my place—the canyon walls somehow channeled it, concentrating the roar, not like that of the sea, but more like a Midwest supercell about to turn the sky sickly green and hit you with three funnel clouds, triple fucking tornadoes. He pushed in the front door, made from three-inch-thick fir planks cut and milled from this land. No key was needed because there was no lock; none of my hippie neighbors on the ridge had locks. (It was a stark contrast to Klaus's on-the-grid six-bedroom Tuscany-style chateau on the tableland overlooking the hamlet. He had a reinforced steel door with three locks and two security cameras trained on it.) Likowski flicked a wall switch, glanced at the voltmeter in the kitchen. "Better turn on the hydro."

While Likowski was out back opening a valve on a pipe that carried Elk Creek water to a Pelton turbine, I studied the living room, furnished with a brown leather La-Z-Boy recliner and matching sofa. It was immaculate. A warm deep tangerine hue emanated from the paneling. The one-by-four tongue-and-groove Doug fir had darkened to that shade with age and composed all surfaces: ceiling, walls, floor. Bookcases, loaded with volumes, lined two of the walls and were big-leaf maple—the only wood that had not come from this land. I knew Likowski had traded some of his Death Wish bud for the maple, milled up in town.

It was the cleanest home of any of us off-gridders. Somehow, Likowski was even able to keep it free of the smell of must, which afflicted every dwelling on the damp coast, including mine. The lights suddenly brightened with the distant hum of the turbine. When Likowski rematerialized, he announced he'd fired up the stove in the sweat lodge. In his hand was a baggie of Death Wish. He poured whiskey, lit six oil lamps, turned off the twelve-volt electric lights, and we smoked his weed and listened to vinyl records on a Pioneer stereo system—Traffic, Emerson, Lake & Palmer, the Stones, all thundering out of three-foot-tall speakers. It became clear as we talked that something had changed for Likowski after seeing Eddie. He seemed to be letting go of his anger, not just with me but with everything. It wasn't resignation—Likowski's steely determination was still contained in the intensity of his gaze. But something was different.

I lay back on the floor, head spinning from the whiskey and Death Wish. With "Sympathy for the Devil," it all came back.

The helicopter went north up the coast, racing over verdant mountains, slashing canyons, and golden meadows. The men in the bay behind me were dressed for battle like a special ops team: black assault rifles, camouflage pants and shirts, bulletproof vests bulging beneath, floppy camo bush hats. All the men except for the rifleman leaning out the open door wore dark aviator sunglasses. The rifleman, strapped in with a harness, studied the land below with binoculars. I couldn't help but think of them as soldiers, even though they weren't: one was a federal DEA agent, two were local sheriffs, and the other two were city cops on loan, one from Pomona, the other from Riverside. The pilot wouldn't reveal what agency he was associated with. When the chopper darted into a canyon and flew low over the canopy, I flashed on the previous summer when I was with the Salvadoran military, flying over guerrilla-held territory near the Honduran border. The coastal rain forest of California was as thick and ominous from the air as any Central American jungle.

The helicopter swung around a headland.

"Holy shit!" the cop in the door exclaimed. "Two suspects—one's armed!" The cop dropped the glasses.

By the time the pilot pivoted the aircraft in position and the gunner raised his scoped assault rifle, the two men had vanished into a patch of Pacific willows. A riderless white horse galloped south down the beach.

"That's Cowboy's horse! I'll bet they're near their grow!" the pilot, a heavyset cop with one and a half chins, said. "Let's find Cowboy's garden!"

We flew over the canyon, but not too low, in case the suspects took shots at us. They treated it like war. The pilot and the cop in the door scoured the canyon for Cowboy's weed patch.

"Is that it?" the pilot asked loudly. He swung the aircraft so the cop in the door could train the binoculars on a spot below the canyon's rim. The pilot then glanced to his right and squinted, studying my press pass—he'd forgotten my name. "We'll get one for you, Will."

I didn't want one. They were putting on a show for my story. One cop had a boom box blasting the hits of the Rolling Stones. Really? I mean, really? Was this part of the theater? Nevertheless I enjoyed "Sympathy for the Devil," faint as it was over the roar of the engine and blades. The kick-ass dope I smoked back home had probably been harvested by hippies somewhere below me. The weed I'd smoke later in the year was growing down there right now. I peered along with the cops, but if I sighted a patch, I sure as hell wasn't going to say anything. It was likely that at least one or two of the cops behind me also smoked weed. Just as every cop is a criminal...

They were officers simply doing their jobs, just as I was a reporter doing mine. My assigned role was impartial observer—just the facts, ma'am, the five Ws. The story played straight yet with enough flair to make the copy readable, good enough to land on the prime real estate, A1, left column. Their role was "enforcing the law." I'd interviewed Van de Kamp numerous times when Van de Kamp was Los Angeles County district attorney. He was really a liberal Democrat, but now as top cop in the state, he had to go along with the politics of his position and of the moment—Deukmejian was in the governor's chair, and Reagan had the White House. Everyone was just doing their jobs. It was 1984.

The pilot gave up on finding Cowboy's patch. He swung the chopper north over a few more canyons. "I think we've got one!" the pilot yelled.

The landscape spun in front of me, and I looked straight down at a weathered house with only two square corners; the other end came to a point like the bow of a sailing vessel. A mast protruded from the point, from which flew a flag: EARTH FIRST! There was a clenched green fist. I smiled. Last summer I'd interviewed Dave Foreman, one of Earth First!'s cofounders. Foreman and I drank a case of beer between us, sitting in the back of Foreman's truck parked out in the desert on a hill overlooking Lake Powell's Wahweap Bay. We started drinking in the early evening, and we didn't finish the case until dawn's light colored the horizon. I'd been on a boat that afternoon with Interior Secretary James Watt, who was there to celebrate the twentieth anniversary of the reservoir. An Earth First! houseboat, adorned with life-sized mannequins dressed as the Beach Boys, circled Watt's boat. Speakers blasted the group's music—Watt had banned them from performing at the July 4 celebration on the Capitol Mall because their music was not "wholesome." I was a good journalist, I sure was. I worked both sides. I'd hang with the smug and smiling robot in a white cowboy hat called Watt for an hour. But I preferred drinking and smoking all night long with the underdogs. And all those sinners saints…

"There!" the pilot said. In the thick chaparral of the canyon wall there was a tiny spray of unnaturally off-color green amid the olive-hued brush. "We're going in!"

The chopper shot across the canyon, aiming for a flat spot in a meadow atop the headland on the south side of the canyon. It was a rough landing because of the wind. Cops poured out, commando style, weapons at the ready and sheathed machetes flapping at their sides, rushing downhill into the fog of brush. The pilot cut the engine. There was the sound of slashing coming from the chaparral as the cops used their machetes to clear a route to the site. Wind rushed past the silenced machine, which shuddered in the gusts. The pilot jumped out. I followed. The cop held his assault rifle up to guard the airship. I was supposed to hang with the helicopter in a hot zone, according to the ride-along agreement with CAMP officials, but these guys didn't care. I crashed into the brush. Sap filled the air, green and sweet. The slope was so steep that I mostly slid and fell. In an opening through a patch of buckthorn, I paused, saw the ship house across the canyon, almost at eye level. When I caught up with the officers, they stood in a circle around six mature plants.

"Purple Kush," announced one cop.

"You're looking at thirty thousand dollars," another cop said.

I scribbled those quotes in the notebook, nodding seriously. But I knew better. I'd spent time with growers. These plants at best had a half pound of bud on each. The market price of bud was well-known, as if posted on a commodity exchange: $1,500 per pound if it was good sinsemilla, or about $4,500 for those six plants. They appeared well cared for. I wondered about the grower losing that income as the cops hacked at the base of the plants, which were then stacked in piles and hoisted by two cops onto their shoulders. I was last in line on the climb up the slope. Weed slapped me in the face. Resin, sticky and total skunk, clung to my nose and cheeks. Near the top, a

*chunk of bud the size of an enchilada fell off. It landed in front of me. I stuffed
the bud into the right pocket of my jeans.*

*We flew north and swept low over a lagoon. A naked man and woman
were swimming, pink and in sharp contrast to the dark water. "Nice tits!"
the cop in the door, his glasses trained on the woman with long brown hair,
shouted. The couple gave the cops the finger. The cop in the door and the
pilot flipped birds back. The cops laughed. I wasn't supposed to hear or see
what just happened. The cops knew that it was de facto off the record by
the unspoken rules of the game. They knew the Times editors would never
publish those parts. It's how journalism worked. Or maybe I just fucked up
by not trying to put it in, a self-censorship based on numerous past lost
battles with the desk. I didn't have much time to write that piece, not sure I
did it justice, but even so it ended up as a column one. A week later I was back
in the bang-bang in El Salvador.*

Now Cowboy rolled another joint of Death Wish, and he studied two
hundred or so vinyl albums, arranged alphabetically on the lower
shelves of the big-leaf maple bookcase. I'd eventually told him about
my first visit to the ridge, via DEA helicopter, and he'd shook his
head ruefully and laughed, joking that I was lucky whoever that was
hadn't shot us down. My admission had been a turning point in our
friendship. Somehow it had increased his respect for me, and we'd
grown closer after that. Sadness crept up on me, and I sunk deeper
into the well-cushioned La-Z-Boy.

"Hey." Likowski wasn't looking at me, but he held up a record,
Moby Grape's self-titled first release. "How's this?"

"Sure," I said.

"Heard it the day it dropped." Likowski nodded appreciatively,
savoring the memory. "The DJ played the entire album without
vetting it. You could hear the crinkling of the shrink wrap coming off
on the radio."

"Where the hell did you live that you had that kind of station?"

"Cleveland—" he answered before he could stop himself, his eyes
shooting up to glance at me and then away, my stunned expression
visible.

"So you took the dead baby's name," I said.

Likowski got busy studying album titles without really looking at them. Led Zeppelin's *Physical Graffiti* was now in his right hand.

"What part?" I asked.

He pretended not to hear my question—he clearly realized he'd slipped. His eyes remained on the spines of his massive vinyl collection.

"What part, man?"

"Doesn't matter," he said.

"Yeah, it does. How long have we known each other?"

"Tell me something: Was where you came from ever a contingency for being allowed to live here?"

"No."

"No. And did it ever make a difference to me? Or anyone else here?"

"No."

"Okay."

He placed *Physical Graffiti* on the turntable, lowered the needle, and cranked the volume to end my questioning. By the time "Trampled Under Foot" rocked from those eighty-pound pressed-wood speakers, we wielded air guitars and hammered on air drums, dancing around the living room, singing along:

> *I can't stop talkin' about love...*
> *Bldddyouboop, bldddyouboooooop!*
> *Yahh, yahhhhh!*

We fell, panting, on the floor.

"Why'd you let it slip now?" I asked him as I caught my breath. "About Cleveland."

He laughed until he was hoarse.

"What?"

"You just won't let up, will you?"

I shrugged.

"Wanna fire the BAR?"

"You have a BAR?"

"My dad brought it back from the war. I got some tracer ammo a few years ago."

Likowski went to a closet with a trapdoor to the attic and used a stepladder to fetch the Browning automatic rifle—an illegal weapon as far as civilians were concerned. We went out into the small meadow in front of the house, Likowski jostling the ammo belt into position and clicking the gun to full automatic. Then he unloaded it into the sky, with Zeppelin still echoing in my head and the Death Wish making it all incredibly beautiful and overwhelming, the tracer lines like reverse-flying meteors set against the Milky Way.

When he was done, he handed me the weapon. "I'm going to need your help tomorrow."

"All right," I said, knowing not to press too much.

Then Likowski put another belt into the BAR, and I took my turn strafing the heavens. I owned guns—you'd be an idiot to live here and not have one—but almost never fired them. The last time I did, it was for shotgun pruning: a drooping Doug fir branch dozens of feet up an old-growth tree was blocking my view of the ocean from the hot tub. I bought four boxes of shells and blasted the base of the branch with my 20-gauge shotgun until it snapped and fell. As cool as that was, firing the BAR was immensely more satisfying.

I woke up on the sofa. A hard rain blasted the roof. It was noon.

"Let's go, couch potato!" Likowski emerged from his bedroom and immediately suggested we take a hike.

"A hike?"

"First, read this, writer man. I've got a story for you."

Likowski tossed a folder that landed on my chest. I rubbed my eyes while he went off to hand-grind coffee. The folder was marked in big block letters written with a black Sharpie: "CALIFORNIA DEPARTMENT OF FISH AND WILDLIFE." Inside were letters to and from the agency about Elk Creek drying up and dead coho smolts. One of Likowski's letters to the agency said:

> I have owned my land since 1973, and until Two Galaxies Enterprises LLC purchased its parcel adjoining my property and upstream on Elk Creek,

it flowed at a rate of eight gallons a minute in September and October, the lowest flow months, in 1973, the driest year on record. In the wettest year, 2009, the rate was eighteen gallons a minute. In 2016, the creek ceased flowing in August. This past summer and the one before, it went dry in July. Attached please find my annual flow logs.

"Two Galaxies?" I asked when I staggered into the kitchen.

"J.D.'s operation," he said.

I continued reading the files inside the folder at the long slabwood table. Likowski set a coffee in front of me.

"I'm going after that son of a bitch," he said. "Fish and Wildlife has called me to Sacramento to give a deposition about my flow logs. I'll need help with that."

"Looks like you are doing a pretty good job on your own."

He stiffened. "You said you'd help me."

"I did. I'm just not sure what I can do."

I began to hand the folder back.

"Just *keep* the information, Will," he said with uncharacteristic tiredness. "I'm the only one who has it right now—well, and Lara knows some of it. But I can't stick it just with her."

His voice wasn't just worn; it was pleading.

He didn't say anything as I tried to catch his gaze—I had just remembered something. "Lara mentioned that woman who came by, snooping around. She said she was scary."

Likowski shrugged. "When did you hear about that?"

"At Craig and Maggie's. The Fourth. You still weren't in a talking mood."

Likowski nodded. "She was strange."

"You think they sent her to spook you?"

Likowski shook his head slowly. "I'm not sure why she showed up, man."

He slammed the final swallow from his cup of coffee. "You want to know everything I know? Later. For now, come along."

Likowski led the way as we ascended the trail, the rain now misting. I was in good shape, but it was hard to keep pace after the night we'd had. I'd nearly forgotten about the incorruptible vigor that ran through my neighbor's seventy-two year-old body. Still, despite my hangover, I was glad to be back on good terms with him. I had missed him, missed hanging out, which could go on for days, as this was beginning to.

Once topside and on the ridge road, we passed Zoë's gate, went up the steadily worsening track, and hiked to the highest point on McGee Ridge, where I'd never been. It was early fall and yet it felt like deep winter. Our pants were mud-caked to our knees by the time we arrived at the ruins of Jenny's meth lab, where the dirt road dead-ended. We turned to face the sea from this lofty perspective: both the sky and ocean were the bluish-black hue of a three-day-old shiner on a cage fighter. Robinson Jeffers wrote that the Pacific is an eyeball on the earth—you can see the curvature on the horizon. But on certain days that eye can be the socket of a cadaver. The breakers were a half mile out, fifty-foot-tall mountains of water smashing against the continent. The rain had ceased. White streamers of fog suddenly appeared, born before our eyes; plumes that boiled up the headland by the score. By the time they reached us they merged and merged again, until they united into small clouds that blew over our heads, becoming part of the bruised heavens. My cabin, almost two thousand vertical feet below in the cloud factory, was an anonymous speck.

Jenny's meth-cooking barn was en route to the trail that would lead to an overlook of J.D.'s mansion and his greenhouses. The barn was close to collapse—it leaned ten degrees to the lee of the prevailing winds. Years earlier cops had splintered in the door during the bust; Pineapple Expresses had blown in all the windows. Hundreds of swallow nests crusted the upper walls and rafters. Rusting canisters marked with skulls and crossbones littered the floor amid broken lab glassware. Likowski and I peered through one of the shattered panes.

Jenny and her two henchmen with identical Travis Bickle–style Mohawk haircuts were the scourge of the ridge. They drove the road too fast and there were near-miss head-on collisions. They once stopped Eddie and demanded to know who he was and where he was going; Eddie flashed his Uzi and they backed off. But the most talked-about incident occurred in 1998 with Manny, a budding botanist and tree nerd in the doctoral program at the university in town. His thesis was on how the lack of fire in the previous century had changed the ecosystem. Manny discovered survey records from the 1880s that showed all of McGee Ridge barren, save for one lone tree that the pioneer mapmakers had recorded in their drawings. Manny had taken core bores in Likowski's forest, and he wanted to test the trees on top of the ridge to determine their age, and Thomas's land was perfect for the study. Likowski connected Manny with Thomas. That afternoon in 1998, Manny drove up the McGee Ridge road and, fearing getting his Buick LeSabre stuck in the puddled trail, parked a mile from Thomas's, extracted the core borer and other tools, and hiked the remaining distance.

Now here's where the locals will all tell it to you the same: When Manny came around a bend, three people materialized from a patch of young fir—Jenny and her Mohawked sidekicks. *You're trespassing!* Jenny snarled. She presented a terrifying sight: face scabbed, hair shooting wildly from beneath a black Grateful Dead cap with the grinning skull bedecked with red roses logo. She held something Manny couldn't quite see in her right hand. He stammered, forgot Thomas's name amid the rush of adrenaline. Thomas and his visitors had a legal right to use the easement. *I'm going to see—going to see—* as the Mohawks threw him to the ground and pinned him on his back, each sitting on an arm. Jenny climbed atop Manny and took hold of his pants, ripped open the button and zipper, pulled his underwear down. Then she took something to his crotch, and suddenly Manny was writhing. Thomas lived another quarter mile up the road, and with the wind fiercely blowing through the trees, Manny's piercing screams went unheard into the wilderness in the opposite direction.

After Manny's incident with the cattle prod, I kept my loaded .45-caliber semiautomatic Colt on the passenger seat when coming in and out, my hand on it whenever I saw Jenny and the Mohawks on the ridge road.

"At least they didn't murder anyone," Likowski said.

I nodded, scuffling my right foot in the debris near the door, kicking aside glassware. A flask clattered across the floor. We all were happy when Jenny was sent away to the Central California Women's Facility.

We hiked down another jeep trail that followed the spine of a ridgeline. We turned off through woods and poison oak thickets and emerged in a clearing on an open and windy point, looking down on a mansion that could have been designed by Gehry—perhaps it was—a whorl of sweeping metal that gleamed white even on the dreary day; the metal points of the three-layered structure evoked a ship's sails, a perversion of Zoë's much more organically designed Ark. A massive photovoltaic solar array was south of the manse. Three greenhouse structures were in clearings on the downslope of the canyon to the east. Likowski pulled binoculars from his pack, and we took turns studying the operation; then he took pictures with a long-lens SLR Canon.

Just then there was the sound of a helicopter in the north. It neared. The white-and-blue-striped Sikorsky S-76, which at certain times of the year came once each week, roared right below us, so near I could see the pilot's eyes beneath a blue-and-white ball cap without the binoculars. I turned the glasses on the machine as it landed in a clearing to the immediate north of the estate; Likowski put the camera on video. Two people scurried to greet a man who stepped out while the blades were still turning. J.D. crouch-walked, wind blowing his blond hair, cut razor ragged by a talented hairstylist. His baby-smooth face was quite narrow, his jaw sharp. He was perhaps forty, forty-five. He wore a collared white shirt and black leather jacket. The trio vanished into the mansion.

"Why'd you film him?" I asked.

"Evidence. Whatever his full name is, he just flew over those greenhouses. He can't say he doesn't know. Look at them," Likowski said, pointing to the three massive greenhouses. "They bulldozed cuts into the mountain. There's sediment load. That alone is a huge violation. That and taking so much water from the creek. This is our huge lucky break."

We retreated and hiked cross-country through a forest. It took a lot of bushwhacking to come out on the dirt road that ran up the ridge.

We went to Zoë's turnoff. At the crest of the hill we looked down at the Ark against the backdrop of the whitecapped Pacific. The house seemed even more askew, listing a good foot lower on the eastern side. The roofline bowed in the middle, like the back of an old horse. After a full minute of study, we went to the ocean side of the dwelling. The red couch I'd brought from Stanford had long since rotted and rusted into oblivion. Four other couches I trucked north in the aughts were skeletons of orange rusted springs and gray frame wood. Wind whistled against the Ark's eaves. We zeroed in on a new addition: a shiny dead bolt on the back porch door. We peered in the window. Everything looked precisely as we'd left it that day I rode out with Eddie, save for one thing: Zoë's tuba was on the couch.

In unison we yelled, "Zoë!"

I ran around to the front. There was an identical dead bolt on that door. We looked all around the exterior. The Volvo remained unstarted, the cable still unhooked from the battery. We again peered in the back window at the dull brass instrument, speculating where it had been and how it got there, but none of our theories made sense.

"It had to be Klaus," I said hesitantly. "Right?"

Likowski invited me back for dinner. "Bring your recorder," he said before he headed down his trail. I wondered what that meant. We hadn't talked about my selling, our estrangement. Our two days together had been like old times, except that, at a certain point, I realized Likowski didn't want my company. He *needed* it.

I went home and napped for several hours, then packed the recorder and hiked down Likowski's road at dusk. He was cooking when I entered. Led Zeppelin blasted as he prepared a hindquarter from a deer he'd shot. We smoked weed. While the roast cooked, we danced to the Stones and Hendrix; between records he talked about his love for Lara. In Lara he saw salvation: Lara was rebirth; Lara was breaking with his past. For the first time, astonishingly, he hinted that maybe he should leave the ridge, use his place as a getaway. Where would they live? He had no idea, but somewhere else part of the year. Italy? Maybe.

I didn't believe him. It wasn't that I thought he was blowing smoke—I wondered if he was lying to himself about leaving the ridge. But his face had softened considerably from the morning we drove to see Eddie in jail and even more from when I'd left him early that afternoon. And there was possibility in his voice. He'd spent an hour on the phone with Lara before I arrived.

After feasting on the venison roast, we smoked more Death Wish and ended up in the sweat lodge. We burned sage in honor of Zoë and speculated more about the tuba's sudden appearance in the Ark. We wanted to believe Klaus found it, but where? I didn't see it that night I nosed around for clues. I looked in every cupboard, box, closet—all over. I didn't tell Likowski that I'd ask Klaus about it the next time I interviewed him. I was still keeping secrets even as Likowski was opening up.

He motioned for me to come to the top bench. He showed me a Signal message on his phone from Jon Barry, a man I'd heard about for years. It took a minute for my eyes to adjust to the brightness of the screen that dripped condensation.

> The dep price is $1,600. The fall price, it's going to be under $1,200, my friend. Listen to the Floyd, man. Money. It's a hit. Don't give me that do-good bullshit. If you were depping I'd buy all you could grow. You have to change and get with the times.

I handed the phone back. "Scroll down." He wanted me to see his reply.

> We had a good run, Jon. 49 years. But all things must end. I leave you with three words: You. Are. Fired.

Likowski knew he didn't have to explain what I'd already heard dozens of times. His customer base had aged out. They didn't want to roll joints or use pipes; it was all about vaping. Artisanal weed like his was passé; ergo, he couldn't grow weed the way he wanted to anymore and make any money. To earn the same income that he once did, he'd have to grow a lot more, which meant depping, which meant a lot more work. Each afternoon you had to pull black tarps over greenhouses a little earlier to fool the plants into thinking it was fall. After the midsummer harvest, another crop could then be grown in the second half of the season. Instantly, along with doubling the crop, you doubled all the crop-planting chores: clipping shade leaves, hiring trimmers, etc. Weed had been a way to make a living and exist comfortably on Likowski's terms, to shun the kind of stress found in the world outside. Expansion meant reading less, listening to fewer records, missing out on rides down to the shore on AOC, and, most important, less time spent with Lara.

We sat in extended silence.

"Get your recorder," Likowski said finally. "I'm going to tell you about Ohio."

I had to catch myself from running into the house to fetch it. "Sure," I responded extra casually, like all he had to tell me about was a comedy show he'd caught on Netflix.

"Did you bring extra batteries?" Likowski asked when I came back.

I said I had as nonchalantly as possible. Before he could start speaking, his phone pinged with a frantic reply from Jon Barry, all pretense at punctuation abandoned. Likowski showed me the screen with a sad smile.

> Fired whats this bullshit?!!! I cant pay more the world is changing you dont need a weatherman to tell you which way the winds blowing if you want to make more you're gonna have to dep getoff yr ass grow more get bigger.

Likowski hammered out a reply with his thumbs, brief and to the point, along the lines of what I could tell was simply *fuck you*. He tossed the phone aside and stood up. "Come on, Will."

"What about Ohio?"

"We'll get to that, don't worry."

We went outside to cool off in a rusting bathtub filled with cold creek water, fed by a poly pipe that was the outflow of the Pelton hydro generator. We then stood shoulder to shoulder, staring into the night. It was really dark on the ridge, especially down in Likowski's forest where the starlight didn't reach through the canopy. I jumped when a barn owl hooted. It was more of a screech, like what I imagined the strange woman might make if she were hiding and watching, wanting to scare us.

"So listen," Likowski said in a quiet whisper, "I need your help with something else. I've buried jars up on the hill, a jar every two years or so ever since I came here. Now I forget exactly where they all are."

"How much?" I asked. On the ridge, buried jars were as close as most people got to a 401(k).

"Two hundred and fifty thousand," he said.

I whistled.

"Never really thought I'd have to dig them up. Always thought I'd keep making more dough, but I'm going to have to start spending some it," he said, adding, "Soon."

I nodded. There was nothing to say. To be sure, no Social Security was due Likowski, simply because he'd never paid a dime into it.

"Plus..." He hesitated, looking—if it was possible for the Marlboro Man to look this way—sheepish. "I want to map it all out for Lara. She'll have no clue if she has to do it without me, not the way it is now."

"So what are you asking?"

"Help me find them tomorrow and rebury them, so I can map it out more exactly for her."

I grimaced. "Maybe I don't want to know about those jars."

He waved a hand dismissively as we went back inside. "You're going to know everything else about me."

"Hope you have some time—it's a long story," Likowski said as he splashed water on the heated volcanic rock mounded over the wood-burning stove, ceremonial stones that he and Zoë had collected far to the east in the Modoc lava beds, the site of the final stand of Chief Kintpuash and fifty-two warriors who resisted the U.S. Army for months in 1873. Sure, I had time. I had as many nights as it would take to hear Likowski's story about another failed insurrection, one that I had grown up longing to understand.

"This is about COINTELPRO," Likowski said, "the Weathermen, from back when we thought we could change the world—some heavy shit, and I'm going to tell you all of it. It's worth somebody knowing."

Bursts of steam filled the chamber and speaking was impossible as we adjusted to the punishing heat of the sweat lodge.

"Just get it right, Will," he said finally, once the steam dissipated.

We spent hours in the sweat lodge, the recorder running, and Likowski purging his past. Why? You don't ask when the character decides to reveal. You just collect the story. Dr. Specter speculates that maybe Likowski wanted it all in print for his unborn child; he and Lara had been trying. Maybe he was noticing the rapidly diminishing time he had remaining on this planet. Maybe he knew I was going to get most of the story anyway, and that no matter how good I was, I would surely have to fill in huge gaps and plug in missing pieces. So he surrendered for the sake of accuracy.

The low morning sun filtered through the towering fir when we finished, and I fell asleep on the couch. Once again, I didn't wake until noon.

We put alfalfa hay in AOC's stall, got shovels and rusted rods from the barn, and ascended the hill into the old-growth fir. The house was a hundred feet below us. We sat side by side for a minute with arms resting on our knees. Our breath was visible in the still air, as was a new and sharper picture of Likowski.

In the 1970s Likowski had employed Tupperware to bury his cash; in later years, plastic mayonnaise jars with plastic screw lids. No steel, to avoid the risk of some treasure hunter with a metal detector. At the start he'd buried containers about twenty feet west of the trees; in later years he switched to twenty feet on the downslope. "But I think I buried some on the east side of a few trees."

"How many are we looking for again?"

"Twenty-five," he said offhandedly.

We got to work. I thrust a steel rod into needle-covered ground in the spots noted by Likowski. It wasn't exactly soil. A fir forest has a layer of duff a foot or more deep, and Likowski said the containers were another foot or so in the mineral earth below this layer. I kept poking and poking west of a white fir; my lower back grew sore. I must have stabbed that rod into the forest floor four dozen times. Despite the forty-degree afternoon, I broke into a sweat. Then I hit something. I got a shovel and dug, exposing a dark olive-green Tupperware. My mother had Tupperware just like it when I was in high school; our entire kitchen was olive green: the stove, the refrigerator, the linoleum. I shouted. Likowski scrambled up the slope.

"You were way off. No way is this twenty feet," I said, pointing to the nearest trunk thirty feet distant.

Likowski shrugged. "It was one of the first ones."

He unsnapped the lid, and the Tupperware exhaled gently. Inside was another container, which opened to reveal a third and smaller one, like a matryoshka doll. In the final one was a plastic-wrapped bundle of C-notes with vulcanized rubber band marks; the bands had crumbled to dust. The notes stunk of must but were otherwise well preserved. One was issued in 1934, signed by Secretary of the Treasury Henry Morgenthau Jr.

"I wonder if stores will think they're fake when I go to cash 'em," Likowski said.

We probed and excavated until twenty-five Tupperware and mayonnaise jars were lined up in a row on the hill. Likowski replaced the old Tupperware with contemporary plastic jars, then we reburied them in the meadow where his grow was located. We used a tape measure to mark off a grid, each jar ten feet from the others, in perfect squares, naturalizing the surface with old horse and cow dung to hide the new holes.

"What about when you put in plants next spring?" I asked.

He didn't answer right away, just finished drawing a carefully measured map with coordinates plotted off of landmarks such as rocks and trees. He put the map in a brown envelope, wrote Lara's name on the outside, and pinned it to a corkboard in his office.

"I'm finished," he said.

There was a long silence that I didn't dare break, because there isn't much to offer someone quitting what he's done for nearly fifty years.

I arrived midway in the timeline of Likowski's existence on this coast. But we didn't really become friends until the winter solstice in 1999, at the annual fire that had its roots in those early years not long after the original hippie settlers bought land from McGee. You could tell the history of this region in its fires, colossal and small, chaotic firestorms and controlled burns.

The women from the community built a big bonfire next to the creek in Zoë's canyon, an event organized by Lauren McGowan, who had the thirteen women hold hands in a circle around the blaze, and she announced, I want to declare the formation of the Order of Hildegard, our secret society. We will meet here in the forest each month. We will read our favorite books by the fire. We will sew leaf dresses. We will cook strange but nourishing soups in a cauldron and will generally act like native witches with no worldly concerns. Your talent for singing wicked songs cannot go to waste in civilization. We will sing them here in this wilderness. We will not be pious. We will make mischief. We will have fun. I am so excited I can't properly say. Thank Goddess!

This was where, after the Ark was finished, Zoë and Lauren built the Hansel and Gretel cabin. Thereafter, the Hildegards put themselves in charge of the annual winter solstice fire, which moved to the beach but migrated back to Zoë's land after rangers banned the practice. All that late summer of 1999, the Hildegards had work parties in preparation for the twenty-fourth annual fire, dragging coyote brush and fir starts to a growing pile in the middle of Zoë's meadow. I had always been away on the solstice, so this was my first. It rained hard all day on December 21. I phoned Zoë to see if the ceremony would still take place. She scoffed, "Of course. We always have the solstice fire, rain or stars."

Fire is how I became close with Zoë. In 1996 she decided she wanted to do restorative burning on her land to reclaim a meadow that had grown in with fir trees. Because of the temperate climate, more or less a rain forest in the winter, fir put on a lot of biomass, about 2 percent annually, with this growth something like compound bank interest. A tree is not 20 percent larger in ten years. It is 50 percent bigger. The sapling in a meadow today will become a sixty-foot tree in about twenty-five years. Already I was losing the meadow on my land. Zoë's plan was to do a thirty-acre burn. This drew fierce opposition from Bill, Alma, and others on the ridge. They called for a meeting at the community center.

For thousands of years, Native Americans burned, *Zoë announced at that meeting, in the start of a lengthy speech justifying the project, her eyes filled with the untamed gleam of a German shepherd raised to guard a scrapyard.* Meadows are just as important as old growth. I am seeing a lot fewer hawks and owls than when we first moved here. Above the road, it was all meadow. Remember that lone Doug fir at the top of Baker's table? The fir have grown in so much that you cannot even see that tree anymore. If there are no meadows, there are no insects and flowers and mice and bats, or gophers for the raptors to consume. It goes right up the food chain to bobcats and coyotes. *She concluded:* Saying that we should not burn is the same as saying the Native Americans should not have been here. *I stood and publicly agreed with her plan—the only other person at the meeting to do so. This support was the most romantic words I could have uttered. Zoë invited me to the Ark for lunch the next day and we had our affair that summer. That winter she did the controlled burn, only there was nothing controlled about it. The fire exploded and jumped her lines, and it grew to a hundred acres. Only heavy rain that night stopped the blaze.*

That December 1999, I joined ninety hippies, smoking dope or drinking from bottles, milling around a brush pile twenty feet tall, thirty wide, in the center of the meadow created by Zoë's burn three years earlier. All the women were in fancy dresses, worn beneath grubby raincoats or ponchos. The men were rather plain, in plaid shirts and Carhartt jeans. Someone voiced doubt about the fire.

"I'll get it going," Zoë declared, removing her raincoat. She wore a long white cape.

"Pray to the Goddess!" Lauren shouted.

Another neighbor said, "Think you'll burn down the ridge tonight?"

Zoë scowled and lit the fire dripper, a steel canister the size of a diving air tank, filled with a mix of kerosene and diesel fuel, with a spout that drizzled dripped fire—kind of like napalm. She walked around the pile spreading flame in a jagged line. The brush ignited, billowing wet smoke for about a half hour, and when it really caught, tongues of flame leaped thirty and forty feet. Orange faces on the lee side, out of the smoke, stared at the inferno. It was soon reduced to a bed of rippling coals.

All heads turned when, out of the night, Likowski and Eddie arrived on horseback. Bill whispered to me that it was the first time Likowski had ever showed up. Likowski and Eddie tethered the animals. Eddie fell back from the crowd, and Bill thrust a bottle of Wild Turkey in Likowski's hand and hugged him.

Zoë went around with a wicker basket. People spat into it, so I did too, even though no one had explained the significance. After the ninety were done spitting, Zoë tossed the basket into the coals. Then Zoë went through the crowd with stacks of blank paper, pencils, and bows and string for those who didn't come with these items. Most of the ninety had them.

"What's this for?" I asked.

"Write down something you want to purge," Zoë said. "Something bad from last year. Something you want to change. Then you fold the paper and tie it to the branch I'll bring around. You can't tell anyone, or it won't work."

I used one of Lauren's purple ribbons to tie my wish on a six-foot-long Douglas fir branch Zoë held aloft. Bill tied his with sisal twine. As the branch traveled around the circle, there were ribbons of every color, old shoelaces, copper wire, nylon fishing line, clothes pins. Eddie had migrated even farther away from the circle of hippies. With the ninety-some papers of wish and regret adorning the sapling, Zoë solemnly approached the embers, setting it on the coals. The fir burst in a yellow flash; there was a resounding sizzle. Zoë jumped back.

The crowd was silent. No one moved until there was music from a boom box, some kind of ambient chill. Alma began a slow dance, twirling among the crowd, trailing a long scarf in her left hand. Someone joined her, then another, until a third of the crowd moved in slow interpretive motion. The wind increased. Intermittent drops of rain peppered our faces. Then an icy northwest wind blasted us, the full storm hitting out of Alaska. Finally, we scattered for vehicles. Likowski and I crouched beneath someone's flatbed truck, waiting for the squall to blow past. Zoë scaled the hood and then the roof of the truck, where she spread her arms to face the wind and near-horizontal rain that struck hard as pebbles, the white cape flapping wildly.

> *Blow, winds, and crack your cheeks! rage! blow!*
> *You cataracts and hurricanoes, spout*
> *Till you have drench'd our steeples, drown'd the cocks!*
> *Your sulphurous and thought-executing fires,*

Vaunt-couriers to oak-cleaving thunderbolts,
Singe my white head! And thou—

When the storm abated a half hour later, some two dozen of us remained.
We stood in dumb primal awe, staring at the deep bed of shimmering embers, just as hairy Neanderthals must have viewed fire.
"Fire," Likowski, standing next to me, said. "Purification."
We passed joints and bottles. Most of us resumed dancing. I wondered where Eddie had gone; his horse was still tied to the fir. Likowski sat close to the embers, staring at the spot where the message-adorned fir had immolated. He was oblivious to his neighbors twirling around him. About a quarter mile away, Eddie sat atop a hill, hunkered in a raincoat, watching the gyrating hippies. At the outer edge where the fire glow ended, where light met the night, he saw Indians cavorting in the shadows.

7

JUSTICE

Another year was closing out, the sun setting farther and farther south into the sea. I'd witnessed it disappear over the sharp blue horizon from the meadow rail perch; now it was close to midnight, moonless. I was in the crow's nest. A distant ship slowly vanished over the northwest horizon.

I descended and went into the night. Sparkles glittered as my headlamp beam raked the frosted brown meadow. I lifted the cover off the hot tub—water steamed. The thermometer showed 101 degrees. Wisps of smoke came from the chimney pipe of the Snorkel stove. I opened the damper, took off the metal firebox lid, put some limb rounds on the embers to push it up another degree or two. Surf echoed in Elk Creek Canyon. I floated near the surface to be in the warmer water, hugging the submerged firebox. Hydra was ascending in the southeast sky. On a clear night like this, each of Hydra's heads was visible; its long, snaking body would whip across the horizon in a few hours. Hydra is a winter constellation, at its zenith just before dawn. It's my favorite. It keeps my hours. But my mind was on the nearest star. I recalled something Baker told me over a bottle of Hennessy I'd brought to his homestead when we negotiated the deal. He'd leaned close, and the oil lamplight intensified the yellow of his decayed teeth—I tried not to inhale to avoid Baker's foul breath: *When you're ten, a year is one-tenth of your life. Now it is one-sixty-fifth of mine. You try to hit the goddamn brake, but instead you end up putting your foot on the goddamn gas.* And I asked, *But doesn't living in the country slow down time?* Baker bellowed, *NO! The sun. The sun! In the city you don't pay attention to it. Here you see time moving. The sun races across the sky, drops into the sea. Every fuckin' day! Over 'n' over. Do you understand?*

I didn't then. But I did now, decades later.

For the first time since the 1970s, the hippies didn't hold a solstice fire. No longer did they want to honor the sun's movement; more than a reminder of Zoë, who always organized the event, it was a confirmation that we were all growing old.

The Candlelight had six patrons: three barflies on stools, two young women hovering over whiskeys at a corner table, and me. I sat in the window booth, my face catching the red neon glow of a Pabst sign. Across the street in a park, two men in their mid-twenties, with dreads and scraggly beards, played hacky sack. A woman in a soiled long blue dress and a red bandanna covering her head sat next to the trio's big road packs; a brown pit bull with a blue bandanna tied around its neck lay on the lawn at her feet. It was nearly one week after the anniversary of Zoë's disappearance.

I ordered a vodka martini and studied a printout of the indictment against her son. I'd reported on many trials and knew quite well that the American system of justice, as anyone who has worked within it or covered it knows, is not even a sausage factory, for that cliché is unkind to sausage factories. For white people, mostly rich white people, it functions most seamlessly. For those who are neither white nor rich, they must be educated and persistent, must have the knowledge to put screws to the system. If you shout loud enough, long enough, it's not that someone will listen and then properly do their job; they'll simply want to do just enough to shut you up, to cover their ass, to win the next election, or to quietly put in their final three years before drifting off to collect early CalPERS retirement. Or, if you're lucky, your squeaking wheel catches the attention of someone still young and naive enough to believe the system actually works and wants to do her job, and that's what happened with the case of the *People of the State of California v. Klaus S. Vanderlip*. Now justice would no longer be put off by appeals and delays. Tomorrow morning it was time for the show. Klaus's trial would begin in front of Judge Maria V. Muñoz, twelve jurors, and four alternates in room twenty, in:

> the State of California v. Klaus S. Vanderlip,
> defendant, that there is probable and/or reasonable
> cause to believe the crime(s) of PC209 (b)(1); PC261(a)

(2) x 3; PC288a(c)(2)(A) x 5; PC289(a)(1) x 2; PC245(c); PC422; PC667.61(d)(2); PC220(b); PC243(a) x 2; PC459; PC667.61(d)(4) has/have been committed by KLAUS S. VANDERLIP (D.O.B.) 8/2/66.

That the lead prosecutor was a twenty-seven-year-old woman was significant: Bridget Marshall was a brand-new ADA, and this was her first major case since she graduated from the UC Berkeley School of Law. It was also the first time a big grower in the county had ever been tried for sexually abusing trimmers. A surprise in the indictment: there were two other women besides Tammie who came forward. One of them, based on the date and details, was the young woman whom Likowski and I had seen that night in 2015, when Klaus rushed out of the Purple Thistle and we found her wounded in the bathroom.

The filings also told me Klaus had some high-priced legal talent. Barlow, Skruggs & Cohen represented the rich and famous facing sexual abuse and murder charges. From the perspective of their clients, they had an excellent track record. But acquittals weren't cheap. If the trial went on for two weeks—and with appeals—the bill could easily approach a half million dollars. Klaus didn't have that kind of money. He was clearly overextended, and Zoë had not been declared legally dead—that couldn't be done for another four years— so under California law her estate was frozen until that irrevocable declaration. Where was the money coming from?

I ordered a second martini and remembered the very special tour Klaus gave me twenty years earlier. We'd met here, at the Candlelight, where he hired trimmers looking for work. Back when I wrote about weed for the *Times*, in my wildest desires I never expected a "get" like a private tour of an indoor grow. Journalism of that kind required repeat meetings, months of personal investment, a long marination process—time I didn't have in the '80s. As it was, I had to fight with the desk for two weeks to stay clear for a project. But Klaus had been young and eager back then, excited to show off.

I watched the woman in the dirty blue dress join the men playing hacky sack, her long black hair swaying wildly as she bounced the sack off her knees and elbows. I no longer had a desk dictating my days, but I could not imagine any future point in life that I'd have time to idly spend an afternoon engaging in a game like that solely because I had nothing else to do. Baker was correct—I'd watched the sun race across the sky for too many years. With far fewer sunrises remaining on my horizon after turning sixty, I had no days to waste.

By the time I finished the second drink, the hacky sack players were gone. I walked over to the 'Ran and went to a corner table in the back. Likowski and Lara were already there, and I sat down across from them. When Tammie arrived, she took the chair to my right. We exchanged vague, distracted greetings and ordered. Lara knew Emily, our server; Lara came here often. Emily understood why we were here—everyone in town who read the alt weekly or listened to the hippie radio station was aware that the trial was starting—and she had the sense to keep away once she brought our meals. We sullenly ate local albacore sashimi, albacore rolls, tempura; none of us was sure what to say to Tammie, who looked unslept and nervous.

"I'm scared," Tammie finally said, staring into her uneaten clam miso soup. Her huge brown eyes lifted to study each of us.

"Of course you are," Lara said. "It is hard. But it is so good, what you are doing."

"I want to thank you for being here with me. I could not do this alone."

"We thank you for being brave," Likowski said.

"I am not so sure I am." Tammie began crying.

"Maybe we should talk of other things," Lara suddenly said, reaching across the table to take Tammie's hand. "Things not about tomorrow."

Tammie nodded affirmatively.

Lara looked at Likowski. "Danny, tell a funny story."

Likowski was freshly shaved, and he'd had a good haircut that afternoon. A boyish grin came to his face. His eyes beneath his bangs crinkled at the edges.

"Will, remember when you confessed about being in that CAMP helicopter? How you saw two guys on the beach, one with a white horse? And we realized it must have been me and Johnny?"

"Yeah."

"And how I said you were lucky someone didn't shoot you down?"
I nodded.

"Well, I didn't tell you just how lucky."

"Go on," I said cautiously.

"So Johnny and I had just met up. He came out of the canyon
when I was coming up the beach on Luther. That's when we heard
the chopper. I got up to run into the willows, but Johnny, he just
keeps sitting there. 'Let's go!' I yell. But he doesn't move. Next thing I
know, he picks up his AR-15, takes aim with his elbows on his knees,
squinting through the scope. He says, 'In 'Nam, the VC would go for
the tail rotor. Ping! If they nailed it, we'd be fucked. Like sittin' ducks.'
I really think he's going to pull the trigger and I drop down next to
him. 'If you do that, they'll strafe us. Strafe the whole damn valley.'
He just looks at me with these dead eyes that are saying, like, *So what?*
So I say, 'Just don't,' or something like that, and stare back, hoping I
don't look too fucking petrified, and we're having this staring contest
with the goddamn CAMP helicopter shuddering overhead. And then
Johnny blinks. And he lowers his gun, kind of annoyed. I'm not sure
what would have happened if I'd blinked first."

I took a long, slow drink as Lara looked at him incredulously.
"That's your idea of a funny story?"

Likowski shrugged and began laughing, which grew to a full-
blown guffaw so intense he clutched his chest. That got Tammie
giggling, and then all of us were laughing.

We were done eating when I asked Tammie what she planned to
do after all of this was over.

"To become legally American so I can go to college."

"You can go to school in California if you're undocumented," I said.

"Yes, you can have the America dream," Lara said, as Emily refilled
our water glasses. "I came here for the America dream."

Emily, a woman in her mid-twenties who wore round glasses and
had a round face, started giggling.

"Why are you laughing?" Lara asked.

Emily looked embarrassed. "Sorry."

"No, it is okay," Lara said. "Last time I was here, you told me you
had dreams."

"But they are impossible. I have a college degree and look what I'm doing." Eyeing Likowski and me, Emily added, "Your generation, especially the boys—you got the last of that pie."

"In Italy we don't even have dreams," Lara said. "My father lost his business. Companies hire no one. It's all on contract, the pay very low. It is very bad here. But it is much more bad in Italy. So I came to America. First I was back east. For two years. Then I came to this crazy place with all of its crazy people. I was told by someone that everyone here has a screw turned just a little bit different. They were being polite. So this is the end of my America road. Here I am realizing how the America dream never existed. But at least it keeps you going. That is the only utility it has. You have to dream. I am following a dream too, even if I fear it is just a mirage that will lead me to a desert of disillusion."

"By the time I pay off my loans and can afford to have children, I'll be too old," Emily said.

"I am thirty-six," Lara said. "Not much time. Another dream?"

I muttered that the future looked pretty bleak.

"I will dance in the apocalypse," Lara asserted, nodding her head. "I will roast marshmallows on the flames. Yes, it is true the future is dark." Her huge eyes were now inches from Likowski's. "But our child, she will dance. She will sing. She will have happiness. Even with the bad things to come. It is human. It is natural. She may not have the America dream. But she will find another."

Likowski kissed Lara lightly on the lips and they continued looking into each other's eyes. "Tell them," he said.

"I got the news today," Lara said excitedly. "Berkeley. I got in!"

"They have a lot to teach you about writing news—you buried the lead," I said, joking. I'd written a letter of recommendation for Lara's application to journalism school months ago and had entirely forgotten. I looked at Likowski. I wanted to ask what the couple was going to do about Lara's husband, but I didn't go there. "How are you guys going to navigate the distance?"

"We're moving to Berkeley," Likowski said.

I froze; possibly my jaw dropped. I never could have imagined these words coming from Likowski's lips. The Likowski I'd known all my life dissolved before my eyes.

He nodded affirmatively at Lara and ignored my gaze. "At least while Lara's in school."

The next morning, when I entered room twenty, Likowski and Lara were already there, along with Doc, Alma, and Bill. Tammie was absent—she would be testifying in a few days and wasn't permitted to attend the proceedings. Klaus sat next to three Barlow, Skruggs & Cohen defense attorneys, just flown in from New York City. My neighbors, who sat with us on the left side of the room, were hopeful that the process would work, certain that Klaus was headed for San Quentin. But I had a feeling of dread festering in the pit of my stomach, which only intensified as the court filled with spectators, mostly Klaus's acolytes, who packed the other side.

I studied the jury box: twelve jurors and four alternates. I'd sat through jury selection, heard all their backstories. There was a college professor, a nurse, an artist. But there was also a rancher from the east county and a grower. I tried to parse their faces, but I knew it was a fool's game to bet on what a jury will do. Klaus wore a crisp white button-down shirt and slacks. His attorneys knew better than to put a tie on him, but they did have him cut his hair. The long flowing blond mane was gone, and in its place was a styled short cut. For the first time it struck me: Klaus was in his mid-fifties. He had never looked his age; when he made a grand entry at the Purple Thistle, he could be mistaken for a man of thirty-five, forty at best. Now he looked older, stunned, unslept. He was on some kind of meds. It wasn't speed, that's for certain. Yet his eyes filled with sudden defiance when he set sight on the people's table. Bridget Marshall wasn't much older than the trimmers on his grow.

Marshall outlined nineteen felony counts against Klaus, including three counts of forcible rape, six counts of forcible oral copulation, kidnapping, false imprisonment, assault by means likely to produce great bodily injury, criminal threats, two counts of sexual battery, and sexual penetration by a foreign object. "You are here because the defendant, Klaus Schöen Vanderlip, raped or assaulted three women." Marshall described the attack on Tammie: "She worked trimming marijuana for the defendant. She was at home on the night of September eleventh, when the defendant showed up at her door and demanded sex. Fearing for her life, she removes her clothes, and when he cannot maintain an erection, he chokes her to the point of near unconsciousness. She had difficulty breathing. Strangulation can cause brain damage." Marshall outlined the felony counts against Klaus for the other two assaults—Klaus told one of the women that if she were to tell anyone about the rape, he would freeze her body and then take it out into the Pacific to be eaten by great white sharks.

Robert C. Chambless, the lead attorney for Klaus's team, took copious notes while the young DA spoke. Chambless's blue-gray two-ply cotton herringbone suit, made by Windsor Custom, the clothier for Wall Street hedge fund managers and high-end lawyers, cost just over $1,000. He was happy to tell me this when I later chatted with him during a break in the proceedings. I knew he'd talk: Barlow, Skruggs & Cohen specialized in trying cases in the press. He had slicked-back black hair, and he smelled of a custom mix that contained oud, a scent that has been described as "regal, rich, and addictive." When it was his time to present, Chambless, six-three and commanding, strode slowly to the jury box, where the men and women caught whiffs of oud.

"Ladies and gentlemen, in the coming days you will hear discussion of 'strangling' and other things that sound violent. You or I may not agree with this kind of activity, but some people engage in sexual role-playing. Mr. Vanderlip is one of them. As far as Mr. Vanderlip is concerned, he was role-playing and these women were consenting to sex. Mr. Vanderlip has been an upstanding member of the community and has never before been in trouble with the law. Every Fourth of July, he puts on a fireworks show, at great expense, for the community. He donated twenty thousand dollars for the skateboard park behind the community center. He in fact is often referred to as the mayor of the community. As for the three incidents you just heard about, with the first, no DNA from Mr. Vanderlip was found on the samples collected by—"

Objections were made, but it didn't matter as he continued.

"The assertion is that Mr. Vanderlip brutally raped a woman who is a close neighbor with two other women who could be coming home at any minute. That defies credulity."

A woman a few seats to the left of Doc began weeping. Someone from the Klaus side of the spectator area hissed, and another woman sneered. Judge Muñoz pounded the gavel. "Visitors to this court *must* remain quiet, or the court will eject you."

Chambless continued: "As far as Mr. Vanderlip is concerned, these are romantic incidents turned into something else, something sinister. Could this be false 'recovered memory'? Or worse? Some people hope to profit—"

"The people object!"

Chambless went on for another twenty minutes, spinning the people's account into a harmless and fun long-running sex and drugs party. I went home and showed up back in court only once in the coming week and a half. I slipped in and left early that day, didn't talk with anyone. I didn't cover it gavel to gavel because I wasn't covering it; I was living it. Watching Klaus's attorney was too depressing. I read about the proceedings in online accounts, and there wasn't much to say about the trial other than this: Those on Tammie's side of the courtroom believed from what they witnessed that the jury could come to no other conclusion than to find Klaus guilty. Those on Klaus's side swore he was going to get off on all charges. I knew that Tammie had been powerful and compelling on the stand, but Chambless had lacerated the other two women, one who had a long criminal record, including selling meth. The jury went into deliberations after closing arguments that Friday. I went home and sulked all weekend.

I stayed in a hotel in town to be in court Monday morning, fresh and well slept. I slipped into the seat next to Lara. "Where is he?" I whispered.

"He was driving up this morning. He should be here any minute."

Apart from Likowski, everyone else was present. I looked beyond Lara at the rest of our group and smiled weakly at them. I hadn't seen Likowski in over a week, but I knew what was happening. He wasn't coming. He didn't want to be here for this.

On the other side of the bar, Klaus, in his courtroom uniform of slacks and button-down shirt, sat slumped, looking exhausted, eyes on the mahogany tabletop. Soon, Judge Muñoz appeared and the jurors filed in. The judge asked the jury forewoman to stand and address the court with the decision; that woman read from a piece of paper: "Your Honor, our jury is deadlocked and each person is standing firm. We cannot come to a unanimous verdict."

Three, four full seconds passed. Klaus's head remained down, staring at the table. He showed no response, yet on both sides of the room, spectators' jaws were agape.

The air in the courtroom gathered into a sudden collective gasp. Somebody cried out, whiles others cheered. Judge Muñoz pounded the gavel. Bridget Marshall whispered to another ADA—both deflated, stricken—but Marshall recovered and asked the court to speak. "The defendant is a flight risk, Your Honor. He has a ticket booked for Berlin out of San Francisco International Airport on Friday. We ask for a no bail hold while the state considers its options to retry this case." There were subdued murmurs when the judge ruled that Klaus would be released immediately after relinquishing his passport.

I gave Lara a quick embrace and slipped out, striding past the elevators, nearly running down the stairs.

I drove as fast as I could over the Cougar. I put my truck in four-wheel drive and navigated the steep track down to Likowski's house. It was early afternoon when I parked in the turnaround about a hundred yards from his front door, slammed the truck door, and called out for him. The afternoon was particularly quiet. Approaching the house, I saw the door was open and paused. I jumped with the sudden guttural cry of a flicker woodpecker, just as I caught sight of his body sprawled beyond the threshold.

I reverted to the old me—the reporter in El Salvador, Bosnia, Nicaragua, the Philippines. When you're in the shit you can't fall apart, or you end up one of the corpses at the side of the road. You function. So I took stock as best I could. I wanted to learn as much as I could, as quickly as possible, before I called the sheriff. Once the detectives showed up, they would begin "investigating," which is to say that absolutely nothing would be done. *It happened south of the Cougar. It was a grow. Case—cold.*

It helped that my friend's body was facedown, already stiff with rigor mortis, the floor stained black with dried blood. I'd seen enough bodies in conflict zones to know that he had been shot many hours earlier, probably last night. A fully automatic weapon was used; a line of splintered wood ran from the lower right corner to the upper left of the door. I made a sweeping motion with my hands, finger on the trigger of an imaginary machine gun; the bullets in the ceiling to the left matched that arc. With the door open like that, and no signs of it being forced, Likowski probably knew the killer. I snapped pictures, kept moving.

Unable to step over his body, I went around and entered the house through the kitchen. Likowski's office was torn up—the floor was littered with the contents of his file cabinets. I went to the corkboard; the brown envelope containing the map, with Lara's name on it, was missing. I ran back outside and climbed the trail to where Likowski and I had reburied the jars filled with cash. Empty mayonnaise containers were cast aside next to twenty-five holes. Here I stopped, dropped to the ground for a moment, shaking but unable to cry. The place was too toxic, too scary. Getting up again, I hurried back to the house.

Heart pounding, I took pictures of everything, from the inside of the refrigerator to the contents of the garbage pail, to be certain I wasn't missing details that would be useful to know, things I might find later studying the pictures. Then I took the ladder from the kitchen and went to Likowski's bedroom. I climbed through the closet hatch and brought down the BAR and all the clips of ammo and stashed them in my truck. I was about to leave when I remembered the horse and hurried down to the barn to check on AOC, who was stabled as normal, the hay fresh and with plenty of water in her trough. I spoke gently but avoided the animal's eyes before rushing out. Only then did I call the sheriff, get into my truck, and in low gear creep back up the trail, piecing together what I knew and imagining what I didn't.

Deaths from sudden violence are often preceded by the exquisitely ordinary. Teeth are brushed. Clothes to be worn are chosen from a closet. Shoes are tied. In an overseas nation riven by war, you wake up each day expecting to die, and these small things are appreciated as they are accomplished, if only for the fact that you are alive to do them. Americans are robbed of this joy because of the illusion that the United States is not a conflict zone. No victim of a mass shooting expects to die going to school to learn, a club or outdoor concert to dance, a cinema complex to watch a film, a church to worship, a small newsroom to report on local events. It's the same for individual victims of violence: The convenience store clerk shot dead by the robber. The unarmed black motorist stopped by the cop for a broken taillight. The inner-city mother watching television in her house, in the path of an errant bullet fired two blocks distant...

For his part, Likowski was relishing the quiet on the ridge after so many recent days in town. Tomorrow he'd go to hear the jury's verdict, to support Tammie, and rejoin Lara, but he would live in the moment and enjoy this day. It had stormed that morning. Rain thundered against the metal roof. Likowski had been awake for an hour, yet he remained in bed. No preparation was necessary for the coming season—he'd made that decision to quit and he had no regrets. He'd always loved the off-season, and now he was living in permanent off-season. For the first time, he was able to blot the stream of chores. The chain saw could be sharpened tomorrow. The hydro intake could wait a few days for its monthly cleaning; enough current was being generated to charge the bank of L-16s. The eaves of the cottage outbuilding could rot for another year. The sight of all that was undone had long been a source of anxiety, but he'd reached the point of surrender. One can work ceaselessly, yet new tasks immediately emerge. "Done" is a word never uttered by anyone with an off-grid homestead.

At eight o'clock he fed wood into the Jøtul. He donned rubberized pants and a raincoat and went to the barn to place hay in AOC's stall. Despite the gear, he was rain-soaked by the time he got back in the house. He warmed by the stove. Then he moved into the kitchen, blasting the college radio station as he ground coffee beans in the hand-crank mill for a cappuccino, cooked scrambled eggs on the propane gas range, and used the broiler to make toast, spread with almond butter and topped with wild blackberry jam that he'd canned last summer. He lingered at the long hand-milled slabwood table *after breakfast, reading the latest print copy of* High Country News. *He removed a steak from the twelve-volt Sun Frost freezer to thaw.*

At six o'clock Lara phoned. They didn't talk long because she was going dancing with Tammie. "Tammie needs to burn off steam. She is very worried about tomorrow. I love you."

"I love you."

Likowski hung up and cooked the steak, fried potatoes with fresh rosemary, made a salad with mizuna from the garden greenhouse. He read the New York Times *online at the big table while he dined. At nine o'clock, he poured two fingers' worth of Wild Turkey 101. He stoked the firebox for the night, dampering the flue. He sipped whiskey and read the last pages of Robert Graves's* Lawrence and the Arabs *by the light of an Aladdin oil lamp, his feet extended on a stool next to the stove. There was shuffling on the porch, which was odd. No one ever came unannounced this late. He put the book down and peered out the window, didn't see anything. He opened the front door to peek. Likowski started to say something—a greeting or a question— but never got out the words. A burst of fully automatic gunfire tore into him. He bled out fast.*

8

1963–1979

He's very old, Larry told his wife.

He's only fifteen!

It don't matter—you're old when you die.

Larry knew. He'd seen plenty of kids die around him on Okinawa. The summer before his sophomore year of high school was the worst of it. The doctors weren't sure why Don was wasting away. They guessed it was some kind of autoimmune disorder. Don painted the room black in early June when he still weighed 121 pounds. All four walls. The ceiling. Black window shades blotted daylight. His parents allowed him to do this because he was dying. By July 4, Don couldn't get out of bed. He ran a fever. He dropped to just below a hundred pounds on a five-ten frame.

His room was in the northwest corner of the 950-square-foot bungalow at 1220 Cindy Lane. The street was named after the daughter of the developer who built the tract in 1947. It was exactly like every other home on the block: it had a forty-foot-wide front lawn, thirty deep; no trees; white clapboard siding; brick stairs with black iron railings; a front door painted blue; blue awnings; blue window trim; pale azure-tinged asphalt shingles. Most houses on Cindy Lane were purchased by veterans and their wives, women who took their husbands' surnames and lost their first, as in becoming Mrs. Larry Lapinsky. Men wounded in the war, in head or body, came home to factory jobs. Larry had a limp from the Japanese sniper's bullet that he took in his right leg. The first bullet struck his backpack; the canteen had saved him. Men like Mr. Lapinsky went to the factory by day, and when they returned the women had dinner waiting for them. Mrs. Larry Lapinsky, whose name was Mary, often made dessert from a Betty Crocker box cake mix; all that was required was water and two eggs. The eggs were unnecessary but were included in the directions because psychologists hired by General Mills said the process of adding them made the women feel like they had done enough baking to win praise. At night these couples infrequently copulated in master bedrooms, each measuring eight by thirteen feet. The first child born at 1220 Cindy Lane was Damion, named after his paternal grandfather to satisfy Larry. Mary hated the old man. From the start she called him Don. Rose arrived fourteen months later.

When they were old enough for school, Don and Rose left each morning carrying brown paper lunch bags with bologna sandwiches on white Wonder bread, celery and carrot sticks, and leftover Betty Crocker cake wrapped in wax paper. The frosting always stuck to the wax paper. Mary remained home to do laundry, clean the house, prepare meals. Each weekday started the same: laundry first thing after the kids went off to school. To save money, she used the suds saver setting: soapy bluish-gray water filled the tub next to the machine and was sucked back in by the washer for the next load. The family had just purchased a natural gas–burning drying machine, a godsend for Mary in the brutal Great Lakes winter. Larry was reluctant to "waste" money on the appliance. His mother lived her entire life without one, he argued without success. Before the purchase, Mary waited for rare sunny days so the laundry could be hung on lines outside. She ironed everything, including underwear. She was so precise that even fitted sheets were indistinguishable from top sheets. In the early afternoon Mary dusted and vacuumed, using the Model 30 Electrolux with chrome skids and a rounded aluminum art deco hatch. Larry didn't want to buy it either. *A broom was good enough for my mother.* Mary once again prevailed. *Your mother didn't have wall-to-wall carpet.*

Each Wednesday, she drove the station wagon to the A&P supermarket and spent twenty-five dollars and change on a week's supply of food. Larry's factory job paid just over $5,000 annually, and this covered the mortgage and groceries, and there was enough left over for summer camping weekends at Marblehead on Lake Erie, using the pop-up tent trailer stored at the end of the drive and a fourteen-foot boat for perch fishing, plus two weeks of vacation in Florida. From outside appearances, it was a happy family. But the turmoil in that small house was profound. Larry Lapinsky, who endured many blast concussions in the war, often erupted in screaming fits aimed at his son. *Wait till the marines get you! They'll teach you! You'll learn.*

Mary fought back. The kids cowered, but there was no place to hide in the tiny home. A benefit of the terror was that it drew the siblings close. For a young male at that time in America, Don treated his sister with a great amount of respect. When Don grew large enough, he shielded her from their father. Rose was a tomboy who tagged along when he and his buddies went on marathon hikes through the woods. Don taught her how to start a one-match fire in the dead of winter, using only materials available in the forest. Favored was wild grapevine bark, whose stout vines climbed trees. If it was raining or snowing, Don showed her how to strip the dry bark from the underside of the vine, which was stringy and turned into a brown fuzzy ball when rolled in the palm. It flamed like gasoline and burned long enough to ignite damp twigs. She became adept. When they held fire-building contests in the woods, Rose always beat the boys. She became involved in whatever Don was doing—only she did it with more gusto. Friends wondered if it was competition. She simply wanted to be what she saw as an idealized version of her older brother.

All through Catholic elementary school, Rose looked up to Don from two grades behind. The nuns didn't understand why. Don was a middling student.

That fall before Don fell ill, Mary ritualistically turned on the black-and-white television to *The Jack LaLanne Show* on ABC. She'd started watching the program the previous year, when the scale told her she'd gained fifteen pounds since her wedding day. Jack stood on a set with his dog, Happy, and a chair, which he said *can be your biggest enemy or your best friend—Americans spend too much time sitting in one.* He announced, *Let's get up on our feet, and give me a great big smile. I'm going to show you how to get rid of those ugly pounds! Firm up your waist!* Using the chair's back for support, he thrust one leg into the air behind him and announced for viewers to do the same. *Lift this leg, then this one, one-two, three-four.* Organ music played. Mary dutifully followed along using a kitchen chair she'd dragged into the living room. *Down to the floor, reach up to the ceiling, one, two, three—*

The show was interrupted by the word "BULLETIN" appearing on the screen. *President Kennedy has been shot in Texas.*

Mary was glued to the set. He was their president, the first Catholic man to hold the highest office in the land. When Larry got home that evening and the family sat at the dinner table, he waved his hand dismissively at the set in the living room, exploded in a rant about how there was too much attention being paid to the assassination. *He's just one guy! Just one guy!*

In early August 1964, Don suddenly started feeling better. He ate voraciously. By Labor Day, he'd regained twenty-two pounds. He started his sophomore year at the public high school. His room remained painted black. He earned Cs and Ds that fall. He told his teachers he was still not feeling well, but they believed this was just an excuse. *He's just being lazy,* his English instructor told the math teacher in the break room. *That kid is smart.* Rose, still at the Catholic middle school, was getting straight As.

In high school, Don was an outsider. He spent all his free time in the woods. He turned eighteen in his senior year. That meant registering with the Selective Service. He soon received a notice to report for a physical. He tried to beg off by citing his illness. The draft board didn't buy it. He was classified 1-A.

Don had no college plans; he had figured he'd take some time and go to school in a few years. But after a draft notice arrived in the mail, informing him to report days after graduation, his outlook suddenly changed. Even with bad grades, a state school would enroll him. He went to Kent State University that fall—a college deferment would keep him out of the army.

He scammed that first year, did enough academic work only to avoid being kicked out, which meant he'd end up in a jungle halfway around the planet. In the second year, he started reading all assigned books. He read others that had nothing to do with school: Dick Gregory's *Nigger*, Michael Harrington's *The Other America*, George Orwell's *Homage to Catalonia*. He got straight As. He made the dean's list. Amid this he discovered a small leftist fringe. Outsiders like him gravitated to it. He went to the Students for a Democratic Society meetings just to listen. Despite the SDS presence, Kent wasn't a radical school. It's where the sons and daughters of factory workers went to college. Students came from homes with parents who were racist at worst, conformist at best, and often both. The majority of students had values that were working class—provincial, socially conservative. Most aspired to replicate their parents' lives, albeit with white-collar jobs. They started out freshman year as clones of their parents and many left exactly the same four years later. But some didn't.

In the fall of 1969, the start of his junior year, Don stopped going to a barber. He discovered weed. Rose entered the university as a freshman. A counselor told her she could get into Ohio University or even Oberlin with a scholarship. But she desired to follow her brother. She now dressed like a hippie girl: tie-dyed scarfs, beads, bangs. She immediately began going to the SDS meetings. If anyone had asked around campus, no one would have placed Don's name with the movement. By that December, however, everyone knew her. She often spoke at a bullhorn during protests.

College deferments were replaced with a lottery. His number was 221, which made him unlikely to get called up. But no way would he leave school. By March 1970 Don could tie his hair back in a ponytail. Now he looked like a radical. Maybe it would finally get him laid. The ponytail was for the SDS women who refused to shave their armpits and legs. He imagined their untrimmed bushes, but he'd never seen one in real life. The SDS girls went out with the older guys with full beards, or they had flings with visiting Weathermen who traveled a circuit as much for easy sex as to foment revolution. The Weathermen bragged to the SDS women about planned bombings, told tales of being tear-gassed and beaten by cops—total chick bait. Don still had a baby face and barely needed to shave wisps of whiskers. The women he knew best weren't political. They were like the girls in high school: all had long-term boyfriends or were virgins holding out for marriage and life in the suburbs. Parma and Strongsville were waiting for them. Among his women friends was a girl named Sandy Scheuer. He couldn't imagine sleeping with her.

By now he had more than just long hair. He really was becoming a radical. A level of anger had reached a tipping point. Maybe it began in 1968 with the Tet, the deaths of Martin and Bobby. Maybe it was hearing too much of the domino theory his entire life; growing up with duck and cover, with the daily air-raid siren that blew at noon sharp; watching the Russians on TV parade missiles that were actually made of plywood. Maybe it was the Nevada test site, the detonation of Boxcar. *Be very, very afraid of the Ruskies.* Radioactive strontium was in his bones, everyone's bones, from those tests. *We bombed ourselves.* Maybe it was My Lai, a story broken by the *Plain Dealer.* Maybe it was *The Smothers Brothers Comedy Hour* being canceled by CBS—

Or maybe it was everything. He absorbed the message of the movement: *They lie. They lie. They lie.*

There was Nixon. On Thursday, April 30, 1970, Nixon announced the Vietnam War would officially expand into Cambodia with ground troops. College students all over America protested. Clandestine shout-filled meetings were held on the Kent State campus that night and into Friday morning. Some talked of taking up arms. *We have no choice but to do something,* Rose told her brother.

What do you mean?

Sometimes violence is the only solution.

I don't know. What about Gandhi?

On Friday, Don took part in the burial of the U.S. Constitution on the campus commons. He helped dig the hole. He could do that. *It's dead!* someone shouted from a bullhorn as the document was lowered into the ground. A bell rung.

He wasn't out that night and the early Saturday morning hours when hundreds of students swarmed from campus into downtown Kent. Bonfires were set in the middle of the street. Five banks were targeted, as was a military recruiting office. Windows were broken. Shouts erupted against Nixon.

Another meeting was held that night. Don sat in the back, as always. Mostly he watched. He almost never spoke. The meeting was heated, people talking and shouting over one another.

I'm not going to sit here and not do anything!

Burn the motherfucker down.

Torch it!
You in?
Hell yeah!
Damn straight.
Yes.
FUCK YES!
The last before him to speak was Rose. *Yes,* she said resolutely.
Don?
Yes. His was the quietest voice in the room. Someone passed out emergency flares.
Break windows. Light 'em up, then throw 'em inside.

They pocketed the flares. As the night matured into May 2, helicopters filled the sky. Two thousand students surrounded a long one-story wooden building that housed the Reserve Officer Training Corps, which trained students who would go into the military after college. Stones were thrown. Windows broken. Flares were ignited, like giant sparklers waved by running children. Burning flares flew into the open windows. They were strangely beautiful sputtering over the heads of the mob.

We are just children.

Where was his sister? Was she even here? Maybe she was back in the dorm. She could have been among them in the dark, a dozen or twenty feet away, and he wouldn't know. Faces were shadows. They were not students. They were one creature howling against the military-industrial complex. He didn't feel strong, however. The flare remained in his jacket pocket. He couldn't bring himself to light it.

Firefighters arrived. Someone had thought to bring a machete; it was used to cut hoses while others wrested hoses away and sprayed firemen with torrents of water. Flames rose into the night sky. Hundreds of rounds of .22-caliber training ammunition exploded like firecrackers. By the time the cops arrived to take control, the ROTC building was ashes.

Sunday morning found the campus oddly calm. He'd sat outside through the night, sleeping on the lawn for perhaps an hour near dawn. As the day brightened, he watched students playing softball near the burned building. Rose showed up with one of the heavily bearded SDS members, a senior; the couple was holding hands. They'd thrown their flares. He lied and said he threw his.

That afternoon Republican governor James A. Rhodes arrived on campus and faced television cameras. He spoke to his downstate cracker constituency as well as those who lived in the working-class suburbs of the steel cities. They constituted Nixon's "silent majority" and favored stopping communism in the jungles of Asia and whacking billy clubs on the heads of these hairy boys and girls who needed to be put in their place. *They're worse than the brownshirts and the communist element, and also the night riders and the vigilantes. They're the worst type of people that we harbor in America,* the governor announced. Then he left. That night at 10:30, martial law was declared. Some six hundred National Guard soldiers were pulled off duty in Cleveland, where they had been involved with busting a Teamsters strike.

I don't like this, Don, a kid named Turchon said to him the next morning. He was a friend of Sandy's. *Let's get the fuck out of here.*

They found Sandy in a parking lot near Prentice Hall, on her way to class.

Fuck going to class, Turchon said, and they began to leave campus.

National Guard troops rushed back and forth, seemed confused as they tried to drive students to disperse; tear gas canisters smoked. Some students threw stones. Then thirteen seconds of gunfire from soldiers near a pagoda atop a hill—between sixty-one and sixty-seven shots from M1 rifles. A bullet hit Sandy's neck. Don didn't remember hearing the shots, just the pink mist of her blood. Nearby, ROTC member William Schroeder, who had been on his way to class with books in hand, lay dying. Four dead. Nine wounded. Someone shouted that they were all being killed. John Filo snapped the picture of Mary Ann Vecchio, a fourteen-year-old runaway, with her arms upraised in anguish.

Don staggered away with Turchon, leaving Sandy behind. Why had the bullets missed him? A laugh came from his throat, a laugh he'd never before heard in himself or anyone else. *Why?* He didn't know that it wasn't really a laugh, just the same crazy sound made by those who'd witnessed the Spanish Inquisition, Manassas, Wounded

Knee, Verdun, Okinawa, Iwo Jima—any of the millions of horrors that preceded humanity that May day.

The cover-up began immediately: the Guard was fired upon by a sniper. No one saw or heard the mythical sniper. No guardsman was shot.

They lie. They lie. They lie.

His father insisted on talking.

Tell me what happened.

I don't want to.

Don's eyes were on the brown Formica of the kitchen table. He'd come home and slept for three days in his old black-painted room. A bottle of Jim Beam sat between them. When Don glanced up, his father now stared at the table. Dad looked ancient. Older than he'd ever seen him. When his father came to his room at midnight asking to talk, he looked shrunken as he slowly moved down the darkened hall toward the kitchen.

You don't talk about the war, Don said sullenly, breaking the long silence. *Why should I talk about what happened?*

This is different.

Is it?

Okay, you want me to talk about the war? I'll talk about the war.

There was sudden alarm in the old man's eyes.

I've seen a lot. Guys shootin' themselves in the legs to get off the island. A guy sat down, like this. His dad pantomimed someone putting the butt of a BAR on the ground, muzzle in mouth. *He pulled the trigger. The whole clip went into his head. I was right next to him. Everyone wanted off that island, one way or another. Bunch more happened. Fuck all that. What I want to tell you about is when we got to the bottom of the island. We were mopping up. We went through this sugarcane field. At the edge was all this coral rock. That's where the Japs hid. There were all kinds of caves, lots of 'em were holed up in 'em. I'm walkin' along, and I see this dead woman. She's in a crack between the rocks. She was killed by one of our bombs. Her head was practically blown off. There's this little boy, clinging to her like she was still alive. I picked him up. He was like two, maybe three. He was so scared. I had some sugar cubes, gave him some. I carried him back to the rear. They wanted me to put him on one of the trucks. I didn't trust 'em. Lots of guys were just shooting prisoners, even babies. I seen it. So I took him to the corpsmen. Once he got there, nobody could hurt him.*

Don's instinct told him to just listen. He took a sip of Jim Beam. His father glanced away.

I wonder if that kid still remembers me. His father picked up his glass, downing the whiskey in one gulp. *That's what I want to remember. That kid ending up okay. The war was bullshit. Good war, my fuckin' ass. Vietnam is just more bullshit.*

Dad, I love you—

Mr. Lapinsky waved his hand dismissively. *Shit happens. Then you get over it.*

There were the bloody clothes: the tan polyester jacket and white shirt. He continued wearing them.

I don't want to forget. Jesse Jackson wore Martin Luther King's blood on his clothes for days.

Jackson's an opportunist. He wiped that blood on his shirt. It was all for show.

Her blood sprayed all over me. I didn't put it there. Are you saying I'm an opportunist?

No! I'm just saying it's creepy.

I loved her.

You thought you loved her. You're still a virgin.

You don't know.

I know. Girls talk too.

I don't want to— It doesn't matter either way. I mean love in a cosmic way. You can love without sex.

I understand. But it's upsetting Dad. Mom says she thinks it reminds him of the war.

Okay, I won't wear them around the house.

He drove. They'd borrowed their parents' Buick Skylark. The orders: take a low-profile car, something that no one will remember. The Ohio night came at them. On her lap was a map given to them at a meeting in Cleveland. *Stay under the speed limit,* she said in a town where they got gas.

We don't have anything on us.

We don't want a record of us being stopped on the way down. We get stopped, we have to call it off. Remember what they said?

You think they're right, that there's a mole? This was the fourth time he'd asked.

Sure. But they can't prove anything. We'll give it to Bob. No one else will know for sure. We won't leave any prints. We can deny everything.

What if he's the mole?

Don't bring that up again. Please.

Bob was the heavily bearded SDS senior. He didn't like Bob, and not because he was sleeping with his sister. Something was off about that guy. Bob had invited them to the meeting at a safe house on the south side of Cleveland, at the edge of the valley and its smoking steel mills. The safe house was owned by a retired steel worker who had been a leader in the 1937 Little Steel Strike by the Steel Workers Organizing Committee. The SWOC had been crushed with violence by police and company goons, so the old radical was sympathetic to the SDS and Weathermen. The man had another house in the suburbs where he lived. Don thanked the owner for allowing him to stay rent-free. *Don't thank me, brother,* the old guy said. *Just make America mean what it stands for. That's all I ask.* They'd slept there May 18 and 19, waiting for Bill Ayers to show up. He'd been underground since the Greenwich Village place blew up, killing two, including his girlfriend.

Bob and Rose took one of the bedrooms in the south side house, and they spent most of the time behind its closed door. There were also two SDS women—they had the other bedroom. Were they lesbians? He'd never before met a lesbian, so he wasn't sure. He crashed on the living room floor in a sleeping bag. That night he heard sex sounds coming from behind the women's door.

There wasn't much to do. By day he listened to the radio. The second afternoon WHK-FM announced a new release by Crosby, Stills, Nash & Young, a song called "Ohio." *What if you knew her / And found her dead on the ground.* Weeping, he ran from the house. He vowed never again to listen to the song. Panting to catch his breath, he stood at the brink of the valley, where house-sized flames burst from stacks and the ground rumbled from the rolling operations.

On May 20, Ayers arrived with two Weathermen. Ayers wore round Lennon glasses and had short hair, a mustache; he more resembled an earnest, boyish college professor than a radical on the run from J. Edgar Hoover's FBI. Ayers explained they needed explosives for new operations; they'd lost much of what they had in the Village disaster. He showed no emotion, was businesslike. This impressed everyone. One Weatherman drew a detailed map of a coal company's downstate operations. That Weatherman had grown up in Columbus and used to hunt deer on those lands. He knew of an explosives bunker deep in the woods. It was unguarded, in the middle of nowhere. He and Ayers couldn't go; they were too high profile. Don and Rose volunteered. Don reasoned: *If Ayers is okay with Bob, I'll be okay with Bob.*

Now, two days later, they were on the mission. Rose fell asleep. He reached beneath the black-and-white-checkered sweater his mother had given him the previous Christmas and fingered the shirt stained with Sandy's blood. He needed it for the mission.

They found an abandoned farmhouse the Weatherman from Columbus had told them about: *You can pull inside the barn, sleep in the car, no one will see you.* It was 3:00 A.M. Rose awakened briefly once the car was in the barn, fell back asleep. He clicked closed the door and walked around the old farmstead. The brick two-story house, with all its windows shot out, stood atop a hill. The moon was one day away from full. Bats flitted about in its light. A breeze stirred newly leafed-out oak saplings growing in what had been the front yard. Across the valley was a high rock wall gleaming in the moonglow; the cliff was created by the strip-mine company that had blasted and shoveled to reach a seam of coal at the base of what once was a hill. The only attempt at reclamation was the planting of locust trees on the rubble. Even in the dark it was clear that most of the locust were dead, scraggly skeletons silhouetted against the shale edifice. They were near the Ohio River. Appalachia.

He tried to nap a little but wasn't even sure if he really slept. They got moving late. Again he drove. They were confused at a fork, took the wrong one down a gravel road. He backtracked. At noon they came to the explosives bunker, built into a hill. He drove right past it for a half mile and pulled to the side, removed a heavy green military duffel bag from the trunk, put on a green military jacket a friend gave him after coming home from Vietnam. She took the wheel and drove off. He walked back to the bunker. The duffel bag contained wrenches, a crowbar, chisels, a sledgehammer, a black Magnum flashlight with a red plastic dome, tight-fitting gloves. The Weatherman had offered a pistol, but Don didn't want it.

There were plans and backup plans. He was to sit in a box elder forest on the hill above the bunker and spy through the afternoon to see if guards patrolled. He'd wait until dark. Break in. Stack the explosives behind the bunker ready for loading. Walk four miles back to the paved road. Rose would drive by precisely at midnight. *I'll throw a burning cigarette from the car*. They didn't want her flashing lights in case he'd been busted and cops were hiding. That would give her away. He'd blink the red-domed flashlight three times. *That means things are cool*. If he wasn't there to blink the flashlight, she was to assume he was busted. She was to drive home. If something went wrong, he was on his own. The Weatherman from Columbus told him to walk southeast. *It's woods for miles, all the way to the river. Cross roads at creeks if you can, go under bridges, crawl through culverts. Don't be seen. Stay in a straight line. Get outside of the perimeter the cops will set up. They won't be looking for you ten miles away. The farther you go, the better off you'll be. Run hard. Run fast.* The plan was then to walk north, parallel with the Ohio River, by night. He was to avoid highways. He had a map that showed railroad tracks. He'd follow them. Sleep by day. Get to Wheeling. It might take a week. There he could get a bus home. He had a small pack filled with tins of tuna, corned beef hash, and sardines and a compass.

He went deep into the box elders, napping with his head on the duffel bag of tools. Hours passed. No one drove down the road. A red-winged blackbird trilled. Water must be nearby. A doe strolled past; the deer didn't see him. *I am one with the earth.* Dusk. It was a chilly spring. He was cold and pulled a black wool watch cap low over his ears. Full dark came. Yet he remained sitting. He looked at the watch. *Now.*

He moved downhill. The full moon didn't help. It had clouded over. He clicked on the flashlight. The Weatherman didn't remember how the bunker was built, other than it was made from cinder block. *If you have to, sledge through the fucking wall to get in.* In the red glow he studied a thick steel hood over a heavy padlock. But the three-quarter-inch steel plate door appeared to be simply bolted to the cinder block—eight lag bolts, two hinges. Could it be this easy? He killed the flashlight and took a wrench to the bolts, working by feel—they came right out. Just like that. When the last was extracted, the steel door fell into the soft dirt, firmly dug in. It weighed several hundred pounds. He needed the crowbar. It took all his energy to pry open the door fifteen inches.

He slipped inside. Sweating and panting, he paused to listen. Kept imagining the sound of tires on gravel. He squeezed outside to be sure. Silence. Back inside, he turned on the flashlight. In the red glow: boxes labeled DETAGEL. There was also TNT. *Both are extremely stable,* Ayers had said. It took a strong blasting cap to set off each. *Get an equal amount of ammonia dynamite and TNT if you can, as much as you can.* He guessed each box weighed fifty pounds. He forced them through the partially open steel door. The first fell with a thud; he jumped back, terrified.

He worked fast. Continued hearing imaginary tires on gravel. *Get this part over. Get out to the highway.* His ears rang from the pressure of his beating heart. It was necessary to climb over the tumbled boxes to exit. He carried the boxes behind the bunker. Five hundred pounds. That's all he felt they should take. They didn't want the Buick riding too low, which would draw the suspicion of cops looking for moonshine runners.

Put the door back. Make it look like nothing is wrong if coal company security drives past.

He pushed against the door, using the crowbar to lift the base as much as possible. After fifteen minutes of struggle, the steel plate was still three inches away from the block. He couldn't get the bolts back in. It would have to do. He hoisted the pack, slung the bag of tools over a shoulder, and ran down the road. The duffel bag was heavy. In a half mile he ditched the bag in a culvert. He made the paved road at ten o'clock. Fearful of falling asleep and missing Rose, he paced to remain awake. He remembered the bloody shirt beneath the sweater and army jacket; he fingered it.

Precisely at midnight, a car came down the road. Cigarette sparks flew from the driver's window. He flashed the light. Rose was excited, asked questions. *I'll tell you later. Let's go!* It seemed to take hours to travel the few miles down the gravel road. Eight cases fit in the Buick's huge trunk, two were left behind. They drove north, never going over the speed limit, arriving at the south side safe house at dawn. Bob was there. Three women, all strangers, were also present. He didn't like that. Few people were supposed to know. Now a whole damn crowd knew.

One of the SDS women was Sara. She was tall, blond, with a pixie haircut and almost nonexistent breasts. Cute. For two days, he and Sara slept next to each other on the living room floor. The other two women were in a bedroom. He suspected that Sara also might be a lesbian. After the two women left to drive a box of Detagel back east, Bob and Rose went to Kent for a couple of days, leaving him and Sara alone in the house. Without asking, she put both of their belongings in one of the bedrooms and left him wondering why she had done that. That night he had sex for the first time. She was menstruating.

Her blood is still on me.

The FBI came to their parents' house. The agents said it was because they wanted to talk about Sandy, Mary told her daughter by phone. *Bullshit,* Rose told Don. *They know.*

Two days after the FBI visit, Larry Lapinsky went to an old trunk in the attic of the home on Cindy Lane. He extracted a .45-caliber Colt semiautomatic pistol that he'd taken off the body of a marine from Texas, Angus Roberts, who'd gotten hit on Sugar Loaf. Larry went into the garage, sat on the floor, pulled the slide back, put the weapon in his mouth, and pulled the trigger.

Don wanted to turn himself in so he could go to the funeral. Rose scoffed. *I'm going to stay underground.* If she had any hesitation, she didn't show it.

Don wrote a letter to the FBI, tapped out on a Royal typewriter that was in the south side house, that he would surrender on the condition he be able to attend the funeral. He was set to give it to a friend from Kent State to deliver to the cops, when the retired steelworker who owned the house stopped by. *Don't do it, kid. They'll lie to you. They'll say they'll let you do that when they talk with you on the phone. You'll be behind bars the day they bury him. Don't trust 'em.* The old SWOC organizer was right.

He talked with his mom from pay phones, a different one each time. Mary was staying with her sister. She couldn't sleep in that house. *I'm not going back there, Don. I'm going to sell it.*

There was only one object that belonged to his father that he wanted. One night, Don walked south on the railroad tracks that followed the Cuyahoga River, several miles to the suburb where he'd grown up. Don stole through the backyards of neighbors to avoid being seen by agents who might have the house staked. He went through the back door—there was a hidden key in the garden—then straight to the basement for a crowbar. A huge trunk was in the attic. Dad's war stuff. As he suspected, Dad had locked the trunk after extracting the Colt. That's how tool and diemakers are: precise, even at the end. He pried the lock off. Inside were military medical records, Japanese silk flags, other war souvenirs. Atop them was a heavy green duffel bag. It contained the BAR and stringers of bullets. His dad had been a BAR man. Dad had hidden it in the duffel bag, and they never checked when he got off the ship in San Diego. Don hoisted the bag and went out the back door, sprinting behind the homes of neighbors, following the tracks to the safe house.

Sara went to Ann Arbor, Michigan, to visit friends. Don drew inward. He hated being in the safe house with his sister and Bob, who he was now convinced was an informant. He considered leaving. But how? And go where? To avoid the couple, he walked the south side streets, sat beneath the Clark Avenue Bridge by day. At night he drank at Tymocs, a bar full of old Russian men. He stared into beer after beer, listening to them bitch and moan about triflings, the kind of talk he'd grown up with. If such conversation among the Slavic blue-collar workers were set to music, it was the song of his people. Late at night he wandered along the rim of the valley filled with flames coming out of the mills' stacks, inhaling its sulfurous air, avoiding going back to the house for as long as possible. Rose and Bob argued a lot. She was edgy, confrontational. Yet two weeks after the suicide, when Bob was out getting groceries, he couldn't put it off any longer. *I think Bob's the informant. That's why they came to the house.*

She raged. Rose had absorbed their father's temper. It couldn't be true. *If he were, we'd be busted by now.*

He couldn't think of a counterargument, other than that was perfect cover for Bob. They had a huge fight. Rather, she had a fight. Yelling wasn't going to convince her. When she was shouted out, he fell asleep. A few days later, Rose and Bob went to Chicago with some of the TNT. It was the last time he ever saw Rose.

A few days later, Sara returned from Michigan. He announced to her that he was in love. She wasn't.

I want to sleep with other people—men and women.

Women?

I'm bi.

He was confused.

Bi-sexual.

They argued. She went back to the girlfriend in Ann Arbor. He was now utterly alone in the house. He needed to earn money but couldn't use his real identification to apply for jobs. He took a bus downtown to the county building and researched death records. He found a baby who had died about the time he was born—Daniel T. Likowski. The kid lived for six days. He liked the similarity, and a Slavic surname matched his appearance. *You will be reborn Likowski.* He got his birth certificate with the official seal and then forged in that kid's name—he learned how from *Steal This Book*, by Abbie Hoffman. With that he took a driving test and was issued a license. *AMF—adios, motherfucker. It was nice knowing you, Damion Lapinsky.*

Dan Likowski got a job in a car wash, worked a lot of overtime, and saved money. When he had enough dough, the newly minted Likowski would head to the coast. Vanish into the counterculture. Get back to the land. No one knew about his fresh identity. Not any of the Weathermen. Not Rose. Not even Sara—they had a few emotional telephone conversations that summer. He'd learned from the heist that if you were going to do something illegal, if you wanted to get away with anything, *tell no one. Act alone.* He hoped FBI agents didn't find him before he could make it to the West. *Some shit's coming down.*

He spread maps of California around the bedroom of the safe house. He loved maps. Looking at them sent a tingle down his back. There were so many blank spots north of San Francisco. Empty land. A place to be free. What did land cost? He went to the big public library and studied real estate ads in the Sunday *San Francisco Chronicle*. He'd need money but didn't know how he'd get it. But he'd buy land out there. Somehow. At night he read the first issues of a new magazine, *Mother Earth News.* There were articles about making a Plains Indian teepee, buying land and setting up a homestead, growing your own food.

By summer's end he'd saved enough from the car wash job to pay $175 for a blue 1962 Ford Falcon. The body was rusted at the fenders, and there was a hole eaten through the rear passenger-side floor, but the engine had low mileage. In September, the Weather Underground announced a fall offensive. All over "Amerika," as they spelled it. *Boom. Boom. Boom.* Bombs everywhere. Sara was Don's contact person. She came down from Michigan and asked him to take the last of the Detagel and some TNT to Weathermen in San Francisco. She gave him an envelope. Inside was $260 in twenties—gas, food, and hotel money. He was given a phone number and a name: Syd. *Call Syd collect when you get close.* He was supposed to take part in a bombing. And then she kissed him, to his surprise. They fell into bed.

He was happy to drive west. He was nervous. He concentrated on forgetting that there were explosives and a machine gun in the trunk. *I'm going on a backpacking trip in Colorado,* he rehearsed. But no cop stopped him. He drove night and day, slept in rest areas to save dough. He grew excited when the Front Range materialized like an apparition on the horizon. He'd never been in the West. Colorado's Loveland Pass blew him away. *Love-that-land.* Then came the Nevada desert. The Sierra. All called for him to linger. Yet he kept moving. What he remembered most about his first moments in San Francisco was the Pacific Ocean air. He'd never inhaled air like that.

Meanwhile, in Chicago, the Weathermen used some of the TNT to blow up a statue of a police officer that honored seven cops killed by an anarchist's bomb on May 4, 1886. Rose drove that night (Bob had mysteriously vanished the previous week). She took two Weathermen to the corner of Randolph Street and Kennedy Expressway. One Weatherman set the device on the twelve-foot pedestal between the legs of the bronze cop dressed in the police uniform of the 1880s. At quarter past one in the morning, there was a thunderous explosion. One leg of the statue was blown dozens of feet away. Forty windows shattered in nearby buildings. Rose made the telephone call to the Associated Press and read a printed statement she'd been given: *This is to honor the four innocent labor leaders who were hanged after Haymarket. Remember Kent State! It's another phase of our revolution to overthrow racist and fascist Amerika! Power to the people!*

Two weeks later Rose went to visit their mother, who was at the Cindy Lane house boxing up belongings, a FOR SALE sign out front. Rose had been dropped off a few blocks distant and was in disguise; she had on a black babushka like those worn by Polish *stada baba*, old women. Moments after she passed through the front door, it was kicked in by the FBI. *Where's your brother, Rose?* they screamed, putting a gun to her head. *Where is your fucking brother? Where's your FUCKING brother!*

On October 1, Likowski met Syd near the Panhandle of Golden Gate Park. Syd had weed. They took a walk into the park and got stoned in a redwood grove. The dope hit him hard. He attributed it to being so tired from driving that long last stretch from Nevada. *I sell grass for a living,* Syd told him.

Then Likowski drove Syd in the Ford Falcon to the Sunset District. It was foggy, exotic. The Pacific Ocean smelled like a freshly opened raw oyster. He inhaled deeply while he waited by the trunk of the Falcon. Three Weathermen emerged from a house and unloaded the Detagel and TNT. Syd vanished. The others invited him inside. At the kitchen table, where they sat drinking whiskey, the Weathermen showed him blasting caps they'd made by dissolving mercury in reagent-grade nitric acid and how they'd use the explosives. The Weathermen outlined the operation, but they didn't reveal the target for security reasons. He'd learn the night they went out. He listened politely, nodded, was very agreeable.

At three in the morning, he told them he was going out to the Falcon for a sleeping bag. He opened the driver's door and put the key in the ignition. He'd done the delivery—he'd made that promise—they had, after all, let him live for free all summer. But now it was SDS: *AMF*; Weathermen: *AMF*. As he crossed the Golden Gate Bridge, he couldn't imagine any human being had ever felt as exhilarated as he did at that moment. He was heading north into the blank spaces on the map spread open in the passenger seat.

He was free. He was Likowski.

Back-to-back storms came off the Pacific that December. By the end of the month, Likowski's tent was shredded by the unrelenting wind. Gusts were strong enough to bowl him over when he walked south on the black sand beach to the World Leisure Time subdivision. He slept in a half-finished model home in the new development. The roof was not yet sheathed. Rainwater cascaded through seams in the plywood. He found a corner on the first floor that was dry and rolled out his sleeping bag. The surf was menacing. Wind shook the windowless structure.

He awoke before dawn and swiped a thick roll of polyethylene plastic and lugged it north back up the beach to his camp near the mouth of a steep canyon. Waves striking the rocks sent white plumes of water shooting forty feet into the air. He moved one mile farther back into the canyon, where there was a rare grove of redwoods, which were more common a few miles inland. One of the trees was hollowed out at the base. The wooden cavern was large enough for him to lie down in with his feet sticking out. He leaned fallen redwood limbs against the trunk and wrapped this frame of sorts with the plastic sheeting, forming a half teepee. He built a cooking and heating fire at the entrance, and mostly the smoke didn't blow back inside.

The Ford Falcon was twenty-four miles away by foot. It had broken down on the drive north from San Francisco. He had it towed to a town on the highway, where it was now parked behind the Tan Oak Café on Main Street. In exchange for a few days of painting in the restaurant, the owner allowed him to park the car there until summer. After finishing the work, he walked west to the beach in late October and set up camp. He survived on mussels and abalone harvested at low tide. He didn't yet know the urchins were good to eat or he would have consumed them as well. Sometimes he was lucky and he'd find a stone crab in a tide pool; the taste provided variety. There was rock kelp and sea palm. Once every two weeks he'd trek to town to buy broccoli, a few cabbages, using what remained of the Weathermen's money. Hitchhiking was problematic. If he didn't get a lift, it was nine hours on foot. Construction workers at the development who lived in the town got to know him, and he'd time trips for shift changes; they'd pick him up. If a sheriff's car rounded a bend, which happened infrequently, he was prepared to run into the forest. But the cops paid him no mind.

In early January he went to a phone booth outside the Tan Oak Café and extracted a card from his wallet:

JON BARRY
JON BARRY ENTERPRISES LTD.

He'd kept the card given to him back in October by the man whose pseudonym was Syd.

It's thin, Likowski had observed dryly, as they smoked a joint not much thicker than pencil lead.

Barry was used to this reaction. He loved seeing people smoke his product for the first time. *Tell me how thin this joint is after we smoke it.*

Likowski only knew the Mexican dope they got back in Ohio that needed to be rolled into stogies. His head reeled, and when he stood to pee behind a redwood tree in the park, he nearly fell over.

What is that—doctored shit? Likowski exclaimed.

No, man, it's just pure weed. Sinsemilla.

Barry told Likowski that he flew to India after reading about the Beatles making their meditation pilgrimage. He went to the northwest corner of the country and discovered a variety of marijuana, Kush, grown in a mountain valley. He smuggled seeds home and had them propagated to create poundage of seed stock.

But you only grow female plants. This shit, it's the Cadillac of cannabis. Not that ditch weed people keep trying to pawn off on me. Not that lame-ass Mexican Mary Jane, man. This is the future, Barry said, holding up a baggie of bud. *You going back to Ohio?*

Likowski shook his head. *Fuck no. I'm heading north. Going to try to get back to the land.*

You want to grow some plants, I'll set you up. Call me.

Barry and Likowski occupied a window seat at the Tan Oak Café. It was late afternoon and the place was empty. The sun blasted through the glass on Barry's tanned face. Even Likowski knew he was good-looking, and he was normally unable to judge the looks of a man. Barry was still a bit soft in the face from youth. He'd grow even more handsome in a few years. Likowski wondered why a guy who was so attractive was dealing marijuana. He should have been in politics or the movies. It was California, after all. Barry wore a crisp white Lands' End shirt, cream khaki pants.

Likowski looked rough. His blue jeans, washed in the stream using rocks to beat the dirt out, were in tatters. His blond facial hair had grown out but wasn't yet forceful enough even at his age to thicken into a decent beard. His hair was nearly down to his shoulders. It would have been longer, but Likowski used scissors to trim it. He braved bathing in the fifty-two-degree ocean every few days when there was sun, yet there was an odor about him.

Order anything you want, Dan. On me.

Likowski got a sixteen-ounce T-bone steak with a side of onion rings. *Mind if I get an extra salad?*

Knock yourself out.

Likowski chewed the bone bare as if he were a coyote. It was the first beef he'd consumed in months. And the salads were equally savored. Barry had French onion soup and fruit, which explained why he was so thin. Barry smiled as they ate. Likowski was self-conscious but so famished that he didn't care. *He must think I'm a rube,* Likowski thought. *That's why he's smiling.*

Truth was Barry delighted in what he was seeing. This kid was literally and figuratively hungry. Barry liked that Likowski was from the Midwest, had a blue-collar background. *Those kids know how to work. Give me one of them for every ten Ivy League hippies.* So many of the kids who came out after the Summer of Love were dreamers. Going back to the land was a fantasy. They had options, a way out. They didn't last long. *One winter in the fucking piss howling rain up here, no electricity, using smoking oil lamps, shitting in the woods, hits them hard. They hightail right back home. Become dentists and accountants and chain store managers. Normal people. Squares.* Barry could smell bad investments a mile off. In the worst-case scenario, even if only one in three people like Likowski came through, Barry was still going to end up a rich man.

When the waitress brought dessert, Barry announced, *Okay, let's get down to biz, Don.*

It's Dan.

Barry took a swig of coffee, hot and black. *Don,* he asserted, smacking his lips.

Likowski's eyes darted wildly, to the door, the street—looking for agents of the bust that was about to come down.

Relax! Barry said when he saw the alarm in Likowski's eyes. *When the guys saw that you'd booked, they freaked. They figured you were FBI. They wanted to bail on the Marin operation. So I made some calls, got the scoop. I don't care what you call yourself now. But if you and I are going to do business, we're going to have to be absolutely honest with each other. If I give you ten Gs in twenties, you're never going to have to count it. It's going to be ten grand. Okay, Dan?*

Okay.

Right now, the going rate for Mexican weed is about a hundred a pound. The stuff I want you to grow, I'll pay four hundred—

Per pound?

Per pound. No stems, no leaves, no seeds. I won't pay for good shit. That won't cut it. I only buy great shit. Cadillac shit. The best. And to grow the best, it's gonna take a lot more work than you've ever done in your life.

I'm not afraid of work.

Barry smiled again. He pushed the empty plate aside and set a thin aluminum Halliburton case on the table. From it he extracted a volume with an orange marijuana leaf on the cover, *The Cultivator's Handbook of Marijuana,* by Bill Drake. *A friend of mine in Berkeley just published this. It's the go-to guide. If you follow what's in it, you're going to grow me some kick-ass shit. It tells you about starving the plants of nitrogen, how to sex them, blah, blah, blah. But the secret is the seed stock. You need the right genetics. The right heritage and a fucking lot of hard work. You can't go wrong if you have both.*

Barry extracted a repurposed small glass olive jar filled with a half inch of seed. *Here you have the genetics. Indica. More than you need, in case you lose starts to mold.* Next came three one-hundred-dollar bills. He pushed the jar and the bills across the table. Likowski's eyes widened. *You're going to have to buy chicken wire to keep the deer out. Irrigation pipe. Et cetera, et cetera. I'll deduct this the first time I pay you. It's an interest-free loan.*

Likowski stared at the C-notes. He was reluctant to touch them. *But what if I—what if—*

If you fuck up or fuck off, I'll write it off as a loss, no hard feelings. But I have a hunch you are not going to fuck up or fuck off. You bought a one-way ticket, man.

They shook on the deal. Barry paid the tab with another one-hundred-dollar bill. While they waited for change, Barry asked, *Where you going to grow?*

In the canyons—up the coast.

Barry whistled. *Hard-core. Guerrilla. Good.*

Barry gave Likowski a lift back to the beach in his red Jaguar XKE, throttling fast on the winding coastal road in the redwood zone where the road was paved, until they hit the bad sections; they slowed to a bouncing crawl when they entered the Douglas fir forest at the switchbacks and the gravel. The engine sounded frustrated. It was a car built for the interstate, not rural roads that were simply improved horse-drawn wagon trails.

Jesus! This car costs at least twenty-five, thirty grand, more than a house, Likowski thought. His mind was wrapping around $400 a pound and how many pounds he would need to purchase land. A pound and a quarter would buy an acre of mediocre real estate; two to two and a half pounds would get him decent property. But you didn't buy just an acre or two. The smallest parcels he saw advertised in the classifieds of the *San Francisco Chronicle* were forty acres. Most were eighty or more. He'd need a lot of pounds; he would grow them.

They arrived at the sea, where the road dead-ended at the sad development. They shook hands again. Likowski hoisted his pack and marched north along the beach dotted with Volkswagen-sized pieces of driftwood. The marine layer was thickening. Barry leaned against the passenger fender. He extracted a pack of Winstons from his breast pocket, cupped his hands to light a cig with a Zippo. When he spun the knurled reel there was a satisfying ignition and smell of kerosene fuel. He snapped closed the lid. He smoked and watched his newest grower vanish into the mist.

First there was identifying where he would grow. The site needed three key elements: remoteness, water, and sun. The day after meeting Barry, Likowski hiked ten miles farther north on that wilderness coast. Numerous canyons shot off the steep oceanfront range. Each had its own personality. He "read" each canyon over the ensuing two weeks. Some had good south-facing flats, but he feared there would be no water in late summer. He made this judgment by studying the springs emerging from canyon walls. He intuited which springs were robust by the plant life. He didn't know then what they were called, but he could tell that one species favored the wettest spots—he'd later learn these were Pacific willows. He didn't need a field guide to identify the watercress he discovered growing in the muddy pools below some springs and stuffed his mouth with sprigs. If 'cress grew, there was year-round water.

He paid sixty-two dollars to have the Falcon repaired and made a deal with the owner of the Tan Oak Café to paint the rear fence to be able to continue parking it there. He didn't want to draw attention by leaving the car at the trailhead. He drove to the city an hour north. He salvaged things from trash bins behind restaurants and businesses:

five-gallon plastic pails, lengths of rusting steel rebar. One afternoon he found a Royal typewriter in perfect working order. He went to a secondhand tool store and purchased a shovel, machete, mattock, clippers. All these were backpacked in. He'd need at least one three-hundred-foot roll of chicken wire for each six plants and twenty-five pounds of chicken manure for a single plant. *The Cultivator's Handbook of Marijuana* told him to expect anywhere from a half pound to one pound per plant, depending on the soil and other conditions, but if he fertilized heavily, he'd get one pound of trimmed bud from each. He wanted at least forty plants. There was no particular logic to this decision. It simply sounded like a manageable number. The book promised there would be loss to many unforeseen mammalian enemies: a type of vole known as a wood rat, deer, or two-legged thieves. And there was powder mold, sludge mold, spider mites, russet mites, broad mites—though with the exception of the brown sludge mold, these weren't as much of a concern for outdoor plants. Even if he lost three-quarters of the crop, his realistic expectation was to end up with $4,000.

After doing all the math, he figured on seven rolls of chicken wire and one thousand pounds of chicken shit. *Jesus! That's a lotta shit. Do I really need that much shit?* He went to the big garden supply center in town. The clerk was suspicious.

Big garden, the clerk, a large woman with snowy hair, said. *And early.*

Prepping, Likowski said. *It's a new garden. There's lots of work to do.*

Watcha gonna grow?

Tomatoes, zucchini, peppers—you know, the usual.

Have you thought about gophers?

Likowski had not thought about gophers.

When the world ends, two things will survive in this county: poison oak and gophers. If you don't protect your "peppers," you'll find a wilted plant, and when you pull on it, the stem will come out with no roots. The gophers eat everything. You're gonna want to protect the roots. She instructed how he'd have to make cages to place in the ground, to keep the animals from the roots. *Even though it's galvanized, it'll eventually rust out. But you'll get two or three seasons from it.*

She led him to quarter-inch mesh galvanized wire. He added three rolls of it to the order. He bought sulfur; mouse, rat, and gopher traps;

ratchet straps. When he backed the Falcon into the loading bay, he wasn't sure he could carry everything. He lashed the rolls of wire to the roof with ratchet straps. Bags of chicken shit filled the trunk, the back seat, the passenger seat. He pushed and stuffed them all in, kicking the last two into place with his feet. No way could he drive this load down the 101 and not get pulled over. There was a twisting back road in the eastern edge of the county that went through the mountains. The Falcon groaned on the grades, and he prayed for the car to not break down. *Just forty more miles, old girl.* He patted the steering wheel.

It was one in the morning when he reached the end of the road at the development. The trailhead parking area was deserted. He'd prepared a staging area a half mile north, back in the dunes, where he'd dug a huge pit in the sand. He hauled everything to that site, to get the vehicle emptied as fast as possible. By half past two the car was unloaded. He spent the rest of the night and through dawn ferrying everything to the hole. The wire went first; he used the ratchet straps to make a shoulder harness to take two at a time. He tried four bags of manure on each shoulder but couldn't handle that; he ended up with three on each side. After he plopped the last bag into the hole, the sun was on the mountains. He shoveled sand over everything and then naturalized the site by using a coyote bush to smooth over the sand.

Day by day, he dug out his supplies and packed them on his back at night to the canyon where he lived and a second canyon to the north. Both grow sites were above rock slides and log jams impassible to cows and ranchers on horseback. It was March when he began prepping sites. This meant leveling ground, making chicken-wire cages, erecting fences. He worked from morning till dark, hacking, chopping, digging, moving earth. If he had more money, he would have installed a drip irrigation system, but he was nearly broke. He'd water by hand. He developed three springs, digging them out, building up rock-lined pools from which to dip water. The final step was to purchase food with the last of the money Barry gave him—pounds of coffee, sugar, dried noodles; spices: pepper, oregano, rosemary; an assortment of kitchen garden seed: lettuce, tomatoes, pole beans. He also bought fishing gear. He now had everything he'd need for the next six months, including the typewriter, books, the BAR. Between April and October, he'd sit on his crop, wouldn't go back to town.

He found a certain Zen in the work. He labored all daylight hours. Carrying water was the most arduous task. At night he journaled on the typewriter and wrote poetry by the light of a kerosene mariner's lantern, inside a teepee covered in the sheet plastic. This structure was in the center of his main garden. As the plants grew it felt tropical, especially at night when he lay on the ground among the cages, looking at the stars, the fronds splayed against Andromeda. He was sorry when he had to start pulling off the big shade leaves once the buds started forming, to increase resin production.

The kitchen garden also did well. Pole beans climbed the sides of the teepee. Romaine lettuce flourished. There was good fishing at the mouth of the canyon that contained his main crop and camp. He caught surfperch and cabezon, which had turquoise flesh that turned white with cooking. There were mussels, abalone, and the occasional crab. He now knew to eat the urchins, raw and over white rice. There were steamed beans, wild miner's lettuce, watercress, and romaine salads. Nights were cold. The chill made the marijuana plants turn from green to a purple hue. Or was that their genetics? Either way, they were growing increasingly handsome. He stroked the young buds as one would pet a kitten.

Up to July, his life existed in a U-shaped world: the path a half mile down to the beach, north a quarter mile to the next canyon to tend the other patch. Late that month he arrived to chaos at the second grow: the chicken wire was smashed down, half the plants were broken over. No fence was going to keep out a black bear, who went after the fish remains he'd used as supplemental fertilizer. A week later, he returned to the surviving plants and found skeletons of stems. Wood rats—four-legged locusts—had discovered a way inside the chicken wire. He'd been chasing them away from his main patch and trapping them. He abandoned the grow in the second canyon.

By August when the buds were ripening on the plants at his main site, it had been four months since he'd spoken with anyone. Twice he saw people walking on the beach in the distance when he was fishing. Each time he retreated to the canyon before they neared. He felt one with the mountain lion that lived upcanyon. He saw its prints in the sand and once heard a distant roar that was more of a snarl. He felt more and more feral. He stopped looking in the mirror that hung from a stunted alder next to the now-dry creek.

At night he smoked the weed. It was already crazy strong. He'd sit facing his campfire and wonder if a human could rewild himself, like the dog in *The Call of the Wild*. The newspapers he bought in the town had stories about Japanese soldiers being found in the jungles of the Philippines—they'd remained undetected for decades, unwilling to surrender. In theory he could dwell in this canyon for twenty-five years, just like those Japanese marines. *Would I go mad? Or die from some minor ailment—even an impacted tooth?* But he would die free. That night, inspired by Thoreau, he typed out: "In wilderness is found liberation from the totalitarian state." He hung that sheet of paper next to the door.

In late September, he began harvesting and hanging the buds upside down on strings looped overhead inside the teepee. The smell of bud was so overpowering that he had to sleep outside. He was losing a percentage of the buds to mold and grew alarmed. But the problem stabilized. He now carried the BAR with him any time he left camp to fish. He was alone, yet the weapon felt good in his hand or over his shoulder. The tomatoes ripened and the carrots were ready. He savored the new tastes. He felt very alive.

When the bud was sufficiently dry, he wrapped it in cellophane bags, which he packed tightly into the five-gallon pails he'd gotten from trash bins; they had tight-sealing lids. There was a lot of bud to harvest. When a second pail began getting heavy, he knew he was in good shape. He prepared to emerge from camp the second week of October. He stashed the BAR and other valuables a mile upcanyon, along with four pails of bud. He hiked out, surprised to see pieces of wreckage from a fresh plane crash that had been hauled next to the landing strip. He hitched to town to call Barry and get the car. He drove it back and parked at the development. One pail squeezed into a pack; he carried the other three in hand. He was paranoid on the hike out and the drive to the big town up north.

Barry's hotel room door was ajar. Likowski, all four pails in two hands, used a foot to push the door in. The drapes were drawn tight, the room dark. Barry was sprawled on top of the still-made bed, smoking a Winston. He had on a blue Brooks Brothers shirt, crisp blue jeans, penny loafers. He leaped up, closed the door. Likowski pried the lid off one of the pails. Barry extracted a cellophane bag. *Holy shit! These buds are beautiful.* He inhaled deeply. Barry broke off a piece of bud and rolled a joint. He ignited it with the Zippo. They toked and talked. Barry fell back on the bed. *This shit is amazing!*

Barry procured a scale. He set each bucket on it, wrote down the weight. He dumped the contents of one of the buckets out on the bedspread and then weighed the bucket.

Minus the buckets, twenty-seven pounds, fourteen ounces. Let's call it twenty-eight pounds even.

Likowski's head reeled as he did the math. *$11,200! Jesus fucking Christ. That's more than double my old man earned in the factory, and he put in all that overtime. And mine's tax-free...*

Barry turned serious. *But I can't pay four hundred, like I said.*

Likowski looked stricken. Before he could protest, Barry cut in.

I'm paying you five, man. Five hundred a pound. For shit like this? I'll move this in two weeks. Or less. He slapped Likowski on the back. *I had you there, man.*

The men laughed. Barry set the aluminum Halliburton case on the round brown Formica hotel table.

You want it in twenties or hundreds?

Ten thousand in hundreds. The rest in twenties?

Sure.

Barry pulled out a bound stack of hundreds, wrapped in a band marked $10,000. Next from the case emerged two stacks of twenties with $2,000 bands around them. Likowski had never held so much cash in hand. *Fuckin' A! Fourteen grand!* He was surprised at the compactness of $10,000—the tightly bound bundle was exactly three-eighths of an inch thick. Barry had forgotten about the $300 advance. Or maybe he just didn't care? Likowski didn't bring it up.

No one's paying like I am. I want a long-term relationship, my friend. This bud is the future. I'd love to have ten more guys just like you. I only ask one thing, man: next year, grow more. A lot more.

By his third summer of growing in the canyon hideout, Likowski had ninety-six of the gorgeous purple plants that were just beginning to bud out. He was looking at a harvest of at least seventy-five pounds. This crop would make him. With the money saved and buried from the forty-one pounds from his second summer of growing, he would have enough that fall to pay cash in full for good land.

On August 2, just after noon, he heard a helicopter. U.S. Coast Guard choppers flew parallel with the beach on patrol all the time, so he ignored it until the sound of the blades came up the canyon. The machine hovered directly above. It wasn't the Coast Guard. The unmarked chopper sped away. Likowski grabbed sheaves of typed papers with his name on them, anything else that would identify him, and stuffed them in the pack, along with provisions—tins of tuna, a jug of water. The money was buried in plastic jars miles inland. Frantically, he looked around. *What else? Fuck it. Go!* He slung the BAR over a shoulder and raced upcanyon. He was now total guerrilla—in monster fit shape, and he knew the country as well as the mountain lion. About a half mile upstream, he ascended the south wall of the canyon, scrambling goatlike up the sheer face to a ridge. He doubled back to a spot in thick young fir, where he looked directly down at his patch hundreds of feet below. He lay on his back, panting, staring at the blue sky through the fir branches. He rolled over on his belly and watched.

Cops armed with shotguns and rifles sprinted up the canyon in combat crouches. Just as they came around a bend and upon the patch, the helicopter materialized. Cops machete-hacked the plants, stacking them into a pile in the creek bed. Smoke rose. By its dark color, he surmised gasoline was used to burn them. Over $35,000 went up in that pyre. The chopper circled in a widening gyre, searching for him. He buried his face in the earth and didn't look up until the helicopter went away. At full dark he stole along the ridgetop, crawling east through choking brush, through places it seemed that no one had traveled on foot since the time of the Athapaskans.

The ranchers weren't happy about the longhairs. The Jones and Edwards families made jokes. *How many hippies does it take to screw in a light bulb? None, hahaha. They screw in the back of VW buses. Those kids smell. The women don't shave their legs or armpits.* But Bill McGee liked young naked women in the swimming hole, hairy or not. He ripped off his clothes and jumped right in the water with them; at night he went to the beach bonfires, and he danced, drank, and smoked their dope.

McGee made a living selling ranches to other ranchers, though he wasn't a real realtor. He was having trouble unloading a two-thousand-acre spread, over three square miles sprawling over a ridge south of the river that happened to be named after his great-grandfather, Thaddeus McGee, who had married into the Jones clan. The parcel had been on the market for five years. It had been logged with clear-cuts in the early 1960s, and then came the '64 fire. The south-facing slopes were especially slow to heal—the earth baked in the relentless summer sun, drying out fir starts amid choking coyote brush and poison oak. It would take a century for marketable trees to come back. The meadows, overgrazed by sheep, were now dominated by invasive rattlesnake grass. No smart local wanted that land.

McGee put down $80,000 on the piece, owner financed, with a balloon payment due on the remaining $1.3 million in five years. He surveyed and platted it into parcels, with most 40 or 80 acres, plus a few 160s. McGee sold only to hippies whom he liked, which generally meant that if a hippie bought him several drinks, he was ready to do business at $800 per acre for the tracts with harsher and steeper exposures, $1,000 per acre for prime parcels. After deducting costs for subdividing, he estimated that he'd clear one hundred grand, worth his trouble. And he viewed the hippies as an infusion of life. He wanted them to create a community center in the old, abandoned schoolhouse.

The first piece to go into contract was a fifty-acre parcel with a sweet house site on a flat table of about five acres with a commanding view of the Pacific. It was sold to Baker, a tall and quiet Vietnam veteran with a young wife and a toddler. Baker had been hit by a mortar round, and he walked with a limp. McGee liked Baker, who lived with his family in a tent on the river bar. *I tried getting a regular job, but I didn't fit in,* Baker told McGee over a drink. *We bought a house in the burbs. Our neighbors never came over. Never wanted to talk to us. But one day, all of a sudden, they all come over. It was the day I started painting the house. Black.* McGee sold below cost—$600 per acre. He wanted Baker on that ridge.

But Baker wasn't going to build a house in the meadow. He had his eyes on the old-growth forest of wolf trees on the north slope and the brushed-in fire-scorched downslope of Elk Creek Canyon. Baker built a camping platform out of recycled old-growth redwood beneath the tallest tree in the ancient forest, to remain hidden from the air. He cut sheet metal and folded the pieces into tall cones that he painted military camouflage green and brown, and he scattered plants in them next to emerging fir starts. McGee was clueless. McGee saw marijuana as something exotic that could only be grown in India or Mexico.

By that summer of 1973, after McGee had sold about half of the two thousand acres, he sat with Likowski in the Candlelight. They were at a corner table, away from the gnarly long-haired crowd at the bar. McGee and Likowski were on their third Smirnoff vodka martinis.

I've got an eighty that's perfect for you, McGee said.

Likowski couldn't spring for any of the $1,000-per-acre tracts. He wanted a forty, but those had already been sold off.

It's my last good eighty going for eight. McGee produced a plat map that showed the parcel straddling Elk Creek. A name was scrawled on the adjoining property: "McGowan"; another corner of the property touched "Baker." *It's in the bottom of the canyon. But there's a great house site right here,* McGee said, pointing west of the creek. *And another spot down here at the bottom, but there's no ocean view. The water in that creek is far out. Water just blows down that canyon most of the year. There's good hydro potential. I think you're gonna fall in love tomorrow.*

Likowski showed up early using McGee's directions on a hand-drawn map. He drove for the first time on the road that ran parallel to the river to the sea, reaching wind-ravaged bluffs. Stunted fir were twisted and bent like oversized bonsai, pointed permanently southeast by a never-ending gale out of Alaska. A dirt track jagged uphill to a headland—there was an increasingly expansive blue water view. At the nine-hundred-foot elevation, the grade leveled off. The road went around a point that plummeted to the surf. Likowski hit the brakes and looked down on a red-tailed hawk soaring a few hundred feet below, in silhouette against the white breakers. It was like being in an airplane. If he could make a deal with McGee, he wondered if he would ever get used to this view. The road continued climbing. He crossed a cattle guard that rattled ferociously beneath the tires of his old Ford Falcon and came to an open area. A dirt trail shot off down into a canyon.

He parked. He was to meet McGee at noon. It was ten o'clock. Meadow grasses, browned by the summer sun, swayed in a stiff wind. He grabbed a satchel and walked down the trail, flanked by emerging second-growth fir some ten feet tall and robust poison oak. A few hundred feet down was a relatively flat area. Upcanyon was a stand of old-growth Douglas fir wolf trees. He continued on to Elk Creek, still flowing strong for August. His guessed the flow at about six gallons per minute. He cupped a hand and drank deeply. He returned to the old growth, set the satchel at the base of the largest branchy specimen, and climbed its ladderlike limbs. At a hundred feet, he clung to the trunk some eighteen inches thick; he felt the sway of the tree. There was a view of the river where it met the sea. He clambered to a large branch twenty feet below. He sat on it, legs dangling.

There were shouts of *hello!* McGee was early. Likowski scrambled down. The men exchanged greetings and walked the perimeter of the steep property as best they could, ending at the creek, at the spot where Likowski had drunk its water. They sat on a mossy bank. McGee told him the price wasn't negotiable—eighty acres, $64,000—but that terms were. Because Likowski was putting down nearly half, McGee agreed to finance for five years at 5 percent interest, with the balance due in a balloon. Likowski extracted a brick of one-hundred-dollar bills from the satchel: three $10,000 stacks held together with blue rubber bands. McGee, barely giving it a glance, placed the money in a small backpack. No one ever counted. It wasn't cool. *It'll get recorded at thirty-four thousand,* McGee said. *This never happened.*

Likowski was left with just over $2,000 to his name. That money had to last. There were payments to make until he sold the next season's crop to Jon Barry; he also had to purchase new supplies. If he was raided and lost all his crop, he'd lose the $30,000. *Failure is not an option,* he thought. He had a plan. Full-bore guerrilla. His mantra: *Scatter the patches.*

The men shook and headed up the trail. Halfway, a boy of seven or eight with long blond hair came bounding down the old jeep road. He looked up, startled.

Your mother must be early, McGee said.

The boy merely nodded shyly. He turned and ran back up the trail.

Wo bist du? a woman's voice shouted from above.

Ich komme! the boy yelled.

When Likowski and McGee topped out, a white VW van was parked next to the Falcon. A woman and man stood in front of the vehicles. Both were blond—the man looked very European. The woman was tall and thin. *Meet your new neighbors,* McGee said. *Helmut and Arden.*

Arden is my legal name, the tall woman, looking at McGee, said with a slight German accent, extending her hand. *I go by Zoë.*

For two days after the close of escrow, Likowski indulged in the glow of ownership. He walked the jeep road to where the Falcon was parked, each step on land that he owned. Dipping his hand in the creek, he drank *his* water. When he urinated to excrete that water, he smiled. *I'm pissing on* my *land.* On the third day, it was time to get to work. In the coming months, he explored the farthest depths of two dozen canyons stretching south for eight miles from McGee Ridge. He climbed their walls. He learned all the springs, studied all their branches and feeder streams. On a carefully drawn map, he marked the most promising sites, ranking them on a five scale based on three categories: sun exposure, late summer water potential, and, most important, difficulty. He hoped the cops wouldn't climb dangerous cliffs for just a few plants. The harder to get to, the better. If the cops weeded some patches, they'd miss others. Even if they hit ten patches, he'd still have more than half of his crop.

At most he placed six plants at each spring site. Most had three. There were sixty-four plants in nine canyons. He never camped near the patches. Never pitched a tent unless it was rainy, and when he did, he collapsed it at dawn. Never slept in the same spot twice. Never had a night fire. Between voles, soil conditions, springs that ran dry, stem mold, and termites that infested some stems, he lost nineteen plants. The survivors yielded twenty-six pounds. When he met with Barry at the hotel in town, he apologized for not having more weight.

A few of my growers got weeded. Two were arrested. They're still in jail. You survived the year, man. That's success, Barry said. Top-quality bud was in short supply. Demand was up for premium bud in Los Angeles. He pulled a ten-grand bundle of hundred-dollar bills, a five-grand bundle, counted out $600 in twenties. *Consider it a government price-support program,* Barry said of the raids as he set the money on the round table.

Likowski felt flush enough to start the long process of building a house. He traded in the Falcon and bought a used four-wheel-drive Toyota pickup. He got a bargain on a chain saw mill. Now he needed raw timber. He cut the limbs off a tree he'd felled from the old forest, broke the trunk into sixteen- and twelve-foot sections. He lashed a long, stout chain around the circumference of a section, hooked the chain to the rear of the truck he'd backed uphill. The wheels spun. He couldn't get the log moving. It wasn't a one-man job. This was when Eddie came into the picture.

Eddie Edwards needed work. The previous day, he'd seen a sign posted in the window of the general store next to the post office:

HELP WANTED
PART-TIME. $4 PER HOUR.
GENERAL LABOR. LEAVE CONTACT INFORMATION IN STORE.

He left a note with Bonnie, the clerk. Four bucks an hour was more than twice the minimum wage, and he wanted the job. Eddie dressed. He didn't bother with breakfast beyond downing a piece of bread spread with jam. He went straight to the barn to work on his truck. Just after ten, his mother, Rosina, hollered out the door. *Someone wants you on the phone.*

You still interested in work? the voice on the other end said.

Yeah!

I'm at the store, Likowski said from the pay phone outside. *You free now?*

Yeah!

Let's meet at the Dugout. Ten minutes.

Eddie was five minutes early and waiting when the Toyota pulled up to the Dugout. Likowski liked what he saw. Eddie was muscular. His wide face was eager. He'd work hard. It wasn't as if Likowski had a choice, however. A majority of hippies grew marijuana and didn't want to work for four bucks an hour. And all the kids from the ranching families, save for Eddie, were wary of the newcomers. Eddie was the sole applicant.

Likowski, he said, reaching his hand to shake. Eddie's huge hand engulfed his. Eddie had hand enough for two men.

What's your name?

I go by Likowski.

Okay, Llllik-kow, L-likoski—

Kow.

Eddie ordered a hamburger. He told Likowski that his relatives hated the hippies but that he was in love with one of them, a girl named Liz. *I'm looking forward to seeing her when she comes home at Christmas,* Eddie said.

After lunch, Eddie leaped in Likowski's truck and they drove up to the ridge, where they donned hard hats. Likowski backed the Toyota to the twelve-foot length of trunk. Likowski had felled several understory trees that were some eight inches thick at the base to use as long pry tools.

Pecker poles, Eddie said. *That's what my dad called 'em.*

Likowski hooked a chain to the trunk. Then he put the truck in creeper gear while Eddie wielded one of the massive poles, leveraging it to rock the trunk as the engine gunned. Slowly at first, but with increasing speed, the log began sliding. Likowski floored it—he didn't want the trunk to dig into the earth and cease moving. The log picked up speed and gained on the truck, going faster and faster. Likowski spun the steering wheel left and barely escaped having the log smash into the Toyota. The log continued on, bowling over the mill set upon the sawhorses; the chain jerked the truck backward, pulling it fifteen feet even though Likowski's foot was hard on the brake pedal. Then everything came to a stop. Eddie raced downhill. With the realization that all was okay, both simultaneously burst into laughter.

Uh, maybe I'll pull a little slower next time, Likowski said.

The men rested with their backs against the giant log and drank deeply from a jug of water taken from the creek. Eddie rolled on his side to face the end cut. He counted the rings.

One-hundred-six, Eddie said. He furrowed his brow as he did the math. *That m-means this part of the tree is from 1868.* He glanced uphill at the stump. *The bottom's older. So the tree was here when the Indians were around.* Eddie thought about the raging eyes of Elwin on the wall of his bedroom and how they must have looked when he pulled the trigger and killed the Native Americans.

The mill wasn't damaged. They used pecker poles to raise the massive log and wedge small rounds underneath. They moved the mill next to the log. The ladder was set on stout sawhorses parallel with the log and acted like railroad tracks for the chain saw to cut the trunk into slabs. Likowski had purchased a chain with a special kerf for long cuts. The men donned earmuffs. Likowski fired up the chain saw, began moving it along the ladder rails. A furious snow of chips flew. The smell of Doug fir pitch, sweet and balmy, filled the air. The edge slab, worthless, was set aside.

Let's start with two-by-fours, Likowski said. *Fuck nominal. Let's go true size.* Likowski cranked the setting over at exactly four inches.

Likowski was in excellent shape, but pushing the chain saw along exhausted him. Eddie took a turn halfway through. He was monster strong. Likowski, panting, watched as Eddie made it look effortless. Likowski leveraged a pole beneath the slab as Eddie neared the twelve-foot mark. Still, the saw bounded up from the pressure of the slab beginning to break free; Likowski put his full weight on the pole to hold the wood up until Eddie forced through the last of the cut. It dropped with a thud. It took all they had to pull the green slab out and place it on the side.

Let's make one two-by-four and call it quits for the day, Likowski said.

They reset the mill for two inches. They cut the next slab and then reset the mill for four inches and ran it across that slab. The board fell. Eddie lifted the two-by-four and set it on the tailgate of the Toyota. *It's beautiful,* Eddie said, stroking the wood.

It wasn't that things went twice as fast with Eddie's help in the ensuing week—it increased by a factor of three. During lunch break on the fifth day, the men sat with their backs against a Doug fir trunk. Likowski's eyes were on the growing stack of two-by-fours and six-by-sixes. The flat now resembled a lumber yard. The wood gleamed white. Interior finish boards would come later. That required a planing machine that used electricity, which meant a Pelton wheel powered by water piped from the creek. The nearest utility lines were over three miles away.

Damn, you work hard, Likowski said. *I can't pay you four bucks an hour. I'm giving you five.*

Nope, we made a deal, Kow. A deal's a—

We'll see, Likowski said.

Two days before they'd finished slicing up all the rough wood from the five trees that Likowski had felled, he stood back and watched Eddie muscle through a cut.

I've got an idea, Likowski said when Eddie turned off the chain saw. *Have you thought about growing marijuana? We could partner. Would you be interested?* It wouldn't just double the poundage of bud Likowski could grow—it would triple. Eddie knew the canyons; he'd grown up riding horses down the beach. With a partner, they could take turns tending. Eddie still had horses, and once Likowski learned how to ride, a horse would bring him home four times faster than walking; he could have time to read books.

I dunno. Maybe.

Think about it, Likowski said.

As Likowski slowly built his house at the bottom of Elk Creek Canyon, he also built his brand. Because he'd partnered with Eddie, it gave him free time to dabble in a quest to create the next generation of monster bud. He was perfecting a new variety by crossing Barry's seed with Purple Thai, a sativa, and Panama Red. It made for a plant that was a deep electric burgundy in the afternoon sun; he called it Death Wish because it was so powerful. You wanted to die if you smoked too much of it. It rapidly became Barry's best seller in Los Angeles and the Bay Area. Once people tried it, they wanted more. Other growers wondered how he was doing it. Likowski was a general in the arms race for strong weed—no one was keeping up with him, and his weed fetched a premium price of $900 per pound. His secret, one that only Eddie knew, was that he was practicing light deprivation; he did a crossbreeding with the first crop, and the next crossbreeding had seed from that hybrid by October. Because of depping, he was able to accomplish in three years what took other people six. But he refused to dep his main crop. Depping wasn't pure. His weed was sun-grown, natural.

All through the early years, Likowski remained a mystery to his neighbors. Max and Rita had a house next to the river, where grid power ended, halfway between the hamlet and the hippies on McGee Ridge. The elder couple also had a phone. The river house became a locus for the emerging community. Max and Rita developed a system to notify their neighbors on the ridge if they had phone messages from relatives and friends in distant cities, posting different colors of eight-by-ten-inch card stock in their front window. Purple meant Zoë and Helmut; green, Lauren; blue, Alma and Bill; and on through the rainbow. When all hues of primary colors were taken, latecomers grew creative. One sheet was on purple stock with a triangle cut from yellow paper mounted in the center, another was red stock with a black diamond, and so on. There were fifty-six different sheets. Everyone on McGee Ridge had one—except Likowski. He never showed up at social events at the community center or the July 4 bash at Craig and Maggie Johnson's place. When they drove off the mountain, Zoë Vanderlip and her son sometimes caught flashing glimpses of Likowski at their outer gate, when he rode Luther, his white horse, in a gallop across the road, on his way to the canyon grow sites. He never stopped to talk.

9

IF SIX WAS NINE

Hard rain fell. It struck flesh cold as snow—it wasn't even cracking forty degrees Fahrenheit. Yet three twenty-somethings huddled outside the Fault Zone, one vaping, the other two smoking cigarettes. I was an hour early for meeting up with Lara. The day after finding Likowski's body, I went into coping mode, which is to say I began investigating; she was my first interview. Witnesses said Klaus was at a restaurant on the plaza having dinner with his lawyers until close to the time Likowski was slain. Sure, it could have been a hit initiated by Klaus, but I doubted that scenario. He didn't seem to have much in him now, wounded as he was by his past and threatened by the retrial; he likely saw far more value in playing the victim than in killing his old mentor.

I ordered a coffee and took a seat near the window and read through my notes. I'd already called around about Lara's husband, Frank Serranto. He wasn't dirty as bail bondsmen go. He specialized in marijuana arrests and growers spoke highly of him. He preferred dope busts for two reasons: growers paid cash, and he believed his clients weren't criminals. Election records showed he had donated $10,000 to ballot initiatives to legalize marijuana, which presumably reduced his business.

Promptly at three, Lara came through the door. She wore a blue wool logger's watch cap and a faded Vietnam-era U.S. Army jacket that Likowski wore at Kent State and had given her. Water drops beaded on the cap and jacket. I rose to hug her. She mumbled hello, rapidly took a seat, and looked down at the table.

"Your husband—"

"He didn't do it!" she snapped in a voice foreign to the one I knew from the sweat lodge and dinners at Likowski's. Her eyes were full of fire.

"He's the obvious choice," I said gently. "If the cops ever get to this, they are going to ask you these questions. It's a story as old as the Bible. The jealous husband—"

"It wasn't him!" she said in a near shout. She caught herself and looked around the coffeehouse. Most patrons wore headphones hooked to devices and were oblivious. "*Mi scusi*," she said softly. "Listen to me. When I met Frankie I called him 'my geezer lover.' Everyone thought I married him for a green card. It wasn't that at all. I'd never met a hippie. He showed me many discoveries. He opened my eyes to so many factors. It was magic, even though he was important, impo—how you say— There is no delicate way to say this. His dick didn't work too well."

"Impotent."

"Yes. He had cancer—of the prostate. I warned him that I like sex. That I would have lovers. Maybe many lovers. It was understood. He just didn't want to know about them. He didn't mind the little ones, the ones that come and go, uh, how you say, 'flings.' But Danny was different. I wanted to have a child with him. When Frankie learned of our plans, he got very upset. Then Danny was shot..."

She cried. I handed over my unused napkin. She wiped the tears.

"So he was angry?"

"Not upset angry. Upset sad. We had a talk two days before Danny died. Frankie knew he was going to lose me. He said, 'I understand. I knew it would not last. I just hoped it would last longer.' There is a Tibetan Buddhist retreat he goes to. So he went there."

"When?"

"Saturday. The night before Danny was shot."

"Where is it?"

"Santa Cruz. In the mountains."

"He could've driven back."

"You can call I guess and see if he was there. But I am telling you, he did not shoot Danny. It is not his way."

"Does he own a machine gun?"

"He has guns, but I do not know if they shoot like that."

We drank coffee for another hour. I asked who was going to get Likowski's land. She had no idea.

"I cannot think about that," she said when I brought up the missing money. "I don't care," she said. Lara periodically broke into tears. "I cannot remain here. It is too..." She looked at the empty ceramic cup in front of her. "Too heavy on my mind. I am thinking of going back to Italy."

I asked about going to school at Berkeley. She shrugged. My last words to Lara were not to make any rash decisions. Rain still sheeted down when we emerged from the coffeehouse. It was dark. As Lara walked down the block away from me, she seemed so diminished. But perhaps I was projecting my own state of mind.

I stayed in town that night after coffee with Lara. The next morning I called the Buddhist retreat—Lara's husband was still there. Then I went to the courthouse and county administrative offices. My primary mission was to look up the property records for Two Galaxies Enterprises but also to see if anything had been filed regarding Likowski's estate. I sat on a stool in the recorder's office and typed in the corporation's name in the computer and nearly fell off my seat: a deed transfer came up on the screen from the Daniel T. Likowski Living Trust to Two Galaxies Enterprises LLC. Likowski's eighty acres had sold for $1.5 million, recorded the previous day. A living trust is created by someone putting their affairs in order. In one of these documents the creator of the trust names an executor and spells out how their assets will be distributed upon their death, so an estate does not have to go through court probate. Likowski was taking care of business. A living trust is not part of any public record. No name was on file with the assessor, so it was impossible to tell who had inherited the place.

I dug deeper on Two Galaxies Enterprises LLC, incorporated in the Caymans. As for the land itself, J.D.'s acreage was registered solely in the company name with the county assessor. The state's division of corporations had a president and secretary listed, but their names didn't appear in any databases. They were either exceptionally private people or fictional. I researched the voluminous legal cases in which Two Galaxies was cited, focusing on several lawsuits filed in Connecticut. A section of one suit named several dozen companies that did business with the litigant, "Two Galaxies Enterprises, aka JDK Group." JDK was a hedge fund managed by James David Kammerman. A *New York Times* business blog post said JDK's primary strategy was investing in firms owned by Russian oligarchs, but that it also was now involved with companies in the marijuana industry—online payment systems and vaping oil. The article said that "J. D. Kammerman could not be reached for comment." Other stories described Kammerman as reclusive and press shy.

Everything stunk about Kammerman: Likowski was on the verge of testifying against him in Sacramento about the water diversions; the hearing was scheduled for April. And now here was the sudden purchase of Likowski's land immediately after his death. But who had sold it? Who had Likowski's given it to, if not Lara?

I spent the remainder of that night composing a letter at my desk in the crow's nest. The next morning, when there was enough sun on the photovoltaic panels to turn on the printer, I folded the document after it came out of the machine and placed it in an envelope. I went up my road and walked south past Zoë's gate. A half mile beyond, signs announced NO TRESPASSING in foot-tall letters. There was a solar-powered keypad entry gate and two cameras mounted on tall steel poles on either side. Confident my presence would be detected, I climbed over the gate and walked uphill. The forest floor glistened in shafts of sunlight that found a way through the canopy.

Around a bend, the rutted dirt road forked. The right branch was paved with concrete wide as an interstate, and it led to a huge structure with an angular metallic roof visible through the trees: Kammerman's mansion. The track to the left went down to the greenhouses. Here a man with an assault rifle stepped out of the woods onto the dirt fork, about one hundred feet from me. A second man materialized from behind a big Douglas fir next to the road leading to the manse; what little existed of his hair, dyed Goth black, was cut in a Mohawk—Earl, one of Jenny's former partners. Needless to say, Earl had not aged well. His face was heavily lined. He was missing two front teeth. And the .45 pistol in my coat pocket wasn't going to help with any problems I might have with him.

"You're trespassing," Earl growled. "Leave now."

"Tell Mr. Kammerman I have evidence that connects him to the murder of Dan Likowski. Here's a letter for your boss. I've left a copy and all the documentation with friends, told them I was coming here this afternoon. I want to talk with him."

"He don't talk to no one," Earl said, stepping toward me. He took the letter.

"Well, I hope he gets in touch before I go to the cops. Have a good day." I turned on my heel and went down the long lane toward Kammerman's gate, not looking back. Only then did I begin shaking. How had I gotten here? From searching for Zoë to hunting Likowski's killer?

I was tapped out, didn't want to see anyone, ignored the ringing phone. I spent the next few days with my back against a tree down in the forest, nights in the hot tub, the .45 always nearby. I had a lot of time to think about Likowski and the arc of his life interlocking with Zoë, Klaus, all our neighbors, and the larger history that haunted them in postwar America. Through them all it became clear that the end of the sixties had an agonizingly slow death, one that outlasted the decade itself. That night Likowski drove over the Golden Gate Bridge in 1970, he knew nothing would change. Likowski understood this much when he watched the ROTC building burn: The students were lashing out as children might, in what amounted to a tantrum against the monstrous entity arrayed against them. They were just helpless children fighting the military-industrial complex.

I could relate. In my youthful naïveté, I thought I could change the world with my work. Could Zoë and Likowski and even me be blamed—if "blame" is a word that should even be used—for exercising the option to vanish into this wilderness, to be so audacious as to attempt the creation of something new, a society inside the legal and political confines of a nation that had betrayed us, would continue to betray us; to create, even on the smallest of scales, something that was true to that nation's purported values, or at least the ideals we espoused and fought for in our youth? When we disappeared behind the sanctuary of these redwoods, we never wanted to look back at Amerika.

There are markers for when the sixties ceased: Hunter S. Thompson argues it was Altamont; others point to the sixty-seven shots fired at Kent State; Joan Didion cites that night on Cielo Drive. But they're wrong. The conclusion of that decade occurred over five hundred miles north of Benedict Canyon, and it didn't happen until a half century later.

Craig Johnson sawed, shaped, and carved the coffin in that week before the coroner released Likowski's body. An excellent weed grower, Craig was an even more adept woodworker. (I knew this because I'd hired him to make new cabinets in my cabin after I landed a good book advance.) Craig invested sixteen-hour days into that coffin, making it from fine-grained locally milled Douglas fir and laurel, and he forged wrought-iron handles. There were six inlaid panels, three on each side, depicting a delicate marijuana leaf, a riderless AOC at a gallop, and Likowski's Toyota 4x4 truck. The coffin was stained and covered in several coats of acrylic sealer—a work of art with Likowski inside that now sat on the floor of the stage at the front of the community center.

I'd come early. The hall was empty save for me and Likowski's remains. I set my coat on a chair in the front row and studied the white clapboard walls lined with dozens of posters from all the cabarets that had ever been held since the hippies took control of the old schoolhouse. The first, from 1974, was titled *California Dreamin'*. It depicted a bearded flower child with long hair, a bandanna, and a tattered cape; he was meditating in a meadow surrounded by flowers. A butterfly flew next to his ear, and a thought bubble came out of his head that showed the Golden Gate Bridge in the upper left, a van chugging along on a road heading north; there were redwoods, and in the bottom right were hippies on a beach, a surfer. The posters from the middle years depicted the realities of hippie life. One cabaret was called *Fixin' a Hole*. The artwork showed rainwater leaking from a ceiling into a bucket and a woman next to an infant in a crib. One of the last, *The Times They Are a-Changin'*, reflected fears about falling weed prices. The freaked-out, wide-eyed hippie looking in a window of Ye Olde Smoke Shop was a characterization of Likowski, wearing his cowboy hat and very much resembling the Marlboro Man. Written above plates of bud displayed in the window: HARVEST SALE! and PRICES SLASHED! Name tags were marked BULLSHIT. GREEN CRACK. Prices ranged from $4.99 to $5.99.

I stared at the coffin four feet away. People filed in. No one talked. There was just the sound of feet shuffling on the old pine flooring. A half hour before the service, every chair was occupied; people sat on the floor, up the stairwell. All windows were opened and latecomers crowded outside each one. Then Lara and Tammie arrived. Bob and Alma gave up their seats in the third row; they joined the others looking in from the exterior. Likowski wasn't at all religious. There would be no preacher. Doc Anderson would fill that role. Already, he stood at the microphone, holding a paper with the eulogy written on it, but he never looked at it. Instead, as he spoke, he folded it into ever smaller squares until he couldn't anymore and replaced it in his pocket.

"I first want to address the elders, most of you as I look around this room, and from what I can see of those of you in the windows. When we came here almost fifty years ago, us men with far more hair on our heads and less in our ears and on our lower backs, we desired to leave society. We took part in the first Earth Day. Some of us read Rachel Carson, and we understood that society had to change but that society wasn't going to change, and if we were going to have any impact on ourselves, we had to create a new society for ourselves. We all had different motives that drove us here. I wanted a place that was away from America where I could speak in English, and I don't mean that in a xenophobic way. In this hemisphere that left my choices as Canada and Belize and Guyana—and here. I didn't want to live in Belize or Guyana or Canada. We all shared the same desire, and what united us was our trying to create something new, something beautiful.

"We lived in teepees and tents, and we literally built our houses and our world with our own hands. We focused on the base of Maslow's pyramid. We developed water systems. We put roofs over our heads. We planted beans, we planted carrots, we planted kale before anyone out there back where we came from knew what the hell kale was. Mizuna too. We lived off the land. We shot wild pigs and deer. We harvested mussels. We used to find pearls in them—I haven't found a pearl in years. That may be telling us something. Some of us got cows and goats, and we didn't know anything about how to raise cows and goats, but we learned. We viewed growing a carrot or raising a cow as a revolutionary act. Each carrot was one that we didn't have to buy from Safeway, from some corporate farm using seeds from Monsanto, chemicals from Dow, oil from the Middle East.

"But we discovered that man and woman cannot live by carrots alone. Our way of life was not all that sustainable. We had to burn nearly a full tank of gas each time we went back and forth to town. Carrots didn't buy clothes for our children, fence posts, nails, feed, a whole bunch of things. Many of us discovered that marijuana could provide us with an income.

"People on the outside have no idea how very difficult work this was back in those days. People planted beneath camouflage netting in forest openings; they guerrilla farmed like Dan Likowski and Eddie Edwards down the coast; they had big baskets and ran to cover plants each time they heard a helicopter. Carlos, I know you're out there somewhere, I think you still have PTSD every time you hear a helicopter. One of our neighbors—I see Thomas sitting on the stairs—he grew in the tops of trees, in what pretty much were giant hanging flowerpots. Thirty plants in fifteen trees. Each day, twice a day, Thomas climbed eighty feet into the canopy of those fifteen trees, jugging water by rope. Do you know how heavy water is? I know because I helped him one day. You had to be crafty. CAMP wasn't looking in the tops of trees. Each dollar was hard-earned.

"I am not a grower. I don't mean what I'm about to say with any disrespect to my neighbors who grow, and I know that my income as a medical doctor derived from that work, but we in fact, pardon my pun, were sowing the seeds of our own destruction. We didn't think of the endgame. We thought a day like today would never happen. I wonder how the outcome could have been different. We are here to mourn the death of our neighbor, our friend, Dan Likowski. But we are also gathered here today to mourn us. All of us have died a little bit with his passing.

"I had a revelation last night when I was walking along the river, thinking about Dan, thinking about what I was going to say today. The water ran dark and fast. The wind was in the willows, in the fir in the hills—that *whoo-whoo*ing of the wind that we all live with—and if I closed my eyes, these sounds transported me back to 1972, the first year on my land, when I lived in a tent on the bank and I was more in tune with listening to the voice of the river and the earth. The ecology of the river has changed, yes, there are almost no salmon left, but

I'm certain the river and the wind in the trees sounded the same as 1872 and 1772. What is one hundred years to this ecosystem? That's one-billionth of one second in the scheme of nature. I realized that we're just the latest chapter in a long history that is particular to the American West. We live in a land of successively doomed societies, each usurped by violence, cultural or economic imperialism. The Native Americans had this land from the Ice Age forward. Then Coronado arrived in what is now called Mexico. I say 'arrived,' but that began the conquest, the defeat of the indigenous peoples of western North America, until the Spanish themselves were defeated by Winfield Scott and what is now the state of California was stolen from the Mexicans—Aztlán. The mountain man was defeated by the pioneer. We hippies defeated the children of the pioneers. And now we hippies are being defeated by agribusiness that is making marijuana into just another industrial product.

"Our way of life is gone. Maybe we were our own worst enemy. Where did we fail? What went wrong? I don't know, there is no precise moment that I can think of. Perhaps this end was inevitable. What is not inevitable—and now I am speaking to the younger people, the second generation, the third generation—is controlling what we do with this change, controlling what we do with loss. For in loss is the true nature of an individual revealed. We have become an aggressive and secretive culture that tolerates sexual trafficking, that tolerates rape, that tolerates treating people as disposable commodities. There's an epidemic of missing people in this county. The world out there, what Edward Abbey called 'syphilization,' has also grown uglier, darker, and maybe we are just a microcosm of that society, a society riven with greed. But I would still like to think that we are better than outside society. I know that so many of you are good people, you treat your workers well, like you, Sequoia. But we are being overshadowed by the few bad players. We need to fight against the culture of darkness. I know I'm sounding like some kind of evangelical preacher, but I don't know how else to say it.

"This community, what is left of it, has suffered severe blows in the last year. The disappearance of a matriarch, Zoë Vanderlip. And now the violent death of Daniel Likowski, a man we all loved. We don't know what happened to Zoë. We don't know who killed our neighbor, or how his death and her vanishing fit in the mosaic of the downward spiral we have been in, but we do know there is some connection, and what we do know is that we have to stop this descent. And as we now go to bury one of our own, we should honor Daniel Likowski by living as he did, in peace, with love, and remembering why we came here in the first place, if not to change the world, then to change our own worlds."

Doc Anderson sat. I expected a stream of eulogies. I'd planned on talking. I had a long speech about what Likowski confessed to me that epic night in the sweat lodge, about his stealing the explosives, flirting with the Weather Underground, changing his name, running from the law for decades, and I was going to capstone that magnificent tribute with, *In the end, they never got him.* And the kicker, Abbie Hoffman: *The first duty of a revolutionary is to get away with it.* Likowski got away with it. But I didn't give that eloquent homage. What could anyone say after Doc Anderson's eulogy, a requiem not just for Don Lapinsky / Dan Likowski, but for all of us? I sure as hell didn't want to stand up. We were all simply numbed by the death and seared by the eloquence of Doc's words.

I looked at my fellow pallbearers—Doc, Sequoia, Bill, Andy, Johnny Gray—and without a word we stood and each took one of the wrought-iron handles created earlier that week by Craig on his forge. We lifted the coffin and carried it out into that sunny March day, to an ancient farm wagon with massive gray wood-spoked wheels drawn by AOC and Buck, now being cared for by Craig until Eddie was released from custody and he could reclaim his horse. We slid the coffin into the wood-plank bed of the wagon, pushing it against two massive speakers. Pallbearers got to ride on the cart, so I jumped up and leaned against the deep red-golden inlaid marijuana leaf on the coffin. Others went to cars and trucks for the funeral procession. Craig took the reins. Bill sat between the speakers; he hit "play" and Jimi Hendrix's "If 6 Was 9" boomed. The coffin vibrated against my back from Jimi's guitar as the long line of vehicles inched behind us at horse speed.

We rolled north, through the hamlet, with Bill DJing songs from the *Easy Rider* soundtrack. It was sunny, but the temperature was in the mid-fifties. We passed the Purple Thistle, where strangers seated at window tables stared blankly. Clouds of fog hung in the hills to the east. I looked over the coffin in the direction of McGee Ridge, also lost in a fog bank.

The road leveled out on the table, and we reached the cemetery overlooking the hamlet. Craig halted the wagon fifty yards from the site of the interment. Everyone else jumped off, but I remained on the wagon, legs dangling over the side. It was my moment to say goodbye. I closed my eyes and conjured Likowski. When I opened them, I did a three-sixty. To the south, the red-tiled roof of Klaus's house rose just over the tops of a line of fir. To the immediate north was a grove of towering century-old eucalyptus. Vehicles parked at the edge of the main road, and people streamed beneath the iron entry arch. The Asian woman I'd talked with at the Purple Thistle last year was amid the mourners. She walked directly to me, wearing a jet-black knee-length merino wool dress and Dior shades.

"Hello, Will."

I just stared at the woman. I was in no mood for her bullshit.

"My name's J.J."

She extended a hand to shake. I hesitated only a second.

"How'd you know him?" I asked. My voice sounded dead and cold to myself.

"I'll tell you after."

It was only then that I saw a tear run down her cheek; she removed her glasses to wipe it away. Her eyes were red from crying.

"Okay."

She went off and was lost in the crowd.

We slid the coffin off the wagon and carried it to the edge of the hole, lowering Likowski with straps into the depths of the earth.

Bill let the strap slack. He lit a joint and spoke to the coffin. "Remember what it was like in the old days? Before it was legal. They sent their best to get us, but it wasn't good enough." Bill took a drag from the joint. He held in the smoke an abnormally long time, pausing for great effect. He exhaled. "We were better, Kow." He gently tossed the joint into the hole, ending his private eulogy.

Neil Young's "Sugar Mountain" blasted from the wagon speakers as my neighbors took turns shoveling dirt and smoking weed. Then I noticed a woman, a stranger, standing alone beneath the eucalyptus. Arms tightly crossed, she could have been in the stands at a sporting event, watching the opposing team she absolutely loathed. The woman had thin white hair and a wrinkled face, and she wore a loose-fitting black dress and woolen black coat, the black leather strap of her purse lashed across her chest like a bandolier. Craig, next to me, was murmuring about the time Likowski helped rescue a horse trapped on an island when the river was in flood. I barely listened. I was focused on the woman in the trees, who noticed me observing her; she looked away. I headed toward the eucalyptus. As I neared, the woman began moving. I hurried after her. Eucalyptus bark, reminiscent of human skin shed after a bad sunburn, crunched loudly beneath my feet.

"Hello, my name's Will Specter," I said, extending a hand as I caught up to her. She refused to shake and kept walking.

"How did you know him?" she demanded in a tone just short of hostile.

"I was his neighbor. I live right above his house. How about you? How did you know Mr. Likowski?"

"I never knew that man!" she said firmly, but growing agitated. "And the other one died a long time ago."

"I'm not sure I understand."

"No, no," she said, "You wouldn't."

I studied the old woman, whose steely eyes grazed mine briefly, and in that moment something familiar flickered. Before I could ask anything else, she walked away with a hand held up to keep me at bay.

"Please," she said quietly. "I want to be left alone."

After the service, J.J. followed my battered 1995 Chevy truck to the ridge in her Ferrari, which were now parked side by side in front of my cabin, an anachronistic pairing if there ever was one. This plan had been hatched with limited conversation and as others made their way to a gathering at Doc's house.

By the time we opened a second bottle of wine, Hydra was high in the southern sky. J.J. wanted to tell me a long story and it began with her family history, which she insisted I needed to know in order for me to understand her connection to Klaus, and Zoë. Her paternal grandfather, Jingwe, was a general in Chiang Kai-shek's army who fled to Taiwan after 1949, where he was called *nèidì zhū*—mainland pig. Her maternal grandfather, Shau-Jin, was a physicist who came to America before the war. He taught at Caltech, where he met Tsien Hsue-shen, the scientist involved with the Manhattan Project, who helped make the atomic bombs ultimately dropped on Japan. When McCarthy was at his zenith, Grandfather Shau-Jin and Tsien were accused of being communists. Tsien was deported to mainland China, Shau-Jin to Taiwan. J.J.'s parents met in Berkeley when they came to the United States for college. They were caught up in the sixties, running away from family and personal histories, and just like the white hippies, they disappeared into the redwoods. Her parents bought 120 acres in the foothills of the Trinities, at the end of a long dirt road. J.J. was born on the homestead, an only child.

"They really went dark," she whispered. "They retreated from the world, even more than Likowski. But at least I had my books."

"Were you the only—"

"The only Asian growers?" she cut me off, saving me from asking the awkward question. Her smile was a little crooked, generous but tough. "No. There was a Japanese man." This man, J.J. told me, had lived on the ridge near Zoë back in the 1970s. "But I was the only Asian girl in grade school," she added.

Like Zoë and her son, J.J.'s mother moved to town her freshman year of high school, where she met Klaus. She came down to the Ark several times in those early years of high school. J.J. appeared to be the child Zoë longed for. She studied furiously, and because of her 4.0 average, a 1590 SAT score, and her essay about her parents being Mandarin-speaking weed growers (with a statue of Guan Yu, the red-faced god, set amid the marijuana plants), she was offered a place in the Class of 1988 at Stanford. The admissions committee must have loved her file. Diversity. Brilliance. And a great backstory. That she was interested in computers and engineering surely made committee members further swoon; back then, she was truly a pioneer for women in STEM. J.J. made a lot of money in the Silicon Valley, both during the dotcom era and the later boom; she now lived in Woodside, not far from Neil Young's ranch.

It was after midnight and the wine was nearly gone. We stepped outside, and as we did J.J. drew close and put her arms around me; we kissed. We ended up in the hot tub. Later, I held her with her back against my chest, as she floated on top of the hottest water. We faced the Milky Way and Hydra.

"Do you know what Helmut did to Klaus?" she asked. I nodded. She confirmed what I'd suspected. "I think what happened to Zoë also had an impact."

I agreed.

"She told me about it one night. It started when she was nine or ten, and it went on for a long time. That is some serious trauma to pack in your luggage. And it got handed to Klaus."

She climbed out of the hot tub and I followed. We sat naked in the cold air, bodies steaming. Then she told me about something that happened between them in eleventh grade: Klaus pinned her when they were having sex. He finally stopped and apologized when he realized he'd scared her—in fact, he began to cry. Still, after that, she distanced herself from Klaus. It was more than that incident. They were diverging anyway, as people do in high school. Nerds with nerds, jocks with jocks. He had already fallen in with the stoners. Being an over achiever, J.J.'s circles rarely overlapped with his as they approached graduation. Decades later, she was drawn to reconnect. They met occasionally for dinner, when he was driving south to his Malibu place or she came north.

"He's not as bad as you think," J.J. said. "I know how that sounds. Yes, he has done bad things. I believe he raped those women." She fell silent for a minute, and then she gestured to the distant shadowy peaks of the Coast Range. "If he hadn't grown up here, with everything that was done to him—the place itself *does* something to some people. And then there was—there is—Zoë. Have you seen what Chinese parents do to their children? Jingjing in Mandarin means 'perfect essence.' Chinese parents name their children what they most fear they will not become. My mom puts Zoë to shame. She pushed me hard. But Zoë pushed him too."

"You still love the kid Klaus *was*," I affirmed. "You think he's still in there somewhere."

"I believe we never lose ourselves entirely; we just lose sight. He's lost sight," she said, more to herself, before shuddering.

The surf was loud and growing louder with wind coming off the sea. We were cold and plunged back into the 104-degree water. J.J. dipped her head. When she came up she shook her hair and wiped water from her eyes.

"Why'd you come?" I asked her.

"To the funeral?"

I nodded, and she stared up at the black expanse above us.

"I guess this was my funeral for Zoë," she said finally. "She loved Klaus so much. I always admired it, even if it felt like too much."

"Do you think Zoë killed herself?"

"Yes," she said resolutely. "She didn't want to see what was about to happen to Klaus. She was tough."

I must have looked sad. She embraced me again, her skin against mine feeling incredibly alive in the hot water. "I have to go now," she said quietly, and rose again out of the water.

"But it's after three in the morning."

"I have to go."

I hate flying. It has nothing to do with fear. Each day spent in an airport and cocooned in a metal cylinder hurtling through the lower levels of the stratosphere is one lost day from life. But here I was, circling over the Mojave Desert on the descent into McCarran International Airport. I didn't want to waste the nearly two days of driving time.

Rose Warner had not been difficult to find, and her postrevolutionary history was all in the public record. After her conviction on explosives and weapons charges, she was sentenced to the Alderson Federal Prison Camp for women in West Virginia. She served only two years.

While in prison she became an evangelical Christian. When she was released, she moved to Orange County in California, where she married Harry Warner, a developer who was also devoutly Christian, and joined him in his business. They built tract homes in places like Fountain Valley, where there was no fountain and no valley, and Lake Forest, where there was no lake and no forest. Rose became involved in Republican politics. She gave testimonials about how she had repented for her Weather Underground days, and she donated heavily to Republican candidates, including Reagan when he ran for president in 1980. Then the couple invested in a Las Vegas project that went belly-up. Harry died in 1998. Rose still lived in Vegas—I had an address from property records. The deed remained in her husband's name.

I rushed away from all the clanging slot machines and headed to the rental car desk. Soon I was navigating the looping roads of suburban Las Vegas, past identical red-tile-roofed homes crammed next to one another, past identical abbreviated front yards of decomposed granite or pebbles spotted with stubby palm trees or cacti. The GPS took me to one of them, windows shrouded by drawn curtains. I rang the bell. When nothing happened for a long time, I knocked loudly. The door eventually opened—just a crack, only wide enough to see Rose's right eye and its familiar gaze. I was looking at the woman from the eucalyptus grove at Likowski's burial. I can't say I was surprised. This had been my hunch. It was midafternoon, but she clearly had just woken up; she looked awful.

"Hello, Mrs. Warner, we met at the funeral."

"Mr.... Mr. . . ."

"Specter. Will Specter. But just call me Will."

"Mr. Specter, I don't feel like talking." She started to close the door.

"Rose!" I said, and she hesitated. "I had to come by, to ask about the sale of your brother's property."

"What good was it to me?"

"But being sold that fast, right before the funeral, to a guy he hated—it doesn't look good."

The door reopened just enough to show a single tired eye again, framed in countless lines; she was old but looked older.

"I only discovered that my brother left me his property when some woman telephoned two days after Don was killed. After some negotiations we came to terms. I had no idea about any man or his relationship to Don."

"It's a lot of money, Mrs. Warner."

She let out a long sigh. "I suppose he told you about me."

"Yes."

"I suppose he told you that I ratted him out, that I spilled my guts to the FBI to save my own hide."

"He didn't use those exact words—"

"His perspective is warped! There is a lot more to that story, Mr. ..."

"Specter. But just call me Will. I'd like to hear your side of things. I promise I won't take up too much of your time."

The door opened wide. She beckoned me to enter, waving weakly with her right hand. The house had an open-floor plan and everything was white: the faux marble floor tiles, the walls, all the furniture. Rose sat on a long white West Elm couch. I sat in a soft white recliner opposite.

"His view is skewed by the fact that he never repented and continued a life of illegality, how he made a living, how all of you grow marijuana—"

"I'm a writer. I don't grow."

"Are you going to write about my brother?"

An honest answer risked immediately losing her and being thrown out of her house. Or she would spill. The needle of my instincts shot wildly back and forth—it could go either way.

"Yes."

"Please do not portray him in a heroic manner. He was a coward. I remained to pay the price for our crimes. I went to prison. I paid my debt to society. He never paid his. He ran off. Gone!"

Rose launched into a long story about how in prison she found Jesus and repented, how her brother lived an illegitimate life and died by the hand of that sword; she talked about my neighbors smoking weed and dancing after the burial and how she was horrified. "It was not a proper funeral. Do you understand how broken our mother was by Don vanishing? He never once tried to get in touch. We assumed he had died. Our mother wept almost every day. On her deathbed, she was delirious. She cried out, 'Don! Where is Don? Why isn't Don here?' Do you understand why I am angry?"

She told me Likowski had phoned her about two years ago. She thought it was a scam. He convinced her and said it was time for reconciliation. "He invited me to visit. He begged me. But I wouldn't have it," she said, not without some pride. "I told him I would talk with him but I didn't want to see him. Too much time had passed for reconciliation. It was like talking to a ghost."

"Then why did you come to the funeral?"

"I went solely for our mother. She would have wanted me to be present. I could not have lived with myself if I had not done that for her. I said my prayers—for her." Rose admitted that she also went for herself—she didn't have long to live. She had cancer. She reflected on her life and talked about her long-deceased husband. "We were very successful, Mr. Specter. We were successful because of hard, honest work. Plain, simple hard work and believing in God. God blessed us. When we lost everything, it was God's will, God's way of testing us. Please do not portray me as 'evangelical.' I am not evangelical as it is defined by the media. I do not belong to any church. Those of us who believe in the Word are not a monolithic group. Harry and I never went to church. We read the Bible every day. But church, never. All these churches, they have the cross as a symbol. You see these churches with three crosses. That is the mark of the Beast, plain and simple. Six-six-six. Three crosses. Those crosses don't mean anything other than crucifixion. They do not represent salvation. They all have the cart before the horse, they have everything backward. The cross is an instrument of death, not of life. The way I read the Bible, it condemns those people. These evangelical churches, they all act like the preacher is God. Those who believe in these preachers are following false gods. There is only one to follow, his name is Jesus. The Bible says there is no other name under heaven given among men whereby you must be saved—"

"I have to ask," I said. "Why do you think your brother wanted you to have his property?"

"Guilt, Mr. Specter. Pure, unadulterated guilt."

I remained silent. When she added nothing, I didn't push—her eyelids were drooping and she looked worse than when she'd opened the door.

"Thank you, Rose," I said gently. "I appreciate you talking to me. Before I go, just one last question. What are you going to do with the money?"

"I am donating it to the state Republican Party. You can check with them. It is all in the public record. Money I do not need. Not now. I have been living on my Socialism Security."

"If you call it 'socialism,' why do you take it?"

"I was forced to pay into it. I put money in, I'm going to take it out. A fool I am not."

On my way home from the airport, I stopped at the Purple Thistle. It was nine o'clock, but the place was empty save for a couple seated at a table and an old rancher at the far end of the bar.

"Hey, Will," Jake said.

I sat on a stool at the bar. It was almost a month after the hung jury. "I was hoping to find Klaus."

"Haven't seen him."

My skepticism must have showed.

"Seriously. No one's seen him around."

"Looks like that's bad for you."

"Yep. Business is way the hell down."

"If you have any of that Weller 107 left, I'll have one. Neat."

Jake tore the seal off a fresh bottle, an indication that indeed Klaus had not been around. No one other than Klaus could afford it. I pounded the Weller. I went to pay, but Jake said, "On me."

I drove to Klaus's and pushed the gate buzzer. I left my car parked in front of the locked gate and jumped it to walk up the quarter-mile drive. The house was dark. There were no vehicles present. I knocked loudly. All the shades were drawn. It felt like no one had been around in days.

I went home and fired up the hot tub, spent two hours in it until Hydra appeared low on the horizon, the .45 within reach at the tub's edge.

A shout awakened me early one morning. "Specter!" I pulled back a tiny corner of the blind. A ragged man with a black Mohawk and dressed entirely in black stood outside my cabin. I opened the door a crack.

"What's going on, Earl?"

"Mr. Kammerman will meet with you. Friday."

"Where?"

Earl looked at me as if I were an idiot. "The house."

"When?"

"Ten."

"Morning?"

"Night," Earl said as he turned away.

"Don't be so gabby," I said to Earl's back.

It was Wednesday. I had two days. I locked my front door and went to my bedside, where the BAR leaned against the wall. I thought about my early journalism life, when I'd alternated working in factories and going to college until a gig came up at a small newspaper and I dropped out. I couldn't believe someone was paying me to write words and not operate a lathe or Bridgeport milling machine. The paper's circulation was publicly listed at thirty-three thousand, but the publisher pulped ten thousand copies to inflate what he charged advertisers. Pay was $120 a week gross, $91 take home.

In that newsroom you were either on your way up or on your way down the ladder of journalistic achievement. I wanted a larger playing field, I wanted the West, but a steady stream of self-addressed stamped envelopes filled my mailbox, returning the clips mailed to California with failed applications. I needed a big score. I'd heard about an underground dog-fighting ring and did some digging, got connected with sources. *Ohio Magazine* commissioned the story. I went undercover to training fights. Those dog fighters were more paranoid than meth cookers, and they all had guns. When the guys started trusting me, I was invited to the clandestine fighting pits, where there was serious betting. I packed my father's .45 from the war. Dad, who grew up on the tough south side, always said, *Once you pull a gun, you'll have two choices: use it, or back down. And if you back down, you'll have that gun shoved up your ass.*

Would I have shot a dog fighter? Maybe. That's how bad I wanted that story so I didn't end up back in the factories, which was a distinct possibility. Finally, one of my stories—this one—got noticed; it won awards. Mike, the assistant managing editor at the *Los Angeles Times*, heard me speak at an Investigative Reporters and Editors conference. We went to dinner that night and he asked me to come to the *Times*. I'd been plucked from the journalistic Little League to play in the majors. Yet the fairy tale came with a price tag. Mike wanted a risk-taker, someone childless and single. I was sent to all the hot spots: El Salvador and other conflict zones, and Mexico, to cover the cartel murders. The more I succeeded at these assignments, the more I was typecast for being willing to jump into a fire. So I had to keep jumping into fires.

I was a wreck by Friday evening. I took a deep breath and walked up my road, but I left Dad's .45 behind. People knew I was going in, and Kammerman wouldn't be stupid enough to Khashoggi me. It was a new moon. At the outer gate, a bumper glistened as my headlamp beam raked a white SUV. The vehicle had tinted windows. The driver's-side door opened, a leg emerged. I braced. Out jumped a thin woman with a pixie haircut.

"I'm Nicky, Mr. Kammerman's personal assistant, West Coast." Nicky was dressed in black jeans and a black blouse. She was about thirty-five, and her demeanor was strictly business as she opened the passenger door before I could say that wasn't necessary.

She sped uphill. The gate with the threatening signs automatically swung in. The SUV went up the expansive concrete lane. The mansion and the gleaming white metal exterior, illuminated by floodlights, came into view. Floodlights? The dwelling was as off the grid as my place.

"Mr. Kammerman is attending to business and regrets that he is running about fifteen minutes late. I do hope this does not inconvenience you. He asked that I give you a tour, if you would like."

I followed Nicky up granite steps to a fifteen-foot-tall door with massive hand-forged iron hinges. The wood was dense, four inches thick. I felt the edge.

"Bubinga," she said.

The room, entirely of white marble, had a twenty-foot ceiling. A grand spiral staircase led to an upper level. The chamber was sparsely furnished. There were dozens of light fixtures and the room's brightness was astounding. "All the light!"

She asked if I'd like to see their power system. Nicky led me into a well-stocked kitchen, twice the size of my cabin, with two Viking stoves and a Sub-Zero fridge. Beyond was a dining room with a table that seated twenty-five and a bank of windows facing the dark sea. We exited through French doors and went past a pool that had steam coming off the water. There was a long stucco building with a red-tiled roof. Nicky opened the door and flicked on a light. Before us was an epic battery bank.

"Rolls Surrette cells," Nicky said of the nearly three-foot-tall batteries. My four L-16s weighed about the same as just one of the three-hundred-pound cells. "There are ninety batteries wired to store thirty-six thousand amp hours of power. You are probably wondering how we charge them."

Nicky opened the door on a room containing a Cummins two-thousand-kilowatt diesel generator. "Last year it was only needed on two days."

Nicky went through yet another door leading to a balcony overlooking a hill sloping into a canyon and the sea. Below was an array of photovoltaic panels that reflected starlight so intensely that our faces were cast in a faint blueish light; it hadn't seemed so vast when Likowski and I looked down on it from the top of the mountain.

"Mr. Kammerman intends to expand this array by ten thousand watts so that the generator will never have to be used. His goal is to be absolutely carbon neutral." Nicky looked at her watch. "I believe Mr. Kammerman should be ready."

We wound our way back through the battery building and the kitchen, returning to the marbled entry room. Discreet music played, one of those Café del Mar collections of ambient chill-out. A low round marble table had an urn marked COFFEE, another marked HOT WATER, two cups, a tray of teas, and various sweeteners. There also was a brown legal envelope stuffed thick with papers.

"Please have a seat. Mr. Kammerman will be down shortly."

I sat in one of the well-padded black leather chairs, and Nicky left the room. Five minutes passed. I tapped my fingers to the music. Then footsteps sounded. Kammerman appeared at the top of the staircase. He was about five-six and was possibly the thinnest man I'd ever seen. He wore a long-sleeved white silk shirt, which contrasted nicely with his deep blue eyes; despite his sleight build, he was quite handsome.

"Mr. Specter," Kammerman said as he descended. I stood and we shook. "I would say it is a pleasure to meet you, but not given the topic." He spoke softly and I had to strain to hear. We sat. "Coffee or tea?"

"Coffee, please."

He spoke as he poured. "Let me get right to the point, Mr. Specter. I have nothing to do with the unfortunate tragedy regarding Mr. Likowski. I'm terribly sorry about what happened to your friend."

"And I'll get right to the point, Mr. Kammerman. Two days after Likowski was murdered, someone from your LLC contacted his sister about buying his place. Two days. That defies—"

"We have compiled data on all surrounding properties. We were aware of the living trust when it was filed. My goal is to purchase any contiguous parcels as they become available. When my people contacted me about the unfortunate death of Mr. Likowski, as tragic as that was and as cold as this sounds, it presented us with an opportunity."

"But Rose Warner's name was not on the document."

"Perhaps you did not dig deeply enough." A wan smile came to Kammerman's face.

I waited a moment before reminding him: "Likowski was also set to testify against you."

"I was quite aware of his complaint filed with the Department of Fish and Wildlife. I was proactively involved with the department and his deposition would have been unnecessary. We are in the process of mitigation. We are installing five fifty-thousand-gallon stainless steel tanks to store rainwater for the dry season. As you can see from your brief tour, we have a lot of roof from which to collect water. In addition, I have contracted with a Mr. Pell to build a dam on Elk Creek, which will charge the groundwater table. We will have the ability to release extra water in the late summer for the salmon. There in fact will be more water, colder water, which the salmon prefer, in Elk Creek than if we were not present. I welcome you to visit once everything is installed. I care about the environment, as you can tell from having seen our power system."

He picked up the manila envelope off the marble table and removed a picture of a haggard woman. "Do you recognize this person?"

I studied the photograph. "No," I lied. I was looking at the same woman Lara had taken a photograph of through Likowski's kitchen window.

"She worked in Alpha."

"Alpha?"

"That is the name of one of our structures. There is Alpha, Beta, and now Gamma. She did not technically work for me. She is an independent contractor, if you will. I do not employ people here at Sky Ridge—"

"Sky Ridge?"

"What I call the farm. Let me confess my personal interest. In the scheme of JDK Group, what we are doing here does not even register as pennies. The real money will come from distribution and supplies when marijuana becomes legal nationwide. Do you realize the metric tonnage of marijuana that is annually consumed in this country? It is simply stunning. The real money will be in CBD oil. Can we be really off the record?"

I nodded.

"We are developing a stable seed strain that is seventeen percent CBD and just point-six THC. It is the ideal medical marijuana. We are registering the brand. Soon there will be no growing here at all. The isolation of Sky Ridge was a plus in the developmental phase for this strain. Now for commercial purposes, the isolation is a hindrance. With it now being legal, we have purchased a warehouse near Coalinga for indoor growing. We will scale up.

"I created Sky Ridge for a different reason. My favorite parts of the year are when I am here. Once I retire, which I hope will happen soon, I'll be full-time here. For the record, I do not intend to do any harm to Mr. Likowski's property. My plans will honor his legacy. I will tear down his house and renaturalize the site. I will do more to restore Elk Creek. I'm quite eager to see salmon once again spawning in the lower reaches in the cold water released by our new dam."

I steered him back to the woman, whose picture I kept staring at on the table next to my coffee.

"Sarah Kimberly Johnson was attached to Alpha. She vanished immediately following the murder of Mr. Likowski. It is in my interest to protect my business interests, so I had my people investigate. Ms. Johnson has been spending numerous hundred-dollar bills in Los Angeles. We believe she is the one who killed Mr. Likowski."

"How are you so sure? Maybe she's just blowing her pay."

"She's spending more than she would have earned. Far more. All of the documentation is here. She has a history of petty theft and dealing methamphetamines."

"Any violent crimes?"

"No."

"Jumping to murder is quite a graduation."

"Money has ways of motivating people, Mr. Specter."

"Of course."

"I was trying to figure out how to get this to the authorities when your letter was emailed to me. I'm asking you to hand this over. Say that you did the investigation. But please keep my name out of it."

Kammerman looked perplexed as I began chuckling.

"Mr. Specter?"

"I was born on a Wednesday, but not last Wednesday. Frankly, I think you are bullshitting me."

"I understand how you might feel that way." Another wan smile. He combed bony fingers through his blond hair. "I was having suspicions about my workers. Can we remain off the record?"

"Sure."

"There are video cameras hidden in the woods around the property and at points on the road on the ridge. I had those installed at the end of last summer." Kammerman pulled out his phone and tapped the screen. "On three different occasions Ms. Johnson went down the trail leading to your friend's home."

He handed over his phone. There was a grainy video of the woman, looking around nervously as she walks down the turnoff at Likowski's place. I had the chilling realization that if Kammerman had a camera at the front of Likowski's road, there was one hidden at my outer gate.

"All of your neighbors bury money on their land. It's a well-known fact. Ms. Johnson was also going around to others on the ridge. We also have evidence of that. It appears she was scouting. Mr. Likowski presented the easiest target because he lived alone. No one else was as solitary. Between the videos and the fact that she is now suddenly spending so many one-hundred-dollar bills, my people feel it is evidence that she is the person responsible."

"Why don't you just give all of this to the police yourself? You don't need me for that."

"In my business I value privacy. I do not want to be involved."

Kammerman's phone rang. He glanced at it, alarmed.

"Apologies. I must take this. It will be just a few moments."

Kammerman walked away at a fast clip and went down a hall. There was the steadily diminishing echo of footsteps on the gleaming white Italian Carrara marble. He reminded me of other wealthy people I'd gotten to know through my reporting and books and by teaching at an elite university. A good number are possessed by a particular kind of loneliness. It's been like that for a long time. Extreme wealth of Kammerman's level placed him in a special league of solitude. William Randolph Hearst cobbled a gilded world at San Simeon nearly four hundred miles down the coast from Citizen Kammerman, and it left me wondering: What was J.D.'s Rosebud? Something in his past drove him to want to live out his final days in this place of wind-borne and fog-bound madness. He was no different from the old hippies save for the fact that he was insanely wealthy.

But this was just a fleeting thought. I was more interested in the file on the table in front of me. I picked it up and studied the woman's picture. The envelope contained credit reports on Sarah Kimberly Johnson, criminal records, surveillance photos of her apparently spending those hundred-dollar bills, printouts of all the addresses she had lived at in Los Angeles. If Kammerman was snowing me, it was an elaborate con job. Or a fairly easy setup of an extremely vulnerable and powerless human being.

I put the file down when I heard the ascending echo of returning footsteps. I'd play along with Kammerman—I had to see where things led. But that didn't mean I'd be truthful with him. Kammerman stood before me and again asked me to take the file to the authorities.

"Okay, I won't use your name with the cops. For now. I can't promise about the future if things get sticky. I won't lie under oath."

"I would not expect you to. I hate to have to cut things short, but I have to be at SFO to catch an early-morning flight to Ukraine. It leaves in"—he studied his watch—"four hours and fifteen minutes. Nicky can drive you back to your gate."

I told him that wouldn't be necessary. Kammerman handed me the brown envelope. "In case we need to talk, how do I get a hold of you without having to deal with Earl?"

Kammerman extracted a card from his wallet. "This has my cell phone and private email."

"Do you answer?"

"I will for you. Under other circumstances, I would say meeting you has been pleasant," Kammerman said, shaking my hand.

The heavy bubinga door closed with a thud behind me. Without a moon, the ocean was especially dark as I made my way home. About a quarter mile before I got to my gate, the chop of an approaching helicopter grew louder. I was on my road at the crest of the hill when the Sikorsky came in for a landing at Kammerman's. Before I got to the cabin, I heard it lift and fade into the southern distance.

I took the San Luis Obispo exit. A downtown storefront advertised espresso, fresh smoothies, and shakes. The shop had a tin ceiling and time-darkened brick walls. University students and millennials, eyes firmly planted on laptops and smartphones, occupied all chairs. A twentyish woman with spiky blue-tinged hair and three tiny silver rings in her left nostril stood behind the counter. Her tattooed arms were unhappily crossed. She wanted to be jamming on a guitar, maybe drums. Singing? But not working here.

"I'd like something crazy. Could you make a beer milkshake?"

She stared at me. "Why?"

"Why not?" I asked. "Have you read *Cannery Row*?"

"No."

"There's a character named Doc. He was driving south to L.A. and he decided he needed a beer milkshake. Doc got his in Ventura. I didn't want to wait that long for mine."

The woman crossed her arms and now looked defiant. "Red Robin sells one—"

"You're kidding."

"It's on their menu."

"Is nothing sacred?"

She smirked. The nostril rings twitched as she assessed the geezer standing before her. I took her disaffection as a challenge.

"I hate chains. I don't want to go to Red Robin. I'd like you to make me one."

"We don't have beer."

"What if I brought you a beer?"

"We're not allowed to do that."

"Who'll complain? You're working alone. I'll leave a good tip." I reached into a pocket and flashed a baggie containing a rolled joint of Death Wish inside.

"What are you?"

"Not a cop."

"Didn't think so. But what are you?"

"A writer."

"And what are you doing here?"

"If I tell you, will you make me the beer milkshake?"

"Maybe."

"Steinbeck loved beer. A poet bet him that he loved it so much that he'd have a beer milkshake someday. That's how it ended up in the novel. I told a friend that story and it made him laugh like hell. I promised him that we had to have a beer milkshake together someday. But we never got to do that. He died last month. I'm doing this for him."

Her attitude suddenly changed. Maggie agreed to make the drink. I walked two blocks to a convenience store and bought a six-pack of

India pale ale. It seemed right for a beer milkshake. I returned and handed over a single bottle. Maggie made the shake and I pulled out my wallet.

"On me," Maggie said. I slipped her the joint.

"My friend who's gone grew it. Organic. Pure. Sun-grown. Made with love."

"I have to know," she asked, fondling the doobie. "Are you bullshitting me about your friend?"

"I never lie. Especially not about something like that."

I sat at a corner table and drank the shake. By now all gen z and millennial eyes ignored laptops and phones, watching the reality show starring me, a theater of unpixeled, unrecorded life, as I downed it. I smacked my lips.

"So?" Maggie asked.

"Great!" I set the tall fountain glass on the counter. "Thanks."

Driving south toward Santa Barbara, I fought the urge to throw up. Yet I had no regrets. Some things you just have to do.

I readied for meeting Sarah Kimberly Johnson by pulling the slide back on the .45, chambering a round. I let down the hammer and stuffed the weapon in my right coat pocket. I closed the truck door. I was hundreds of miles south of the ridge, yet the air was frigid as the north coast. Night in Los Angeles is like this when the wind blows strong off the Pacific. Before me was a nondescript midcentury modern eightplex, a clone of thousands of apartment complexes that occupy the San Fernando Valley: taupe stucco, cycads and palms in front, windblown hamburger wrappers and soft drink cups littering flower beds that hadn't seen blooms in decades. Pointed metal spikes attached to cinder block perimeter walls, angled outward like black rattlesnake fangs. Signs announced SE RENTA. A light was on in unit five, upstairs on the right. I ascended concrete steps poured into rectangular steel forms that rumbled a metallic thunder. Anyone worried about unwanted visitors would have plenty of warning. A television blasted in unit four. Screaming voices, a man and woman fighting, rose over a Spanish telenovela. A baby cried. I paused outside unit five. No sound came from the interior. My right hand was in the coat pocket. I knocked with the left, stood to the side.

"Who is it?" a female voice asked.

"Domino's."

"I didn't order pizza."

"It says right here you did. A call came from 818—"

As I read the rest of her phone number that was in the file Kammerman gave me, it resonated true enough for her to open the door a crack. I stared into the face of Sarah Kimberly Johnson. Her eyes widened. I stuck a foot in the opening. No one else was inside. I'd cased the unit all day long, had to piss in a McDonald's thirty-two-ounce supersized soda cup three times and then dump it out the open door so as not to have to leave the stakeout. Johnson had come and gone once—alone. That skinny little meth freak was strong. I thought my right foot was going to break.

"Ms. Johnson, I need to talk with you before I go to the police. Kammerman says you killed Likowski. If you did it, you're fucked. I'm going to call 911 right now and turn you in. If you didn't do it, I'm the only one who can help you. Open the motherfucking door! Please!"

The pressure relented a little.

"Who are you?"

"A writer. Will Specter. I live above Likowski's place. We were friends."

"Why should I trust you?"

"Because you've got no other option."

Just as her door swung in, the door to unit four opened. A big man wearing boxer shorts and a white wifebeater stepped out. He glared menacingly. "You okay?"

Johnson stuck her head out. "It's all right, Berto. Thanks."

She looked me up and down. My hand was still inside the coat.

"C'mon in. You're not going to need whatever you got in that pocket. I don't got no gun. My parole officer catches me with one, I'm back inside."

There was a lumpy orange couch, a coffee table, a lamp without a shade on a lone end table, and not much else in the apartment. "Have a seat."

"I'm not going to stay long." I left the coat on, sat with my buttocks barely on the nasty sofa that smelled of moldy bread and looked like an ideal haven for bedbugs.

She sunk back on the couch next to me and looked into my eyes. "Jesus fucking Christ. Just what I need. I didn't kill him."

"Look, Sarah," I began, pulling out a notebook and a digital stick recorder.

"I go by Kim," she said.

"Okay, Kim, I met with Kammerman last week. He says you vamoosed right after Likowski was killed—"

"When I heard about that shit, I got the hell out of there."

"If you didn't do it, why'd you run?"

"You got a record like mine, you know the cops are going to come knocking. I figured they'd bust the grow at least. Or frame me. I ain't going back to prison. Believe it or not, I've been clean two years. Things used to be different. I went to college—"

"You're spending money. Hundred-dollar bills. Lots of them. Someone dug up jars of hundred-dollar bills buried at Likowski's place—"

"They didn't come from your friend."

"Then where from?"

She fidgeted.

"Tell me."

"Can we keep this between us?"

"Yes."

"Kammerman's a fucking idiot. He doesn't know a damn thing about growing. We depped in the big greenhouse. The first crop was good shit. The second crop was that medical crap. He never knew about the first batches. Figured the plants were just growing slow when he came in August. We got about two hundred pounds of bud off the books. Both years."

I smiled. This got her to relax—a little. "Split how many ways?"

"Three."

"Not a bad haul. That's, let's see, about a hundred-sixty grand in your pocket, no?"

"Pretty close."

"But it's hard to believe Kammerman didn't notice. What if he came back and caught you?"

"He has no fucking idea how weed grows. He only came in the fall around regular harvest. He doesn't know about depping. We figured the worst he'd do if he came early was fire us. We were ready to quit anyway. I was makin' about ten bucks an hour. You won't tell?"

"No. There's justice in that."

"How?"

"Never mind. So why are you living in a dump like this?"

"My son. Paying the damn lawyers to keep him outta prison. And I want to make the skins last till I figure what's next. I'm clean. You may not believe it, but I am."

"That doesn't explain why you went to Likowski's place and checked him out. You asked for water, went to see Bill and Alma, and Andy too."

"Earl didn't have connections to sell that much weed," she said of her coworker with the Mohawk. "I was lookin' to talk to them about their connections. But those dudes on that ridge, they're all so fuckin' paranoid. They freaked when I showed. So I never asked. We had to find connections down here on our own."

I stood, gathered the recorder. "Thanks, Kim."

"That's it?"

"Yes. Do you have email?"

"Yeah. You ain't gonna call the cops?"

"Nah. Write it here," I said, passing the notebook and pen. "I'll be in touch, let you know what I find."

Kim wrote with her right hand.

"Oh, a silly question," I asked, slipping the pad into the coat pocket next to the Colt. "What hand does Earl write with?"

She pondered a moment. I recalled Earl taking the Kammerman letter with his right hand. Memory is a funny thing, though. I wanted to be sure.

"Right. Yeah, his right. I would have remembered if he was a leftie."

I didn't want to be late for the meeting with John Martucci, a partner in the law firm that hired the private investigator for Kammerman. When I had mentioned Kammerman's name to the secretary I was put on hold; she came back and said Martucci would take my meeting later that morning.

While hunting for a parking spot, cars followed me as I trolled for an opening. I tried keeping my eye on the rearview mirror, but with traffic I couldn't really tell. I blew it off to paranoia. Or were they really watching? Then I came upon not one but two open spots. I was late and ran to the law offices, barely having time to catch my breath as I announced myself at reception.

Almost instantly, Martucci emerged. "Mr. Specter?"

I extended a hand.

"Shaking hands, that is something I never do," Martucci said. He raised his right hand and said, deadpan, "I wave."

I waved back. Martucci could pass for an actor playing a big-wheel corporate lawyer in a Hollywood film—just over six feet, jet-black hair, slightly tanned, angular cheekbones, eyes that burned into a visitor. Intimidating. He ushered me into a conference room paneled with black walnut and offered a seat. I remained standing. I reached into my satchel and pulled the report Kammerman gave me. "This has your law office's name all over it." I plopped it on the table. "We're talking about murder, Mr. Martucci. Things the California Bar would be most interested in hearing about."

"We have done nothing wrong. And certainly Mr. Kammerman took no part in a homicide."

"What about that raft of bullshit Kammerman tried to pawn off on me, about Kim Johnson being the killer? Your report fingers her."

"We have come to know more than we did when that report was written."

"So why didn't Kammerman let me know that?"

"You will have to ask Mr. Kammerman that question."

"You have a legal and moral duty—"

"There is an answer. Please sit, Mr. Specter."

I took a black leather chair facing Martucci, whose elbows rested on the surface of a dark wood conference table. His fingertips went into a power pyramid. "I presume that you are not recording this conversation. You understand that California is a two-party consent state?"

I nodded.

"Can we be utterly off the record?"

"Of course."

"I am precluded by attorney-client privilege from revealing too much. Let me just say that I am hired to protect the interests of many wealthy people. It's the job of my office, in broad general terms, to provide a number of such people with information, especially when they face threats from forces outside of their control. We find facts and then present those facts to our clients. I can tell you one thing: follow the money."

"Huh?"

"Robert Redford and Dustin Hoffman. Surely you saw the movie..."

I wasn't surprised. After all, I was in Los Angeles, where an attorney of course would recite words never uttered in real life by the source who gave information to Bob Woodward and Carl Bernstein. The line came from screenwriter William Goldman, who nonetheless understood the news game and got at the core of what any good investigative journalist should do.

"Your neighbor was involved in a certain kind of business, which meant he dealt with certain kinds of people. Follow *all* the money. The answer will lead you to a person known to Mr. Likowski."

"Who?"

"I've already stretched the bounds of what I should reveal. That is all I can say. Good day, Mr. Specter."

There are two kinds of sources: those you have to convince to talk, and people like Sheldon. You can't shut them up. The problem is keeping them on track, steering their digressions back to the matter at hand, which in this case was Jon Barry. I met Sheldon at his house in the Oakland Hills, a sprawling Spanish-style McMansion in the middle of an unkempt meadow that may as well have been a field in the center of Kansas. Sheldon's original mansion burned down in the 1991 firestorm that swept through the Oakland Hills. When he answered his door, I made a comment about the unmowed meadow surrounding the house. "A grass fire ain't nothing. Grass doesn't burn hot. It's the trees! I hate trees! No fucking trees!" he told me, launching into a tirade about the species of tree he hated most: eucalyptus. "They explode like gasoline in a fire!"

That story went on for twenty minutes in the foyer, leading to his telling about buying the two adjoining lots to keep them empty and rebuilding this six-thousand-square-foot house so that it would never burn down. It was hard to fathom that I was talking with one of the biggest vaping oil moguls in California. If you met Sheldon on the streets of Oakland or Berkeley far below us, you'd assume he was a homeless man who saw the face of Jesus in crushed Starbucks cups. His scraggly gray-white beard was as unkempt as his lawn, and his hair looked greasy even when washed; it fell to his shoulders. What you could see of his face was leathery and weathered from years of surfing. He was seventy-six.

"Want a hit?" Barry asked after I'd taken off my shoes and we had migrated to his kitchen. He held up a vape pen, which I declined, but I did accept a Keurig coffee. We went to his living room. My seat, a high-backed leather chair, faced a bank of windows that provided a sweeping view of San Francisco Bay, the city skyline, Alcatraz Island, the Golden Gate Bridge, Mount Tamalpais. Below us the flats of Oakland and Berkeley stretched to the water.

My neighbors on the ridge had connected me with veteran Bay Area and Los Angeles buyers. I interviewed a dozen people in the span of two nervous weeks, with cars appearing in my rearview mirror and trailing for overly long stretches before pulling away, the faces of the anonymous drivers always fuzzy, indiscernible. Everyone I spoke with was close to or over seventy. It was a geriatric history lesson in drug dealing that propelled me back to a different era, the time when my neighbors were all realizing they had to leave square America. A key year for all of them was 1967. The Summer of Love was already over by the time it was discovered by the national media. Yet kids continued flocking to San Francisco, pulled by cultural mythology. But they were also pushed, on the run from a normal that never existed. They shunned replicating their parents' lives in Danbury or Short Hills, in a doorman building on the Upper East Side or, at the other end, a trailer in Kentucky or a clapboard house blackened from the smoke of steel mills. Among them was Jon Barry, who repeatedly came up as I talked with those twelve, among them Sheldon, who met Barry in a history class at Berkeley.

"A lot of us kids hanging around the Haight hustled nickel and dime bags, but Jon, man, he wanted the stars. He saw the future before anyone. Funny thing, he didn't have to sell weed. I mean, he was blue blood. Old money, from back east. His father, grandfather, they went to Harvard. But he came to Berkeley. His parents were pissed. The University of California didn't mean anything to them. Jon wanted to get away from that bullshit. Everyone on campus knew him. It wasn't just because he was SDS and you'd always see him on Sproul Plaza at a microphone. He was really good-looking. He was at all the parties and he shared his weed. That was part of his plan. Nothing was free, not from Jon. He had great shit. So when the time came that you wanted to buy the best weed, you went to him. He turned everything into money. Jon opened a head shop in the Haight. 1967."

He took another hit from his pen. When he exhaled, he continued: "I worked for him for a few months in the shop. He didn't make any money. The shop was a way for him to meet the people he needed to get to know, all the kids who'd come from back east. They wanted to get back to the land even if they'd never been on the land. Jon was amazing. He knew how to talk to the rich kids. But he also got along with the blue-collar kids. Everyone loved him."

Sheldon said those head shop customers began drifting north of the city, into the redwood forests, to farm the Kush seed provided by Barry. He closed the shop in 1973. By then he was buying hundreds of pounds from growers scattered across the sweep of mountains and canyons north of the Golden Gate. In turn he sold to Los Angeles connections. He amassed a fortune. The money kept pouring in, ridiculously huge amounts of it. As a front to launder money, he started an import-export business that dealt in ivory, elaborately carved and some of it very old. Another way he legalized his proceeds was to buy expensive homes in cash—literally—and sell them a few years later to get bank money. His growers became talented at breeding new varieties, blends of indica or sativa from parent stock such as Acapulco Gold, Thai Stick, Maui Wowie. The strains were given names like Vishnu Temple, Zoroaster Zen, and Likowski's Death Wish.

"Yeah, Death Wish," Sheldon said dreamily as he talked about the varietals sold by Barry. "That was great shit. Another one was Raz-Barry Kush. The grower named it in honor of Jon. Growers loved him. Jon, he was damn near evangelical about all of them. He marketed their product and created a demand. His growers got bigger. He got bigger."

There was only one direction for the market: up. By the early 1990s, Barry owned a twenty-room mansion in the Pacific Heights neighborhood of San Francisco. From Sheldon and the others, I heard about the ceaseless stream of beautiful young women who came and went. His yacht sailed out of Sausalito to the coast of Mexico. Copious lines of cocaine were inhaled on the boat—the cocaine often coming from Sheldon. "It was one helluva floating party," Sheldon said. This was the apex for the swashbuckling buyer and his former head shop customers, who now owned 80- to 360-acre spreads in the north. His life resembled that of a modern-day Gatsby told from the party boy perspective, a soft focus dreamworld of fine clothes, dinners at Chez Panisse, sex, helicopter ski vacations in British Columbia, more sex.

But by the late aughts, his life had darkened. The price of bud began its free fall. When Barry's runners opened their black Pelican cases, they passed out fewer hundred-dollar bills. The people both below and above Barry became less pleasant. The big Los Angeles connections bought from industrial producers. The mom-and-pops, who farmed with love and Zen, were marginalized.

The street price on the East Coast wasn't falling, but what Barry's Los Angeles people, those at the top of the weed economy pyramid, paid him wholesale hit the gutter. They were taking the cut when they shipped back east. Why shouldn't he earn the markup? He needed direct East Coast sales to maintain his lifestyle. After he scored a New York connection, Barry used runners to drive loads across the country in SUVs or vans. He paid $1,400 a pound for weed that sold for $3,500 back east. But occasionally a runner vanished with product. To solve that problem Barry scaled up and put all his bud in one basket: he bought a tractor-trailer rig, painted a fictitious moving company's name on the sides, and had his most trusted employee drive it.

"Jon didn't factor in Donner Pass and Sherman Summit," Sheldon said. The elevation of those summits caused pressure changes in some vacuum-sealed bags, bursting them. "When the truck was stopped by the Iowa Highway Patrol, a shepherd caught a scent. The feds turned the driver. Jon got named in the indictment. It was his first bust ever, but it was the mother of all busts. He was fucked."

I knew—I had the police records. Three hundred pounds of bud and 240,000 THC vaping cartridges filled with Sheldon's oil. "He'd already paid me for it," Sheldon said with a chuckle. "And my name wasn't on anything."

Barry faced serious time in federal prison and was blowing all his money on lawyers. He'd lost the yacht years earlier, and the San Francisco mansion was going into foreclosure. His financial difficulties were common knowledge, as was his descent into madness. Was the cause bad drugs, money issues, or a combination?

"I don't know," Sheldon said. "He's batshit fucking crazy. I stopped buying product from him."

Besides losing his mind, Sheldon and the others told me that as the aughts progressed into the teens there was a physical change as well. Photographs of Barry through this period mark how the dashing dealer who once resembled Robert Redford had morphed into a haggard old man with a hard drinker's tan. He grew obese and developed jowls. Oxy came into the picture.

"Last time I saw him, Jon was rambling on about how someone kept calling his cell phone with threats," Sheldon told me. "He said, 'It's a low voice, menacing. The only reason I pick up is that it's a 707 number.' He was convinced it was your friend. He blamed that guy for a half dozen other growers dumping him."

Others had told me Barry said the caller sometimes just breathed heavily into the phone.

"I just couldn't deal with him anymore," Sheldon said. "He bought a MAC-10. Don't ask how I know. I'll just say he'd never been into guns."

"How dangerous is he?" I asked.

"Depends on which day you catch him. Some days he comes off pretty normal. Others, he's whacko-cracko. Frankly, he scares the shit out of me."

When I asked him directly if Barry might have killed his old friend Likowski, Sheldon ducked his head and looked away. For once, Sheldon was done talking, and I was done asking questions.

It took a while to track down all the players who knew Barry and when I was done, I took what I had learned directly to Robert Bogel, who agreed to meet off the record at his office. It was the first time I'd visited the DA's office, sterile and empty save for a desk and a surfboard leaning against a wall. Bogel looked out of place behind that desk—tall, thin, a shock of blond hair. The district attorney told me evidence was thin. "There were no prints. No DNA."

"Did they vacuum the library?"

"Of course. All standard procedures were followed."

"Surely there are camera license plate readers on the Golden Gate Bridge."

"Even if there's a match," Bogel said, "he could say he loaned his vehicle to someone. Or that he was going to dinner in Sausalito."

"What about receipts for gas, food?"

"You know those guys. They only spend cash."

But Bogel agreed with my theory about the killer being a leftie. "Do you know if Barry is left-handed?" he asked.

"No. People can tell me his damn shoe size but not which hand he uses. I'm thinking about an ambush interview."

"I'm not sure that's a good idea."

"Are you going to talk to him?"

Bogel nodded affirmatively but said nothing. I could see the lost cause that it was for the DA, who shifted in his seat and looked out the window. He squinted, as though everything were too bright.

I first crossed the Golden Gate Bridge in 1974, when I was still struggling with college. I took off a quarter from Cleveland State and drove alone out west to backpack in Utah and then check out California. A convertible passed me a few miles north of the span; the car had a vanity plate, BLUEBOY. Back home, no one was open like that about their homosexuality. Odds were that such a tag would get them shot dead. It was just one of the many things about California that I liked. Growing up in Ohio was perpetual winter, a movie in black and white. California was in color. Now, over forty years later, I approached the Golden Gate from the north. I pulled off before the bridge and parked, went on foot onto the eastern walkway packed with tourists. Midway I leaned against the railing. San Francisco, creamy pastels and porcelain in the afternoon sun, was just as gorgeous as it had been all those decades earlier. But it was a mirage. For mere mortals, the price of admission was too high. It was now a tech-bro Disneyland. The San Francisco of Jon Barry's Haight-Ashbury heyday was six feet under.

Barry lived in one of the buildings crowding a hill to the south, above the red roofs of the former Presidio military base. His mansion was indiscernible amid hundreds of windows glinting in the afternoon sun. Barry was certain to lose his case. He faced twenty years in federal prison because of mandatory minimum sentencing. A man with nothing to lose is not the best subject for an ambush interview, which is why I leaned against the railing for a long time. Why hurry? Great clarity comes when you are about to stalk the man who killed your neighbor.

When I got under way, I mindlessly moved through traffic, following the GPS commands of a disembodied British female voice with attitude. I don't remember driving, just that I simply materialized at the address. I found a good observational parking spot because it wasn't a tourist neighborhood. Lawns were dotted with camphor, magnolia trees, Monterey pine, and many unrecognizable Australian species. Barry's home was Spanish style, the lawn spotted with queen palms. Two of the hillside mansion's levels were visible. The dwelling had a red-tiled pyramidal hip roof with dormers, a creamy stucco exterior, and wrought-iron window boxes painted white. There was no garage or driveway. Barry would have to come out or return at some point.

At full dark, a few lights came on. I strolled along the sidewalk, didn't see any movement in the windows. Back in the truck, I sat sideways in the seat, leaning against the driver's door, with a good view of the mansion. Being that it was San Francisco, the night got chilly, and the truck's cab was stuffy. I opened the window halfway down, turned the ignition to run the heater. I sipped on a thermos of coffee to fight nodding off...

"So, you FBI or local?" a voice said.

I snapped awake. My chest seized, what I imagined a heart attack would feel like. I couldn't breathe. The gun remained beneath the seat, even less useful than the BAR stashed in back. There was no going for either one. The voice was behind, coming through the half-open window.

"Why are you here?"

"Who is it?" I struggled to see and braced myself.

A laugh grew into a chortle. "No need to be coy, Roy."

I reached for the gear shift as I sat up and slowly rotated, looking into a chubby face. Even in the dark it was visibly malformed by drugs and booze, puffy and jowly, the head topped with sparse white hair—but recognizable from the mug shot in the federal court case.

"Hello, Mr. Barry," I said quietly.

"And to whom do I have the displeasure of speaking?" Barry wore a black jacket, black T-shirt, black pants. He was quite—to put it mildly—rotund. "Maybe your name's Jack. Yeah, Jack. Like Jack Webb from *Dragnet*." Barry cackled and snapped his fingers as he sang in a melodic falsetto, "*Hit the road, Jack, and don't you come back no more, no more, no more.*"

Sobering, he returned to a normal voice, deep and cigarette gravelly. "Why do you guys keep watching me? You got a million in bail out of my ass. I'm not gonna blow that. I'm not running. Nuh-uh. I'm going to fight the case. Gonna win."

"Name's not Jack. And I'm not a cop."

"Bullshit. You stink of cop."

"No one's ever accused me of that before."

"You're the kind of cop they like: one that doesn't look like one."

I rolled the window all the way down. "Why sneak up on me? What are you doing out here, anyway?"

"Been out walking for hours. That's what I do now. Walk. Walk and think. Feels better outside than in there." He shrugged up at the house.

"Why all the paranoia?"

Barry broke out into the Kinks: "*Para-noia! They destroy ya!*"

I shook my head, looking around, hoping to see someone on the street. But it was deserted.

Barry kept talking: "How much they pay you to do this, man? How many billions do you guys waste? Save some taxpayer dough. I just want to be left alone. Live in my own private Idaho. Dig it? Like a wild potato. Tell your bosses to chase down some real criminals."

"Really, I'm no cop. I'm a writer."

Barry squinted, sized me up as I told him who I was. Then he threw his head back and let loose with a frightening burst of crazy laughter. "So you're him! Asking all over kingdom fucking creation about me! The one who thinks I shot Kow! The 213 number that keeps calling!"

The laughter ceased. He leaned on the truck door with both hands. I could smell his breath. No booze. He didn't smell of dope either.

"I didn't kill your friend." Barry had big eyes like Marty Feldman, the actor from back in the day, which Barry seemed to be musically and culturally stuck in. Sad eyes. *How could a human being have eyes so elastic?* "I didn't," he stressed.

I stared into those elongated ovals boring into me. "I'd like to interview you."

"Let me ask you a question first."

"Sure."

"Why're you so into this? Why are you digging so hard? It ain't normal. In fact, it's pretty fucking weird. Weird! What's in it for you?"

"I'm writing a book."

"Is it about Likowski?"

"A little. The sixties, how the hippies went up north—and weed."

"Am I in it?"

"Yeah."

"You want me on or off the record?"

"On."

Barry rubbed his thin hair. "Cool. Yeah. That's cool. Dig it, man. I'll be in your fuckin' book. On the record. C'mon in."

"No. We can talk here."

"Man, chill out. I ain't gonna shoot you. Why the hell would I do that? Loved Kow. Absolutely loved him. Are you a good journalist?"

"I'd like to think so."

"Then hear me out, man. Shut this thing off and come in."

"No. Out here."

Barry paused for a long time. No way was I going into his mansion. The biggest part of being street smart is knowing when to stay on it.

"Okay," he surrendered. "Have it your way."

"I'd like to record you. For accuracy." I pulled my pocket recording stick out of the cup holder.

"Sure. I got nothing to hide." He reached in a vest pocket and extracted a pack of Winstons, popping a smoke into his mouth with his right hand. He used his left hand to extract a Zippo lighter. His left thumb spun the knurl as his cupped right hand blocked the light breeze coming off the bay. In the flash of light his eyes were blue gray.

I glanced to my right at the blinking light of Alcatraz. Finally, I said, "You're the only one who knew that he'd once been Damion Lapinsky—"

"I never held it over his head. Never used it against him, if that's what you're getting at. Do you know how many crazy-ass people I deal with who've done heavier shit? I buy from all kinds of outlaws. Hell, Kow was a piker. Nothing big in relative terms from what I'm used to. I know a lot of people way out there, man. We're talking Jupiter, Pluto, the fucking asteroid belt. He was only, like, Mars."

"What was he like back then?"

"Same as all of us, man. A hippie on the run. We weren't dropping out. Leary had it right. We were tuning in. Kow was a real go-getter. Gung ho for ganja. Best investment I ever made. He took weed to a whole new level. Death Wish was my A-number-one seller until a few years ago. He hit it early, hit it hard. Me? People probably told you I got into this to get rich. Nope. I got into it because I love the business. Love the mechanics of it. Love the people who grow it. Love the smell of dope. Love everything about it. Everything except growing. Not for me. I'm a fool for the city. Hate getting my hands in dirt. When I die and go to hell, I'll be off the grid. I don't know how they do it. A lot of them up there are living like they did back in the seventies. Some of my growers are still in tents. Tents! Midnight at the oasis, baby. Send your camel to bed. Put a fork in that bullshit, man."

As he went on waxing about the old days, I felt the cold sweat on my palms: *What if at this moment he's listening to those voices he hears in his head?* His puffy jacket was half zipped. *Is he carrying?*

"I hear you and Likowski had a falling out. That you weren't happy when he fired you."

"Sure, I was sad to see him go. But let's get real. By those last few years, I was doing *him* a favor. In the end Kow was my smallest supplier, not even nickel and dime. Pennies. If you're writing about the industry, you have to understand that it's a game. One big fucking game. Sure, the money was good, back when. Hell, look at that place." He nodded toward his mansion. "So I guess you could say that I liked the money. But that wasn't really it. Games change. This one's got new rules now that it's legal. I was keeping up. Kow didn't keep up. He hit a level. Plateaued. Wouldn't dep, wouldn't get bigger. I kept pushing him to keep up. He wouldn't go there. I'm not dissing him. He wasn't any different than a lot of the others. My growers, all of them, work hard. Damn hard. But that's not enough anymore. It's a different world today. Doesn't matter if the weed's sun-grown by fairy elves in unicorn shit. No one cares."

"Isn't that a race to the bottom?"

"Don't romanticize it, Willy. You can't make a buck, you bag it. You got to keep up."

"What about ideals?"

"Ideals?"

"All that hippie peace, love, and harmony stuff—"

"Oh, Willy, you are a romantic. Capitalism won, baby."

"Tell me about Syd."

"Let's not go there."

"Set the scene for me at least. Don Lapinsky drives out from Ohio. What was he like?"

"That's a long time ago, baby. He was wide-eyed, a lot on edge. And it wasn't because of his cargo. He was hungry. That's why I invested in him."

"By giving him seeds?"

"More than that, man! You have no idea. When he bought his spread, I paid off what he owed so he could save some bread. I fronted him dough till he could pay it back. Interest-free. Took him two seasons. Paid it off in full. Starved himself to do it. Told him I'd give more time. He told me, 'No way.' Had that Midwest ethic about money. I'm telling you, I loved that man. He was different."

Barry looked off in the distance and stared at a line of headlights crawling like fireflies across the Golden Gate Bridge. He shivered. I didn't avert my gaze from those pudding eyes. "What about the civic center operation?

Barry shrugged. "Funny thing is he lived his life on the lam and didn't have to. All we did was blow up the women's restroom. Hell, the statute of limitations on that Marin shit had run out. Same with his stealing the dynamite. I had my lawyers check all that out back when he bought his place. He worried someone would run his name, discover who he really was. Said, 'I'll look into it, take care of you, man.' My people told me he could stand on a mountain and shout what he'd done. He was good to go. No one was killed. If someone died, then it's different. But he was in the clear. Even Ayers came out of hiding a hell of a long time ago. Congress declared that amnesty after that COINTELPRO stuff was exposed. But by then he had really become Likowski. He inhabited that cat's skin."

"Were you Weather Underground?"

"Let's not go there."

"Were you involved in that Wisconsin operation when a lab worker died?"

Barry stared at me coldly. I leaped deeper into the hottest place in the inferno. Because I had to.

"People think you killed Likowski."

"I will speak this loud and clear into your recorder," Barry said, reaching to pick up the stick from the window ledge. He held it like a microphone. "*I. Did. Not. Kill. Kow.*"

He set the stick down.

"And I can prove it. I won't call it an alibi. That sounds nefarious. No, I have witnesses. I was here in the city that night, at a dinner party at a friend's house in the Mission."

"I imagine a lot of people owe you favors."

"What are you implying? People saw me that night."

"I've covered a lot of murders. People always think they've committed the perfect crime. They map it all out. But then there's a piece of evidence that comes out, something they forgot to factor in. Or a DA twists someone. That person cracks. Then all of a sudden, everything isn't perfect."

"That so?"

"Here's what I think. Somebody knew about your past and wasn't letting you live with it. You convinced yourself that it was Likowski on the other end of the line, tormenting you, trying to drive you stark raving mad. You couldn't take it anymore. You drove north to confront him. Likowski heard your voice, which was why he opened the door wide and without concern. You hadn't gone with the intention of robbing Likowski's stash, but you saw the map Likowski had pinned up; right now, even that kind of change would help you."

Barry stared at me without revealing any emotion.

"I'm guessing you're still getting the calls, aren't you?"

"Oh, Willy. Willy, Willy."

Something had changed in his voice and he was shifting, moving. I slammed the truck into drive and hit the gas as his hand began to reach inside the jacket. I fully expected bullets to shatter the rear window. Nothing came.

It was long after crossing the Golden Gate Bridge, when I got to the Willits Grade and the chain of vehicles thinned, that it was clear someone was staying a quarter mile behind, slowing when I slowed, speeding up when I accelerated. At the top of the grade the road was swallowed in a bank of fog. There was no calling Bogel or anyone else now.

I let off the gas, but I didn't see headlights in the rearview until the downslope after the summit. I went around a curve and the lights vanished from the mirror. I needed gas. I pulled off in the town that Likowski and I had plastered with Zoë's missing person flyers and paused at the bottom of the off-ramp to see if anyone was behind me. Nothing.

It was one in the morning and the twenty-four-hour service station was empty of customers. I drove slow on my way out of town past some of the poles we'd postered—Zoë's were all gone. I came to the turnoff that led through the redwood forest. The mist thickened in the ancient grove. It was the blackest of Black Fogs. The road, barely more than a single track, S-curved around trees, making twenty miles per hour fast on a sunny day. I crept along in near-zero visible conditions. Still, I knew I was being followed. I couldn't go home—once inside the cabin, I'd be trapped.

I chose a pullout that would hide the truck, backing in behind a tree trunk wide as my cottage. I extracted the BAR and sat in the bed of the truck beneath the thousand-year-old tree. The only sound was the spattering of coffee-bean-sized drops striking the roof and hood—it wasn't storming; fog was condensing in the canopy and fell as if rain. The drops were loud on the steel. A half hour, forty-five minutes went by. I fought to stay awake.

Then came headlights in the mist. I sat up.

The vehicle was crawling, the dull glow of headlamps materializing through the fog, then vanishing as the road curved behind the base of redwoods and reappearing again. The fog grew slowly whiter. I leaped from the bed of the truck and ran three trees over. I lay prone, the BAR aimed at the road. The vehicle appeared in front of me, some kind of SUV. The driver gunned the engine and sped off around the curve. The fog turned red from taillights that diminished and then suddenly went dark as silence returned. There were just two sounds: fog drops slamming the truck and my pounding heart. I trained the BAR on where I'd seen the last red fog.

And then a burst of fully automatic fire came out of the mist. I instantly opened up, emptying the ammo belt. Five seconds or less of absolute terror as the weapon jumped in my hands. Then nothing. Just the ringing silence of blasted eardrums.

I feared the shooter was coming toward me; I pulled the .45 and curled myself up in a ball behind the massive redwood trunk. I was no fighter. But I was a survivor. I listened for footsteps in the forest duff; instead there was the sound of a slamming door, an engine, burning rubber. The fog was again red as the SUV sped away to the west. I went to the truck. The bullets had hit high—all the windows were blown out. I threw the BAR in and sped back to the 101, driving north at thirty miles an hour in the Black Fog, cold wind pummeling my face. At a hotel in town, I pulled into the parking lot and shut off the engine, heart still thudding.

I slept until checkout time and took the pickup to a shop. "Someone used my truck for target practice," I told the guy at the counter.

He shrugged nonchalantly. "Had two of these last month."

I called Robert Bogel. His secretary patched me right through—he was eager to see me. I took a Lyft to the county building and blurted out what had happened in the redwood forest, but he cut me off with a raised hand.

"You haven't seen the news," he observed.

I hadn't. Bogel typed into his keyboard and turned his desktop screen toward me. Orange flames sputtered in the center of the blackness on the screen. "Civilian video. He was driving over the Cougar at around seven this morning and spotted it." County fire responded. When the corpse was pulled from the bottom of the canyon, it came out of a G-Class Mercedes-Benz SUV registered to Jon Barry. "A preliminary examination of the body shows a bullet wound entry to the back of the head," Bogel added, before peppering me with questions. Who wanted him dead? I didn't know. All I knew was that Barry didn't come back to the 101 after chasing me; he took the ocean road and the back way to town, over the Cougar. Somehow en route, he encountered his killer.

After Bogel's office I went to the nearby jail and stood in the blinding white waiting room. When the desk officer returned, he shook his head. "He doesn't want visitors."

I appealed to the cop, but there was nothing he could do.

"Off the record, he's not so good," he said. "Son of a bitch should be doing cartwheels, as far as I'm concerned."

"What do you mean?" I asked.

That's how I learned the lawyer Likowski hired had miraculously gotten a plea deal. Eddie had been sentenced to a year in the county jail and not state prison. That meant with time already served he'd be released in late September. And yet, it was a long time for Eddie to be "not good."

Even with Jon Barry dead, I was paranoid. I drove home the next day after claiming the truck from the shop. I didn't have the stomach to stop where Barry was sent over the edge. I just wanted to get home. When I did, I kept the shutters drawn. But by the fifth evening I felt more secure and began venturing outside with the BAR. I built a fire in the Snorkel stove, and while waiting for the water to hit temperature, I walked the meadow, pacing the fence line with the BAR in hand. When the hot tub was sufficiently warm, I immersed to my neck and dreamed the stars.

The next morning I phoned Bogel to learn of any developments. The coroner had officially identified Barry's remains. No relatives could be reached; it appeared he was headed for a pauper's grave. Bogel told me Klaus had checked in at a luxury rehab facility in Connecticut. Bogel speculated about the shape of the upcoming retrial scheduled for that fall. The defense would be addiction and past sexual abuse. They would use his treatment as evidence that he was on the road to rehabilitation.

I didn't want to leave my ridgetop aerie. What finally got me off the mountain was food—I was running low. I'd neglected my greenhouse gardens for months. One was filled with weeds, and ground squirrels had broken into the other; they ate everything down to vegetable stumps.

Early one morning, I drove to town. After the Cougar's summit, I came to the spot where Jon Barry's $130,000 temporary coffin plummeted. Bogel said the Mercedes SUV had been set afire before it was pushed over the edge. This time I stopped and got out. The path to the bottom of the canyon was marked by blown-out brush on the face of the escarpment. The charred wreckage was one thousand feet below. The county had no budget to haul it up; it would exist there until it rusted back into the earth.

I loaded up with supplies: twenty-five-pound sacks of rice, blocks of toilet paper, seed for the greenhouses, and new tackle for kayak fishing. The pandemic was just hitting the county, and it looked like I'd be hiding out from the world on the ridge for a long time.

I went to Klaus's place and hopped the gate. No one had been around. The house was in foreclosure. Real estate records showed that the Malibu house had been sold at a loss. From Bogel, I learned the facility where Klaus spent eight weeks cost $65,000 per month. I asked where the money was coming from, but Bogel had no idea. Nor did anyone else I talked with, including J.J., who emphatically denied paying for the lawyers or the rehab when I phoned. Despite the fact that Klaus was in Connecticut, rumors circulated: Klaus had been killed by Sotirova, had been disappeared by a lynch mob; he committed suicide in the Trinity Alps; he was in Hawaii with a twenty-two-year-old trimmer. Next I went to the hill above Klaus's grow. It looked like ruins—storm winds had tattered the greenhouses, which were empty of plants. Weeds grew in the roads. I ended up at the Purple Thistle. There wasn't a single car in front. The missing person poster for Zoë remained on the wall near the door. Jake sat on a stool behind the bar, glum. "A lawyer called last week and said it's been sold."

"Who bought it?"

"Some guy named Sotirova. I was supposed to close it down yesterday, but I'm going to keep coming in and workin' till they kick me out."

I imagined Sotirova got the joint for a fire sale price. The proceeds wouldn't generate enough to fund what Klaus had been spending on treatment and lawyers. Had Jake seen or talked with Klaus?

"Nah." Jake offered a Weller on the house, but I wasn't interested. I did notice when he hoisted the bottle that it was nearly empty.

"C'mon," I said. "Klaus has been around."

Jake's denial was a little too emphatic to be believed.

My last stop was the post office. I put the key in my box. On top of a stack of mail was a letter with no return address. My name and box number were in big block letters, like the writing of a child. I used a key and slipped it beneath the seal. Inside was a plain white sheet with letters, cut out from magazines, pasted on the paper:

BARRY GOT BURIED IN THE SHIT

I folded it and placed it in a vest pocket. I drove back to the Thistle and stuck my head in the door but didn't enter.

"Do me a favor," I said to Jake. "Next time you don't see Klaus, tell him I said thanks."

At two in the morning, the jailer came to Eddie's cell. Keys rattled and the door clanged open. "Pick up your belongings at the front desk," the deputy said.

"I don't wanna leave," Eddie, curled up on his bunk, replied. He had been dreaming of his mother and wanted to return to that pleasantly maternal place. Eddie sometimes woke up screaming, which was why they kept him pumped full of antipsychotics. Jailers wrote in their reports that "the inmate believes native spirits or ghosts are trying to kill him." The reality of the tired deputy was not what Eddie wanted to see or deal with. He closed his eyes, rolled on his side away from the cell door, pretending the deputy was not present.

"You have to go. You got early release because of COVID. Let's go. Now!"

The jailer made him put on a mask. Eddie shuffled down the cell tier. His gray and wiry beard, untrimmed for months, made him utterly feral. His eyes were listless, void. A deputy pushed the clothes he'd been arrested in across the counter, along with a pack of cigarettes, a lighter, his wallet; he made Eddie sign a piece of paper saying he'd gotten the items back. He was led to a changing room. As soon as he emerged, he was escorted to the rear entrance, and the door slammed behind him.

Eddie tore off the mask and threw it to the sidewalk. Cars rushed by with terrifying speed on the main drag, so he zigzagged south on back streets. He was hungry. There was no money in his wallet. Behind a McDonald's, he rummaged through a dumpster and discovered a clear plastic bag of hamburgers and breakfast sandwiches. He wolfed two burgers, hoisted the bag over a shoulder.

Dawn found him in the marsh next to the freeway. He curled up deep in a stand of box elders and slept through most of the day. He avoided main roads when he started moving again, and where possible he stuck to woods. When Eddie arrived at the ocean, he turned south on the roadless coast. It was vital that he hide. They were after him. He walked the black sand beach by day.

When the sack of dumpster burgers was empty, he pounded mussels with rocks, eating them raw by sucking on the broken shells; there was kelp and sea palm and a rusting heavy tin can washed up in the driftwood that, when smashed open, contained pork and beans. He stuffed the beans into his mouth.

At night he built a huge bonfire in a canyon, slept fitfully, waking suddenly to scream and throw rocks to keep the Indians at bay. They were far outside the perimeter of firelight, shaking bushes. *Woosh! Woosh!* They danced all around him; they came closer no matter how loud he screamed or how far he threw sparking logs into the dark.

At dawn he began to recognize familiar headlands. He went upriver to the bank, used a root bent like a human elbow to hoist himself up. He paused and stared at Edwards Mountain. He went straight to his barn and wrote a note addressed to Doc Anderson: "Im afraid Im going to hurt someone. Im afraid theyre going to get me." He affixed a rope to the turn crank on a 1955 Oliver hay baler so the line would coil tight, then stood against one of the twelve-by-twelve Douglas fir support beams and circle-wrapped his chest in the rope. He stretched to reach the "on" switch of the machine, which hadn't been used in decades.

Another funeral. We buried Eddie three graves over from Likowski, the nearest open site. A half dozen of us were graveside that afternoon, and I imagined the spirit forms of Native Americans watching from the eucalyptus grove. Hardly anybody came; Lara couldn't bring herself to and Tammie had left town already. The pandemic wasn't the reason for the low turnout. Save for Likowski, Eddie wasn't close to the hippies, and he'd become disconnected from the rancher families who rejected him for cavorting with the longhairs.

"Eddie was caught between two worlds and he belonged to neither," Doc Anderson said over the coffin. The doctor recalled how Eddie came to cabarets at the community center in the 1970s and 1980s. He'd sit in the back, leave when the dancing started. One night Eddie slipped away, and two hours later, after a jug band ceased playing and everyone was filtering out, Eddie was about a quarter mile down the road. *Go home, hippies!* he screamed. There was a gunshot, then two more in quick succession. By the arc of the flashes from the barrel, he aimed at the night sky. *Go home! F-fucking hippies! Go home!*

"And who stepped forward?" Doc asked. "Likowski. He calmly walked down the road and got Eddie to put the gun down. Those men, from very different backgrounds, they ended up like brothers. Our community has lost two unique, powerful, and very important members this year."

After those words, we six got into our vehicles and drove back to our homesteads. I hunkered down for the pandemic. My time was spent walking the woods and meadow by day, dreaming the stars from the hot tub by night. That first week of September, an inversion settled over the coast. It was the mother of all inversions. It went on for days. I awakened those mornings to the sound of the wingbeats of distant ravens, coming in through the open windows that did little to cool the cabin. I lay in bed drenched in sweat, unable to sleep. On the second insomniac night, I walked the meadow naked, barefoot, in honor of Likowski. My feet, peppered with near-invisible prickers, stung; it was my version of wearing a hair shirt. I sprawled like Jesus on the cross atop the water tank just before five in the morning, facing the southern stars. Hydra's head was barely poking above the skyline.

On the fifth morning of the epic inversion, I awakened at noon in yet another sweat-drenched bed. It was a good day to work with water. I placed the needed tools in a five-gallon plastic pail and went down the trail to my springs, to drain the four-hundred-gallon poly holding tank and flush out the mucky sediment collected at the bottom.

The trail was blocked by Douglas fir branches, bent downward because of the extreme heat. I'd never seen the limbs hanging this low any previous fall. Branches that had been a dozen feet over the trail now struck my face, about as close as a tree can get to screaming that it is starved for water. I opened the two-inch petcock and water blasted out into the Pacific willows. I sat at the edge of the spray, basking in the cool mist. After it emptied, I tipped the tank to drive out the last sediment. I lay on dry ground, drifted off to the sound of water from the spring box hoses dripping as they refilled the tank.

Likowski appeared and sat on the slope just above the tank amid the dense stand of stinging nettles, impervious to them because he was dead. I smiled because he was incarnated in the body of his twenties. I asked, "Was it worth it, coming here?" He brushed the blond hair out of his eyes and smiled. "One day here is worth ten in the outside world. Are you still really gonna sell, Will?"

I startled awake before the conversation could continue. A goldfinch sang somewhere in the willows. The finch fell silent. The woods were still. I splashed cold water on my face and went back up the trail. At dusk, I took a beer out to the fence post. I recalled the day Likowski came up the headland a quarter of a century earlier, when we first met. The route wasn't visible: what had been meadow dotted with coyote brush was now a thick forest filled with encroaching fir now thirty to forty feet tall. Dark settled in.

I jumped from the perch. The smell of smoke filled the air, the distinct sweet odor of burning fir. This fire was close. Very close. At that moment came a thumping from the south—a tuba. I shook my head, disbelieving. I cupped my ears. The notes were faint, unclear; then it solidified into "Flight of the Bumblebee."

I broke into a run toward the Ark. An orange glow filled the southern sky as I jumped Zoë's gate and crested the hill. The Ark was fully engulfed in flames that leaped as tall as the brush pile fires the day we burned back in the nineties.

"Zoë! Zoë! Zoë! Zoë!" I screamed, yelling until hoarse from choking smoke.

The tuba fell silent and there was just the roar and crackle of the fire, which created its own wind that pushed the conflagration uphill through the chaparral right at me. I ran, but the flames were coming faster than I could move my legs. Instinct told me to go downhill. *Get to the beach.* I abandoned the road and pushed blindly through the brush, more falling than running, gasping for air. Then the smoke caught up with me and I couldn't see, couldn't breathe. All I could do was continue falling. *I'm not going to make it.* A flash of stars—*I can breathe*—a gust of smoke, more falling, falling, then the down ceased and I collapsed, drenched in sweat, arms bleeding, lungs heaving. I staggered to the surf line, sitting on the wet sand, incoming waves smashing over me; the wounds burned from the salt.

The entire ridge was ablaze. Either my cabin would be there in the morning or it would not. I felt suddenly at peace. Burning Doug fir cones shot heavenward on thermal blasts, sparkling and sputtering in zigzagging lines. I recalled something Likowski said of fire: *It's all just solar energy.* And then I thought of something else he uttered about fire: *Purification.*

A flash filled the sky, followed by a series of explosions that sounded like bombs dropped in war. *Kammerman's place going up,* I thought, *those massive propane tanks.* I went off to a dune, collapsed on my back, lungs burning with each breath. My gaze focused on the constellation Hercules, the ancient Greek hero who battled two strong giants, who prayed to his father, Zeus, for assistance to win the fight. Hercules lives in the sky next to the constellation Lyra, whose main star is Vega, the name rooted in Arabic from a phrase that means "the falling eagle."

@unnamedpress

facebook.com/theunnamedpress

unnamedpress.tumblr.com

www.unnamedpress.com

@unnamedpress